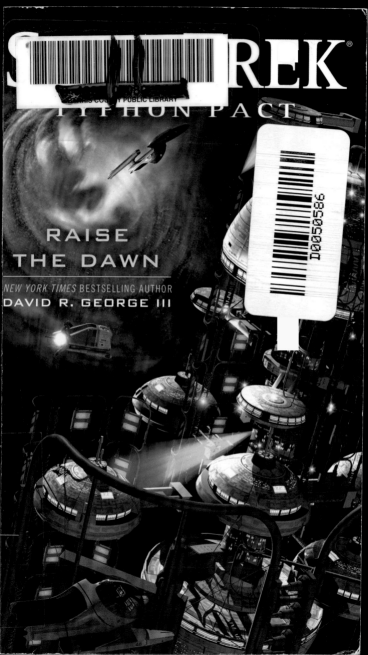

STAR TREK®

TYPHON PACT

RAISE
THE DAWN

NEW YORK TIMES BESTSELLING AUTHOR
DAVID R. GEORGE III

ISBN 978-1-4516-4956-7

Captain [...]
saw the end [...]

She held her injured right arm against her body, feeling the
ache dee[...]
beneath [...]
thrashed [...]
ops. She [...]
just as al[...]

But [...]
planted [...] its nose [...] den[...]
containment for two of the station's reactors. Her crew jettisoned one of the reactors, but the explosions had damaged
the second ejection mechanism. There had been no time for
Ro and her officers to even attempt anything else.

And then, as though the Prophets objected to the
impending loss of Deep Space 9 and all aboard the station, the wormhole had blossomed into existence, a refulgent flower denying the great desert of space. Befitting its
cognomen among the faithful, the Celestial Temple then
delivered a potential savior into the Alpha Quadrant: *U.S.S.
Robinson*. Not a believer herself, Ro nevertheless focused
on the identity of the *Galaxy*-class starship's commanding
officer: the Emissary himself, Benjamin Sisko.

But whatever hope *Robinson* might have brought with
it had vanished as quickly as the wormhole. The Tzenkethi
marauder wheeled around, its tail demolishing Kasidy
Yates's cargo vessel. Suddenly, Captain Sisko's presence on
the battlefield seemed less like a cause for hope than a brutality conveyed by indifferent circumstance.

STAR TREK
TYPHON PACT

RAISE THE DAWN

DAVID R. GEORGE III

Based upon *Star Trek* and
Star Trek: The Next Generation®
created by Gene Roddenberry
and
Star Trak: Deep Space Nine®
created by Rick Berman & Michael Piller

POCKET BOOKS
New York   London   Toronto   Sydney   New Delhi   Ki Baratan

Pocket Books
A Division of Simon & Schuster, Inc.
1230 Avenue of the Americas
New York, NY 10020

This book is a work of fiction. Names, characters, places, and incidents either are products of the author's imagination or are used fictitiously. Any resemblance to actual events or locales or persons, living or dead, is entirely coincidental.

First Pocket Books paperback edition July 2012

POCKET and colophon are registered trademarks of Simon & Schuster, Inc.

For information about special discounts for bulk purchases, please contact Simon & Schuster Special Sales at 1-866-506-1949 or business@simonandschuster.com.

The Simon & Schuster Speakers Bureau can bring authors to your live event. For more information or to book an event, contact the Simon & Schuster Speakers Bureau at 1-866-248-3049 or visit our website at www.simonspeakers.com.

Manufactured in the United States of America

10 9 8 7 6 5 4 3 2

ISBN 978-1-4516-4956-7
ISBN 978-1-4516-4958-1 (ebook)

To Margaret Clark,
An editor whose professional talents and creativity
Only ever helped to improve my work,
And a person whose intelligence, kindness, humor, and friendship
Continue to enrich my life

Prospero: Hast thou, which art but air, a touch, a feeling
          Of their afflictions, and shall not myself,
          One of their kind, that relish all as sharply,
          Passion as they, be kindlier mov'd than thou art?
          Though with their high wrongs I am struck to th' quick,
          Yet with my nobler reason 'gainst my fury
          Do I take part; the rarer action is
          In virtue than in vengeance; they being penitent,
          The sole drift of my purpose doth extend
          Not a frown further.
                    —William Shakespeare,
                         The Tempest, Act V, Scene 1

Each eve brings unexpected light—
A newfound truth, a redemption,
Or some complex revelation—
To vanquish dark and raise the dawn.
                    —K. C. Hunter,
                         Cycles in the Sky, "Nyx and Eos"

In Medias Res

Deep Space 9 exploded.

In the center of the *U.S.S. Robinson* bridge, Captain Benjamin Sisko felt shattered. From where he had fallen to his knees on the deck, he watched the main viewscreen as a massive blast ripped through the lower core of the space station. *The reactors,* he thought automatically, a reflexive response born of his years in command of DS9. Two of the tubular power-transfer conduits that connected the lower core to the midcore fractured, and Sisko thought—he *hoped*—that the reactor compartment might tear away completely, sparing the station further damage and possibly saving the lives of everybody aboard.

What happened? he wondered, incredulous, even as he understood that no answer would suffice. He'd brought his ship home days early from a six-month exploratory mission to the Gamma Quadrant, after his crew had lost touch with Deep Space 9. They'd come through the Bajoran wormhole to a devastating scene. Torpedoes and energy discharges blazed through space as *Defiant* battled a Romulan warbird, and as DS9 itself faced down a Tzenkethi marauder and a Breen warship. Other, smaller vessels—Starfleet runabouts, civilian ships, a Breen freighter—buzzed about, some joining the conflict, others apparently seeking escape.

Sisko had leaped up from his command chair almost as soon as *Robinson* had emerged from the wormhole. Then he saw the smooth, silver-clad Tzenkethi vessel perform a maneuver he'd come to know too well during the Federation's last war with the Coalition. The teardrop-shaped starship whirled on its minor axis, its tapered end whipping around and slicing through the hull of an *Antares*-class freighter.

Maybe it was some other Antares-*class freighter,* he thought in desperation. But no. He'd recognized the old cargo vessel: *Xhosa.* Kasidy's ship.

For just an instant, *Xhosa* had hung in space, cleaved in two, but otherwise intact. Sisko dared hope for the impossible, but then in the next moment, his wishes evaporated like beads of moisture beneath a hot wind. A great fireball bloomed where the vessel's hull had been breached, the ship disintegrating into pieces as it blew apart. *"No!"* he'd cried out, and then collapsed to his knees. "Kas . . . Rebecca . . . no."

He'd felt a hand on his back, and had heard the voices of his crew all around him. But for the second time in his existence, Sisko felt his life draw to a close. More than fifteen years earlier, when the Borg attack at Wolf 359 had taken his first wife, Jennifer, from him, his heart and mind had seemed to spill out, his very essence washing away in a torrent of loss and despair. Had it not been for Jake, and Sisko's need to care for his young son, he couldn't say what he would have done.

Sisko knew that, with her first mate away from the ship, Kasidy had intended to make *Xhosa*'s latest cargo run herself. She'd also spoken about the possibility of bringing their daughter along with her. *I tried everything to save them,* Sisko thought. *I gave up everything. I stayed away so that they would be safe. If I've lost them both—*

On the main viewer, Sisko saw another jet of fire erupt from DS9's reactor compartment. That explosion appeared to trigger another, and a chain of destruction traveled up through the station's central core, and then higher, through the structures that housed the Promenade and the operations center. In his mind, Sisko imagined all the places in which he had spent so much time—the Replimat, Quark's, station security, the infirmary, ops, what for seven years had been his own office. He imagined the detonations splintering their decks, bulkheads, and overheads. He pictured the conflagration engulfing and devouring all of it—along with all those on board.

I wish it had been me, he thought, utterly defeated. *I wish I had been on the station.*

In that terrible moment, Ben Sisko did not see how he could possibly go on.

Commander Anxo Rogeiro, first officer of *Robinson*, NCC-71842, squinted from where he stood in the middle of the bridge as the image on the main viewscreen flared brightly. He watched through narrowed eyes as a succession of explosions climbed up the central hub of Deep Space 9, annihilating the core structures at the heart of the station. The radial crossover bridges ruptured, causing the inner habitat ring and the outer docking ring to fragment. Two of the hooklike docking pylons sheared off and went tumbling through space. Broken sections of the station flew outward in all directions.

Surprised and dismayed by the canvas of destruction painted across the viewer, Rogeiro glanced down to where the captain had slumped to his knees on the deck. With an empty look in his eyes, his mouth hanging open, and the trails of his tears running in quicksilver streaks down the dark flesh of his face, Sisko appeared as stunned as the first officer felt. More than that, though, the captain looked like a beaten man.

Rogeiro understood what had just happened—that Sisko, prior to seeing DS9 blow up, had witnessed the destruction of his wife's cargo ship—though not why it had happened. Rogeiro had reached down to settle a hand on the back of his captain—of his *friend*—in an attempt to offer some small measure of solace through the simple act of providing human contact. He also needed to bring Sisko back to the present, to where three Typhon Pact starships still occupied Bajoran space at the threshold of the wormhole—and one of which continued a firefight against a Starfleet vessel. Rogeiro had already ordered *Robinson*'s shields raised to their maximum level, and if the captain didn't soon regain his composure, the first officer would likely also have to take the ship into battle.

"Captain, the Breen have sealed their hull breach," reported Lieutenant Commander Uteln from the tactical console on the raised rear section of the bridge. "And it appears that the Tzenkethi are on the verge of restoring their shields."

Rogeiro waited a moment for Sisko to reply, but the captain did not react. He gave no indication at all that he'd even heard *Robinson*'s chief of security speaking. Rogeiro looked over to where Lieutenant Althouse, the ship's counselor, sat in her customary position to the left of the captain's chair. She worked

intently at the console beside her. Before the first officer could
get her attention, Uteln spoke again.

"The *Defiant*'s shields are below sixty per—" started the
security chief, but then he stopped in mid-sentence. "Captain!"
he called out, his tone urgent.

Rogeiro peered up at Uteln, then followed the Deltan's gaze
back to the main viewer. There, the first officer saw a large,
curved assemblage spinning through space, its ends bent and
twisted where it had torn out of Deep Space 9's docking ring.
It grew larger on the viewscreen as it neared, apparently on a
collision course with *Robinson*.

Sparing another quick look down at Sisko, who showed no signs
of recovering from his obvious state of shock, Rogeiro removed his
hand from the captain's back and stepped forward. Leaning in past
Lieutenant Commander Sivadeki at the conn, he said, "Move us
out of its path and away from the wormhole." Sivadeki worked her
controls at once, and on the viewscreen, Rogeiro saw the mass of
DS9 wreckage slip away to the ship's port side.

That danger averted, the first officer considered what actions
the *Robinson* crew needed to take next, and in what order. "Set a
course for the *Defiant* and the Romulan ship," he told Sivadeki,
"but hold our position." Then, straightening and turning back
toward the security chief, he said, "Hailing frequencies. Warn
the Tzenkethi and Breen ships that if they don't stand down
immediately, we will open fire on them." With the shields of
the two enemy ships disabled, such an attack would prove
catastrophic for them.

"Aye, sir," Uteln acknowledged.

As the security chief complied with his orders, Rogeiro again
peered over to the ship's counselor. Althouse saw him, quickly
finished working at her console, then stood and darted over
to the first officer. Having joined Starfleet late in her life, the
pixieish blonde nevertheless carried herself with the confidence
that long experience in her field afforded. They stepped to the
side of the bridge together. "I've got a medical team on the way,"
she said in hushed tones. "But I can relieve Captain Sisko right
now and take him to sickbay."

Rogeiro nodded, noting that the counselor had left to him the actual decision of whether or not to remove the captain from command, though only she and Doctor Kosciuszko, the ship's chief medical officer, possessed that authority. "Enter the action in your log, and I'll answer it in mine," he said, matching her whisper with his own. Rogeiro felt tremendous sympathy for Sisko, but he also understood that the responsibility for the lives of the *Robinson* crew—and for perhaps many more lives than that—had suddenly fallen to him. "Escort the captain yourself," he told Althouse. The counselor nodded, then padded over and crouched beside Sisko. She took the captain gently by the arms and began trying to coax him to his feet.

"Sir, there's no response from either the Tzenkethi or the Breen," said Uteln. Obviously mindful of Captain Sisko's condition, the security chief spoke directly to Rogeiro. "Power distribution levels in the marauder—" Uteln cut himself off again, this time interrupted by a series of three tones emanating from his console. He examined his tactical display, then announced, "The wormhole is opening."

The Enterprise, Rogeiro thought expectantly. The *Sovereign*-class starship had been conducting an unprecedented joint exploration of the Gamma Quadrant with the Romulan vessel *Eletrix*—ironically enough, as a means of helping to establish peaceful relations among the worlds of the Khitomer Accords and the Typhon Pact. When the warbird had apparently crashed on a moon with the loss of all hands, and the *Enterprise* crew had subsequently lost communications with Deep Space 9, Captain Picard had contacted Captain Sisko. With neither crew able to reach DS9 via subspace, the two men had agreed that both ships should proceed at once back to the Alpha Quadrant. "On-screen," Rogeiro ordered.

On the viewer, the Bajoran wormhole swirled in a spectacular flurry of blues and whites. As Counselor Althouse accompanied the captain toward the portside turbolift at the forward reach of the bridge, Sisko jerked his head to the right to look at the main viewer. Rogeiro thought he saw the captain's expression harden when he saw the wormhole, but Althouse urged him on, one hand on his arm, the other at his back. The two entered the turbolift, and the doors glided shut behind them.

Rogeiro peered back at the viewscreen and waited to see the Federation flagship appear in the bright center of the maelstrom. It didn't. Instead, the section of DS9's docking ring that had almost struck *Robinson* spun end over end as it entered the wormhole. Then the great vortex rushed in on itself, ultimately vanishing in a pinpoint flash of light, taking the piece of wreckage with it.

Suddenly, *Robinson* shuddered. A roar filled the bridge, and Rogeiro lurched to his left, pinwheeling his arms in order to stay on his feet. The overhead lighting flickered once.

"The Tzenkethi hit us with their plasma cannon," called out Uteln. The ship shook violently again.

"Evasive maneuvers," ordered Rogeiro, and the low-level hum of the impulse drive changed as Sivadeki worked to move the ship. "Return fire, full phasers."

"Firing phasers," said Uteln.

Rogeiro heard the audible feedback of the tactical station as the security chief defended *Robinson*. The first officer looked to the main viewscreen, which had changed to display the Tzenkethi starship. Beams of golden fire leaped from the Starfleet vessel and pounded into the marauder. Obviously restored, the enemy vessel's shields flared, a second skin of bluish light that clung to the easy curves of the ship's hull.

The wreckage of Deep Space 9—*And of* Xhosa, *and of any other smashed ships out there,* thought Rogeiro—littered the surrounding space, the floating bits of debris reflecting the distant light of B'hava'el, the Bajoran sun. It appeared that most of the other, smaller vessels had withdrawn, though he spied one runabout making a frenzied dash past the Tzenkethi ship, pummeling it with more phaser blasts. The marauder's just-repaired shields flared repeatedly, and Rogeiro hoped that it would not be long before they failed again.

A brilliant white bolt shot out from a recessed port on the Tzenkethi vessel, and Rogeiro braced himself for the impact. But on the viewer, the starfield canted dramatically, and the form of the marauder slipped up past the top of the screen and out of sight. Thanks to Sivadeki's efforts at the conn, the plasma blast did not land.

But then something else struck *Robinson* hard. Rogeiro flew backward as the overhead lighting blinked off, and then stayed off. The first officer struck the starboard bulkhead and fell to the deck in a heap, the wind knocked out of him. He struggled to breathe, gasping in the dim illumination thrown off by the bridge consoles.

"It's the Breen," he heard Uteln call out. "They've flanked us."

Even as Rogeiro gulped for air, he cursed himself for disregarding the Breen ship. Its shields had been down and its hull breached, and even though they'd repaired the latter damage, it should have taken them much longer to restore their defensive screens. But as the old Romulan saying told, *Never turn your back on a Breen.*

"Shields down to eighty-seven percent," Uteln said. He waited a beat, doubtless expecting an order to return fire, but Rogeiro had yet to recover. The pause lasted only an instant before the security chief declared, "Firing phasers on the Breen."

Overhead, the emergency lighting finally engaged, bathing the bridge in an eerie red glow. Rogeiro peered toward the main screen in time to see the Breen warship heave into view. *Robinson*'s phasers lashed at it, several beams striking it in rapid succession along its engine housing. Where the weapons hit, pieces of the Breen ship's hull broke off, blasted away into space. The damage surprised Rogeiro, and he realized that he saw no flash of defensive screens under attack, that the Breen must not yet have brought their shields back on line.

How could they fire their weapons, initiate a confrontation with an enemy vessel, without the ability to protect themselves? Rogeiro wondered. *What's so important that they feel compelled to take such a risk?* The first officer briefly considered ordering Uteln to cease firing the ship's phasers, but then the Breen vessel launched bright green pulses of energy into the night. The disruptor bolts slammed into *Robinson.*

"Shields down to seventy-one percent," declared Uteln. "And the Tzenkethi ship is coming back around, weapons hot."

Finally able to breathe normally again, Rogeiro rose and raced back to the conn. When he arrived, Sivadeki anticipated his orders. "Evasive action?" she asked.

"No," Rogeiro said. "Keep us steady."

Robinson quaked again, hard, and Rogeiro had to grip the edge of the conn to keep himself from falling. On the viewscreen, he saw the assault cause the ship's phasers to swing away from their target, after which Uteln stopped firing altogether. "Evasive now," he told Sivadeki, and the image of the Breen vessel quickly slid from the viewer as the lieutenant commander veered *Robinson* away from the enemy ships.

"Both vessels in pursuit," Uteln said.

Good, Rogeiro thought, seeing an opportunity. Slipping past the conn and over to the operations station that sat beside it, the first officer said to Lieutenant Commander Plante, "Show me a tactical plot of our position in relation to the Tzenkethi and the Breen."

"Yes, sir," Plante said, and she worked to give him the information he needed. He looked to the main viewscreen to see a graphic appear there. On it, emblems for the Tzenkethi Coalition and the Breen Confederacy stood in for their respective starships, and the symbol of Starfleet for *Robinson.* The two enemy vessels followed *Robinson* in close proximity to each other.

"Both ships are firing," said Uteln, just seconds before the combined force of a plasma cannon and disruptor bolts battered *Robinson.* "Shields down to fifty-three percent," the security chief called amid the tumult.

"Uteln," said Rogeiro, "lock quantum torpedoes on the Tzenkethi ship, phasers on the Breen. Target their engines. Wait for their closest approach." Then, peering up toward the overhead, Rogeiro said, "Bridge to engineering."

"Engineering," came the immediate response from the ship's chief engineer. *"Relkdahz here."*

"Commander, we need to reverse the engines hard," Rogeiro said. "Can the ship take it?"

"We'll need to maximize power to the structural integrity field,"

said Relkdahz. *"Even then, we can't perform such a maneuver safely more than a couple of times."*

"Don't worry about that," Rogeiro said. "We're only going to get one shot at this. Signal the conn when you're ready. Bridge out."

The ship shook again as it took more weapons fire. "Shields at forty percent," said Uteln.

Looking to Sivadeki at the conn, Rogeiro said, "When engineering's ready, we're going to reverse thrust. Bring us to a standstill as quickly as possible." He pointed toward the tactical display on the main viewer. "Move laterally as necessary. I want you to split those two ships out there as they pass us."

Sivadeki worked her console. "Preparing for reverse thrust," she said. "Plotting our position between the Tzenkethi and the Breen."

Peering back at Uteln, Rogeiro said, "All applicable phaser banks, all applicable torpedo tubes."

Sivadeki looked up from the conn. "Ready here, sir," she said, just as another set of weapons fire crashed into *Robinson*. The emergency lighting wavered, went out, came back on.

"Shields down to thirty-one percent," said Uteln.

"Give us a little wiggle," Rogeiro told Sivadeki. "Don't make it easy for them, but keep us more or less on a straight course."

"Yes, sir," Sivadeki said.

Rogeiro glanced up at the tactical plot on the main viewscreen, then looked to Plante and made a slicing motion across his throat. On the viewer, the tactical display vanished, replaced by a spread of stars. The distant points of light wavered as Sivadeki jogged the ship to port and starboard, up and down. A dazzlingly bright plasma bolt streaked past, losing itself somewhere in Bajoran space, but missing *Robinson* entirely.

Rogeiro heard Sivadeki's console emit a tone, and she confirmed what he hoped: "Commander Relkdahz signals that engineering is ready."

Rogeiro nodded. "Ready on weapons," he said.

"Aye," said Uteln.

To Sivadeki, he said, "Full reverse, now."

"Initiating full reverse," Sivadeki said.

Rogeiro peered at the viewscreen and saw the field of stars steady. Then the tone of the impulse engines changed radically, from a smooth hum to a sound more like metal straining beneath an excessive force. Rogeiro felt the push of his own momentum as the inertial dampers labored to overcome the sudden reversal in thrust.

Feedback tones from the tactical console heralded the launch of *Robinson*'s weapons. "Firing," said Uteln. Just an instant later, the two Typhon Pact vessels hurtled past on the viewscreen, one on either side. Bands of phaser fire extended from *Robinson* to the Breen warship, and a line of quantum torpedoes to the Tzenkethi marauder.

Before the two vessels could vanish from sight into the distance, a fiery explosion consumed the Breen ship. He saw Sivadeki quickly raise a clenched fist, understandably satisfied at the vanquishing of a dangerous foe, but Rogeiro took no joy in the deaths of a starship's entire crew. He'd been left little recourse, though. He'd offered an end to the hostilities he and the *Robinson* crew had stumbled upon, and so he felt no compunction about fighting for the lives of his own crew. But he didn't have to like it.

"The Tzenkethi ship is slowing," said Uteln. "We might have damaged their engines. Their shields are down again, their weapons are off line, and they appear to be drifting."

"All right," Rogeiro acknowledged. "Then we can go help the *Defiant* crew." To Sivadeki, he said, "Set course for the—"

"Sir," Uteln interrupted. "The Tzenkethi vessel is headed directly into a severe ion storm. Contact in less than five minutes."

Damn, thought Rogeiro. He knew few facts about the Denorios Belt, which covered an orbital ring far out in the Bajoran system, encompassing both Deep Space 9 and the Alpha Quadrant terminus of the wormhole. A plasma field of varying density and dimension, and prone to tachyon eddies, acute neutrino disturbances, and intense ion storms, it posed not merely a hazard to navigation, but a threat to the safety of any ships that passed through it. "How bad is the ion storm?" he asked Uteln.

"Bad enough that, without shields, the marauder probably won't make it through intact," Uteln said.

"What's the status of the *Defiant*?" Rogeiro wanted to know.

"Scanning," Uteln said. "Their shields are below fifty percent, but they appear to be fighting the Romulan vessel to a stalemate. The warbird's shields are down to forty percent."

Rogeiro sighed heavily. He wanted to take *Robinson* to join the *Defiant* crew's battle, but the Tzenkethi faced a more imminent threat. Despite their status as enemies of the Federation—something the marauder's crew had just underscored by their actions in the Bajoran system—Rogeiro could not simply let them die.

"Prepare to deploy the tractor beam," the first officer said to Uteln. "Sivadeki, take us to the Tzenkethi." Rogeiro stepped between the conn and ops stations, then walked over to the command chair. He did not sit, though, but turned and remained standing. "Uteln, open a channel to the Tzenkethi."

The tactical station beeped in response to the security chief operating it. "Channel open, sir."

"Tzenkethi marauder," the first officer intoned, "this is Commander Anxo Rogeiro of the Starfleet vessel *Robinson*." He waited for a reply.

"There's no response," Uteln said after a few seconds.

"We know that your engines and shields are off line," Rogeiro continued, "and that your ship is heading into a significant ion storm. We are approaching to assist. Using a tractor beam, we will halt your momentum toward the storm." When he heard nothing, he looked back over his shoulder at Uteln.

"Still nothing," said the security chief.

"All right, close the channel," Rogeiro said. Frustrated, he raised his hands to his hips and peered at the main viewscreen. "You don't want to talk to us, and just a few minutes ago, you tried to blast us out of the sky, but we're going to save your lives anyway." He saw Lieutenant Commander Plante glance over at him from ops, and he offered her a shrug. "That's why we're the good guys," he said. Plante smiled, then turned her attention back to her station. Rogeiro stared at the image of empty space on the viewer, until at last a distant shape became visible. He watched as it grew in size, resolving into the elegant, teardrop-shaped form of the marauder.

"Status of the Tzenkethi vessel," Rogeiro said.

"Their weapons, shields, and drive remain off line," said Uteln. "They are continuing to drift toward the ion storm."

"All right, let's try this again," Rogeiro said. "Hail them."

"Hailing them, sir," said Uteln.

Seconds passed. "Nothing?" Rogeiro asked.

"No, sir."

The first officer shook his head. "Let's get this over with, then," he said. "Lieutenant Commander Sivadeki, bring us to within range of our tractor beam."

"Reducing speed to match that of the marauder," Sivadeki responded. "Employing thrusters to move us into position."

The great silver ship grew to fill the main viewer. Rogeiro saw several black scars blemishing its surface, and a run of ragged metal around the port housing one of its plasma cannon. Up close, essentially in repose, the vessel looked like a piece of abstract art, laid out on black velvet, awaiting restoration.

"Mister Uteln," Rogeiro said, "engage the tractor—"

Robinson trembled. A curtain of translucent white light shimmered across the main viewscreen, partially obscuring the image of the Tzenkethi starship. Rogeiro understood the situation even before Uteln reported on it.

"They've deployed their own tractor beam," the security chief said.

"Sivadeki, full reverse, now!" Rogeiro yelled.

The sound of the impulse engines rose, suffusing the bridge. The hum quickly increased in pitch as *Robinson* struggled to free itself from the clutches of the marauder. Rogeiro hoped that the Tzenkethi crew sought only to alter their trajectory toward the ion storm, but he didn't trust them.

As if to confirm his suspicion, he saw the marauder start to move. It spun around on its minor axis, the tapering tip of the vessel coming up and over at great speed. "Fire phasers!" he called out, but too late.

With a roaring sound unimaginably loud, the tail end of the Tzenkethi starship crashed down on *Robinson*.

We failed spectacularly, thought Commander Orventa T'Jul.

On the bridge of the Romulan vessel *Eletrix,* from the command chair, she gazed at the main viewer, at the bright veins of directed energy that seared through nearby space, at the blaze of disruptor bolts and quantum torpedoes seeking—and often finding—targets. The background patterns of stars swung to and fro, upward and downward, reeling at a dizzying pace as her crew fought both for their lives and for the security of the Empire. T'Jul continued to issue orders in the ongoing battle, though she no longer credited even the possibility of achieving true success in their mission.

No, not their *mission,* T'Jul thought. My *mission.*

Except that her orders had not originated with any of the admirals in her direct chain of command, had not been issued by Fleet Admiral Devix, had not even passed to her from some political leader. *No,* she thought bitterly. *Tomalak brought us to this point.*

The former proconsul to Praetors Kamemor and Tal'Aura, Tomalak had before those appointments spent a lifetime crawling slowly up through the ranks of the Romulan Imperial Fleet, his ultimate military achievement less a product of superior ability, she believed, than of simple endurance. He had arrived aboard *Eletrix* as the Romulan liaison for the joint mission with the Federation vessel *Enterprise,* to aid in communication between the two crews. But Tomalak had brought with him another mission, ostensibly originating with Admiral Vellon, a known puppet of the Tal Shiar.

On the viewer, T'Jul saw a streak of blue-white light an instant before another quantum torpedo detonated against *Eletrix*'s shields. The ship jolted beneath the attack, and the commander knew that time was growing short. Working on weapons and defense, her executive officer, Subcommander Venalur Atreev, provided a temporary fix of the ship's defensive screens, which had dipped below thirty percent. T'Jul heard the sound of disruptor bolts launching, even as the image of the stars on the viewscreen rotated rapidly, Lieutenant Torlanta laboring hard to evade the bantam Starfleet vessel that had unmasked *Eletrix* as it emerged into the Alpha Quadrant from the wormhole.

The burden of T'Jul's failure seemed to envelop her. Tomalak had presented the mission to her as a mere possibility, a secondary plan intended only as a backup should the crew of *Ren Fejin* require assistance. The Breen cargo ship had entered the Gamma Quadrant as part of the opening of Typhon Pact and Khitomer Accords borders to civilian space travel. A Breen engineer had developed a means of converting existing Pact starships to use quantum slipstream drive, but to accomplish that important goal, he required specific equipment that could be found only within the Dominion. The crew of *Ren Fejin* had successfully infiltrated the Changeling-controlled territory and located that equipment, but the machinery's considerable size necessitated a much larger ship to transport it.

Employing materials left throughout the Gamma Quadrant by other civilian Pact vessels, T'Jul and her crew had counterfeited the destruction of their ship, then had traveled to the Dominion to take possession of the equipment. As added layers of protection for *Eletrix* and its precious cargo, an operative had planted bombs aboard DS9, and two cloaked Pact starships had stood guard within the Bajoran system. But the plan had called for the sabotage of the space station and the military support of the Breen and Tzenkethi vessels only if absolutely necessary to secure the safe passage of the Dominion equipment. In the best-case scenario, *Eletrix* would have simply slipped through the wormhole and out of Federation space cloaked and undetected.

Instead, the worst happened, thought T'Jul, though less with bitterness than with a sense of resignation. *Eletrix* had been exposed as soon as it had entered the Alpha Quadrant from the wormhole. Deep Space 9 had been incapacitated, but not before it had engaged the Breen and Tzenkethi starships, which had ended up providing virtually no help whatsoever to T'Jul and her crew. The space station had ultimately been destroyed, further ensuring the disastrous nature of the entire incident, which would doubtless have interstellar repercussions. After such actions by Typhon Pact ships, could a declaration of war by the Khitomer Accords powers be far behind? And with the Federation's military advantage of the slipstream drive, what hope could there be for the Romulan Star Empire in such a war?

All of which makes it even more important that we succeed, T'Jul thought, trying to rally herself. She stood from the command chair and strode to the port side of the bridge, to where her executive officer crewed the weapons and defense console. "Atreev," she said, "precisely how much time do we need in order to cloak?" The subcommander confirmed the exact interval for her, a small amount of time that they had nevertheless been unable to secure for themselves during the battle. "What if we blanket the space between us and the Starfleet vessel with disruptor bolts?" she asked. "Not attempting to strike the enemy, but to interfere with the operation of their sensors . . . to obscure the *Eletrix* just long enough for us to cloak and go to warp."

Atreev appeared to consider the question, even as he worked his controls and launched another barrage of weapons fire at the Federation vessel. The compact but powerful ship seemed a more or less equal match for *Eletrix,* but throughout the course of the battle, the Starfleet crew had gained just enough of an edge to foreshadow the eventual outcome of their encounter. "Our generators are not functioning at optimal capacity," Atreev said. "If we fire our disruptors in the way you suggest, while leaving enough power to cloak and go to warp, we wouldn't be able to defend ourselves in the interim."

Eletrix rocked again as another Starfleet weapon punched at the warbird's shields. When the ship had steadied, T'Jul said, "We're barely able to defend ourselves right now." She peered at the main screen and saw the Federation starship flash across the field of view. "We don't need to win this fight," she told Atreev. "We need to escape it." She looked back at her executive officer, who nodded in agreement.

T'Jul paced back over to stand in front of her command chair. Addressing her entire bridge crew, she said, "It is of vital importance to the Empire that we deliver the Dominion equipment we have aboard. To that end, we are going to lay down a line of fire to obscure the sensor readings of the Federation starship." She gazed back toward her executive officer. "Subcommander Atreev, at the moment of maximum dispersal of the disruptor salvo, you will cloak us."

"Yes, Commander," said Atreev.

Turning to the starboard side of the bridge, toward the piloting console, T'Jul said, "Lieutenant Torlanta, once we are cloaked, you will take us immediately to warp. I want rapid, random course changes at short intervals, until we are certain that we are not being pursued."

"Yes, Commander," acknowledged Torlanta.

On the viewer, T'Jul watched as the Starfleet vessel arced around, its crew clearly intending to make another weapons run at *Eletrix*. The commander waited until it appeared at its farthest reach from her ship, then called out, "Execute."

At once, T'Jul heard the sounds of the weapons and defense station as Atreev worked its controls. On the viewscreen, a throng of bright green disruptor bolts raced into the area between *Eletrix* and the Federation starship. The line of attack looked haphazard, but as weapons began to detonate, the effectiveness of the firing pattern became clear. The output of the exploding disruptor bolts spread out and joined together, forming a transitory but uninterrupted veil of energy in space.

"Cloaking," Atreev said. The lighting on the bridge changed, dimming and gaining a green tint, signaling to the crew the operation of the ship's cloak.

"Going to warp," Torlanta said, but then *Eletrix* shook strongly again. The intensity of the bridge lighting returned to normal at once, its green hue lost.

"The cloak is down," Atreev said, stating the obvious. "Shields down to nineteen percent."

Before T'Jul could ask what had happened, she saw a second, smaller Starfleet craft rush across the viewscreen, a pair of phasers firing from its bow. Behind it, the broad shroud of disruptor energy faded into nothingness. The other Federation vessel sprang forward, quantum torpedoes bounding from its forward weapons ports toward *Eletrix*.

"Return fire when you can," T'Jul ordered, knowing that it would take some time to recharge the disruptors. The deck shifted beneath the commander as the quantum torpedoes landed. Her leg struck the edge of the command chair, and she fell heavily into the seat, a movement that seemed to perfectly capture the sense of resignation that tightened about her. She felt anger toward Tomalak and the Tal Shiar, but also disappointment and disgrace for her inability to accomplish the goals of the mission they had set her. More than anything, loss and sadness threatened to overwhelm her, emotions she sustained both for herself and for her crew. Her time as their commander had been the most fulfilling not just of her career, but of her entire life. She had worked so long and so diligently to attain her rank and her position, and yet her tenure would be short-lived.

For T'Jul knew how the day would end for *Eletrix* and those aboard the Romulan warbird.

Captain Ro Laren closed her eyes and saw the end of her life rapidly approaching. She held her injured right arm against her body, feeling the ache deep within it, the fall she'd taken that had pinned it beneath her still fresh in her mind. Breen disruptors had thrashed Deep Space 9, sending her sprawling to the deck in ops. She had picked herself up, though, and fought back—just as all of her command crew there had.

But DS9 had been compromised when a pair of bombs planted in its lower core had detonated, causing the loss of containment for two of the station's reactors. Her crew jettisoned one of the reactors, but the explosions had damaged the second ejection mechanism. There had been no time for Ro and her officers to even attempt anything else.

And then, as though the Prophets objected to the impending loss of Deep Space 9 and all aboard the station, the wormhole had blossomed into existence, a refulgent flower denying the great desert of space. Befitting its cognomen among the faithful, the Celestial Temple then delivered a potential savior into the Alpha Quadrant: *U.S.S. Robinson*. Not a believer herself, Ro nevertheless focused on the identity of the *Galaxy*-class starship's commanding officer: the Emissary himself, Benjamin Sisko.

But whatever hope *Robinson* might have brought with it had vanished as quickly as the wormhole. The Tzenkethi marauder wheeled around, its tail demolishing Kasidy Yates's cargo vessel. Suddenly, Captain Sisko's presence on the battlefield seemed less like a cause for hope than a brutality conveyed by indifferent circumstance.

At which point, DS9's first officer, Colonel Cenn Desca, had walked up beside Ro and whispered that only twenty seconds remained before the station's damaged reactor would explode. Ro thought of Quark in that moment, and hoped that he had been evacuated and had made it to safety. She also felt an awful sense of helplessness as she peered around at the women and men with whom she had lived and worked, some for just months, but most of them for years. It tore at her that she had let them down, that in the end, all their efforts, all their dreams, essentially came to nothing.

But isn't that the truth of all things? Ro remembered asking herself in what she had known would be the last moments of her life. *No matter what we do, a day will come when we are no longer here.*

The thoughts had struck her even then as fatalistic. *At least we will die together,* she told herself, attempting to recast her final feelings. *At least we will die together in a place where we worked with each other for the greater good.*

And then, almost miraculously, Ro's vision had begun to cloud with white motes—not from being vaporized by a reactor going critical and destroying Deep Space 9, but from the familiar effect of a transporter beam.

Captain Ro Laren opened her eyes and saw the rest of her life stretching before her. She stood in the cockpit of *Rio Grande*, behind Dalin Zivan Slaine, who sat with Ensign Rahendervakell th'Shant at the main control console of the runabout. When the bombs had been discovered in the lower core, Ro had charged th'Shant—an engineer with considerable piloting experience— with aiding in the evacuation of Deep Space 9's civilian population. Along with Ensign Richard Gresham aboard *Rio Grande*, the engineer made several runs to Bajor, ferrying scores of passengers each time. They had just transported another load of people aboard from the station when the *Defiant* crew discovered the Romulan warbird attempting to steal into the Alpha Quadrant through the wormhole. Ro ordered the vessel fired upon, but a Tzenkethi marauder and a Breen warship decloaked, intercepting DS9's quantum torpedoes and phasers. Despite the risk to the civilians aboard *Rio Grande*, th'Shant chose to take the runabout into battle, eventually firing on all three enemy ships.

Just before DS9's reactor had blown up, resulting in the destruction of the station, Ensign Gresham had detected the looming disaster on the runabout's sensors. Th'Shant opted to fly *Rio Grande* within transporter range of DS9, and Gresham beamed over everybody in ops, including most of Ro's senior staff: Security Chief Jefferson Blackmer, Science Officer John Candlewood, Slaine, Cenn, and the captain herself. Ro had never felt happier to see the inside of a runabout, but she could not prevent herself from thinking of the many other Starfleet officers who'd still been aboard Deep Space 9, as well as the civilians there who'd been awaiting rescue.

Through the forward viewports, the Romulan warbird began to fade from sight. Ro understood the implications of that: once cloaked, the enemy vessel could evade detection and escape not only from the Bajoran system, but from Federation space. After all that had transpired—the sabotage on DS9, the attack by the three Typhon Pact starships, the destruction of the station—Ro could not allow that to happen. She could not deny her hunger for justice and even vengeance, but more than that, she felt driven by the need for actionable intelligence. Why had the Pact taken the actions it had, and what did it mean for the future?

"Fire," Ro ordered Dalin Slaine. Highly skilled in the use of shipboard weapons, the strategic operations officer had taken over at tactical for the less experienced Gresham, who had moved to a support console on the starboard side of the cockpit. Slaine reached forward on her panel and worked its controls. Phaser fire immediately shot from the bow and bombarded the spot where the Romulan vessel had just disappeared. For a moment, the energy blasts seemed to stop in the middle of empty space, but then the form of the warbird materialized once more.

Off to port, the wall of disruptor energy the Romulans had created began to disperse, and *Defiant* became visible beyond it. At once, the Federation starship assailed the Romulan vessel with quantum torpedoes. "Take evasive action," Ro told th'Shant, wanting to provide the *Defiant* crew with a clear field of fire. "Then bring us around again." The young officer quickly swung the runabout around in a wide arc, away from the warbird.

"Captain," said a familiar voice from behind Ro—a voice that caused her to force back a smile. She turned to look past the rest of the ops crew to see that one of the evacuees had entered the cockpit from the aft living compartment, where nearly a hundred civilians crowded together. He held a crimson carryall at his side, its strap slung across his shoulder. Ro guessed that none of the people rescued from the station would have been permitted to bring along any of their belongings, but it didn't surprise her that Quark had somehow managed to defy that order. "Do you know when you'll be able to bring us to Bajor?"

"Quark, now's not the time," Ro told her old friend and sometime lover. Her words came out more abruptly than she'd intended, but considering the situation, she would have been justified in having him hauled bodily out of the cockpit. Still, it felt good to see him, to know that he'd escaped Deep Space 9 before the end.

Colonel Cenn walked over to the barkeep—who, Ro reminded herself, also served as the Ferengi ambassador to Bajor—and took him by the elbow. The first officer attempted to steer him back through the aft door. Instead, Quark pulled his arm from Cenn's grasp and sidestepped around him.

"I'm sorry to bother you, Captain," Quark said, his tone noticeably even. He sounded neither angry nor scared, but rather, concerned. "It's just that some of the people back there are beginning to panic." He hiked a hand back up over his shoulder, pointing a thumb toward the rear of the runabout. "Morn's just about ready to open a hatch and abandon ship."

Before Ro could respond, Dalin Slaine said, "Captain, we're coming back around."

Ro held Quark's gaze a moment longer, then looked to Cenn. "Desca," she said, "see if you can calm our passengers down, would you?"

Cenn nodded. Evidently satisfied, Quark headed back into the aft section of the runabout. The first officer followed.

Ro turned back to the main console. Through the ports, she saw both *Defiant* and the Romulan vessel in frozen tableau, the battlefield grown surprisingly still. Lieutenant Commander Blackmer at once sat down at a companel on the port bulkhead and tapped at some controls.

"Bring us to a full stop," Ro ordered.

"Yes, sir," said th'Shant, working the conn to halt *Rio Grande*. "What's going on?" he asked, clearly puzzled by the sudden cessation of hostilities.

"Captain, I'm reading an open comm channel between the *Defiant* and the Romulan ship," reported Blackmer.

"Let's see it," Ro said.

Blackmer operated the companel, and an image appeared on its screen. Ro's second officer, Lieutenant Commander Wheeler Stinson, stood in the center of the *Defiant* bridge. He had dark, wavy hair and a long face, with a mouth that naturally turned down at the edges. Ro had always thought of his countenance as brooding, though he in general had an upbeat, if serious, personality.

"—of the Federation vessel *Defiant*," said Stinson. "*Our sensors indicate that your weapons are off line and that your shields are on the verge of collapse. We demand that you lower your shields at once. Your crew will be taken into custody for treaty violations and acts of aggression against the Federation. We will provide any medical assistance your crew may require."* Stinson stood quietly in the center of the *Defiant* bridge, obviously expecting a response.

Ro waited as Blackmer studied the companel. "I'm not reading any return communication from the Romulans," said the security chief.

"No, of course not," Ro said. In her experience, Romulan arrogance knew no bounds. "Jeff, open a channel to the *Defiant.* I want to speak with—"

The Romulan warbird exploded. Virtually everybody in the *Rio Grande* cockpit flinched, Ro included. The white-hot blast incinerated the Romulan vessel in just seconds, leaving only the smallest remnants behind.

Silence descended on the *Rio Grande* like a shroud. So many lives had been lost that day that Ro already felt shocked to the core by it all. With the apparent self-destruction of the Romulan starship, a numbness began to set in.

A piece of debris floated past the viewports, whether from Deep Space 9 or the Romulan warbird, Ro could not tell. The wreckage snapped her from her daze, reminding her that prior to the loss of DS9, she had ordered all the emergency bulkheads on the station closed. That meant that if large enough sections had survived the destruction of the station, then people might still be alive within them.

"Jeff, open a comm channel to the *Defiant,*" Ro said. "I want to talk to Wheeler." They needed to check on *Robinson* and the Tzenkethi marauder, but after that, they would have to mount rescue efforts, trawling through the debris field in search of survivors.

As long as the day had already been, Ro knew that it would be longer still before she and her crew could rest.

As the tapering end of the Tzenkethi marauder bore down on *Robinson,* Lieutenant Commander Uteln reached for the firing touchpad, even before Commander Rogeiro issued the order for phasers. Over the sound of the ship's impulse engines thrown into full reverse, a tremendous din filled the bridge. The ship jolted severely, in a way that the security chief had never before experienced. On the main viewscreen, through the white haze of the Tzenkethi tractor beam, he saw debris flying away from the point of impact, from where the tail portion of the marauder had plowed into *Robinson*'s saucer section.

Uteln's hand came down on the firing control, and a phaser blast flashed outward at point-blank range. The beam caused a surface explosion on contact, and the Tzenkethi tractor beam immediately ceased. Uteln glanced at the hull integrity indicators on his tactical console and saw alarms everywhere, *Robinson* breached in many sections, on a number of decks, throughout the forward center of the primary hull. Emergency force fields struggled to contain the massive damage and protect the crew from the vacuum of space, but the security chief knew that they would fail; too many areas had been affected, and the grid had been compromised in too many locations. He quickly brought the fleshy side of his hand down on the pad that secured emergency bulkheads in place. He watched as indicator after indicator turned green, realizing that those that stayed red likely signified portions of decking that no longer existed—at least not as an intact part of *Robinson*. Though the emergency bulkheads that remained would protect the rest of the ship and crew, Uteln knew that they could do nothing for those who'd been in the path of the vicious Tzenkethi attack.

Peering up at the main viewer, the security chief saw more wreckage drifting through space—and then, among the pieces of misshapen metal, several bodies. As he watched the scene in horror, *Robinson*'s phasers penetrated the marauder's silver hull. A moment later, the Tzenkethi ship blew up. Chunks of the fractured vessel hammered into *Robinson,* shaking the ship again and again, until at last the remains of the marauder had passed.

Uteln stared at the viewscreen, at what had once again become an empty starscape, but he recalled clearly seeing the bodies of some of his shipmates floating lifeless through the void. He knew that hundreds of Tzenkethi, perhaps more than a thousand, had just been lost as well, and he figured that many of their crew likely had no choice in participating in the attack on Deep Space 9. Still, Uteln found that he could muster little compassion for them.

The security chief suddenly realized that his name had been spoken, and he refocused his attention. The ship's first officer stood in front of the command chair, peering up at him. Uteln replayed in his head what he'd just heard, which had been Commander Rogeiro asking him for a report of the ship's status.

"Checking," Uteln said, consulting the readouts on the tactical console. "The Tzenkethi vessel struck the forward portion of the saucer section, carving out a roughly wedge-shaped gap through the forward parts of decks eight, nine, ten, and eleven. Emergency force fields are ineffective because of the extent of the damage, but emergency bulkheads are sealed and maintaining the integrity of our internal environment. Casualty lists are still coming in, but we have dozens of injured, some critically, and—" He looked at the list that had so far been assembled, and noted the tally at the bottom. "—at least twenty-seven missing." The top of his bald head went cold, a typical Deltan reaction to tragedy.

For his part, Commander Rogeiro looked ashen, the color drained from his swarthy complexion. He started to say something, but his words came out in a low, breathy voice that Uteln couldn't understand. The first officer stopped, cleared his throat, and began again. "What about the *Defiant*?" he asked.

"Scanning," Uteln said, operating his sensor panel. "I'm detecting the *Defiant*, but not the Romulan warbird." He studied the readings of the Starfleet vessel. "The *Defiant*'s shields are functioning at low levels, but the ship is operational." He checked for radiation and residual energy in that area, identifying numbers that, in the current situation, could only be considered good news. "It appears that the warbird has been destroyed."

Rogeiro let out a long breath, apparently in relief. "Are there signs of any other Typhon Pact ships?" he asked.

Uteln broadened the reach of the sensors to include a larger region about Deep Space 9—or about the location that DS9 used to inhabit. "No, sir, I'm seeing no other Typhon Pact ships," he reported. "There's considerable wreckage throughout the area, but there are also a number of smaller vessels, both civilian and Starfleet, unharmed."

Then Uteln spied a sudden fluctuation in the numbers. "Sir," he said, "there's a ship closing on the area at high impulse speed." The idea that the *Robinson* crew and its badly damaged starship would soon find itself in battle once more brought with it feelings of dread and resignation. Uteln worked to identify the approaching vessel, scanning for its transponder beacon. To his relief, he immediately read an ID signal. "Commander, it's the *U.S.S. Canterbury.*"

"All right," Rogeiro said. "Raise the *Defiant,* then I'll talk to the *Canterbury.*"

"Aye, sir." Uteln toggled open a standard ship-to-ship comm channel, then nodded to the first officer.

Rogeiro turned around and faced the main viewscreen. "*Robinson* to *Defiant,*" he said. "This is Commander Anxo Rogeiro, in temporary command."

On the viewer, an image of the *Defiant* bridge replaced the field of stars. A tall, slender man gazed up from the command chair. Uteln noted that he wore the two solid and one hollow pips of a lieutenant commander, and he wondered if DS9's captain had perished on the station.

"*Commander,*" the man said. "*I'm Lieutenant Commander Wheeler Stinson.*"

"What is your status, Commander?" Rogeiro asked.

"*We've taken some damage, but we're still spaceworthy,*" said Stinson. "*We're just beginning rescue efforts. Emergency bulkheads were closed on Deep Space Nine prior to its destruction, so there may be survivors in some of the larger pieces of the wreckage. Captain Ro is coordinating operations from the runabout she's aboard, the* Rio Grande.*" Stinson turned to a console at the side of his command chair. "*I have Captain Ro on another channel,*" he said, working his controls. "*I'm patching her in.*"

On the viewer, Uteln watched as the picture of Stinson aboard *Defiant* shifted to the left half of the screen, while a Bajoran woman, presumably Captain Ro, appeared on the right side. She held her right arm closely against her side, as though she'd recently hurt it. To Uteln, she appeared exhausted, and yet also determined.

"Commander Rogeiro," she said, but then she paused. She cast her gaze aside for a moment, but then looked back up. *"How is the* Robinson *and its crew?"*

"Both are badly damaged," Rogeiro said. "Before we destroyed the Tzenkethi vessel, they took a sizable slice out of our primary hull, and we've sustained casualties."

Ro nodded. *"Are you still functional?"* she asked. *"I know the* Canterbury's *on its way, but we're going to need all the help we can get in our recovery efforts."*

Rogeiro peered back up over his shoulder. "Uteln?"

The security chief verified the current status of the ship with a glance down at the tactical console. "I'm not sure how we'd fare against another marauder," he said, "but all of our breaches have been sealed, and the engines and transporters are working."

Rogeiro turned back toward the viewscreen again. "We're prepared to assist," he told Ro. "Should we coordinate with you or the *Defiant*?"

"With me," Ro said. *"Commander Stinson has another task to take care of right now."*

"Understood," Rogeiro said.

With the urgency required of the rescue operation, Uteln wondered what else could possibly warrant the attention of the *Defiant* crew. On the main screen, he once again saw Captain Ro hesitate and then look away. When she peered back, she finally voiced the question that he thought had been troubling her. *"Where is Captain Sisko?"*

"The captain is in sickbay. He's been . . ." Rogeiro paused as he seemed to search for the appropriate word to use. "He's been injured," he said at last. "But he should make a complete recovery."

Though Ro's expression didn't change, Uteln still perceived relief in her. *"We're working on a grid for our search,"* she said. *"In the meantime, we'll send you coordinates at which to rendezvous. Meet us there, and we'll provide the search pattern."*

"Yes, Captain," Rogeiro said.

The tactical console chirped, and Uteln studied the panel to see that the *Rio Grande* crew had transmitted the coordinates.

"*Ro out,*" said the captain, and the runabout cockpit disappeared from the viewscreen, which filled again with Lieutenant Commander Stinson on the *Defiant* bridge.

"Rogeiro out," said the first officer.

Uteln followed the implied order and terminated the comm signal. When Rogeiro looked up at him again, the security chief said, "Coordinates received, sir. I'm routing them to the conn."

"Sivadeki," Rogeiro said, "when you're ready, take us to the coordinates." He moved to the command chair and sat down, then contacted Doctor Kosciuszko in sickbay.

Uteln returned his attention to the tactical console, where he examined the damage assessments being submitted by the crew from all over the ship. He could already see that *Robinson* would require considerable downtime to effect repairs. *But nobody's going to be able to repair all the people we lost,* he thought cheerlessly. Then he thought about Captain Sisko. In the two and a half years in which Uteln had served aboard *Robinson*, he'd never seen his commanding officer react to anything the way he'd reacted to the destruction of the *Antares*-class cargo ship. From the names Sisko had said afterward, Uteln understood that the captain believed that his wife and daughter had been aboard that vessel.

But he should make a complete recovery, Commander Rogeiro had said. Uteln didn't agree. In fact, he wondered if Captain Sisko would ever set foot on the bridge of *Robinson* again.

Tomalak—for so long a commander in the Romulan Imperial Fleet, and after that, a proconsul for two different praetors— stood on the bridge of the Breen privateer *Ren Fejin,* racing for home. *A home whose walls have grown weak,* he thought angrily. *A home whose leader would gladly allow mortal enemies to walk through those walls, even to topple them, rather than charge the Empire with spending the necessary capital to reinforce them.*

The deck underfoot rattled considerably, but Tomalak

had become accustomed to the rough ride. He longed for his voyage to conclude, but not because of the uncomfortable vibrations that the freighter's engines sent coursing through the ship. Rather, he simply craved success in his first mission as an agent of the Tal Shiar. Tomalak wanted to prove his worth as he embarked on the next stage of his professional career, but more than that, he wished to deliver to the Empire the tools it required to ensure its military superiority over the Federation and its Khitomer Accords allies.

He walked over to the middle of the confined bridge, to where the navigational console projected a holographic sphere. An image of the Breen vessel—a brace of opposing and asymmetric arcs joined together by a connector that looked misaligned—sat in the center of the display. Ahead of the ship, a bright green line—the same color as the horizontal light across the front of the ridiculous Breen helmets—showed *Ren Fejin*'s calculated course. None of the pinpoints that represented the stars correlated to any Romulan sun. As long as his journey had been—from the Empire, to Deep Space 9, to the Gamma Quadrant, to the Dominion, and finally back to the Alpha Quadrant—it would yet require days and days before he would see the familiar lights of home appear on the display. Before he returned to Romulus, though, he would have to visit the Breen Confederacy.

And thanks to the ineffectiveness of the Breen and the Tzenkethi, and the incompetence of T'Jul, he thought, *it's going to take me even longer to get home.* With the loss of *Eletrix,* Tomalak no longer had a ready means of traveling from the Confederacy back to the Empire.

Turning in place, he peered around the bridge. One Breen oversaw ship operations, while a second piloted the vessel. A third, Trok—the engineer who required Dominion technology in order to develop and implement quantum slipstream drive on Typhon Pact starships—stood in a corner. *Perhaps observing,* Tomalak thought of the Breen engineer, *but more than likely simply cowering.* Since Trok's rescue from the clutches of the Jem'Hadar, he had kept to himself, showing signs of emotional trauma through his agitation and reticence. Tomalak surmised that the engineer understood just how close he had come to death; of the thirteen Breen who'd boarded *Ren Fejin* for their mission, only four—along with a Romulan specialist, Joralis Kinn—had survived the near debacle in the Gamma Quadrant.

Taking two steps over to the communications panel, Tomalak felt the inclination to dispatch a coded message back to the Empire, back to Tal Shiar Chairwoman Sela. The idea of sharing word of what had happened, and of laying the responsibility for the failure at the feet of T'Jul and the others, seemed necessary, but he also understood the foolhardiness of transmitting even encrypted communications through Federation space. In the current state of affairs, at least until Kinn reinstated the cloak on *Ren Fejin,* it would take great effort to avoid not just Starfleet patrols, but also civilian vessels. Thanks to the recent agreement to open some of the borders of the Typhon Pact and the Federation to commercial traffic, a Breen cargo ship would not by itself draw attention, but with the fiasco at the mouth of the wormhole, the situation had changed. Sending any kind of message to the Empire, to Sela, would foolishly risk *Ren Fejin's* detection.

And I did not rise for so many years through the Imperial Fleet, he thought, *I did not have starships named after me, I did not have praetors seek out my counsel, because I took foolish actions.* For too long, Romulus had been beset, if not by fools, then at least by leaders who overreached their abilities. Hiren, Shinzon, Pardek, Braeg, Rehaek, Tal'Aura, Donatra, Kamemor—they had all played at Romulan politics and power, and they had all lost. Well, Gell Kamemor had not yet lost, but she would. In Sela, Tomalak had finally allied with the keenest mind and the most fervent patriot he could.

The harsh notes of what sounded like an alarm rang out in the enclosed space of the bridge. The two Breen at the operations and piloting consoles looked at each other and spoke in their garbled electronic argot. Tomalak stepped closer to them, and his translator deciphered the final few words after the alarm ceased: "*—ship in pursuit.*"

Tomalak spun quickly and moved back to the holographic

navigational display. At the edge of the spherical projection, directly aft of the representation of *Ren Fejin,* he saw the form of the Starfleet vessel that had engaged *Eletrix* as soon as the warbird had reentered the Alpha Quadrant. Tomalak observed for just a moment, and in that brief interval, the starship visibly gained on the Breen privateer.

Tomalak hastened to the communications panel, reached up, and pressed the button that initiated an open link. "Bridge to engineering," he said. "Kinn, what's the status of the cloaking device?" Because the agreement that unlocked Typhon Pact and Federation borders to commercial craft explicitly prohibited vessels with cloaks, Joralis Kinn, a specialist in such technology, had traveled to the Gamma Quadrant with the crew of *Ren Fejin,* carrying with him the component pieces from which he could construct a functioning cloak. He had assembled the device, and the Breen had employed it in their mission to the Dominion, but to avoid raising Starfleet suspicions upon their return through the wormhole, he had dismantled it prior to their reentry into the Alpha Quadrant.

"The status is that I'm in the middle of rebuilding it," Kinn replied, the comm channel lending a hollow ring to his words.

"In the middle?" Tomalak said. "Kinn, we've got a Federation starship coming up fast behind us. We need to hide this scow, and we need to do it soon."

"How soon?" Kinn asked.

Tomalak peered over at the two Breen running the ship, both of whom stared back at him—or seemed to—through their snouted masks. "How long before they reach us?" he asked them, pointing over at the navigational display. One of them consulted his panel, then gave an answer enumerated in Breen units of time, which Tomalak quickly estimated for Kinn in Romulan terms.

"That's not enough time," said the specialist.

"It better be," Tomalak told him, "or we're going to be spending time—probably a *long* time—in a Federation prison." Tomalak would never allow himself to endure such a fate, of course, but he clearly needed to motivate Kinn.

"Maybe if I had more assistance," said the specialist, though his tone did not sound especially confident to Tomalak. At present, only one person, the fourth surviving Breen, aided Kinn.

Tomalak looked across the small bridge. "You," he said, pointing over at Trok. "You're an engineer. Get down below and help Kinn."

Trok froze.

Tomalak took a stride toward him. "Go!" he bellowed. "If you don't recall, the Jem'Hadar took down this ship's shields, and we certainly can't outrace or outgun a Federation starship. The only thing we can do is hide, so you better go help Kinn make that happen."

Trok nodded, hesitantly at first, but then more strongly, as though coming to understand the exigency of the situation. He quickly crossed the bridge and exited. Tomalak could only hope that his engineering expertise would function as an asset to Kinn.

Returning to the communications panel, he said, "Trok is on his way. As soon as you can cloak the ship, do it. Then let me know so I can change our course and avoid detection."

"Very well," Kinn replied calmly.

Tomalak closed the channel, then cursed the specialist aloud for his equanimity. The two Breen looked his way, but he ignored them. Instead, he headed back over to the holographic display, where he saw that the Starfleet vessel had already grown noticeably closer.

Tomalak watched the representations of the two ships for a while. As he did so, time seemed to speed up. The gap between the two ships continued to shrink.

When a tone indicated an incoming transmission to the bridge, Tomalak deluded himself for an instant into hoping that it originated with Kinn down in engineering. It didn't. When he moved over to the communications panel and accepted the message with a touch to a control, he immediately heard a male voice speaking in Federation Standard. Even if his translator hadn't interpreted the words for him, and even if his long experience with Starfleet hadn't brought him a significant understanding of the foreign tongue, he could have deduced the speaker's intent from the circumstances.

"*This is Lieutenant Commander Wheeler Stinson of the Federation vessel* Defiant," the man said. "*You are ordered to stop your vessel at once and surrender. You will be taken into custody on suspicion of abetting treaty violations and acts of aggression against the Federation. Please respond at once.*"

Tomalak reached up and opened a communications link. "Bridge to engineering," he said. "Kinn, how long until we can cloak?"

"*You just sent Trok down here a short while ago,*" Kinn said. Though his tone stayed level, his words seemed to suggest that his composure had begun to crack. "*We still need some time.*"

Unfortunately, Tomalak thought, *in addition to shields, effective weapons, powerful engines, and a functioning cloaking device, time is something we lack.* But he said nothing more to Joralis Kinn. Instead, he punched at the control to close the channel to engineering.

Tomalak wondered what he could tell the Starfleet officers who would take him into custody, and those who would follow, undoubtedly with questions. He could claim that the crew of *Ren Fejin* knew nothing of the Romulan warbird that, while cloaked, had followed the Breen cargo ship through the wormhole. He could assert that he'd been duped, or perhaps captured and held against his will. He could, in fact, maintain any number of falsehoods in an attempt to save himself. He understood, though, that even the smallest amount of scrutiny would expose his lies.

The signal that denoted an incoming transmission rose once more on the bridge. Again, he worked the communications console to receive the message. "*This is Lieutenant Commander Stinson of the* U.S.S. Defiant. *You are ordered to bring your vessel to an immediate halt. If you do not, I will be forced to open fire. Without shields, I cannot be sure that your vessel will survive such an assault.*"

To Tomalak, the ultimatum fell short of the strongest form it could have taken. Had the roles he and Stinson played been reversed, Tomalak would have avowed with certainty that *Ren Fejin* and its crew would be destroyed if *Defiant* sent phasers or quantum torpedoes in their direction. Regardless, he knew that the long path he'd traveled from Romulus had finally come to an end—at least for the present.

"Bring us to a full stop," Tomalak told the two Breen. They looked at each other momentarily before turning to their consoles and working their controls. Around them, the sound of the ship changed, the drone of the engines deepening as *Ren Fejin* slowed. Likewise, the shuddering of the deck calmed.

When at last the bridge had completely quieted and stilled, Tomalak drew a disruptor pistol from the hem of his silver, broad-shouldered tunic. The Breen had virtually no time to react before he shot them down. Tomalak had no confidence that they would have kept their silence about the mission once they'd been taken into Federation custody.

Wasting no time, he rushed from the bridge and made his way to the ship's engineering section. Kinn did not appear surprised even when Tomalak aimed his disruptor at the specialist and the other two Breen. Once he had ended the threat that they would reveal the nature of their mission to Starfleet, Tomalak encoded all the relevant information about that mission and transmitted it to Trok's chief assistant, Keln, who would immediately pass it on to Sela. Tomalak looked forward to the time when the chairwoman would secure his release from Federation custody so that they could celebrate what would ultimately become their victory. He then took the time to destroy all of the cloaking equipment, and then to purge the ship's logs.

It occurred to him to take his own life, but he trusted in his own ability to resist the interrogations of Federation authorities. Despite the attitudes of some Romulans, Tomalak found the prospect of an honorable death far less appealing than that of a dishonorable life. And he needed to remain alive, so that Sela could effect his eventual return to the Empire.

Instead, Tomalak deposited disruptor pistols in the hands of the four Breen and the Romulan specialist. He discarded his own weapon as he did so. He briefly lamented the loss of Trok, the Breen who had developed the methodology for creating and installing slipstream drive on Typhon Pact starships, but the engineer had not worked alone, and so surely Keln and other Breen would be able to renew his efforts.

His final tasks aboard *Ren Fejin* complete, Tomalak returned to the bridge and waited. He did not reply to any additional hails from the *Defiant* crew, but since the Breen ship no longer traveled at warp, and since it had no shields protecting it, he knew that the Starfleeters would not fire on him. Eventually, the bright white illumination of a Federation transporter beam appeared before his eyes.

Doctor Julian Bashir sat on the floor of what previously had been a corridor in one of the crossover bridges on Deep Space 9. No longer a part of the demolished station, the dim section of boxlike hull had become a lifeboat, carrying survivors of DS9's destruction drifting through the sea of space. He and the twelve other people with him still awaited rescue, but he felt confident that such salvation would come.

Many lives clearly must have been lost, though, and it troubled Bashir that he had no idea whether Sarina had survived. After bombs had been discovered in the station's reactor compartment, she had stopped by the infirmary on her way from the security office, saying that she just wanted to see him before she played her role in dealing with the crisis. She stayed for only a moment, but he could still feel the warm touch of her lips on his, could still hear the sweet sound of her words—*I love you; be safe*—in his ear.

Captain Ro had assigned Sarina, as a part of DS9's security team, to help evacuate the station's population—first civilians and then the crew. The captain tasked Bashir with safely relocating patients from the infirmary to *Canterbury*'s sickbay, so that they could then be taken to ground-based facilities on Bajor. Afterward, he too aided with the overall evacuation from Deep Space 9. But from the time Sarina left the infirmary, through the disintegration of the station, to the current moment, Bashir neither saw nor heard from her again.

Seated on the deck of the crossover segment, the doctor gazed from the emergency bulkhead at one end of the erstwhile corridor toward the emergency bulkhead at the other. Together, the thick metal doors held in heat and atmosphere, containing the small, habitable environment against the airless, pressureless nullity of space. The lighting panels in the overhead and the artificial-gravity grid embedded in the deck had failed with the loss of power, but emergency chemical lights provided indistinct, yellowish illumination, and a stash of harnesses in a crisis kit allowed people to secure themselves to the deck in a seated position.

All of the people there peered up at Bashir, obviously waiting for him to continue speaking. He knew that the six men, four women, and two children, all civilians, looked to him for leadership, for guidance and a sense of surety that rescue would indeed find them. He had tried to provide it by engaging the youngsters, a brother and sister, perhaps six and four years old, respectively, who had begun to grow restless and, he thought, scared. When the boy, Relev, had begun to ask when they could go home, the mother had looked to Bashir plaintively.

Bashir had related the tale of Beltese, a *pylchyk*—a Bajoran draft animal—and the farmer who used him to plow his fields. Each morning during one particular planting season, when he went to yoke up Beltese, the farmer found different shapes cut out of the grass, leaving behind various dirt figures. This perplexed the farmer. The only thing he could think of was that Beltese was eating the grass and making the geometric shapes, but pylchyks didn't do such things.

"Finally all the plowing was finished," Bashir continued. He noticed that the eyes, not just of the children and the mother, but of all the adults, had turned toward him. He had not intended to gather everybody's attention with his telling of the old Bajoran fable, but he counted anything that took the castaways' minds off their shared plight as positive. "The next day, the farmer was going to begin planting his *katterpod* crops, so he didn't need the plow, but he decided to go out to the pasture anyway. Beltese was there, of course, but that morning, he was standing right beside the place where all the grass had been disappearing. And when he raised his head and looked over at the farmer, that old pylchyk was chewing a mouthful of grass."

"He *did* do it," yelped the little girl, Solay, clapping her hands together.

"Yes, he did," Bashir agreed. "And the farmer gazed down at the dirt shapes, and he finally realized what he was seeing. The circle was B'hava'el, up in the sky. The triangle was a roof, and the square below it was a farmhouse. There were lines that formed fences, and other triangles that represented distant mountains in the background. And in the lower right-hand corner, rows of smaller shapes looked like katterpod plants in full bloom.

"Beltese had created a picture of the farmer's land," Bashir concluded.

"He was a *smart* pylchyk," said Solay.

"Yes, Beltese was a smart pylchyk, and he was an artist," Bashir said. "And that's the point. The farmer thought Beltese was just a draft animal, and Beltese certainly was strong and very good at pulling a plow across a field. But he also was good at something else: making pictures."

The mother put her hands on Relev's shoulders and leaned in toward him. "Just like you can do different things," she told her son. Whether or not she'd ever heard the story before, she evidently understood its message. "You can be a farmer and an artist, you can be a vedek and a champion swimmer. You don't have to be just one thing, or even just two things. You can be whatever you want to be."

"What about me, Mommy?" the little girl asked.

The mother reached out and took hold of her daughter's hand. "You too, Solay," she said. "You can be anything you want."

Solay seemed to consider this for a moment, and then she declared, "I want to be a pylchyk."

Bashir could not stop himself from laughing. Other people joined in, including the mother of the two children, who pulled her daughter to her and hugged her tightly. In such tense conditions, the jollity provided a welcome moment of relief.

Once the laughter had subsided, Relev said, "Tell us another story."

"I think I've talked enough for right now," Bashir said. In truth, something about the tale of Beltese had begun to gnaw at him.

"Ple-e-ase," the boy said, stretching out the word.

"Now, Relev," his mother chided him, "the doctor just told you a story. We need to let him take a break now."

The boy looked down at the deck, plainly disappointed, but he did not protest his mother's decision. For a moment, silence surrounded the group. Then, from the other end of the crossover segment, a voice said, "I know an old legend I can tell." Bashir leaned to one side to peer past the other people. He saw a young, raven-haired Bajoran woman say, "It's called 'Home Are the Travelers.'"

Bashir had never heard of the story, but as all of his fellow castaways turned toward her, he saw no reason to question her choice, especially given its title. He listened as she began the tale, a bit haltingly at first, but then with more self-assurance as she continued. Before long, though, Bashir's mind wandered from her oration and returned to Beltese. He had always heard the moral of that story rendered as some version of *You can be more than merely one thing in your life*, just as the mother had said. But another interpretation occurred to the doctor: *Not everybody is who they appear to be.*

A cynic might regard that less as a moral, Bashir thought, *and more as a caution.* He wondered why he'd selected that particular tale, and then attempted to convince himself that it had been a wholly random choice. *But as Counselor Matthias or some other psychologists might insist, there are no accidents.*

Bashir understood the thoughts trying to rise to the forefront of his mind. Two months earlier, Sarina had reported a conversation she'd overheard in which a fellow member of the crew, Ensign th'Shant, threatened revenge against the Federation for not doing enough to aid the Andorian people with their species-wide reproductive crisis, a perceived failure that had led directly to Andor's secession from the UFP.

Suspicion had fallen not just on th'Shant, though, but also on Sarina and DS9's security chief, Jefferson Blackmer.

At the time, Bashir had vigorously defended Sarina, and indeed, after an investigation, she—as well as the other two officers—had been exculpated. Bashir knew that Sarina had previously worked for Starfleet Intelligence, and that during that time, she had been approached by Section 31. She had even agreed to conduct operations for the amoral, extralegal organization—but only for the ultimate purpose of exposing them and extinguishing their unseen, uncontrolled power.

Bashir knew all of that because Sarina herself had confessed it to him. After they completed their own mission for Starfleet Intelligence in the Breen Confederacy a year earlier, they decided to build a life together on Deep Space 9. Before long, Sarina admitted to Bashir her involvement with Section 31, its intention to utilize her to enlist him, and her goal of finding a means of bringing down the organization.

But she revealed all of that to him only under the strictest conditions, in which she could be certain that they would be neither seen nor heard by any of 31's agents or devices. After that, they developed their own complex shorthand and shifting ciphers for use when discussing how the two of them could effect the end of Section 31. Even so, prudence dictated that they talk about such matters only occasionally.

The allegation of Sarina's possible involvement in a terrorist plot against the Federation—and more specifically, against DS9—had therefore troubled him greatly. Bashir knew that she not only served Starfleet loyally, but that she risked everything in working furtively to put a stop to Section 31. He also loved her, and therefore resented any suggestion of criminal or immoral behavior on her part.

But, looking back over the past two months, the investigation of Sarina troubled him even more. She had been cleared, and for that, he had been grateful, and maybe even relieved, though he had never conceded, even to himself, that he harbored any doubts about her innocence. In the wake of Deep Space 9's destruction, though, he finally asked himself the question he hadn't been able to after the investigation: *why* had Sarina been cleared?

For in truth, she *had* worked for Section 31—and still did. Nobody but Bashir knew the reasons for her involvement with the clandestine organization, and so her membership in it should have raised serious concerns. He could only figure that the investigation had not discovered her association with the group.

But that raises another question, Bashir thought. What else remained undiscovered about Sarina? In the terms of the story of Beltese, how many roles was she playing?

Bashir shook his head, as if that might clear it and dispel his concerns. He felt disgusted for even allowing himself to doubt Sarina. How could he possibly entertain such thoughts about the woman he loved? He'd waited his entire life for Sarina, and then once he'd found her, he'd ended up having to wait nearly another seven years for them to be together. If he couldn't trust her, if he couldn't place his full and unmitigated faith in her, then how could their relationship possibly endure?

Except that I can't be sure if we even still have a relationship, Bashir thought. *I don't know if Sarina's alive.* Once more, the possibility of her death filled him with dread. At that moment, he wanted more than anything to see Sarina's beautiful face, to hold her in his embrace again, to feel the delicate pressure of her lips as they kissed.

With an effort, Bashir forced himself to abandon such thoughts. As the lone Starfleet officer in the crossover segment, he knew that he needed to focus on the dozen people for whom he had become responsible. To help him do that, he chose to concentrate on the voice of the young woman relating the Bajoran legend.

Just a few seconds later, though, Bashir heard something else. A hum rose in the enclosed space, a recognizable drone that in that moment sounded to the doctor like music. He watched with a mixture of joy and relief as the surroundings began to fade, replaced an indefinable amount of time later by another place entirely.

Bashir pushed himself up to his feet from a large, rectangular transporter platform. He saw at once that he had been transported to a cargo hold, several Starfleet officers crewing a console across the compartment. He peered around at the people with whom he'd been set adrift, tallying their number as they stood up to make sure that everybody had been recovered. As he counted to twelve, the mother of the two children caught his eye.

"Thank you, Doctor," she said.

Bashir smiled in response. Then he felt a tug at his pant leg. He looked down to see Relev staring up at him. "Thank you, Doctor," he said.

"Thank you, Doctor," echoed Solay.

Bashir lowered himself to his haunches before the two children. "You are both most welcome," he said.

"Julian?" The voice came from the front of the transporter pad. Even before Bashir rose back to his feet, even before he turned to see Sarina, tears pooled in his eyes. When he saw her—dressed in her Starfleet uniform, smudges of dirt on her knees, her long, light-brown hair pinned up but tousled—he sprinted down the steps to the deck and threw his arms around her.

"Sarina," he said, and he could almost taste the sound of her name on his lips. "You're all right." He intended the words as a simple statement, but they came out more as an earnest plea.

"I'm fine," she said, and she pulled back to face him, her hands on his shoulders, his on her waist. "I was in the docking ring when the emergency bulkheads closed," she said. "Like you, I was trapped in there, but safe, when the station broke apart. The *Canterbury* recovered us." She looked about the cargo hold, indicating that they presently stood on the *Galaxy*-class starship. "Captain Ro is leading the rescue effort aboard the *Rio Grande*."

"The captain survived?" Bashir said, surprised by the news, but pleased.

Sarina nodded. "A lot of people have," she said. "There were about twenty-two hundred left on the station when . . ." She could not finish her sentence—or chose not to. "So far, including your twelve, we've saved five hundred forty-seven of them from pieces of wreckage that were protected by the emergency bulkheads, and that managed to survive the breakup of the station."

Sarina took a step back and inspected Bashir. "Are you all right?"

"A few bumps and bruises," he said, "but nothing major."

"Not everybody's been as fortunate," Sarina said. "There are quite a few broken bones, as well as a number of head traumas. If you're up to it, I'm sure the *Canterbury*'s CMO could use some assistance in sickbay."

"Of course," Bashir said. "I'll head there straightaway." But he didn't move. He stood there and gazed at Sarina, ecstatic that he had not lost the woman who meant everything to him. He stepped forward and swept his arms around her once more. "I love you," he whispered into her ear as her arms encircled him.

"I love you," she whispered back.

Finally, they let each other go. Bashir turned and headed for the cargo hold's doors, on his way to *Canterbury*'s sickbay. He did not think once about the doubts he'd begun to form about Sarina.

Enterprise dropped out of warp, slowing to impulse speed as the ship entered the Idran system. Captain Jean-Luc Picard sat in the command chair on the bridge and watched the main viewscreen, anxious for the light show that awaited. While he knew that he would appreciate the spectacle of the next leg of his ship's journey, he simply wanted to return to Federation space.

"We're approaching the threshold," announced Lieutenant Joanna Faur from her position at the conn.

"All ship's systems ready for the traversal," said Lieutenant Jasminder Choudhury. The ship's chief of security, she crewed the tactical station.

"As soon as we arrive, Lieutenant Faur," Picard said, "take us in."

"Aye, sir," returned Faur.

As he waited, Picard glanced down and to his right, to where his first officer sat. Commander Worf peered back at him. Betraying nothing via any sort of facial expression, Worf leaned toward Picard and asked, sotto voce, "Are you all right, Captain?"

"I'm fine, Number One," Picard said, not bothering to lower his voice. He understood Worf's concern. The crew's time in the Gamma Quadrant had ended more quickly than anticipated, and far more abruptly. The plan for the joint exploratory mission of *Enterprise* and the Romulan vessel *Eletrix* had called for a voyage measured in months, not weeks. But the tragic, and thus far unexplained, crash of the warbird on a moon, resulting in the loss of all hands, had halted the historic undertaking almost as soon as it had begun. With the mission intended as a form of entente between the Khitomer Accords and the Typhon Pact, it remained to be seen how its conclusion would affect interstellar relations. Certainly, the prospect of a breakdown in the uneasy peace between the two factions had caused a noticeable rise in the tensions of the crew. Picard himself, contrary to what he'd just told his first officer, felt tired, and he did not relish having to make a full report of events to the commander-in-chief of Starfleet, Admiral Akaar, or to the Federation President, Nanietta Bacco.

Thinking about his crew and how the loss of the Romulan vessel had impacted them, Picard looked to his left, to the chair of the ship's counselor, Hegol Den. Though some doubted the reality of the loss of *Eletrix,* the image of the warbird's remnants after its apparent crash on the surface of a moon had nevertheless taken its toll on the *Enterprise* crew. Before the captain could say anything to the counselor, though, a resplendent formation of brilliant blue and white light spun across the main viewer. Impressed as always by the appearance of the Bajoran wormhole, Picard watched as the white glow at its center grew to fill the screen. *Enterprise* rushed into the opening.

Inside the extradimensional tunnel, a magnificent display of hues and shapes surrounded the ship. Picard watched as *Enterprise* traveled through sets of great white rings that rimmed the spatial passage. Immense blue and white streamers shifted like waves rolling across an ocean, and concentric circles spread along the unseen walls of the cylindrical conduit like raindrops in still water. In virtually no time at all, the captain knew, the wormhole would allow his ship to travel between a point in the Idran system and a point in the Bajoran system that, in normal space, lay some seventy thousand light-years apart. Such a journey astounded Picard, but the fact that an alien race had actually *constructed* the wormhole seemed unfathomable.

"Captain," said Choudhury, "sensors are intermittent, but they're showing a contact within the wormhole. I'm detecting indications of another ship, but—" Picard heard a series of feedback tones as Choudhury operated the tactical console. "—it's moving very slowly."

"On-screen," Picard said.

On the viewer, the image seemed to change little, but a small, dark object appeared at its center. To Picard, it neither looked nor moved like a starship. He peered at Worf, who shook his head. "Can you identify it, Lieutenant?" he asked Choudhury.

"Trying to, Captain," she said. "The readings are fluctuating, but I'm unable to distinguish any impulse signature. That could be a result of the interference to the sensors, but I can confirm its low velocity."

Picard felt his brow furrow. "We know that numerous civilian craft, including ships from the worlds of the Typhon Pact, are using the wormhole regularly for passage between the Alpha and Gamma Quadrants. Could this be one of those?"

"Possibly," Choudhury allowed, "but why would a ship enter the wormhole and then not ride its currents to its other end?"

"Perhaps it had lost engine power and then could not prevent itself from falling into the wormhole," Worf suggested.

"Perhaps," Picard said, but then another, more disquieting possibility occurred to him. Looking to his first officer, he said, "When Commander Sisko initially traveled through the wormhole, he reported his runabout landing on a planet inside it. Could the crew of this ship be scouting for that world?"

"Before our mission, I read those reports," Worf said. "It

was unclear to me whether that planet existed physically, or only as a manifestation of the wormhole aliens' attempts to communicate."

"Quite right, Number One," Picard said. "I'd forgotten that. But maybe the crew of that ship wish to answer that question for themselves. Lieutenant Choudhury, open a channel—" Picard stopped speaking and slowly stood up. As *Enterprise* had gotten closer, the details of the object had become visible. "That's no ship," he said. "At least, not an *entire* ship."

What looked liked twisted sections of metal first drew Picard's eye. As he observed the object, he saw viewports along one side, all of them dark. It rotated at a leisurely pace as it moved along, but not in a way that seemed deliberate. More than anything, it resembled a piece of wreckage, a portion of hull violently torn from a spacecraft.

"I'm trying to scan the exterior plating," Choudhury said. "Sensor function continues to be problematic."

"Number One, that doesn't look like a part of any Starfleet vessel to you, does it?" Picard asked his first officer.

"No, sir," Worf said, climbing to his feet beside the captain. "It appears too dark . . . too angular."

"I agree," Picard said.

"Captain, I'm able to scan the hull now," Choudhury said. "I'm reading cast rodinium . . . alternating layers of toranium and polyduranium . . . and a main core of keldinide." More chirps arose from her tactical station as she worked her controls. "Captain, according to our ship-recognition routine, the depths and the pattern of the hull layers most closely match those of Cardassian starships."

"But the Cardassians are now our allies," Worf said. "What could have happened to it within Federation space?"

"That's what we need to find out, Number One," Picard said.

"Captain, that appears to be an emergency bulkhead," Worf said as *Enterprise* closed on the wreckage.

All at once, Picard recognized what he saw, and it staggered him. "That's a section of Deep Space Nine." The thought of the space station taking such damage, perhaps even being destroyed, would have been horrifying under any circumstances, but on the heels of the calamity that had befallen *Eletrix* and its crew, the captain feared a link between the two events, and the advent of some great new threat to the Federation.

"Captain," said Choudhury, "I'm reading an atmosphere over there."

"An atmosphere?" echoed Picard. "Then they did seal the emergency bulkheads, so they must have had some advance warning of whatever caused this." He gestured toward the image on the viewscreen, then peered over at Choudhury. "Lieutenant," he said quietly, "are there survivors?"

The security chief tapped at her tactical console, but all her efforts resulted in the muted sounds of failed operations. "Life signs are indeterminate."

"Would it be possible to transport over there?" the captain asked. He already suspected the answer.

"Not within the wormhole," said the security chief.

Picard nodded, then moved into action. "Lieutenant Choudhury, prepare a tractor beam. Lieutenant Faur, I know our velocity is limited by the wormhole's structure and its physics, but push the *Enterprise* as best you can."

As both officers acknowledged their orders, Picard returned to his chair, and Worf followed suit. On the viewer, the ruined section of DS9 slid off to port and out of sight as *Enterprise* passed it. Given the sporadic operation of the sensors within the wormhole, Picard hoped that they would not encounter similar problems with the tractor beam.

"Ready for towing, Captain," said Choudhury.

"Make it so," Picard ordered. "Reverse angle on viewer."

The main screen switched to display the space aft of *Enterprise*. There, a translucent white energy field connected the ship to the lost section of the space station. "The tractor beam is functional and holding," said Choudhury.

Seconds passed. Picard kept his gaze on the viewscreen, hopeful that the tractor would perform long enough to allow *Enterprise* to reach the Alpha Quadrant still hauling its potentially precious cargo. The otherworldly beauty of the wormhole had suddenly lost its appeal to the captain.

And then the sets of circles and the undulating streamers and the stirring raindrops vanished, replaced on the main viewer by a whirlpool of light that marked the wormhole's entrance. An instant later, it had collapsed in on itself and closed. "We have cleared the wormhole," announced Lieutenant Faur.

"Very good," Picard said. "Viewer ahead."

For a moment, nobody said anything. Picard knew that every member of his bridge crew dreaded what they would see. The captain himself expected to see a badly damaged Deep Space 9.

But when the starscape changed on the viewer, it showed no space station at all.

"Lieutenant?" Picard asked.

From the tactical console, Choudhury spoke in low tones. "Captain, Deep Space Nine does not appear anywhere on sensors. But . . . there is a tremendous amount of debris in the area. I'm also reading several vessels: the *Canterbury* . . . a number of runabouts . . . some civilian ships."

What the hell happened here? thought Picard. He wanted to know, and at the same time, he didn't. He had witnessed so much death and destruction in his life, particularly during the last few years. And yet he hadn't grown inured to it; in some ways, he found it more difficult to deal with now than ever he had. Of course, it didn't require the abilities of a counselor to figure out that his marriage to Beverly and the birth of their son had everything to do with that.

"Lieutenant Faur, bring us to a full stop," Picard said. "Lieutenant Choudhury, are sensors showing any signs of life aboard the section of the station?"

"Something has affected the hull," Choudhury said. "I'm still getting interference." She looked up at the captain. "We won't be able to use the transporter either."

"The hull fragment might be small enough to bring aboard," Worf suggested.

"Lieutenant?" Picard asked.

Choudhury consulted her readouts. "Aye, sir," she said. "Not in any of the cargo holds, but we can bring it into shuttle-bay one."

"Make it so." Picard stood up. "Mister Worf, have Doctor Crusher and an emergency medical team meet me down there, as well as security officers and an engineering squad. If there are any survivors, maybe they can tell us what happened here. In the meantime, I want you to contact the *Canterbury* to see what they know."

"Yes, sir."

Picard paced quickly to the nearest turbolift, entered, and specified his destination. As the car descended, he asked himself why he hadn't contacted Captain Euler aboard the *Canterbury*. Some cataclysm had resulted in the destruction of Deep Space 9, and since Euler's ship had been stationed at Bajor, it seemed likely that he would have information about what had happened. Worf could just as easily have investigated the space station's lost hull section for survivors.

Except that there might not be survivors, Picard thought. They could find the section of hull completely empty. *Or we might find it filled with corpses.*

Picard realized that his answer lay with the latter possibility. As *Enterprise*'s chief medical officer, Beverly needed to be there, and so he wanted to be there as well, to shield her as best he could from the specter of more death. He thought about that for a moment, about the way in which his decision-making process had changed since his marriage and the arrival of René. Since he had in no way compromised the ship or the safety of his crew, he decided that he could easily live with that.

The lift completed its vertical descent, then glided horizontally toward the aft end of the ship's saucer section. Eventually, it eased to a stop, and its doors parted. Picard stepped into the corridor outside the shuttlebay to find Beverly waiting there with a pair of her nurses, as well as two engineers and two security officers. Beverly carried a tricorder in her hands, and a medkit slung over her shoulder, while the engineers clutched pairs of long, thick work gloves. The security officers had arrived with phasers perched on their hips and beacons strapped to their wrists.

"Have you been informed about what we're bringing aboard?" Picard asked the group.

"Yes, Captain," Beverly said.

Picard nodded, then stepped toward the shuttlebay doors, which opened at his approach. Inside, the vast deck reached all the way to the aft end of *Enterprise*'s primary hull. All of the ship's support craft sat on the inner half of the bay, or hung suspended from the overhead there; the outer half of the deck stood clear. At the far end, a wide hatch, protected by a force field, stood open to the stars, the ship's warp nacelles visible to either side.

Between the engine structures floated the hull section from DS9, its movement controlled by the tractor beam that still tethered it to *Enterprise*. As Picard and his officers watched, the fragment of hull neared the ship. After a minute or so, a spray of blue pinpoints sparked as it broke through the plane of the bay's force field. It took another minute for the tractor to deposit the wreckage on the deck and disengage.

Picard approached the hull section. It measured perhaps twice as tall as one of the ship's shuttles, and three times as long. Up close, the gray metal looked tattered, as though it had been torn apart as easily as one could tear through paper.

Beverly deployed her tricorder. "I'm having trouble scanning through the hull," she said.

"Lieutenant Choudhury reported the same interference," Picard said. He turned and addressed one of the engineers, a young Bolian named Falnam Edrel. "Ensign, how can we open the emergency bulkhead?"

"We may have to find a port and hook up power to it," he said. "But the Cardassians usually build manual overrides into such structures."

"See what you can find," Picard said. The two engineers walked over to the wreckage, donning their work gloves as they did so. The captain turned to the remaining officers. "We don't know yet what happened to Deep Space Nine, but they had time to seal their emergency bulkheads. We have no idea who or what might be inside, or even if there's anybody or anything inside at all. But I want everybody to exercise extreme caution."

"Understood," Beverly said, obviously speaking for the group.

"Sir?" said Ensign Edrel. "I think we've found something." Picard walked over, and Edrel pointed to where a metal panel had been slid aside. Inside, the captain saw a series of three *T*-shaped handles. "These are probably the manual door releases," Edrel said. "If the emergency bulkhead and the hull surrounding it haven't been too badly damaged, we may be able to open it."

Picard turned and nodded to the security officers. They positioned themselves outside the emergency bulkhead and drew their phasers. "Go ahead, Ensign," Picard told Edrel.

"Yes, sir," the engineer said. The other engineer, a female crew member whose name Picard did not recall, moved to the bulkhead, where she reached into a recess with her gloved hands and took hold of a short bar. Edrel turned the first handle. When it had made a complete revolution, a loud noise erupted from one side of the bulkhead, a sound like large locks releasing.

Edrel twisted the second handle, and earned a similar result. When he completed spinning the third handle, the bulkhead actually moved, telescoping into itself several centimeters. The other engineer, her hands still buried in the recess, pulled, and the bulkhead opened a meter or more.

Picard waved the engineers away, and one of the security officers approached the opening. He aimed his phaser, then switched on his beacon, shining its light through the opening and into the hull section. "Captain," he said, "we have two bodies."

"Go," Picard told Beverly. She quickly headed for the opening and followed the security officer inside. Picard stepped in after her.

Within the broken piece of DS9's hull, the security officer adjusted his beacon from a narrow beam to full illumination, then set it down. The setting looked like a simple section of corridor. Two women lay supine on the deck, not far from each other, tethered in position by several straps. Neither of them wore Starfleet uniforms, though one wore vestments of some kind. As Picard got closer, he saw that one appeared human, the other Bajoran. He could not tell if they were breathing.

Beverly kneeled down beside the woman wearing the robe and worked her tricorder. "This one's alive," she said, then held out the device in the direction of the second woman. "So's the other one."

"What kind of condition are they in?" Picard asked.

"Good," Beverly said. "They both have some contusions, but nothing serious. There are no broken bones and no head injuries." Beverly closed her tricorder and stood back up. "I'd like to transport them to sickbay so I can do full workups on them."

"Of course," Picard said. He started to reach up to activate his combadge, but then one of the two women—the human—stirred. Beverly saw her move too, and she quickly bent to help the woman raise herself up on her elbows. Picard walked over and squatted down as well.

The woman peered up blearily, first at Beverly, then at Picard. "Where am I?" she said, her voice gravelly.

"You're on board the *U.S.S. Enterprise,*" Picard said. "We recovered you from what appears to be a section of Deep Space Nine that had been adrift in space."

"Yes, yes, the station," she said. Then she seemed to remember something, and she pushed herself up higher, trying to see around Picard and Beverly. "Is Nerys all right?" she asked with a tone of great concern.

"You friend is fine," Beverly said. "You're both fine." The news seemed to calm the woman.

"May I ask who you are?" Picard said.

The woman nodded. "Yes," she said. "I'm Kasidy. Kasidy Yates."

I

Awaked an Evil Nature

Prospero: I pray thee, mark me.
        I thus neglecting worldly ends, all dedicated
        To closeness and the bettering of my mind
        With that which, but by being so retir'd,
        O'er-priz'd all popular rate, in my false brother
        Awak'd an evil nature; and my trust,
        Like a good parent, did beget of him
        A falsehood, in its contrary as great
        As my trust was; which had indeed no limit,
        A confidence sans bound.
                    —William Shakespeare,
                    The Tempest, Act I, Scene 2

August 2383

1

Sela's boot heels clacked on the stone floor, sending echoes along the narrow tunnel through which she walked. Two men from her security detachment followed behind her at a distance, their own footfalls adding to the cacophony in the enclosed space. Set into the walls at long intervals, lighting panels did a barely sufficient job of banishing the darkness that gripped the ancient subterranean passage. The recirculated air caressed the exposed flesh of Sela's face with an uncomfortable chill, like the threat of an ill wind as the sun sets and the night impends.

The chairwoman of the Tal Shiar led her guards at a brisk clip, striding with determination toward a meeting she had never wished to have, but for which she had still developed contingencies. Her mind brimmed with broad facts and intricate details, with unanswered questions and necessary suppositions. Sela had always understood the possibility that she might have to deliver the report that she carried with her on a data tablet, and so she had planned for it, but she didn't like it. To her way of thinking, the word *contingency* equated to failure: one need enact a secondary plan only if a primary plan has not succeeded.

But now two *of my stratagems have failed,* Sela thought, her jaw tightening. She remained uncertain how far back the latest events had set her. She had already lost so much time thanks to the incompetence of the Breen. Sela had helped the Confederacy purloin Starfleet's schematics for the quantum slipstream drive, only to see the Federation mount a covert operation and eliminate everything the Breen had subsequently accomplished, including not only a slipstream-equipped prototype vessel, but all copies of the drive plans.

You will have to work harder than all the others, her father had always told her, and he had been right. As a half-breed, born of a human mother, Sela had found it impossible even to trade on her father's rank and position—General Volskiar had commanded *IRW Victorious* through many successful campaigns—and so she'd had to work from the periphery. But she internalized her father's wisdom, and never undervalued the importance of sheer diligence.

Before rising to chair the Tal Shiar, Sela had served as a personal operative to the praetor, and before that, as a proficient officer in the Imperial Fleet. Throughout her career, she advanced as the result of indefatigable effort, and as she did so, she learned the value of careful planning. But she had never anticipated the ascension to the praetorship of somebody like Gell Kamemor—a nonbeliever in Romulan exceptionalism, and an apologist for, and even an appeaser of, the Federation. And Sela never could have foreseen the string of events, improbable in the aggregate, that had allowed it to happen: the assassination of nearly the entire Senate; the descent of Shinzon into madness; the Remans' successful struggle for independence; the schism of the Empire into factions led by Tal'Aura and Donatra; and the need for the Romulan people to accept nutritional and medical assistance from the Federation. Even after all of that, it had still required the deaths of both Tal'Aura and Donatra; the death of one of their likeliest successors, Senator Xarian Dor; and the deaths of the war hawk Pardek and Tal Shiar Chairman Rehaek—only then had enough opposition fallen to permit the elevation to praetor of a populist like Kamemor.

Sela reached the heavy door standing closed at the end of the tunnel, a bright lighting panel in the ceiling above it reflecting dully off its satin-textured metal surface. She reached up and placed her hand on the security plate beside the door, knowing that she'd already been under surveillance for some time. After the many lethal disruptions of the government in recent times, the Senate had increased security considerably—though not always visibly—in and around the Hall of State.

The scanner emitted a yellow glow as it examined Sela's hand. On the screen beside it, her image appeared, along with the details of her service record. As always when she saw herself, Sela noted the alienness of her own features: eyebrows that hugged the lines of her eyes, the flatness of her forehead, the shocking yellowish color of her hair. She despised the human elements of her appearance, the details that set her apart from her fellow Romulans. Yet she had chosen never to alter them, never to surgically effect the changes that would allow her looks to fall within the Romulan norm. Instead, she let her differences drive her to overachieve, and she chose to project the impression that her differences made her better, that they singled her out as an exceptional individual among an exceptional people.

The door slid noisily to one side, withdrawing into the wall. Sela turned back to face her guards, who could proceed no farther. She nodded curtly to them, then paced through the door and up a set of worn stone steps.

The Tal Shiar chairwoman strode through the door at the top of the stairway and into a circular courtyard. Night had established itself earlier, and the silver orb of Elvreng had risen high in the sky. The pale light from Romulus's second moon filtered through the windows in the cupola that topped the courtyard, draining the color and contrast from the scene. Between the doors that ran along the perimeter, white beams of light reached upward, the indirect illumination further brightening the area, but restoring none of its tint or texture.

Sela crossed to the set of tall, wide wooden doors that dominated the courtyard, to where a pair of *uhlan*s stood watch. In the ashen light, the chairwoman could discern the faces of the two guards no more than she could the elaborate scrollwork in the doors. Still, she knew the names of the two men—Voster and Strak—and could run down both their professional and personal histories. The idea that power relied on knowledge had been a cornerstone principle of the Tal Shiar since its inception.

"Chairwoman Sela to see the praetor," she said, identifying herself to the guards, although in addition to recognizing her, they also would have been informed in advance of her late visit.

"Praetor Kamemor is expecting you, Chairwoman," replied Uhlan Voster. He turned and, beside the doors, pulled twice on a braided rope that Sela knew to be gold, but that looked white in the moonglow. Then he leaned into the large doors, which slowly opened inward, and he stepped aside. Sela passed between the two guards, who then followed her inside.

As the doors closed decisively behind her, she peered around the praetorial audience chamber. Gell Kamemor had inarguably altered the character of the place during the six hundred days of her administration. Although pairs of columns rose majestically all around the room, creating niches filled with artwork and reaching up to a magnificent mural on the ceiling, the once-regal setting possessed a commonplace atmosphere. Despite the gleaming black surfaces of the floor and walls, despite the throne that sat on a raised platform at the far end of the room, the large conference table and the chairs arrayed around it commanded the space and marked it as a simple, workaday venue. Stark white lighting buttressed the utilitarian effect.

Such details, Sela knew, had always troubled Tomalak. He did not go so far as to suggest that appearances trumped substance, but he did believe that such things mattered, particularly for somebody in Kamemor's position. Sela did not concern herself with such minutiae, but she could not argue that the praetor succeeded in delivering a message with the refashioning of her audience chamber.

The chairwoman did not see Gell Kamemor. As Sela moved farther into the room, the praetor emerged from behind the dais, where an entrance led into Kamemor's private office. Though more than a couple of decades past her first century, the praetor maintained a healthy physique, and her lustrous black hair had not yet begun to gray. She wore traditional robes, of a gray that matched the color of her eyes.

"Chairwoman Sela," Kamemor said as she crossed in front of the dais. Never once in the many times Sela had met with her in the audience chamber had the praetor sat in her throne. "I trust from your sudden request for a meeting at such a late hour that something of considerable import has brought you here." She spoke with an ease that suggested word of events in Federation space had yet to reach the Hall of State.

Kamemor stopped near the head of the conference table,

and Sela strode over to face her. "I'm afraid that I do, Praetor," she said. "Our observers have reported a major confrontation within Federation space. I'm sure that you are familiar with the Bajoran star system."

"Of course," Kamemor said. "That's the site of the artificial wormhole that connects to the Gamma Quadrant." She paused, then, with a tone of concern, asked the logical question: "Has the Dominion sent the Jem'Hadar back into the Alpha Quadrant?"

"No," Sela said. "I'm afraid that such a situation might be easier for you to deal with." The chairwoman lifted the data tablet she had brought with her and activated it. She pretended to consult the information on its screen as she said, "At the Alpha Quadrant terminus of the wormhole, two Federation starships, as well as the Starfleet space station positioned there, engaged in battle with three Typhon Pact starships."

Kamemor's lips parted, but she did not immediately respond. She reached out a hand to the back of one of the chairs at the conference table, as though to steady herself. "'Battle'?" she said at last. "Not a *skirmish*? Not a few weapons discharges that might be ascribed to an accident, or to some overzealous tactical officer?"

"No," Sela said. "The exchange of arms apparently lasted for some time, resulting in the destruction of the space station and all three Typhon Pact vessels."

The praetor seemed thunderstruck. She stood speechless for a long moment, then pulled out the chair and slipped down onto its seat. When she peered up at Sela, her complexion had taken on a ghostly pallor. "How many dead?" she asked quietly and without inflection.

"We don't have word on that yet," Sela said. "But the number probably totaled in the thousands on the three Pact ships, and as many on the station."

Again, Kamemor said nothing. She peered toward the floor, though Sela doubted that the praetor actually saw anything, since she appeared so deep in thought. Sela waited. Eventually, without looking up, Kamemor said, "You mentioned Typhon

Pact *starships*." The deadened quality of her voice had given way to a note of anger. "By which you mean to say *military* vessels."

"Yes," Sela confirmed. She expected that the praetor's ire would only increase.

Kamemor raised her head and stared up at the chairwoman. "What were Typhon Pact *starships* doing inside Federation space?" she asked. "Other than the *Eletrix* setting out for its mission with the *Enterprise,* and the civilian vessels that have been allowed, there's no reason—no *legitimate* reason—for military ships from the Pact to enter Federation territory."

"We don't have word on that yet either," Sela said.

"No, why would you?" Kamemor said, apparently more to herself than to the chairwoman, but Sela took note. "Whose ships were they?"

Sela had known that the praetor would raise the question. Before she answered, the chairwoman pulled a chair out from the table, turned it to face Kamemor, and sat down herself. She glanced again at her data tablet, as though confirming the facts she intended to impart.

"The ships were a Tzenkethi marauder, a Breen warship . . . and a Romulan warbird."

Kamemor stood up, holding Sela's gaze as she did so. Then the praetor turned and walked calmly back in the direction from which she'd entered the chamber. For an uncomfortable moment, Sela thought that she intended to leave. Instead, Kamemor stopped along the wall, in a bare alcove between two sets of columns. There, she placed her hand flat on the wall, and a panel slid upward to reveal a communications console. She touched one of several buttons on it, then waited.

Sela stood up, but forced herself to remain calm. She considered it a possibility that Kamemor might call for a security contingent to take the chairwoman into custody, but in such a case, it would serve no point for Sela to run. "Praetor," she said, "I do have additional information for you."

"I'm sure you do," Kamemor said without turning from the communications console, which suddenly blinked to life. Even at a distance, Sela recognized the unruly head of gray hair that belonged to Proconsul Anlikar Ventel.

"Praetor," he said, his voice still heavy with sleep. *"Is everything all right?"*

"Anlikar, I want you to reach Admiral Devix at once," she said, naming the man who commanded the Romulan Imperial Fleet. "He's in space right now, but I don't care how far he is from Romulus. I want a *real-time* connection with him before the night is out."

"What's happened?" Ventel asked, sounding more alert.

"Reach Devix," Kamemor said again. "Then get to the Hall of State as soon as you can." She looked back over her shoulder at Sela, then back to the communications screen. "I think we'll be convening the cabinet, and then probably the Senate as well."

"Praetor, what—" Ventel started, but Kamemor cut him off.

"Do what I asked," she said. "Then get here."

"Yes, Praetor," Ventel said. *"At once."*

Kamemor reached up and touched a control. The display went blank. Leaving the panel open, she walked back over to face Sela once again. "Do you know what's going on?" she asked the chairwoman. The flatness of her voice made it difficult for Sela to know whether or not she intended her words as an accusation. Under the semblance of innocence, Sela chose to interpret them as a simple question.

"It's difficult to know with the paucity of information we have at this point," she said. "We don't even know who initiated the fighting."

"The Typhon Pact did," Kamemor said without hesitation, her voice rising as her anger returned. "Three unauthorized starships in Federation territory. I don't care if the Starfleet vessels did fire first; it was the Pact's fault for being there illegally. If three Federation or Klingon ships arrived at one of our most important ports, what would you do? Invite them to partake of some ale?"

"No, Praetor," Sela said, acting appropriately chastened. She had never seen the praetor so upset.

"So tell me, what do you *think* is going on?"

"My suspicion," Sela said, "is that rogue elements within the Typhon Pact are seeking to undermine the recent lessening of tensions between the Pact and the Khitomer Accords."

"If so, then they have doubtless succeeded in that goal," Kamemor said, visibly appalled at the idea. "This is not the first time since I've been praetor that 'rogue elements' have jeopardized interstellar peace," she continued, making obvious reference to the theft of the quantum slipstream drive schematics from Starfleet's Utopia Planitia Shipyards—an operation that, unbeknown to the praetor, Sela herself had set in motion. "I understand the distrust and fear of the Federation—and of the Klingons and the Cardassians and all the powers we habitually call our enemies—but what I don't fully comprehend is the desire to bring them down at the cost of Romulan lives. Let's say that we could destroy the entirety of the Khitomer Accords. Even in the best possible conditions, even if every single battle turned our way, how much of our own blood would we have to spill to make that happen?"

Sela said nothing. She herself did not understand how Kamemor, so clearly an intelligent woman, could not see the tremendous threat in allowing the Federation and its allies to sustain a first-strike capability, which the slipstream drive provided them. If the Khitomer Accords powers—which included the overly aggressive Klingon Empire, a sworn enemy of Romulus—ever chose to press that advantage, the price paid in Romulan lives would prove horrifying. But Sela said none of that, knowing that any attempt she made even to explore the possible motives of the "rogue elements" would eventually bring her under the praetor's scrutiny.

"And it's not even a question of numbers," Kamemor went on. "Even the loss of a single Romulan life—of any life—that could be prevented by averting war is worth the effort to establish and maintain peace. Which is why I need you to find out who's coordinating these rogue actions on the Romulan side."

"Yes, Praetor," Sela said. "After what just took place, we may already have an idea."

"Tell me."

"The warbird involved in the battle at the wormhole," Sela said. "It was the *Eletrix*."

"What?" Kamemor said. She placed her hands on her hips and paced away from the conference table. When she had reached the center of the room, she turned back toward Sela. "What about the joint mission? Did the *Eletrix* destroy the *Enterprise*? Were the Breen and Tzenkethi ships in the Gamma Quadrant as well?"

"We don't have any of those answers at this time," Sela said. "But the commander of the *Eletrix* is Orventa T'Jul."

"Should that name mean something to me?" Kamemor asked, walking back over to the table. Fortunately for Sela, the praetor left starship assignments and other such matters to the Imperial Fleet—though, when it suited her purposes, the chairwoman did not.

"Before being promoted to command of the *Eletrix*, she served as second-in-command aboard the *Dekkona*," she said.

"The *Dekkona*," Kamemor repeated. "That was the ship involved in stealing the slipstream drive plans from Starfleet."

"Yes," Sela confirmed.

"And so you're saying we have our traitor."

"It seems an unlikely coincidence," Sela observed, knowing well that T'Jul had never been involved in planning either the operation at Utopia Planitia or in the Gamma Quadrant, but had merely been following orders. The assignment of *Eletrix* to the latter mission, though, and therefore of T'Jul, had been the result of careful planning. The chairwoman had not anticipated failure, and certainly nothing on as grand a scale as had occurred, but she had contrived to send *Eletrix* on the joint mission with *Enterprise* for the specific purpose of having T'Jul available as a scapegoat. That T'Jul had likely died in the battle at the wormhole only amplified her value in that role.

"I want you to investigate T'Jul," Kamemor said. "Let's make sure that her presence on the two missions wasn't the result of chance. And if it's not, then I want to know who her compatriots are—beyond the Empire, but most especially within it."

"I'll start on it at once."

"Is there anything else I need to know?" Kamemor asked.

"No, Praetor," Sela said. The operation had failed, but at least the chairwoman would not need to contend with the complications that would have arisen had any of the personnel or vessels involved been captured.

"Keep me informed," Kamemor said.

Sela nodded her acknowledgment, then stepped back and headed for the doors. One of the guards opened them for her, and she exited into the courtyard. In seconds, she had picked up her security detail and started back through the underground tunnel that had brought her to the praetor's audience chamber.

By the time she boarded the shuttle that would return her to her office at Tal Shiar headquarters, she'd already decided to move forward with her next attempt to obtain the quantum slipstream drive from the Federation.

2

Federation President Nan Bacco tried to calm her rising anger as she stared across the room at *Bridge over a Pond of Water Lilies* in its ornate gilt frame. The impressionist painting, she knew, had endured for nearly five centuries, surviving three world wars and more attacks on Earth than she could probably list. Oil-based pigments on a simple piece of canvas, not quite a meter wide, and even shorter along its vertical dimension, it had been painted by a man after whom the situation room in the Palais de la Concorde had been named. Bacco had often wondered what Claude Monet would have thought about his idyllic creation adorning a place too often given over to conducting the business of war. As she peered at the artwork that morning, though, she thought about the fact that it antedated the United Federation of Planets by more than a century and a half. *And with the way we're going,* Bacco thought, *I'm not sure we're going to last as long as the painting has.*

"One thousand ninety-one," she said, still seething as she looked back down at Admiral Akaar and repeated the number he had just supplied. "Is that the final count?"

"It's close," Akaar said. He sat directly across from Bacco at the large, round conference table that went a long way to filling the floor space of the situation room. Starfleet's commander-in-chief, Akaar had notified the president of the shocking events at Deep Space 9. "The ships have canvassed the Bajoran system in search of other sections of the station that might have survived its breakup. It's still conceivable that they could find more survivors, but the rescue effort has been so extensive that such a possibility is dimming."

"Do we have a breakdown?" Bacco asked. "How many civilians, how many Starfleet officers?"

Akaar reached forward and picked up a personal access display device from the tabletop. Reading from it, he said, "Four hundred sixty-one civilians dead or missing, six hundred thirty Starfleet personnel." He set the padd back down, though he continued studying its display. "That's strictly from the station. We also have thirty-two dead on board the *Robinson,* two from a runabout, and an unknown number of casualties aboard civilian ships." He looked up then and fixed the president with what she recognized as an earnest expression. With Akaar's enormous size—a Capellan, he stood more than two and a quarter meters tall, and carried a toned physique to complement his height—his stare equated to a viselike hold. "The crews managed to evacuate or rescue more than fifty-five hundred people from Deep Space Nine. Considering the circumstances—two bombs detonating and three Typhon Pact starships attacking—that's a remarkable accomplishment."

The president nodded, not so much an agreement as an automatic response while she tried to process everything that had happened at Bajor. Beneath the outrage she felt at the duplicity of the Typhon Pact leaders—and of Praetor Kamemor in particular—Bacco also felt extreme fatigue. She had always understood—or thought she had—that the presidency would bring with it tremendous pressure, but the almost unremitting nature of it throughout her term had worn her down. She often joked about escaping the burdens of her position by not standing for reelection, but with all that had happened, she had begun to seriously think about the prospect of stepping aside.

Not that there's any guarantee that I'd get reelected anyway, she thought. Would citizens consider her record and decide that the Federation had finally and permanently beaten back the Borg threat during her administration, or would they say that the Borg had killed more than sixty billion people on her watch? Would they see her as the leader who stood up to the new and continuing threat of the Typhon Pact, or as the woman who allowed a founding member of the UFP to secede?

And what will they think if I take us into another war? The Dominion, the Borg, the Typhon Pact—maybe the Federation needed to ask itself why it had so many adversaries. *And the Pact doesn't even count as just a single enemy, but as six,* Bacco thought. *Or at least five, since we don't really have much of a history with the Kinshaya.* But the Breen, the Tholians, the Tzenkethi, the Gorn, and the Romulans had all been clashing with the UFP for a long time.

Except that I'd thought things had gotten better, Bacco thought. *With all of the Pact worlds, but especially with the Gorn and the Romulans.* After all, the praetor had approached Bacco with a proposal for a Khitomer Accords–Typhon Pact summit, and when the Boslics had subsequently hosted such a gathering, Kamemor had spearheaded efforts to move all the players away from even a cold-war footing and toward peaceful coexistence.

But that wasn't really what she did, Bacco thought resentfully. *Obviously, I was set up. We were all set up.*

The silence in the room suddenly penetrated Bacco's thoughts, and she realized that everybody present waited for her to take the lead in the meeting. She looked around the table at the others: her chief of staff, two members of her cabinet, and a second Starfleet admiral seated beside Akaar. The president glanced at Esperanza Piñiero, who sat beside her, making notes on a padd. Then Bacco took a deep breath and said, "The Typhon Pact has committed an act of war, but it seems unlikely that they actually *want* war. And I know that we don't. So why did the Typhon Pact do this?"

"Whatever their reason, they haven't announced it to us or to anybody else," said Jas Abrik. A Trill who had once served in Starfleet, rising to the rank of admiral, he served as security advisor to the president. "There's been no public word on events from any of the Pact governments, and none of our sources have picked up even any private discussions."

"Frankly, I don't care what they *say*," Bacco avowed. "I care about the reality of the situation. I want to know what their true motives were."

Across the table from the president, Admiral Alynna Nechayev glanced up at Akaar, who offered her a curt nod. "We can't be sure," said Nechayev. "It's possible that they set out to do precisely what they accomplished in destroying Deep Space Nine. Or they might have sought to secure the entrance to the wormhole for themselves."

"Is that really a possibility, that they wanted to take possession of the wormhole?" asked Raisa Shostakova, the Federation's secretary of defense. Her peculiarly short stature and poor posture betrayed her status as a native of the human colony on the high-gravity world of Pangea. "I don't see how they could reasonably hope to accomplish that with just three starships. Even if they'd managed to defeat the Starfleet forces there, how could the crews of three vessels realistically expect to hold a position against the might that Starfleet would throw against them?"

"Controlling the wormhole could be something they needed to do only temporarily in the pursuit of some other goal," Nechayev suggested.

"Or the Pact might have intended to send reinforcements," said Safranski, a Rigelian and the secretary of the exterior.

"We've seen no other incursions into Federation space," noted Shostakova, "and no massing of ships along our borders."

"We did not *see* the incursion into our territory of the three Pact starships that attacked Deep Space Nine," Akaar said, "because we were not meant to do so." The laconic admiral often said little during meetings, which lent additional weight to those things that he chose to say.

"So you believe that we're on the cusp of an invasion of cloaked ships?" Bacco asked, aghast at the thought of the Federation returning to war.

"No," said Akaar. "At least, not an invasion exclusively by the Typhon Pact."

"What?" Safranski exclaimed. "Then by who?"

But Bacco discerned Akaar's reasoning. "The Dominion," she said. She stumbled over the words, not wanting even to think them, let alone utter them. The mere suggestion of renewed hostilities with the Gamma Quadrant power chilled her. With the Cardassians and the Ferengi now signatories to the Khitomer Accords, which already included the Klingons, with Starfleet sufficiently if not completely rebuilt, and with the tactical advantage of the slipstream drive, the Federation and its allies could stand against the Typhon Pact. They would pay a fortune in blood and treasure, but they would prevail. For a while, that estimation alone had allowed Bacco to sleep at night, knowing that it would keep the Pact at bay. The recent attempts at entente by the Breen and the Gorn and the Romulans had further solidified the president's belief in the possibility of a durable peace. But the events in the Bajoran system had just razed any such hopes. *And if the Typhon Pact has established an alliance with the Dominion—*

"Yes, the Dominion," Akaar said. He looked to Nechayev, who presented the argument.

"Reports of the incident at Deep Space Nine indicate that two vessels exited the wormhole: a Breen cargo vessel and a Romulan warbird. As a part of our agreement with the Typhon Pact to open our borders, we also allowed scores of their civilian ships to cross into the Gamma Quadrant. Although we prohibited them from even approaching Dominion space, and took steps to monitor their movements, we can by no means be assured that some ships did not actually visit the Dominion.

"Further," Nechayev continued, "the Romulan warbird involved in the attack on Deep Space Nine was the *Eletrix*—the same vessel that was teamed with the *Enterprise* on the joint mission. Captain Picard reports that the *Eletrix* crew apparently fabricated the crash of their ship on a moon before returning surreptitiously to the Alpha Quadrant. The time between the former event and the latter would have allowed the *Eletrix* crew time enough to travel to Dominion space."

Bacco felt overwhelmed. Upon learning of the incident at Deep Space 9, she had called the meeting with her highest-level advisors for the purpose of dealing with the new threat from the Typhon Pact. She found it dizzying that she suddenly found herself listening to suggestions that the Federation might face another war with the Dominion, which not that long ago had come exceedingly close to defeating the entire Alpha Quadrant.

"What do you recommend?" the president asked. She peered not at Nechayev, but at Akaar.

"All of this is conjecture," he said. "We need more information."

"It would make sense," Nechayev said, "to send a ship into the Gamma Quadrant to determine if there is a Jem'Hadar force headed toward the wormhole."

"And if there is?" Shostakova asked. "It would be difficult enough to face the Typhon Pact in a shooting war. We can't also take on the Dominion and hope to survive."

"No," Nechayev said. "Which is why we'd have to collapse the entrance to the wormhole."

"Why not just destroy the wormhole completely?" Safranski asked. "That would permanently put an end to the danger of a Dominion attack."

"We can't destroy the wormhole," Bacco said. "Alien beings live there."

Safranski nodded. Bacco wondered if he had momentarily forgotten the denizens of the wormhole, or if he hadn't considered preserving their lives a priority. "So we don't destroy the wormhole," Safranski said. "We just close it. Do we even know how to do that?"

"I . . . don't think *we* do," Nechayev admitted. "But there is somebody in Starfleet who might be able to make it happen."

"Captain Sisko?" Bacco asked. The president knew of Sisko's status as a religious icon among the Bajoran people, thanks to his discovery of the wormhole more than a dozen years earlier. She also understood that he had been one of the few to communicate with the aliens who had created and resided within the interquadrant bridge.

"Yes," Nechayev confirmed.

For a few seconds, nobody spoke. The president assumed that, as with her, it would take some time for everybody to deal with the prospect of a new Dominion threat. It felt harrowing to Bacco even to consider the idea.

Finally, Security Advisor Abrik said, "I agree that it's important to think about all possibilities, to investigate the viable ones, and to plan for realistic eventualities. And we should definitely perform reconnaissance on the Dominion. But we've seen no evidence since the end of the war to suggest that they are plotting a renewed offensive. Both the *Enterprise* and the *Robinson* have spent time in the Gamma Quadrant recently, and although neither crew entered Dominion space, neither did they report observing anything noteworthy on routine sensor sweeps. If anything, the Founders and the society that serves them appear to have become isolationists. So if the Typhon Pact hasn't entered into some form of alliance with the Dominion," Abrik concluded, "we need to explore what other reasons they might have had for attacking Deep Space Nine."

"Strictly speaking," Akaar said, "it wasn't an *attack* on the station, but a *defense* against it."

"Pardon me, Admiral," said Safranski, "but such a characterization seems absurd. The crew of Deep Space Nine didn't violate interstellar borders, fly the station into the sovereign territory of a Typhon Pact state, and open fire on their assets."

"When the Romulan warbird exited the wormhole," Nechayev explained, "it was cloaked, following closely behind a Breen cargo vessel. Because of heightened security on Deep Space Nine, the *Defiant* crew checked for cloaked ships and discovered the warbird. It was only then that the Romulan ship fired on the *Defiant*, and that the Breen and Tzenkethi ships uncloaked and attacked the station. So it may be that the Pact ships planned to fight if necessary, but that they did not intend to do so if they could avoid it."

"They could have avoided fighting by not being in the Bajoran system at all," Safranski said. "But the *Eletrix* crew faked the destruction of their own starship, then apparently tried to abscond back to the Empire."

Bacco saw Abrik's mouth drop open, before he said, "Which would leave Captain Picard, Starfleet, and the Federation in the uncomfortable position of having to explain why only the *Enterprise* crew returned from their joint mission with the Romulans."

"Propaganda," said Akaar.

"Demonstrating that the Federation could not and should not be trusted," Abrik said.

"But to what end?" Safranski asked. "Who could they hope to sway to their cause by such an action? As far as we know, there are no major powers giving consideration to joining the Typhon Pact."

All at once, Bacco saw the political—and practical—goal. "What about Andor?" she said.

Beside her, Piñiero reacted with an expletive under her breath.

"The bombs planted on Deep Space Nine were covered in Andorian writing," said Nechayev. "If they had nothing to do with that, if the Typhon Pact actually planted the bombs, but the Federation accused Andor, then that might further alienate them."

Again, the room quieted as everybody seemed to consider what had just been said. As she thought about it, though, something did not make sense to the president. "It doesn't add up," she said.

"Respectfully, Madam President," said Abrik, "it does make sense, and it's perfectly in keeping with the complex subterfuges that the Romulans have historically perpetrated."

"But that's just it," Bacco said. "You know the Romulans. We all know the Romulans. They do nothing without excruciatingly detailed planning. They might not have wanted a battle at Deep Space Nine, but they did prepare for one by having the Breen and Tzenkethi ships there, and probably even by having somebody plant those bombs on the station. When the crew of the Romulan warbird had to fight, the fraud they perpetrated on the *Enterprise* crew was therefore exposed, which tells me that any propaganda value they might have gained from their ruse could not have been their primary aim."

"No," Akaar agreed. "Clearly the Romulans hoped to sneak the warbird through the wormhole and back to the Empire, but if they couldn't, they were willing to fight—perhaps in an attempt to ensure that the warbird returned to the Empire." He reached up and placed his massive hands flat atop the table. "The Romulan vessel was carrying something."

"What?" Abrik asked.

Akaar shook his head. "I don't know, but obviously it must have been something they acquired in the Gamma Quadrant."

"Whatever it was," Nechayev said, "they didn't want us to know about it, because once they'd been defeated and were on the verge of capture, they destroyed the warbird along with themselves."

"Not all of their vessels were lost, though," said Akaar.

"What?" Bacco asked. "I thought you said that all three Typhon Pact starships were destroyed."

"All three were," Akaar said. "But the *Defiant* captured the small Breen cargo vessel that the *Eletrix* followed through the wormhole. And it carried a single living passenger: Tomalak."

"The former proconsul?" asked Safranski.

"And the Romulan liaison to the *Enterprise* crew during the joint mission," said Nechayev.

"Where is he now?" Bacco wanted to know.

"We've had him transferred to the *Enterprise*," Abrik said, "where he's been placed under arrest."

"Has anybody spoken with him?" Bacco asked.

"Captain Picard's security chief spoke with him briefly," Nechayev said. "She described Tomalak as 'talkative, but not forthcoming.' The captain is awaiting word from Starfleet Command on how to proceed."

"And Starfleet Command awaits word from Federation Security and the Federation president," Akaar said.

"What is your recommendation, Admiral?" Bacco asked.

"Let Picard take a run at Tomalak before they turn him over to Federation Security," Akaar said. "The *Enterprise* crew has experience in such matters, as well as some history in dealing specifically with Tomalak, who spent many years in the Imperial Fleet."

"Jas?" Bacco asked, soliciting his advice.

"I agree with the admiral," Abrik said, "with the proviso that Tomalak should be remanded to Federation Security within a few days . . . a week at most."

Bacco looked back to Akaar, who nodded his accord.

"All right," Bacco said. She turned to her chief of staff. "So where are we?"

Piñiero dragged a finger across her padd, then said, "The first action needed is to assess the possibility of a Dominion attack."

"We've got four starships in the Bajoran system right now," Nechayev said. "We can have one of the crews make a recon run into the Gamma Quadrant."

"Send the *Defiant*," Akaar said.

"Yes, sir," said Nechayev. "I should also point out that we probably want to demand that all of the civilian Typhon Pact ships return immediately to the Alpha Quadrant through the wormhole and then vacate Federation space. We may even want to send escorts for them to ensure compliance."

"We should also recall all civilian Khitomer Accords ships from the Typhon Expanse," added Safranski.

"Agreed," Bacco said. "Admiral, whether or not we have any immediate need to fear the Dominion, I don't want to antagonize them, so let's not send more than a ship or two to bring back any Typhon Pact vessels."

Akaar nodded.

To Secretary of the Exterior Safranski, Bacco said, "For Khitomer Accords ships in the Typhon Expanse, contact Iliop." The Berellian served the Federation as its secretary of transportation. "Have him handle the recall. Tell him that I'll contact Castellan Garan and Grand Nagus Rom to make sure he doesn't run into any issues with the Cardassian and Ferengi crews. And if he pushes back at all, tell him he should be grateful that the Klingons chose not to allow any of their vessels into the Expanse."

"Yes, Madam President," said Safranski.

"I think we also need to fortify our presence in the Bajoran system by assigning a number of starships there," Akaar said. "Essentially, we need to replace the security that Deep Space Nine afforded."

"That makes sense for the short term," Bacco said. "I've already spoken briefly with Bajor's First Minister, and I'll be contacting her again to keep her apprised of our response to events. I know that she'll be looking down the road for a more permanent solution than simply a few starships, which would bolster security but wouldn't replace the other functions of a space station at such a strategically and commercially important location. I'll be addressing the Federation Council in closed session later today, so I'll broach the subject of constructing a new facility at the mouth of the wormhole. You should discuss the matter with your admirals as well."

"I also recommend that we strengthen our presence on our borders with the Typhon Pact powers," said Jas Abrik. "Not so much as to provoke a violent response, but enough to let them know that we've got our eyes on them. They've already committed acts of war. I know you've made it clear that's not what you want, ma'am—that's not what any of us want—but we have to let the Pact know that we are prepared for it, that we will brook no further actions. With the Cardassians and the Ferengi on board, we have enough matériel to increase our strength at the borders without weakening ourselves elsewhere."

"Admiral?" Bacco asked Akaar.

"It'll be a balancing act," he said, "but we can do it. We should also increase patrols specifically searching for cloaked ships. Once you've spoken to the castellan and the grand nagus, I'll contact Central Command and the Treasury Guard."

"Very good," Bacco said. Perhaps paradoxically, having concrete actions to take provided an effective means of combating her exhaustion. "More than anything, I think we need to find out *why* the Typhon Pact did what they did. Whether they were trying to forge an alliance with the Dominion, or to erect a framework for their propaganda, or to bring something back from the Gamma Quadrant, we need to know. And we'll start with Tomalak." She stood up, and everybody in the room followed her lead. Looking across at Akaar, she said, "Admiral, I want to speak with Captain Picard and Captain Sisko, so I'd appreciate it if you'd stay." Then, peering around the table, she said, "The rest of you may leave. We'll meet again soon."

A chorus of *Thank you, Madam President*s went up in the room. Jas Abrik and Safranski exited together. As Admiral Nechayev spoke quietly with Akaar, Bacco turned to her chief of staff. "What do you think, Esperanza?"

"I think there are definitely those in the Typhon Pact who see the Federation as a threat, and who therefore counsel taking up arms against us," Piñiero said. "And I think you're correct that the Romulans are pushing that agenda."

Though her chief of staff agreed with her, Bacco found the validation unsettling. "I trusted her," she said.

"She seemed genuine at the summit," said Piñiero, plainly understanding that the president spoke about Gell Kamemor. "And nothing we knew of in her personal or professional history suggested otherwise."

"I'm not so sure," Bacco said, remembering back to the briefing materials she'd received eighteen months earlier, when the Romulan Senate had appointed Kamemor to the praetorship. "As an ambassador around the beginning of the century, she delivered the Treaty of Algeron and effectively imposed it on the Federation and the Klingon Empire, which essentially ended the hopes for the trilateral peace they'd been negotiating for months."

"But if you look at some of the other writings about those events, Kamemor had some admirers," Piñiero said. "The Federation ambassador at the time firmly believed that she opposed the contents of the treaty, the new Romulan policy of isolationism, and the termination of the peace talks. And in Captain Harriman's memoir, he said the same thing, but he went even further; he called Ambassador Kamemor a true patriot, which he defined as somebody who worked for the betterment of their people, no matter how difficult or unpopular such a stand might be within the Empire."

"But that's just it," Bacco said. "She *didn't* fight the treaty or the cessation of negotiations."

"Not in front of the Federation and the Klingons, she didn't," Piñiero said. "But Ambassador Endara and Captain Harriman both seemed to think that she *did* oppose it within the Empire."

Bacco shrugged. "Well, maybe she was reasonable and sought peace back then," she said, "but maybe absolute power *does* corrupt absolutely."

"I see that every day, ma'am," Piñiero said, a devilish glint in her eye.

"Believe me, if I had absolute power, I wouldn't be here," Bacco said. "I'd be back on Cestus Three, in the middle of a hundred-hectare estate outside Prairieview, where nobody would bother me, and all I'd have to do would be to catch a Pike City Pioneers game when they came to town."

"As if you wouldn't miss the glamour of the presidency," Piñiero said.

Bacco laughed. It felt good, even given everything with which she had to contend—or perhaps *because* of that.

Across the room, Admiral Nechayev finished consulting with Akaar, and she headed for the door. Before exiting, she turned to Bacco and said, "Thank you, Madam President." Then she left.

Bacco circled the conference table and joined Akaar below the Monet painting. "Admiral," she said, craning her neck to look up at him, "I want to talk to Captain Sisko about the wormhole, just in case we do have an issue with the Dominion. We should see how feasible he thinks it would be to close it from our end, whether that means negotiating with the aliens inside it or finding some technological solution.

"I also want to talk to Captain Picard about his crew's

interrogation of Tomalak. We should tell him all of our suspicions and hypotheses."

"Yes, ma'am," Akaar said. He waited for Bacco to take a chair, then sat down beside her. Opposite them, on the wall that had been behind the president during the meeting, hung a large viewscreen. Bacco nodded to Piñiero, who had taken a different seat at the table, off to the side. The chief of staff reached for a set of communications controls in front of her.

"Zachary," she said, "President Bacco and Admiral Akaar want to speak with Captain Benjamin Sisko aboard the *U.S.S. Robinson.*"

"*Right away,*" came the immediate reply. Zachary Manzanillo assisted the chief of staff, and had done so ever since Piñiero had resigned from Starfleet and joined Bacco's staff during her time as governor of Cestus III. A moment later, the viewer activated, and the emblem of the United Federation of Planets—a pair of stylized wheat stalks cradling a blue and white field of stars— appeared in its center. As always, the president marveled at the complex communications technology that had been installed in many places throughout the Federation, and that allowed her to speak in real time with people located all over the quadrant. Sometimes, it would be necessary to maneuver ships into place to boost the comm signal, but the real-time network continued to expand.

After a moment, the UFP emblem vanished, replaced by the face of an olive-skinned man with wavy black hair and dark eyes. Bacco had spoken with Captain Sisko before, during the schism in the Romulan Empire, and so she knew that she had not reached him. She noted that the man wore three solid pips on the crimson neck of his uniform, making him a commander.

"*Admiral Akaar,*" the man said. "*I'm Commander Anxo Rogeiro. I'm Captain Sisko's first officer.*"

"Commander," Akaar said, and in the single word, Bacco thought he sounded more than a little displeased. "I'm sure that you recognize President Bacco."

Rogeiro's gaze shifted from the admiral to the president, and then his eyes widened in what must have been an involuntary reflex. *"Madam President,"* he said hurriedly, noticeably flustered, though he quickly reigned in his reaction. *"It's a pleasure to make your acquaintance."*

"Commander," Bacco acknowledged.

"Perhaps you can explain to me, Mister Rogeiro," Akaar said in a serious tone, "why an eyes-only message for Captain Sisko has been answered by his first officer." As a rule, all communications Bacco made to specific Starfleet officers carried an encoding designating them exclusively for that officer.

"My apologies, Admiral," Rogeiro said, *"but Captain Sisko is currently in sickbay and unavailable. At the moment, I'm in command of the* Robinson.*"*

"Was Captain Sisko injured during the attack?" Bacco asked, then realized that the answer seemed self-evident.

"The captain was . . . hurt, yes," Rogeiro said. Bacco took note of both the commander's hesitation and the careful phrasing of his response. *"As I said, I'm in temporary command of the ship, so if I can help you—"*

"Commander," Akaar said, "the president and I expressly need to speak with Captain Sisko. Have him contact me the moment he's able."

"Yes, Admiral," Rogeiro said.

"Akaar out." Piñiero touched a control, and the image of Commander Rogeiro aboard the *Robinson* vanished, replaced once more by the Federation seal. Turning to Bacco, the admiral said, "With your permission, Madam President, I can speak with Captain Sisko as soon as he's available, and get you the answers you need."

"That will be fine," Bacco said. "Shall we contact Captain Picard then?" But even as Piñiero worked to have a channel opened to the *Enterprise,* the Federation president thought about Benjamin Sisko, and wondered about the manner in which Commander Rogeiro had replied to her question about the captain. Though she could not say what, something seemed wrong.

3

Ben Sisko's eyes fluttered open. He looked up at the overhead, but he did not immediately recognize his surroundings. He felt disoriented. He'd just been dreaming, he remembered that, something light and comfortable. Rebecca running around the *moba* trees . . . giggling and waving her arms . . . jumping into piles of leaves.

Sisko watched her from the porch. As he leaned on the railing, he called out to her. Except that the house in Kendra Province had no railing, he knew that. But of course it didn't matter. In the dream, his hands rested on a railing, on *their* porch, at *their* house. And as Rebecca ran and threw herself down on the ground and rolled around, she laughed, a high-pitched squeal that resonated with the joy of a six-year-old.

She's so happy, Kasidy whispered into Sisko's ear, and he glanced sidelong at his beautiful wife. He reached an arm out and sent it around her waist, drawing her close. *I love you,* she told him, her breath warm in his ear.

I love you, he said, never more certain of anything in his life.

As Sisko lay on his back, reliving the images and emotions that sleep had brought, the sounds of the ship began to seep into his reverie. He could feel the soft thrum of the impulse drive, heard somewhere not too distant the occasional tones of equipment being operated, and became aware of subdued voices, the words spoken too indistinct to distinguish. Above him, the overhead looked the same as on every ship he'd ever served—*Livingston, Okinawa, Saratoga*—though not like the distinctly Cardassian architecture on Deep Space 9.

Deep Space Nine, Sisko thought. In the next instant, he saw the inner core of the station erupting in a series of explosions, saw the habitat and docking rings blown apart, broken into pieces. *Kasidy,* he thought, and then the image of *Xhosa* recurred to him—*Xhosa,* sliced in two by the whiplike action of the Tzenkethi marauder, and then blowing up.

"Kasidy," Sisko said, so quietly that he could barely hear

himself. "Rebecca." His voice cracked, more whimper than whisper. He felt hollow, as though the very essence of him had drained from his body, leaving behind an empty shell.

Still on his back, Sisko turned his head and looked to the right. He saw a bio-bed beside him, and two more beyond that, each of them filled with a member of his crew. On the other side of sickbay, a nurse studied the medical readouts on the display above a crewman's head. Sisko waited for her to leave, then dragged his legs over the side of his own bio-bed and slowly sat up. He paused there, not wanting to make himself dizzy by rising too quickly, then pushed himself to his feet.

"Captain Sisko," said a voice. Sisko looked over and saw Doctor Kosciuszko padding over to him. With his auburn, shoulder-length hair pulled back from his face and his smooth features, *Robinson*'s chief medical officer appeared years younger than Sisko, though the captain actually knew the opposite to be true. Kosciuszko stopped directly in front of him, placed a hand on the captain's upper arm, and gently applied pressure. Sisko had no choice but to sit back down on the edge of the bio-bed. "Let's take a look at you," Kosciuszko said.

"I'm fine, Doctor," Sisko said, but even he could hear the strange, impassive sound of his voice.

"Captain," Kosciuszko started, but then he lowered his voice and spoke less like a physician and more like a friend. "Ben," he went on, "you've suffered a considerable shock. You need to take it easy."

"What I need, Doctor," Sisko began strongly, but then he didn't finish his sentence. *Because I don't know what I need,* he thought. *Or I do know what I need, but I can't have it.*

"Ben," said Kosciuszko, persisting in his personal approach, "you've been under sedation, so you may be feeling a little off. But you should know that all the enemy starships in the Bajoran system have been destroyed, and we've been engaged in rescue operations."

"Rescue?" Sisko said, feeling a flicker of hope.

"A number of sections from Deep Space Nine's rings remained intact after the station's destruction," the doctor explained, "and emergency bulkheads allowed hundreds to survive."

"From Deep Space Nine's rings," Sisko repeated numbly, understanding that Kosciuszko had spoken very specifically, omitting the possibility of crews on ships in the system surviving the attack.

"Yes. There were no escape pods," Kosciuszko said. "I'm sorry, Ben."

Sisko said nothing. What could he say? In addition to ignoring the will of the Prophets and causing so much pain and suffering to the people he loved, he had left his wife and child. He had hoped in doing so to spare them, but they had paid the price of his hubris anyway. In the end, not only had he lost them, but he had thrown away the last two and a half years of their lives. *The last two and a half years of my life.* He could have stayed with them, could have shared all that time, could have spent those days showing them how much he loved them.

"Ben, I don't want to return you to duty anytime soon," Kosciuszko said, "but I need to tell you that Commander Rogeiro's been down here a couple of times. When you're ready, Admiral Akaar wants to speak with you."

Sisko nodded.

"I want you to lie back so I can check your readings," Kosciuszko said. "You're probably hungry too, so afterward, we can bring you something to eat."

The captain allowed Kosciuszko to guide him back down onto his back. As the doctor turned to examine the readings on the medical scanner at the head of the bio-bed, Sisko closed his eyes. In his memory, he saw Rebecca: in the moments after her birth, when he walked into the Shikina Monastery to find Kasidy holding her; in their home in Kendra, watching her crawl for the first time; and later, on their trip back to Earth to visit Sisko's father, seeing her manage to take a few halting steps. He recalled hearing her first word, which had sounded satisfyingly to him like *Da-da,* but that he and Kasidy later realized had been *Ada,* the initial syllables of *Adarak,* the nearby town.

Sisko tried to remember the last time he'd spoken with Rebecca. Due to the *Robinson*'s loss of contact with Deep

Space 9, it had been longer than the three days he and his daughter normally went between messages. *Was it when Rebecca was so anxious to finish talking so she could go out and play in the snow?* he asked himself. It troubled him that he could not precisely conjure up the last image of his daughter he'd seen on the companel in his quarters.

Rebecca has been fixated on coming with me aboard Xhosa, Kasidy had told him in that message. It hurt terribly to think that Sisko himself had kindled Rebecca's interest in space travel, in her mother's cargo ship and his own starship. And she'd also enjoyed visiting Deep Space 9 when he'd taken her there.

Rebecca has been fixated, Kasidy had said.

Sisko opened his eyes. *Rebecca's been fixated.* Did that mean that Kasidy had definitely decided to bring Rebecca with her? When she'd gone on her shipping run, could Kasidy have left their daughter back on Bajor?

Is it possible?

Hope sprang up within Sisko—a desperate, unconvincing mixture of expectation and self-delusion. He clung to it like a drowning man to a piece of driftwood. He swung his legs from the bio-bed once more and hopped to his feet. The doctor, he saw, had moved across sickbay, to where he and a nurse ministered to another crew member.

Sisko strode quickly across the compartment and past the main surgical bed. He skirted a low rolling table filled with medical instruments, then passed through an archway and into the corridor that led to Doctor Kosciuszko's office. Pleased to find the room empty, Sisko raced inside and directly over to the desk, where he turned the computer interface around to face him. He activated it with a touch. "Computer, open a channel to Bajor, Kendra Province. I want to speak to Jake Sisko." If Kasidy hadn't taken Rebecca with her aboard *Xhosa,* she likely would have left her with Jake and Korena.

"All extraship communications must be routed through the bridge," replied the computer.

Of course, Sisko thought. In a crisis, the crew would limit communications. "Computer, override subspace security limits, allow extraship communications from this location. Authorization: Sisko kappa zero five one seven."

"Security override accepted," responded the computer. *"Extraship communications permitted at this location."*

A rush of excitement buzzed through Sisko, but he hesitated. In that moment, between the despair of the past and the hope for the future, he could pretend that Rebecca had not gone with Kasidy, that his daughter had stayed with Jake and Korena, and that even now, she lived. But once he contacted his son, once he had confirmation that Rebecca had indeed traveled with Kasidy on *Xhosa*'s shipping run—once he knew with certainty, he could never *not* know. His daughter would be dead, and she would always be dead.

But he had to know.

Except he remembered that Jake and Korena had recently visited Earth. Their trip had been intended partly as a vacation, but also as an opportunity for Jake to reapply for admittance to the Pennington School. *Are they even back on Bajor yet?* If not, then Kasidy obviously couldn't have left Rebecca with them.

"Computer, open a channel to Kendra Province on Bajor," he said. He didn't hear anybody behind him until she said his name.

"Ben."

At first, Sisko felt sure that the voice had spoken inside his head. He understood that the loss of his wife and daughter had been too much for him, that something within him had broken. He didn't move, *couldn't* move. And then the computer asked him to specify the destination for his message, and that seemed to prompt him. He slowly turned.

Kasidy stood in the doorway.

Sisko's jaw fell open. He blinked once, and again, then slammed his eyes shut for one second, two seconds, three. He knew that he had lost his mind.

But when he opened his eyes, Kasidy still stood there.

"Oh, Ben," she said, and she rushed into his arms. He felt the warmth of her body against his, heard the susurrus of her breathing. He held her so tightly that he thought his arms might break with the effort.

"Kasidy," he said. "What about—?" But he could say no more.

She turned her head against his shoulder to face him. "Rebecca's on Bajor," she said. "She's fine." Then she buried herself back in his embrace.

When they began to tremble together, Sisko thought that she had begun to cry. But then hot tears spilled down his own face. Where earlier he had felt hollow, relief filled every part of his being.

Ben and Kasidy stood that way for a long time.

September 2383

4

Tomalak sat in the only place he could reasonably do so: on the built-in, cushioned platform that ran across the width of the compartment's inner wall. The space seemed comfortable enough, if spare: three featureless walls, a washbasin, a mirror, and elimination facilities with a small privacy screen. As a prison, it sufficed, though it did not impress him.

Neither did the woman across from him, on the other side of the force field that formed the fourth wall of his cell. Oddly enough, though human, she had a face that Tomalak found surprisingly Romulan. With dark eyes, high cheekbones, and straight bangs, she needed only an upsweep of her eyebrows and a sharpening of her helices to pass for one of his people, he thought.

No, not only that, Tomalak realized as she paced from side to side in front of his cell. She'd also have to sever the absurd length of hair she'd bound up in a tight wrap that stretched down her back. *And she'd have to keep her mouth closed too,* he thought, which forced the sides of his lips up in amusement.

"Have I said something humorous?" the woman asked.

"Not at all," Tomalak said. "Though I wish that you would."

The woman stopped walking and regarded him for a silent moment. "I wish I could, Proconsul," she finally said, "but there's nothing funny about the deaths of more than four thousand people."

"Nor have I suggested that there is," Tomalak said. "Especially since you tell me that more than a quarter of those were Romulan deaths."

The woman resumed moving to and fro. She'd identified herself as a lieutenant and the head of ship's security, but the foreign sound of her name had left Tomalak unable to retain it. "I don't think I needed to tell you about the destruction of the *Eletrix*," she said. "I think you already knew." She enunciated her words in a mild accent that Tomalak did not recognize. "After all, when you headed into the Gamma Quadrant three weeks ago, you were a member of its crew."

"And so I was," Tomalak said. "But things change."

"Do they?" the lieutenant said. "So are you claiming that at some point during your time in the Gamma Quadrant, you left your position aboard the *Eletrix* to join the crew of a Breen freighter, and that there's nothing more to your story than that?"

"I must admit," Tomalak said, "that does sound implausible for a man with such a distinguished career in the Imperial Fleet."

Again, the woman stopped pacing. "You are welcome to treat this matter lightly," she said. "But I can assure you that *you* will not be treated in the same fashion."

"No?" Tomalak said, rising to his feet. "Am I to conclude, then, that I am to endure more of this 'brutal' questioning?" When the *Defiant* crew had first transported Tomalak over to *Enterprise*, the lieutenant had appeared at his cell to ask him about what had transpired in the Bajoran system. Her rudimentary interrogation had made it easy for him to say much but reveal nothing. For the next three days, the *Enterprise* crew had essentially left him alone, until the lieutenant arrived just a few moments earlier and renewed her questioning.

Tomalak strolled forward until he stood opposite the woman across the threshold of his cell, peering at her from close range. He could sense the energy of the invisible force field that separated them. "Tell me," he said, "with your questioning, how am I to survive beneath the crushing weight of such imposed boredom?"

"You do yourself no favors with your intransigence," the lieutenant said. "Whatever your plan, you've failed. Instead, you face a long incarceration, with little chance of ever seeing your home again. If you're bored now, just think how decades of imprisonment on Earth will feel to you." The woman offered him a slight, tight-lipped smile. He gave her credit for so effortlessly mimicking his own expression. "Imagine the tedium of such an existence for a man with your distinguished career."

Tomalak gazed at the woman, feeling a strong urge to reach across the short distance between them and wrap his strong hands around her delicate neck. Instead, with the force field preventing him from doing so, he allowed his lips to part in a broader smile. "I withdraw my earlier statement," he said. "You *do* amuse me." Without waiting for a reaction, he turned and moved deeper into his cell, but not before peering past the lieutenant and taking the measure of what he espied there. His cell fronted on a larger chamber, and he saw a single crewman— presumably another member of the ship's security staff—sitting behind a freestanding console.

When Tomalak looked back at the lieutenant from just in front of the sleeping platform, he said, "You know, Starfleet security could learn a great deal from the Tal Shiar, who really know how to extract information from a subject. Or perhaps you could take lessons from the Breen; they're a bit less subtle, employing their neural truncheons, but they do get results. There are even the Klingons, your own allies, and their blunt but useful mind-sifter technology." Tomalak sat down once more. "Oh, but your Khitomer Accords ban the use of such devices."

"That the Federation treats everybody, including its enemies, with a basic level of dignity and respect is a lesson the Romulan Empire could stand to learn itself," the woman said with a trace of indignation. She started to say more, but then she stopped and looked to the side. A moment later, a familiar figure came into view.

"Lieutenant Choudhury," Picard said, pronouncing the woman's peculiar name. He did not spare even a glance into Tomalak's cell, but addressed the security chief directly. "Have you made any progress with our detainee?"

The woman peered over at Tomalak. Picard did not. "He talks a lot, Captain, but he doesn't actually say much."

Picard seemed to consider that. "You should not count that as a failure on your part," he said. "In my experience with him, your characterization is perfectly apt. Which is one reason that I've decided to speak with him myself." Tomalak did not appreciate being referred to in the third person while present. "If you'll drop the force field for me, Lieutenant."

"Sir?"

Tomalak waited for Picard to reprimand his officer for questioning his order, but it did not surprise him when the captain didn't. Imperial Fleet discipline, Tomalak knew, differed markedly from that of Starfleet. It sometimes amazed him that the Federation even managed to maintain an effective presence in space, considering the laxness of their shipboard behavior.

"You may accompany me into the cell, Lieutenant," Picard said. "But I don't believe that our detainee will be any trouble." At last, Picard turned his attention to Tomalak. "He prefers to oversee operations, not to sully his hands with actual work."

If the captain's comment had been intended to wound Tomalak, to soften his resolve, it failed utterly. Still sitting on the sleeping platform, Tomalak watched as the lieutenant drew her weapon from its place at her hip, checked its settings, then turned toward the console on the other side of the outer chamber. She gestured to the crewman stationed there, and a blur of white pinpoints flashed briefly along the cell's wide opening as the force field deactivated, a low buzzing noise rising and falling with it.

Picard stepped into the cell. The lieutenant followed, and again gestured toward the crewman in the outer chamber. The force field frizzed back into place.

Tomalak watched the two officers with a measure of disinterest not entirely feigned. He did visualize overpowering them—the lieutenant first, so that he could commandeer her weapon—but even if he succeeded and then made it past the other security guard, where would he go? Where *could* he go? The vibrations in the deck, which had begun earlier that day, told him that the ship traveled at warp, and he thought it likely that *Enterprise* carried him deeper into Federation territory, not closer to the Empire.

"Liaison Tomalak," Picard said.

"*Liaison* isn't truly a title, is it?" Tomalak said. "At least, it's not one that seems to bear a sense of much importance."

"I don't agree," Picard said. "In the context of the joint mission between the crews of the *Enterprise* and the *Eletrix,* I think the actual position meant a great deal. It served as a means of familiarizing the two crews with each other, and of integrating their processes and personalities. In theory, the liaison would have facilitated understanding and friendship on a small scale, providing a model for something even greater." Picard paused, and then raised his open hands palm up, conveying a simple feeling of frustration. "But then, we didn't get to test that in practice, did we?"

"Such a pity," Tomalak said, his voice dripping sarcasm. He'd forgotten just how much he despised the garrulous Picard. He looked down briefly, and used the movement to peek furtively over at the security chief. She hadn't left her position by the force field, nor had her attention wavered from Tomalak; her weapon remained leveled in his direction.

"I agree," Picard said, clearly ignoring Tomalak's tone. "So how would you have me address you? Proconsul? High Commander? Your Majesty?"

"You flatter me, Captain."

"I mock you, 'Proconsul,'" Picard said, his features growing hard. "Except that you're not a proconsul anymore. Or are you?"

"No, no longer proconsul," Tomalak said. "No longer high commander. But perhaps if an emperor is ever restored to the throne . . ."

To Tomalak's surprise, Picard moved across the cell and took a seat beside him on the sleeping platform, just an arm's length away. "Bold words from somebody who seems to have been relegated to the position of errand boy," Picard said. "Somebody sent along simply to ensure that somebody else accomplishes *their* mission."

Tomalak understood that Picard meant to bait him, but he refused to allow it. "As you say," he replied.

"Except that you didn't even succeed at that task, did you?" Picard said. "The crews of the *Eletrix,* a Tzenkethi marauder, a Breen warship, and even a civilian freighter, all dead. All but you."

"I did not understand the compulsion of the others on the freighter to take their own lives," Tomalak said.

"Suicide, then?" Picard nodded. "You're asserting that the freighter crew took their own lives?"

"What else?" Tomalak said. "Surely you do not mean to accuse me . . ."

"No, I don't," Picard said, "because that is not within my responsibilities. The task I've been assigned right now is to deliver you to the people who will examine the evidence and decide such matters. But I would suggest that any hand you might have had in murdering five crew members aboard the Breen freighter pales beside any complicity you had in the attack on Deep Space Nine."

"If you will recall, Captain," Tomalak said, "I was not aboard any of the vessels that attacked your space station or any of your starships. I was on a civilian freighter legally authorized to travel to and from the Gamma Quadrant through Federation space."

"Again, that is for others to decide," Picard said. "But be certain of the story you tell. The more lies that pass your lips, the more difficult it will be for you."

"Lies, Captain?" Tomalak said. "What reason do the innocent have for lies? I cannot be held culpable if the crews of other ships attacked—or defended themselves against—your space station and starships. It is not my fault if the rest of the freighter crew chose to end their own lives rather than face capture. That is what some people do."

"Indeed," Picard said. "Clearly the commander of the *Eletrix* felt that way."

Tomalak shrugged. "That is often the Romulan way."

"And of course, she also destroyed whatever precious cargo you were bringing back from the Gamma Quadrant." Picard leaned forward then, so close that Tomalak knew that he could seize the captain's neck and tear the life from him before the lieutenant could even fire her weapon. "Unless the destruction of the *Eletrix* was meant as a distraction," Picard said quietly. "A ploy to lead us away from the true cargo, which you carried aboard the Breen freighter."

Tomalak smiled. "You are imaginative, Captain Picard," he said. "But I also have no doubts that Starfleet has already torn the freighter apart, and since there was no such cargo, I'm equally sure that you did not find anything."

Picard returned a smile of his own, which unnerved Tomalak. "About that, you are wrong. It is true that we did scour the Breen vessel, but we did not find nothing."

Tomalak felt genuinely puzzled. "You are either a liar or a fool," he said. He could not tell Picard that the massive, complex machinery they had acquired from the Dominion had been in *Eletrix*'s holds, not those of *Ren Fejin*. "The freighter carried no cargo back from the Gamma Quadrant."

"Didn't it?" Picard said. The bluff could not have been more transparent to Tomalak, and yet the captain seemed completely believable.

Picard rose and started toward the force field. In the instant he turned his back, Tomalak again envisioned putting a swift and welcome end to his life. But he also knew that the time for escape had not yet come. In the end, he knew that Sela would see to his release, one way or another.

When Picard reached the front of the cell, he motioned toward the security officer in the outer chamber, just as the lieutenant had earlier. When the crewman had deactivated the force field, Picard stepped out of the cell and motioned off to the side. Another officer—a thin woman with wavy blond hair—then followed him back inside, and the force field reactivated behind them. Unlike the lieutenant, she did not carry a weapon at her hip, but rather a small pouch of some kind.

"In searching the Breen freighter," Picard said, "we conducted exhaustive sensor scans. We found two items of particular note: Jem'Hadar DNA, and morphogenic tracer particles. The quantities of each tell us that at least seven separate Jem'Hadar boarded the Breen freighter, along with at least one Changeling."

Tomalak felt his jaw tighten, and he forced himself to relax. "You're lying," he said, but even he thought his tone sounded unconvincing.

"At least one of us is," Picard said. "My motive for lying might be to attempt to get you to admit something to me that you do not wish to tell me. But what would your motive be?"

Tomalak said nothing.

"Obviously, you don't want the Federation to know that the Typhon Pact initiated contact with the Dominion," Picard said, answering his own question. "But that doesn't address what cargo you might have hidden aboard the Breen freighter— unless *you* are that cargo."

"What?" Tomalak said, but then he understood Picard's point. "You think I'm a Changeling."

"Given the information I have, is that not a reasonable conclusion?" Picard said.

Tomalak stared at Picard, unsure how to respond. The captain clearly possessed the evidence for his deduction, despite its being fallacious. If Tomalak could demonstrate the falsehood to Picard, then perhaps he could drive him away from the truth. "It may be a reasonable conclusion," he said, "but that does not make it correct."

"Are you willing to prove that it's not?" Picard asked.

Tomalak almost asked how the captain expected him to do that, but he knew how. Like the Federation, the Empire had fought against the Founders during the Dominion War, and so knew how to unmask them. He also realized why Picard had called in another of his crew. "You may take a sample of my blood," Tomalak said, standing up. He knew that any part of a Changeling separated from its body would revert to its gelatinous state.

"Nurse Gigon," Picard said.

The blond woman reached to the pouch at her side, opened it, and withdrew a handheld device with a clear tube attached to it. As she approached Tomalak, he again considered taking action—perhaps throwing an arm around the nurse's neck and threatening her life—but as before, he decided against it. Gigon lifted the device to the side of his shoulder and pressed it against him. Tomalak glanced at the tube and saw his green blood flowing into it. When the nurse pulled the device away, she withdrew the tube, held it up for Picard to see, and waited.

Nothing happened. The blood remained blood.

"Are you satisfied now of my identity, Captain?" Tomalak asked.

"Oh, I've always known who you are, Tomalak," Picard said. "Nothing that you've said, nothing that happened at Deep Space Nine, nothing that happened on the *Eletrix* or the Breen freighter has changed that."

The captain looked to his officers. "Thank you, Nurse, Lieutenant," he said. The two women moved to the front of the cell, and Picard followed. The security chief kept her weapon trained on Tomalak until all three had exited to the outer chamber and the force field had been reestablished.

As the two women moved out of sight, Picard peered back into the cell. Tomalak expected him to say something, but he didn't. He simply turned and left.

Tomalak didn't know how, but suddenly he had the feeling that the captain had just bested him.

5

As the transporter effect completed and her vision cleared, Ro Laren thought that they had been beamed to the wrong coordinates. She stood in a pool of light that did not extend much beyond the portable, two-person emergency platform on which she and her security chief had materialized. Still, despite her inability to see much around her, she sensed that they had arrived in a large space.

Ro stepped down from the platform, as did Jefferson Blackmer beside her. The hollow scuff of their boots on the concrete floor reinforced the impression of openness about them. Ro glanced up and saw a single illuminated lighting panel in a ceiling at least ten meters above her head. The air smelled stale. "Are you sure this is the right place?" she asked, still peering upward. Her voice echoed back to her from the shadows.

"I verified the coordinates before we beamed down," said Blackmer. "And I confirmed our meeting with both the defense and transportation ministers." They both turned in place, looking around, but Ro could not see beyond the circle of light in which they stood. "Maybe we should contact the ship," Blackmer suggested.

Ro agreed. She began to reach for her combadge when a loud, echoing thud resounded about them. Banks of lighting panels in the ceiling simultaneously activated, illuminating a large, warehouselike space. Ro saw that the portable transporter platform lay at one end of an area that measured perhaps twenty meters wide and twice as long. Great, gray walls stretched unbroken all around, containing no doors and no windows. In addition to lighting panels, air-transfer ducts lined the arced roof overhead. Rows of computer interfaces, companels, and other equipment, all appearing inactive, marched from side to side throughout the space.

Ro turned to look behind her. In each corner of the building there, she saw an enclosed room with a single door. A sizable, solid gate, clearly intended for the movement of large equipment into and out of the space, stretched between the two rooms, in the building's front wall. Above the gate, rows of Bajoran characters spelled out WYNTARA MAS CONTROL CENTER.

One of the smaller doors opened, and a pair of Bajoran Militia officers appeared, both of them conspicuously armed. They took positions on either side of the doorway, and then four other individuals followed them out. Ro had expected both

Bajor's ministers of defense and transportation at the meeting, but it surprised her to see the first minister.

Asarem Wadeen strode directly toward Ro and Blackmer, and the captain stepped around the portable transporter platform to greet her. The popularly elected head of Bajor's government, Asarem had captured an impressive sixty-seven percent of the vote when she'd won her second sexennial term a year earlier. Immediately after the end of the Cardassian occupation, the provisional government had appointed her second minister, a position she held for five and a half years until she replaced First Minister Shakaar Edon upon his assassination. Shortly after that, during the regular election cycle, she'd been returned to the government's highest office by the people of Bajor.

Asarem stopped in front of Ro. The first minister wore a tailored scarlet suit, a color that complemented her long black hair and sienna complexion. She stood more than a dozen centimeters shorter than Ro, but the confidence with which she carried herself and the charisma she projected made her seem larger than life.

"Captain Ro," said Asarem. "It's good to see you again, though I wish of course that it could have been in more pleasant circumstances."

"Thank you, First Minister," Ro said. "It's good to see you, but I didn't expect you here this afternoon. I hope everything's all right."

"As well as it can be, given the situation," said Asarem. "I wanted to welcome you to Bajor in person, and to thank you for all that you and your crew did in evacuating Deep Space Nine. I understand that you succeeded in saving more than ninety percent of the people on board."

"More than ninety percent of the civilians, yes," Ro said. Although she had no desire to correct the first minister, she could not ignore the ultimate sacrifice that so many of her crewmates had made. "Nearly eighty-four percent overall, but we lost almost three-quarters of the crew." The captain felt pressure behind her eyes as tears threatened. In the week since the destruction of DS9, she had fought many times against crying, sometimes successfully, sometimes not. In addition to having to face the deaths of so many of her crew—deaths for which she felt responsible—she also counted many friends, both Starfleet and civilian, among the casualties. She both anticipated and dreaded the memorial ceremony she would lead tomorrow in Ashalla, Bajor's capital. Over the previous seven days, it had been hard enough to console her own crew—and impossible to console herself.

Asarem closed her eyes and bowed her head briefly before looking up at Ro again. "I'm very sorry for your losses," she said. "I offer my condolences."

"Thank you, First Minister."

Asarem waited for what Ro considered a respectful moment, and then the Bajoran leader turned to her left and motioned toward the heavyset man there. "I believe you know the minister of transportation, Kifal Illior," she said. Kifal had thinning brown hair, but a full, neatly trimmed beard. Ro acknowledged him with a nod.

"And this is our new minister of defense, Ranz Vecta," Asarem continued, gesturing to the man at her right. Ro had first seen him on the comnets when Asarem had nominated him to replace the outgoing defense minister, who'd chosen to retire from public life. After Ranz's confirmation by the Chamber of Ministers, the captain had made sure to read up about him. Much younger than the man he'd succeeded, he looked barely older than forty, but his résumé boasted two decades of impressive military service, first in the Resistance and then in the Militia. He stood at least a head taller than Ro, with chiseled features and unusually dark eyes. As with Kifal, the captain nodded to him.

"And you know my aide, Enkar Sirsy," Asarem concluded, pointing out the final member of her party. The first minister did not introduce the Militia officers, who hung back at a watchful distance.

"Of course," Ro said. "It's good to see you, Sirsy." It pleased Ro that Asarem had brought Enkar with her, rather than her other aide, Theno. While the captain usually enjoyed Theno's impertinent attitude, she didn't think she would appreciate it that afternoon.

After Ro introduced Blackmer, Asarem said, peering around, "So, what do we have here?"

"Many years ago," said Minister Kifal, "this installation housed the transportation control center for the province of Wyntara Mas." He turned and pointed up at the writing on the wall behind him. When he looked back, he began walking forward, toward where equipment crowded the space from wall to wall, and the group followed.

"'Many years ago'?" Ro said. "How far back are we talking about?"

"This control center was put into operation not long before the Occupation," he said, which put its age somewhere near the half-century mark. As the group came abreast of the equipment, Ro had no trouble believing that. In addition to the thick layer of dust that covered everything—she noted that everybody's footsteps left trails along the floor—the technology appeared well out of date. "But even after the Cardassians officially annexed Bajor," Kifal continued, "this center continued to function. It coordinated all active transportation for the entire province: ground vehicles, shuttles, and transporters. It even monitored orbital traffic, though it fed that data to the consolidated space center in Musilla. Only later, when Central Command began limiting the movements of Bajorans, did the Cardassians shut this place down."

Ro stopped at a bank of computer interfaces and dragged her hand along the surface of a monitor. Her fingertips left tracks in the dust. "So this place hasn't run in how long?" she asked. "Thirty years? Forty?"

"Actually, after the end of the Occupation, we reopened this center," Kifal said. "It required a great deal of updating, but we brought it back on line relatively quickly. It functioned effectively for three years, until we finished constructing the new planetary operations center."

"So it's been about a decade then?" Blackmer asked. Kifal nodded.

"I don't mean to offend," Ro said, examining the computer interface before her, "but this equipment not only looks old, it looks obsolete."

"Some of it is," said Kifal. He moved beside Ro and tapped at a control on the interface. It blinked slowly to life and displayed a menu of functional options. "As you can see, the overall design appears outmoded, and there's a lag in some operations. But as a part of our efforts to use this place while we built the planetary ops center, we reconstructed the infrastructure that connects Wyntara Mas to other decentralized facilities, as well as to the Militia net."

Minister Ranz walked over, and Kifal moved out of the way to allow him access to the computer interface. Ranz leaned in and worked its controls. A series of additional menus appeared in rapid succession, and he navigated through them until Ro saw a banner that read BAJORAN PLANETARY OPERATIONS CENTER. Ranz stepped through a couple of other menus before calling up a list of names and designations. He scrolled down until he evidently found the entry he wanted, which he selected with a touch. An external technical diagram of a familiar Starfleet vessel appeared. Ro read the label above it: *U.S.S. Defiant,* NX-74205. Below, she saw a shifting set of long numbers that she recognized as orbital coordinates.

"Your ship, Captain," Ranz said.

"Is this in real time?" Ro asked.

"It is," Ranz confirmed. "As Minister Kifal indicated, the infrastructure supporting this installation was upgraded a little more than a decade ago. It's not the most advanced technology, but it is functional. For access to orbital data, we're networked with planetary ops."

"We also understood that Starfleet would retrofit this center with its own computers, interfaces, and communications," Kifal said. "That would obviously increase efficiency. Also, communications relays in orbit of Bajor would link continuously to whichever Starfleet vessels are patrolling the Denorios Belt."

At the moment, Ro knew, *Canterbury, Brisbane,* and *Venture* had been assigned that duty, with *Enterprise* headed for Earth and

Robinson undergoing repairs. Admiral Akaar had ordered *Defiant* into the Gamma Quadrant to verify that the Jem'Hadar remained within Dominion borders. After confirming that, Ro had taken the ship, cloaked, on long tours through the Bajoran system, on guard against additional incursions by the Typhon Pact.

"With a continuous comlink to those ships," Kifal went on, "you can monitor readings from the Celestial Temple." Ro noticed that the transportation minister didn't say *wormhole*, and she wondered what term he would have employed had he been speaking with, say, a human Starfleet captain.

Ro looked around again at the facility. She tried to imagine her crew—*What's left of my crew*—working there, but she couldn't see it. At the same time, she knew that they had few other reasonable choices. "How many personnel can this place accommodate?"

"There are ninety-eight individual workstations," Kifal said. "But during the upgrades, we might be able to expand that."

Ninety-eight, Ro thought, knowing that the equipment that would have to be installed would not increase the capacity, but probably cut it by a third, meaning that the center would probably handle only sixty or so of her crew at a time. *That'll be tight.* Starfleet intended to assign her another two hundred fifty personnel shortly, which would bring her crew up to just over five hundred in number—still nearly four hundred fewer than she'd had on the station. The plan she had submitted to Starfleet Command called for some of her crew to stay aboard *Defiant*, while the rest worked at a ground-based facility on Bajor, until a replacement for Deep Space 9 could be constructed. If *a replacement is constructed*, she thought, realizing that she did not know how Starfleet, the Federation Council, and the Bajoran government would decide to proceed.

But if Starfleet agreed with her proposal to split the DS9 crew between *Defiant* and Bajor, she'd have to figure out how to do that. Normal capacity for *Defiant* topped out at forty, and with space for just sixty in the Wyntara Mas center, that meant that she would have the combined capacity for a hundred crew on each of three shifts; that still left her with no place for more than two hundred personnel. Presently, they pushed *Defiant*'s limits with sixty of her crew aboard, while the other two hundred had been temporarily assigned to the other ships in the system.

Addressing the first minister, Ro said, "I take it that this is the best option available."

"There are obviously more advanced centers on Bajor," Asarem said, "but they are all in heavy use. As I understand it, if we chose to adapt one of those, it would take almost as much time to settle Starfleet personnel into it as here, but then Bajor would also have to modify this facility for the displaced functions, creating far more work overall."

"I understand," Ro said. She regarded Kifal and Ranz. "You've consulted with Starfleet about this proposal?"

"We have," Kifal said. "We believe that with only a few immediate modifications, Starfleet personnel can begin using this center in just ten days. Upgrades would continue after that for another thirty."

"What about security?" Blackmer asked.

"The walls, floor, and roof were constructed with a layer of kelbonite," Ranz said. "It naturally interferes with the transporter, which is why we needed the targeting platform to beam inside. It also has a defensive shield grid, although that could also use an upgrade."

Blackmer peered over at Ro. "We can work with that, Captain."

"Well, it's not a massive, modern space station at one end of the wormhole," Ro said, "but we no longer have one of those, so I guess this will have to do." She still didn't know how she would find enough work space for her crew, but she would do what she had to do. "We're expecting the arrival of a new chief engineer shortly," Ro said, her voice cracking slightly as she thought of Jeannette Chao, who had perished on the station. "When he arrives, I'd like to send him down here to get his opinion, but in the meantime, I'll contact Starfleet Command to tell them that I believe we can proceed."

"Very good," said Asarem. "I'm glad that we can be of assistance."

Ranz reached down and deactivated the computer interface. As he and Ro started forward, back toward the portable transporter platform, the rest of the group did as well. They had only gone a couple of steps, though, when the first minister said, "I'd like a moment more of your time, Captain."

"Of course," Ro said.

"I wanted you to know that I submitted a measure this morning to the Chamber of Ministers," Asarem said. "In it, I have called for the immediate approval of Starfleet's plans for a new space station to replace Deep Space Nine."

"I didn't think that the Federation Council had authorized those plans yet," Ro said.

"They haven't," Asarem said. "Some representatives are arguing that posting starships—*existing* starships—would be a better solution than the huge commitment of time and resources a new station would require." The first minister stopped walking, and so Ro did too. "I don't agree with that assessment," Asarem said. "Since the end of the Occupation, Starfleet has completely altered Bajorans' perceptions of Deep Space Nine. In our daily lives, we no longer referred to it as Terok Nor, nor did we even think of it in terms of its terrible history. For us, it became a symbol of both hope and strength. It sat on the doorstep of the Celestial Temple, and for so long, provided a home to the Emissary of the Prophets. The space station became a part of who we are right now, and even though it's gone, we don't want to give it up."

A sense of pride and accomplishment filled Ro, since she had served as the commander of DS9 for three and a half years. But she also felt shame, for the station had fallen while under her command. She had not slept well in the last week, and didn't expect to for some time to come. When she did not lie awake in bed mourning the nearly eleven hundred who had died aboard Deep Space 9, she struggled to deal with her guilt for allowing it to happen. Again and again, she replayed the final events before the reactor went critical and started the chain reaction that led to the station's destruction. That she had been unable to find the flaws in how she had reacted to the crisis did not assuage her guilt, but instead caused her to doubt her own abilities. If she could not figure out how she could have prevented the loss of DS9 and so many lives, how could she trust herself to safeguard her crew aboard *Defiant*, on Bajor, or on another space station?

Asarem reached forward and lightly touched Ro's arm. The captain realized that her attention had drifted, that she had pulled into herself, and clearly the first minister had noticed. "You did everything you could," Asarem said, as though privy to Ro's inner monologue. "And you saved many lives."

Ro forced a smile onto her face that she did not feel. "Thank you," she said, trying not to choke on the words.

Asarem looked to the side, and Ro did too. She saw that the others in their group had continued on and reached the portable transporter platform at the front of the building, though the two Militia officers remained closer than that to the first minister. To Ro, in a quiet voice, Asarem said, "You think I can't know about what you did in those last hours and moments aboard Deep Space Nine. And maybe I can't, even though I have read a report from Starfleet Command. But I also know what your leadership has provided over time, and I have been told in recent days that your efforts during the disaster are to be lauded."

"Thank you," Ro said again. She appreciated the first minister's sentiments, and this time, she offered Asarem a genuine smile.

As the two women started toward the others, Ro's feelings of loss and shame eased, if only for the moment. But something else replaced their intensity, something that she knew would plague her until she put it to rest. The Typhon Pact had for some reason sent three starships into battle against DS9 and *Defiant*, and they might have prevailed had *Robinson* not arrived in time. But such a victory would not even have been possible, and the destruction of Deep Space 9 far less likely, had the station not been sabotaged beforehand.

Somebody had planted bombs aboard Deep Space 9, and Ro would not rest until she found them out and brought them to justice.

6

Kasidy dragged the spatula across the surface of the cake, spreading the white, orange-flavored icing over the chocolate dessert she'd baked. She swayed gently as she did so, feeling the rhythm of her coordinated movements—feeling, for the first time in a long time, the rhythm of her *life*. She smiled to herself, and even that simple act seemed as sweet to her as the confection she prepared.

Beside her in the kitchen, Ben pulled open one drawer after another, apparently searching in vain. "Are you sure they're here?" he asked. "Maybe I should just replicate more."

"Yes, they're in there," Kasidy told him, mildly exasperated, but somehow even that struck her as a positive emotion. She set the spatula across the bowl of icing, then crouched down beside her husband. "Ben, I said the *top* drawer," she told him as he reached for the lowest one on that side of the kitchen and hauled it open. "Does that look like the top drawer?"

Ben rooted around for a few seconds, pushing around various utensils and checking under some dishware. Finally, he pushed the bottom drawer closed and stood up, shrugging in obvious frustration. Kasidy followed him up. "I already looked there," Ben said, pointing to the top drawer, "and they're not there." As though to prove his claim, he tugged it open.

Kasidy forced the smile from her face as she reached forward and scooped up the package of small candles. She held them up before Ben. "They're not there, huh?"

Ben looked at the candles, then stared down at the open drawer as though it held the secrets of the universe within it. "How did you—? Where were—?" He peered back up at her, then reached up and took hold of her wrist.

Just the feel of her husband's touch sent a charge through Kasidy.

"Are these *Romulan* candles?" he asked with a smile. "Did they come equipped with a cloaking device?"

As Kasidy gazed into Ben's eyes—and oh, how she'd missed

doing that—she slyly lifted her free hand up to the counter. "Don't blame your tired old eyes on the Romulans or anybody else, Mister Sisko," she said, playfully reprimanding him. "You just need to pay more attention to what you're doing." She quickly raised her hand to his face and touched her finger to the end of his nose, depositing a gobbet of icing on it.

Plainly startled, Ben released her wrist and stepped back. "Kasidy Danielle Yates," he said reprovingly, but the shine in his eyes told her something different than his tone. He swatted the icing from the tip of his nose, then made a show of tasting it. "Not bad," he said.

"'Not bad'?" Kasidy asked in mock indignation. "I'd like to see you do any better."

"Next year," he said.

"I'm going to remember you said that," she told him, and she thought that she probably would. The very idea of Ben staying with her and Rebecca for the next year—and beyond—filled her with happiness, but also a strange sense of relief. That odd relief sprang not from the realization that her long separation from the man she loved had finally come to an end. No. Rather, Kasidy felt liberated from the need to understand what had happened to her aboard Deep Space 9, on the fragment of the destroyed station that had carried her and Nerys into the wormhole.

But it's more even than that, she thought. More than having to figure out the meaning of her experiences, she desperately didn't want to have to explain to Ben what had taken place. *If he knew—*

She could not finish the thought. It scared her too much.

"Kas?" Ben said. "Everything okay?"

Kasidy mentally shook herself, trying to shed her thoughts of the past like a dog ridding its coat of water. She wrestled for a moment with what to say, but then a peal of laughter suddenly erupted from the other room. Kasidy and Ben both looked in that direction, though they could not see the living room through the doorway. When they peered back at each other, they both smiled widely, and Kasidy knew that they shared the same joy that all parents must feel when they know that their child is happy.

"What's going on out there?" Ben called lightly.

Another burst of laughter, and then Rebecca yelped, "Jasmine's tickling me!"

"I don't know what Miss Rebecca is talking about," claimed Jasmine.

More laughter. "She's *ticklin'* me!"

Kasidy had appreciated Jasmine Tey from the moment she'd come into their lives, but in the three and a half years since, Kasidy had come to adore her. A former member of the first minister's security staff, both highly trained and widely experienced in law enforcement and personal protection, she helped rescue Rebecca from the Ohalu zealot who abducted her. Afterward, she agreed to "help out around the house" a few days a week, with the understanding that her real purpose would be to provide additional protection for Rebecca. *More protection for Rebecca,* Kasidy thought, *and peace of mind for Ben and me.* But even though the importance of her presence had grown after Ben left to take command of *Robinson,* Jasmine had become less like somebody who provided a service for their household and more like a part of their family.

"Come on," Kasidy said to Ben, nodding her head in the direction of the cake she had baked. "Let's finish this up. They should be here any minute."

Kasidy applied the rest of the icing to the cake, then watched Ben use the decorating bag to spell out Happy Birthday Rebecca! in bright orange letters. Together, they positioned the candles around the edge of the cake. "It's hard to believe she's seven already," Kasidy said, the sweetness of watching her daughter grow into her own, unique person balanced by the bitterness of life's evanescence, of the blissful, bygone times that would never come again.

"I know," Ben said, his voice nothing more than a breath.

When Kasidy looked at him, she saw that his eyes glistened. "Oh, Ben," she said, placing her hand on his arm. As quickly as the seven years of their daughter's life had passed for Kasidy, she knew that the time had gone even faster for Ben. Yes, he had brought it on himself by leaving his family, but that didn't make his melancholy any less real.

"I'm sorry," Ben said as a single tear spilled down his cheek. Without thinking about it, Kasidy stepped forward and into his arms, resting her head against his shoulder.

It had been a week since the last time they had held each other like that, when she had found him in *Robinson*'s sickbay. They had said little that day, other than to explain how each of them had arrived at Deep Space 9 when they had. Kasidy wanted to get home to Rebecca, though, and Ben agreed that she should go as soon as possible. He also promised to follow her to Bajor, a vow she refused to trust. But two days later, after he had conferred with Starfleet Command, and after Commander Rogeiro had taken *Robinson* to Starbase 310 for repairs, Ben showed up on her doorstep.

On our *doorstep,* Kasidy thought.

Chimes rang out from the front of the house, but Ben didn't let go. "They're here," Kasidy whispered to him, and she felt him nod his head. When she stepped out of his embrace, she reached up and dried the track of his tear. Then they both headed through the doorway into the dining area.

Jasmine stood at the front door, holding it open for Jake and Rena. They both wore light jackets—spring had definitely begun to take hold in Kendra Province—and wide, easy smiles. Jake held a small cloth bag in one hand, while Rena carried a wrapped gift tucked under her arm.

"Jake-O!" Ben called out. Kasidy followed her husband as he cut through the small sitting area in front of the stone fireplace on the right. When Ben reached his son, he grabbed him in a manly bear hug that had become something of a ritual for them over the past few days. Jake had long ago surpassed his father in height, but in the last couple of years, he'd also filled out. No longer the lanky young boy Kasidy had first met on DS9, he'd grown into a solid, handsome man. She loved seeing him with Ben.

After everybody finished greeting one another, they all moved off to the left, to the living room proper, where a sofa and several easy chairs sat arrayed before picture windows that offered a tranquil view of the Kendra Valley. Rebecca jumped into her brother's arms—Kasidy had yet to explain to her daughter the subtleties of her half-sibling relationship to Jake—and they flopped down together in the corner chair. As Kasidy sat down beside Rena and Jasmine on the sofa, she noticed through the windows that buds had begun to appear on several of the moba trees. It seemed that everywhere these days, she perceived new life.

"So," Kasidy said, tapping Rena on the leg, "you two never told us about New Zealand." Jake and Rena had arrived back on Bajor from Earth only three days earlier, and they'd been in transit when the crisis on Deep Space 9 had unfolded. Fortunately, Ben managed to reach them before they heard anything about what happened, sparing them any anxious moments about the safety of the family.

"New Zealand was wonderful," Rena said. "Wellington is a beautiful city."

"Oh," Jake said. "Speaking of Wellington . . . before we talk about our trip, Rena and I brought something back . . . for you." He playfully poked a finger into Rebecca's midsection, which sent her into a paroxysm of giggles. Jake reached to the floor beside his chair, where he'd placed the cloth bag he'd brought. "This isn't your birthday present," he said. "It's just a souvenir Rena and I wanted to give you." He handed the bag to Rebecca, whose eyes widened as she accepted it.

"Can I open it, Mommy?" she asked.

"Yes, honey."

Rebecca found the mouth of the bag, which had been closed by a drawstring, and she pulled it open. Then she peered inside and let out a squeal of delight. She overturned the bag and a model starship slipped into her lap. "What is it?" she asked Jake. "I never saw one like this. It's got three nacelles." Like most Starfleet vessels, a pair of warp shells extended upward from the secondary hull, but a third such structure also depended from it.

"That's a *Niagara*-class cruiser," Jake told his half-sister. "And here, can you read its name?" He pointed to the top of the wide primary hull, to the ship's identification.

Rebecca leaned in and studied the letters intently. *"U.S.S.*

Well . . . ing . . . ton," she read, then looked up excitedly. "It's the *Wellington*."

"That's right," Jake said. "And look at this." He took hold of the top and bottom of the model and pulled them apart, the two sections dividing across the midline of the secondary hull.

"Oh!" Rebecca said, then pointed inside the ship. "What's *that*?"

Jake reached in and lifted out what looked like a very large bug, measuring maybe fifteen centimeters from one end to the other—nearly as long as the model of the ship. To Kasidy, it resembled a giant grasshopper. "This is a replica of a weta," Jake said. "It's a type of insect that lives only in New Zealand."

Rebecca held out her hand, and Jake placed the weta on her palm. She studied it for a few seconds. "You know what?" she said. "This can be the alien captain of the ship." She gathered up the two pieces of the model, then scooted from Jake's lap and onto the floor.

"What do you say, Rebecca?" Kasidy asked.

"Thank you, Jake," she said, jumping back up to hug her brother. Then she raced across to the sofa. "Thank you, Rena." Then she threw herself back onto the floor to play with her gift.

"Well, now we've lost her," Kasidy said.

"That's okay," Rena said. "This way, we can tell you about New Zealand. We had a great trip."

"It rained quite a bit while we were there," Jake said, "and the temperature was on the cool side, but it wasn't too bad."

"We did a lot of sightseeing anyway," Rena said, "even when it was wet out."

"Did you get to the Te Papa?" Jasmine asked.

"We did," Jake said enthusiastically.

"That's the national museum," Rena explained. "They've got exhibitions on New Zealand's art and history, on its environment and geology, on the Maori, who are the indigenous people. It's really something."

"And plenty of the exhibitions are interactive," Jake said.

"What about the Botanic Garden?" Jasmine asked. "It's one of my favorites."

"Yes, we went there too," Rena said. Gazing across the room at her husband, she added, "We even had a romantic picnic in the Lady Norwood Rose Garden."

"Romantic and *wet*," Jake said. "It rained on us there too."

"That made it even *more* romantic," Rena said, offering knowing glances to Kasidy and Jasmine.

"I guess the big question," said Ben, who sat in a comfortable chair across the room, "is whether you think you'd like to live there."

"That depends on whether or not I'm accepted into the Pennington School," Jake said.

"I'm confident that he will be," Rena said with pride. "They accepted him once, and now he's a *better* writer. Why wouldn't they accept him again? And yes, I definitely think we can make a home for ourselves there while Jake's studying."

"Actually, I think I really would enjoy spending some time in New Zealand," Jake said. "It seems like a really interesting place."

As Rena and Jake described more of their trip, Jasmine asked lots of questions. She explained that during her secondary education in her native Malaysia, she'd spent a semester abroad in Wellington. Kasidy had never visited New Zealand, and so she listened with great interest. Ben appeared to do so as well, but he didn't say much himself.

That's how it's gone since he's been back, she thought. The two of them certainly talked, but their conversation really remained on the surface. They did speak about the events at Deep Space 9, but not about the two and a half years that preceded them. Nor did they discuss the future.

Forget about the future, Kasidy thought. *We really haven't even talked about the* present.

Since returning to Bajor, Ben had spent his days at the house, but his nights at Jake and Rena's—both before and after the couple had come back from Earth. Kasidy and Ben didn't decide together about the arrangement; it just seemed to happen. And while it removed the pressure of immediately having to reacclimate to each other, and to deal with the awkwardness that their separation had created between them, it also disappointed Kasidy not to have Ben fully back in her life.

Don't push it, she told herself. *Just let things happen naturally.*

Unbidden, the image of the wormhole rose in Kasidy's mind. She pushed it away.

After Jake and Rena finished talking about their trip, Ben suggested that the time had come for birthday cake—to which Rebecca responded by clapping and hopping up and down. *Chocolate cake is just about the only thing that'll pull that girl away from her starship models,* Kasidy thought. They all gathered around the table in the dining area and sang as Ben carried the cake in from the kitchen, its seven small candles alight. He set it down before Rebecca, who had climbed up on a chair. Hewing to an old Earth tradition, Ben told her to make a wish and then blow out the candles. Rebecca looked to the ceiling for a moment, evidently deep in thought. Then she inhaled deeply, leaned forward and, with her cheeks puffed out, extinguished the candles in a single breath.

As she watched, Kasidy made a wish of her own.

7

Denison Morad followed the two security officers out of the landing bay and through a tortuous corridor. The heels of his shoes clipped noisily along the wide metal tube as it twisted toward the functional section of the facility. Ahead of him, the two Tzenkethi moved with such effortless grace that if he closed his eyes on their softly glowing forms, their silent steps would not have betrayed their presence.

The large circular passage not only curved laterally along its course, but also rose and fell, sometimes even as it arced to one side or the other—conforming, Morad had always assumed, to the contours of the Vir-Akzelen asteroid. A series of artificial gravity envelopes, shifting at the crooks in the path, allowed individuals to maintain their footing—at least in theory. As many times as Morad had visited the experimental laboratory, he had not mastered the transitions from one gravitational field to another. He stumbled often, despite closely watching the security officers and attempting to precisely mimic their footsteps.

Of course, I'd stare at those two anyway, Morad thought. The members of alien species almost never attracted him, but something about the Tzenkethi—*any* Tzenkethi, really—always garnered his appreciation. Their flesh in no way resembled the scaled gray of Cardassians, but Morad found the delicate radiance they emitted beautiful. And while their long necks lacked tapering ridges along the sides, they still somehow gave the impression that they did—whether through a trick of color and shadow, or because of some underlying musculature, Morad had never been able to tell.

He trailed the Tzenkethi—one of them a midrange green with yellow eyes, the other of a lighter shade with orange eyes—through the winding corridor, tripping his way past the gravitational transitions, until at last they reached the final stretch. There, mercifully for Morad, the passage leveled and straightened, although that did not signal the end of the changing gravity fields. As the security officers approached the curled, patterned slats of the round door that marked their destination, they moved left, walking up the sides of the tube. Morad knew from past experience to simply close his eyes and do the same. Not looking as they entered the lab would prevent him from feeling disoriented by the change in attitude.

When Morad heard the door iris open ahead of him, he kept his eyes closed and counted out seven more steps. He navigated the final alteration from one gravity envelope to the next with only a small hitch in his stride. When he heard the door close behind him, he at last opened his eyes.

A wide, squat cylinder housed the lab. Equipment both large and small crowded the floor and also marched up the walls, thrumming as they operated. On previous visits, Morad had wondered why the ceiling remained empty, since in his experience, the Tzenkethi typically utilized every surface within a space. But as he peered upward, he at last saw why: the ceiling had been rendered transparent, allowing an unfettered view of space.

"Morad, you are here," said a voice that sounded less like speech to him than a chorus of small bells, though his translator interpreted the words for him. The Cardassian looked down to see the project's lead scientist approaching him. He recognized Nelzik Tek Lom-A from her yellow, almost golden skin and her bright orange eyes. The security officers had apparently departed the lab.

"Your message said you needed me here urgently," Morad said. "Hasn't the large-scale annular confinement generator I brought you satisfied your needs?" Not long ago, Nelzik had demanded the piece of equipment, stating that it could well solve the last technological hurdle and bring the project to fruition.

Morad had heard such claims many times. While he never disbelieved the sincerity of Nelzik and the other scientists, he had come to doubt the prospects of their eventual success. The Tzenkethi had begun their research more than a decade earlier, not long after Cardassia had left Bajor—a time Morad still had difficulty facing. The planet and its system had still offered abundant resources for the Union, including a wealthy supply of forced labor. The discovery of the wormhole and the access it provided to the Gamma Quadrant only underscored the foolishness of his people's decision to abandon Bajor. *How much better off would Cardassia be today if we had stayed?* Morad thought bitterly. *If we hadn't released the inferior Bajorans from their servitude, if we hadn't begun dealing with the hated Federation as anything but the enemies they are, and if we controlled the wormhole and access to the Gamma Quadrant?*

"The annular confinement generator has worked as expected," Nelzik said, much to Morad's surprise. He had acquired it from the Romulans, some of whom understood the great danger of the Federation, against whom both Cardassia and Romulus had fought wars. The advent of the Typhon Pact had initially provided some hope for Morad, thinking that the new alliance would at least keep the UFP in check, and perhaps, ultimately, bring it down. But when the castellan of the Cardassian Union agreed to enter talks about allying with the Federation, he felt driven to take action.

One day, when traveling to Cardassia Prime to deliver a shipment of self-sealing stem bolts, Morad learned that the UFP had donated an industrial replicator to the civilian government—a clear inducement for Cardassia to join the Khitomer Accords. The Detapa Council, in turn, announced that they would place the replicator in operation outside the city of Lakat. As much as it angered Morad for the Union to engage in friendly relations with the Federation, it absolutely incensed him to think of his people accepting its charity.

By the time he reached his destination, his emotions had seethed into a blind range. After delivering his shipment, Morad set course for Lakat. He did not remember consciously thinking about what he would do when he reached the city, but when he arrived, he didn't hesitate to act. He first used sensors to locate the industrial replicator, then confirmed its location by flying over it. Then he banked his ship hard and returned to the piece of Federation machinery. He set a short course on his navigational computer, sent out a distress call, then abandoned ship in an escape pod.

By the time the pod landed and he stepped out of it, his cargo vessel had plunged directly into the replicator. He saw it in the distance, ablaze. He felt guilt when he wondered if anybody had perished in the "accident," but that feeling quickly passed when he realized that anyone working at the replicator deserved whatever happened to them for having contributed to the diminishment of Cardassia.

Morad's trial had lasted longer than he'd expected. Assumed guilty, he attempted through his confession to persuade the archon that his had been an act of negligence and not malice. To his surprise, Archon Makbar ruled on his behalf, settling on a relatively light sentence of one hundred days in the Hutet labor camp on Cardassia IV. Only later would Morad discover that Makbar privately lauded the destruction of the Federation-provided replicator, and that she hoped that after serving his sentence, Morad would join her in the True Way.

Which he had. He resumed his livelihood as a merchant, but began using his connections to seek out like-minded individuals to enlist in the movement. The True Way represented a desire to return Cardassia to its greatest days, when the military—Central Command—provided strength and order, and ensured that every citizen worked to the benefit of the Union. But the movement also pinpointed the Federation as the most dire threat in the Alpha and Beta Quadrants, and in that, support came not just from Cardassia, but from a host of other worlds.

It did not take long for Morad and the True Way to join forces with the Tzenkethi scientists who worked to create what Cardassia *should* have had before it retreated from Bajor. Not long ago, the Romulans, with whom Morad worked, had taken an interest in the project. Injecting considerable amounts of capital into it and providing needed equipment, Tal Shiar Chairwoman Sela over the previous hundred days had, according to the Tzenkethi scientists, advanced their efforts tremendously.

"So the annular confinement generator is working," Morad said to Nelzik. "What is it, then? Do you need additional equipment?" For so long, Morad had sought various pieces of technology for the Tzenkethi scientists. If he had come to question their abilities, he still believed in their overall goal—a goal that he saw would help to restore the greatness of Cardassia. While Nelzik and her colleagues doubtless worked toward different objectives, Morad understood that success in their endeavors would benefit everybody.

Everybody but the Federation and Bajor.

"No, we do not need new equipment," Nelzik said. "We have accomplished our goal."

Morad blinked. He didn't think he had heard the scientist correctly. "You . . . have accomplished what goal?" He could only guess that Nelzik's team had reached some intermediate but important stage in their work.

"Our *goal*," Nelzik repeated. Then she turned in a way that didn't seem possible for a humanoid, rotating her torso completely around so that she faced away from Morad. The scientist pointed across the lab, to where several of her colleagues stood on the far wall. "We are prepared for a demonstration."

She turned back to face Morad, and he realized that she awaited an answer.

"Yes," he said. "Yes, of course. Show me."

Nelzik spun the upper portion of her body around again and made a quick, complex gesture with the exceptionally agile digits of her left hand. Morad watched as the group of scientists began to work at various consoles. Nelzik peered back at him and pointed upward. "Look there," she said.

Morad did as she instructed, gazing up at the field of stars visible through the transparent ceiling. Around him, the pitch of the machinery rose, loudly filling the space. He waited, still not convinced he understood what Nelzik had told him.

Moments passed, and nothing happened. But then a brilliant streak of blue light flashed out into the void, from a point clearly on the Vir-Akzelen asteroid. It looked a lot like a disruptor blast or phaser fire at first, but then other beams splintered off from it, forming a cone comprising the blue rays of focused light. Morad did not know what to make of the display, since it resembled nothing he'd ever seen, and nothing he'd expected.

But then, the formation of the blue beams ceased, and in its stead, a great light bloomed into existence. It swirled and churned, dazzlingly white at its center. Its outer, spinning eddies burned, not with the blue of the beams that had apparently created it, but a fiery red.

Morad watched silently, amazed, his ears filled with the din of the lab equipment, his eyes with the wonderful sight he beheld. He almost could not believe what he saw.

And then the mass of whirling red light collapsed in on itself. In almost no time at all, it vanished entirely. Morad anxiously looked down at Nelzik. "What happened?" he asked, and he heard desperation in his voice.

"You saw what happened," Nelzik said. "We succeeded. There was no need to continue. This was merely a demonstration."

"So what's next?" Morad wanted to know.

"We will begin testing our ability to target the other terminus," Nelzik said, "and to maintain stability and structural integrity."

"How long?" Morad asked. "How long before you'll know whether we can put this into practice?"

"If we have truly succeeded, then not long at all," Nelzik said. "Perhaps only a matter of days."

Days! The news stunned Morad. "Excellent," he said. "What more do you need from me?"

"At present, nothing but your support," Nelzik said.

"You have it," Morad said. "Now go. Begin your testing."

The Tzenkethi turned and headed toward where her colleagues stood. Morad watched her cross the laboratory until she reached the far wall. There, she walked up its vertical surface.

Morad peered back up at the transparent ceiling and out into space. The moments he'd just experienced seemed surreal, since the promised success of the project had for so long failed to materialize. But he had just seen it for himself, and he felt elated by it. It could only mean great things for his people.

Finally, after so much time and so much effort, he thought, *Cardassia will have its own artificial wormhole.*

8

Nan Bacco entered the turbolift that would take her to the fifteenth floor of the Palais de la Concorde and her presidential office. Agent Alan Kistler, a member of the security team assigned to protect her, had preceded her into the car. Her chief of staff, Esperanza Piñiero, and a second agent, Steven Wexler, followed her inside. The agents silently faded into the corners.

"Well, I think that went rather well," said Piñiero. She carried several padds with her, one of which the president had used as a reference for the notes she'd made for her speech.

"It's about time *something* went well," replied Bacco. The doors slipped closed and the lift began to ascend. "But we never should have had to make that argument to the Federation Council."

"I agree completely, ma'am," Piñiero said. "It's still hard to believe what happened out at Bajor."

"I'm not talking about the Typhon Pact," Bacco snapped, her temper flaring. "I'm talking about the damned Council."

Piñiero stood still for a moment without responding. Then she said, "Yes, ma'am," and lowered her gaze to the floor of the lift. "Of course, ma'am."

Bacco cursed herself. Her duties as Federation president had been extremely difficult of late—*When hadn't they been?*—but she certainly didn't need to mistreat the people around her, and especially not somebody like Piñiero, on whom she relied.

Bacco inhaled deeply, held her breath, then slowly exhaled, all in an attempt to bring her frustrations under control. She had worked with Esperanza Piñiero for a long time, all the way back to their days together on Cestus III, and so she knew that her chief of staff understood how the pressures of the presidency could sometimes affect her. Bacco had barked at Piñiero before, and she probably would do so again. But that didn't mean that the president didn't hate herself for it.

"I'm sorry, Esperanza," she said. "And you're right: I should be pleased that the Federation Council finally signed off on allowing Starfleet to construct a replacement for Deep Space Nine."

"'Finally,' ma'am?" Piñiero said. "With all due respect, it's only been two weeks since the attack. The Council usually can't clear its collective throat in that short a span of time."

Bacco nodded, recognizing the truth of what Piñiero had said. Offering a half-smile, she said, "Next time, instead of running for president, I need to try my hand at dictator."

"I think you do all right, ma'am," Piñiero said, straight-faced.

Bacco let the jibe pass. "It definitely wasn't all me this time," she said. "Thank goodness for Krim Aldos."

The Bajoran representative to the Federation, Krim also served on the Federation Security Council. He had been understandably furious about the Typhon Pact's attack in his home system, the loss of more than a thousand UFP lives— many of which had been Bajoran—and the destruction of DS9. Given all that, the president felt grateful that he hadn't lobbied for immediate retaliation. To the Federation Council that morning, he had argued passionately that they not only needed to replace the space station—as opposed to assigning a squadron of Starfleet vessels to patrol the mouth of the wormhole—but that they needed to do so as soon as possible.

"The violence perpetrated on Deep Space Nine and the other vessels represents something beyond an assault simply on the lives and property of Bajor and the Federation," Krim had avowed. "It represents the hostility that the worlds of the Typhon Pact harbor for our very way of life. The United Federation of Planets stands for peaceful coexistence, for the sharing of resources in order to benefit all, and for the exploration of the unknown, in a quest to better understand both our universe and ourselves.

"This cowardly, unprovoked attack tells us who the Typhon Pact is, but we cannot permit it to define who *we* are," Krim had continued, the volume of his voice rising. "Where we have been knocked down, we must climb back up. Where we have been hurt, we must heal. Where we have been pushed, we must hold our ground."

During the speech, Bacco had observed from her position on the platform the reactions of the councilors in the chamber. All of them watched Krim. Nobody moved.

"They have destroyed Deep Space Nine," Krim had gone on, his voice reaching a crescendo. "Do we here today propose that it is too dangerous to rebuild the station, or too impractical, or too costly? Do we propose that the Typhon Pact should dictate to us where or how we should live? The answers to those two questions must be the same, and that answer must be: *No!* I am the Bajoran councilor, and I say that Bajor, a vital crossroads of exploration, diplomacy, and trade, must remain exactly that, and nothing less than that. I say that we must rebuild, and that we must do it *now!*"

Bacco had not risen to her feet and applauded only because, in her position, it would have been neither decorous nor politic to do so. But she wanted to. Fortunately, a great many of the councilors present did stand and clap for Krim Aldos.

"And still," Bacco said, "even after Krim's address, the vote was close."

"But you prevailed, ma'am," Piñiero noted.

"*We* prevailed," Bacco said. "I have no particular interest in whether Bajor has a Federation space station at the mouth of the wormhole. For all I know, it *would* prove just as effective to assign a company of starships there as to spend all the resources in constructing an all-new replacement for Deep Space Nine. But Krim is right: our nose has been bloodied and we've been knocked down. Our only response, short of going to war, is to clean ourselves up, rise, and stand tall."

"And now we're going to do that," Piñiero said. "So as far as I'm concerned, the Council meeting went rather well." She did not smile even slightly, but in the echo of her earlier words, Bacco could hear mischief.

"You don't have to be so persistent," Bacco told her. "I already said you were right."

"Yes, ma'am, I know," Piñiero said. "For some reason, though, I never tire of hearing that—especially from you."

Bacco shook her head as she considered a variety of pithy retorts, but before she could choose one, two quick tones sounded. Piñiero raised one of her padds in front of her and activated it with a touch. As she did, the turbolift arrived at the fifteenth floor and the doors parted.

Agent Kistler exited and looked both ways down the corridor. Then he peered back inside the lift. "We're clear," he said.

Bacco didn't move, waiting as Piñiero continued examining her padd. Finally, her chief of staff looked up. "Madam President," she said, "you have a visitor."

"Where?" Bacco asked, confused. "Here? In the Palais?" She immediately thought of her daughter, but she had just spoken with Annabella yesterday, and she'd been on vacation with her family halfway across the Federation.

Since Bacco had become president, she'd welcomed legions of guests to her office, but, other than in times of crisis, none of them unexpected or unannounced. Because of that, she could not imagine who would presume to show up at her office without an appointment—or who would even be permitted inside the Palais, let alone up to the fifteenth floor. But she could see from Piñiero's expression that somebody had done exactly that.

"Yes, ma'am, he's waiting outside your office," Piñiero said. "It's Slask."

"Slask?" she echoed, her surprise shifting, but not abating. "From S'snagor?"

"That's the one," Piñiero said.

Bacco could tell that her chief of staff had no explanation either for the sudden appearance of the Gorn adventurer. Bacco had befriended Slask when she'd served as the governor of Cestus III, which bordered on the Hegemony. She had not seen him in years, although during the course of her presidency, he had willingly functioned as a clandestine messenger of sorts, both delivering and receiving off-the-record messages for her that would have been difficult to safely transmit otherwise.

"Do we know what he wants?" Bacco asked. When Slask had delivered messages to her in the past, it had always been through intermediaries, never in person.

"He refuses to say," Piñiero said, consulting the padd again. "He says he'll speak only to you."

"I don't like the sound of this," Bacco said.

"No, ma'am," Piñiero agreed.

Bacco looked to the security officer beside her. "Agent Wexler," she said, "I'll go into my office the back way. I need you to see Slask, confirm his identity, and assess his intentions." She highly doubted that either of the security officers with her would have allowed her to meet with Slask otherwise. Turning to her chief of staff, she said, "Esperanza, I'd like you to go too. Since you know him, you should be able to judge how important this is." She shook her head, not pleased with how suspicious her position had made her. "It's not that I don't trust our old friend," Bacco said, explaining more to herself than to Piñiero, she thought. "It's just that we've got so many issues with which to deal right now. I've got to prioritize."

"Yes, ma'am," Piñiero said. She and Wexler stepped out of the lift and headed toward the anteroom outside the presidential office. Bacco assumed that Slask waited there not just with her assistant, Sivak, but also with some number of uneasy, distrustful security officers.

Bacco left the turbolift, and she and Agent Kistler walked toward the rear entrance of her office. At the door, Kistler entered. Bacco knew that active sensors unlocked the entrance only if they read the president's presence there. Kistler confirmed the room safe for her, then escorted her inside.

As the agent took up a position inside the main door, Bacco crossed to her desk. A bright morning shined in at her through the curved windows that formed the outer wall of her office. She glanced quickly at the Tour Eiffel, the centuries-old iron tower that graced the Left Bank of Paris as it overlooked the River Seine, but she gave it no more attention than that. She sat down behind her desk, her mind racing over Slask's unforeseen appearance at the seat of the Federation government.

It occurred to her that the Gorn waiting in her outer office might be masquerading as her old friend. Perhaps the Typhon Pact had sent an impostor as part of another attack on the Federation and the Khitomer Accords. Perhaps he would walk in, draw an energy weapon, and shoot Bacco down. Or maybe he would trigger an explosive device implanted in his body. She imagined the window-walls of her office splintering outward into the brisk morning air and raining down fifteen stories onto the Champs-Élysées, while thick, black smoke rose from the top of the Palais, disfiguring the sky like a scar.

Bacco closed her eyes, uncomfortable with such dark musings. Wanting to put them out of her mind, she tried instead to think constructively, to consider the decisions she would soon need to make. The *Enterprise* crew had arrived at Earth with Tomalak in their custody, as well as with additional information about the actions of the Typhon Pact in the Gamma Quadrant. Admiral Akaar reported to the president that, while under interrogation by Captain Picard, the former Romulan proconsul had allowed the *Enterprise* crew to test whether or not he was a Changeling. Tomalak did so, Akaar explained, because Picard informed him that morphogenic tracer particles had been detected aboard the Breen freighter.

"What the hell are 'morphogenic tracer particles'?" Bacco asked.

"I believe that they exist only in the mind of Captain Picard," said Akaar.

Tomalak's responses to the *Enterprise* captain, though, including his willingness to be tested, confirmed that a Changeling had been present aboard the Breen vessel. That meant that there likely had been contact between the Typhon Pact and the Dominion, a situation that could prove dire for the Federation. Bacco had consequently charged Akaar and his admirals with formulating a plan of action on that front.

The intercom on Bacco's desk chimed, and she opened her eyes. *"Madam President,"* said Sivak, his tone containing no hint of his frequent impudence. The elderly Vulcan—he had passed the two-century mark some years ago—had been a part of Bacco's staff, like Piñiero, since her days as governor. Often irreverent to the point of insolence—surprisingly so for a full-blooded Vulcan—he kept her affairs organized and her office running smoothly, and he also acted as a gatekeeper for her. That he had permitted Slask to wait in the anteroom indicated his belief that the Gorn posed no threat. *"You have a visitor,"* Sivak continued. *"Slask, of S'snagor, has requested a meeting with you. He insists that the matter is urgent, but that it will take up very little of your obviously valuable time."* There, at the end, Sivak had slipped in just a soupçon of disrespect with the use of the word *obviously*. Perhaps strangely, it suddenly made Bacco feel less anxious about Slask's arrival.

Before she could respond, though, the door to the outer office opened. Piñiero entered, followed by Agent Wexler. "One moment, Sivak," Bacco said, closing the intercom channel.

Both Piñiero and Wexler approached the desk. "It's definitely Slask," Piñiero said.

Bacco looked to Wexler. "He passed every security checkpoint and every verification we have, otherwise he wouldn't even be in the building," the agent said, "let alone on the fifteenth floor."

Bacco stood up behind her desk. "All right, then," she said. "Let's see what my old friend has to say." She reached for the intercom and activated it. "Sivak, please send in my visitor."

"Right away, Madam President."

As Bacco closed the intercom, Piñiero moved to the front of the desk, while Wexler moved to the main door and opened it. A moment later, Sivak entered. "Madam President," he said, "may I present Slask, of S'snagor."

A Gorn walked in, the body beneath his green, reptilian hide quite muscular. He had silver, multifaceted eyes, a mouthful of narrow, sharp teeth, and rows of hard ridges beginning at his brow and crowning his head. Bacco recognized her old friend at once.

Slask waited as Sivak withdrew, closing the door after him. Then he said, "Madam President," hissing his greeting in the sibilant language of his people, which Bacco's translator rendered in Federation Standard.

The president gritted her teeth, parted her lips, and thrust her tongue to the front of her mouth. It had been some time since she had spoken the language of the Gorn, and even then, she'd only managed short phrases. Still, she gave it a shot, hissing out a welcome to her friend.

Slask produced a rumble deep in his throat, which Bacco knew would sound to the uninformed like a prelude to attack, but which she recognized as laughter. "You honor me, Madam President," Slask said. "You remember well, and you do far better in my tongue than I could ever do in yours." He plodded across the office toward the desk, his movements slow and methodical. He wore a white, patterned tunic, belted at the waist, along with a buttoned black vest. When he reached the desk, he bowed at the waist.

"You remember my chief of staff, I'm sure, Esperanza Piñiero," Bacco said, eschewing Slask's language for her own.

"Of course," Slask said, and he offered Piñiero a bow as well. "It is good to see you again."

To Bacco's surprise—even though she should have stopped being surprised by Esperanza years ago—Piñiero hissed out her own greeting.

Once more, Slask laughed. "Am I on Earth, or back home on S'snagor?"

Bacco chuckled, though she had begun to feel apprehensive

again. She needed to learn the reason for Slask's visit. She motioned toward the two chairs that faced her desk, and both the Gorn and Piñiero sat down. "So tell me what brings you here," Bacco said.

"First," Slask said, "please forgive me for coming at all. I know that our relationship, beyond the personal, has proven useful to both of us since you began serving as Federation president. That has been possible primarily because our friendship is not something widely known. By my coming here to speak with you directly, I have obviously put that secrecy at risk."

"I trust your judgment," Bacco said, and she meant it. In the time she had known Slask, he had demonstrated a quick and analytical mind, as well as a keen understanding of political life. "I believe that you would not have come here yourself unless circumstances warranted such an action."

Slask nodded, a movement that involved not just his head, but the whole of his upper body. "I think you will see the importance of my visit," he said. "I am, of course, aware of the attack on the Federation in the Bajoran system, as well as the destruction of your space station. I do not know if this will mean much to you, but I have ascertained from a source I trust that Imperator Sozzerozs never approved such an action, nor is he pleased that it has taken place."

"I do appreciate that," Bacco said, thinking back to her interactions with the Gorn leader at the summit on Cort, which she had thought had gone well. "But those sentiments would take on much greater meaning if the imperator were to issue such a statement in public."

"I agree," Slask said. "But we both know that there are other forces at work. From what I understand—and from what seems evident to me, based on Sozzerozs's reaction to the attack on the Federation—the Typhon Pact is still finding its way. The alliance remains relatively new, and it is large and in some regards unwieldy. There are differing points of view between individual governments, and also *within* individual governments. While the Hegemony and the Federation have had difficulties in the past, we have also shared long periods of calm, and even of peaceful interaction. I believe that Sozzerozs presently has no interest in engaging in battle with the Federation, but I am also mindful that he will not wish to antagonize any of the signatories to the Typhon Pact who do."

"Signatories like who?" Bacco asked, although she already knew the identities of the UFP's enemies. Still, she wished to hear Slask's assessment.

"The Tzenkethi, of course," he said.

"Of course," agreed Piñero. "Everything that's gone wrong within the Coalition for the past two hundred years is the Federation's fault."

"The Breen too, I think," Slask said. "And the Tholians."

Bacco waited, but Slask said no more.

"Not the Romulans?" she finally asked. More than anything, Praetor Kamemor's disingenuous attempts to sow peace among the worlds of the Khitomer Accords and the Typhon Pact—and more specifically, between the United Federation of Planets and the Romulan Star Empire—maddened Bacco. At least the Tzenkethi never prevaricated about their hatred for the Federation. It galled the president that Gell Kamemor had held out an olive branch across the negotiating table while holding a loaded disruptor pistol beneath it.

Bacco could only wonder why all sides had not yet gone to war, other than that she and the Federation Council had called for calm. But the president also knew that she could not allow the Typhon Pact to commit such acts with impunity. Starfleet had militarized along the Federation's borders, and Bacco and the Council agreed that, should the Pact perpetrate another act of aggression, the UFP and its allies would have to react strongly. Chancellor Martok and the Klingon High Council already beat the drum for war—especially to fight the Romulans.

"No," Slask told her. "Not the Romulans."

"It seems to me that you might not have all the details about what took place at Bajor," Bacco said. "But one of the vessels in the attack was a Romulan warbird—a warbird that was supposed to be engaged in a peaceful mission of exploration with a Starfleet vessel, but whose crew faked its destruction before returning to Bajor to join the attack."

"I am aware of all that," Slask said. "And I have something for you that I hope will speak to those issues."

"That you *hope* will speak to those issues?" Bacco said. "You don't know?"

"No, not with certainty, Madam President," Slask said. He reached to the inside of his vest. Wexler took a step forward, clearly to make sure that the Gorn did not produce a weapon—even though the heavy security within the Palais de la Concorde made such a possibility highly unlikely. Instead of a weapon, Slask withdrew a small, flat, translucent rectangle, which Bacco recognized as a data storage chip. "I am happy to deliver messages for you and to you," Slask said, "but I do not examine their contents."

"For that, I am grateful," Bacco said. "Who is the message from?"

"It is from Gell Kamemor."

Bacco shot to her feet even before she knew that she meant to do so. "What?!" She strode out from behind her desk and across her office, along the front windows. When she reached the far end of the room, she spun around to address Slask again. "*Why* would the praetor send me a message? To gloat over her success in killing a thousand Federation citizens and destroying a space station vital to our interests? To apologize for doing so? 'Oh, I'm sorry, I didn't mean to fake the crash of one of our starships and then send it to attack your people.'" She hied back to her desk and peered down at Slask. "There were *civilians* on that station. There were *children*."

Slask gazed up at the president without saying anything, and only then did Bacco realize that she had been yelling at him. Very slowly, Slask reached forward and placed the chip on her desk. When he spoke, the hiss of his speech had become a whisper. "I know that there were civilians and children on your space station," he said. "That is why, when Praetor Kamemor made it clear that she wanted to deliver a message directly to the Federation president, but not through official channels,

I deemed it important enough to risk my own reputation by personally visiting you on Earth."

Bacco dropped her head. All at once, the strength drained out of her. "Yes," she said. "Yes, of course. Please forgive me, Slask. I'm . . . it's been a difficult time." To Bacco, that excuse had begun to wear thin. She reached down and picked up the chip. "Thank you for doing this."

"If I may ask," Piñiero said, "how did you come into possession of the message?"

"I would rather not reveal my . . . contacts," Slask said. "I am sure you understand."

"Yes," Piñiero said, "but if we can't be sure of the chip's provenance . . ." She allowed the question to dangle unfinished.

"You can be sure," Slask told Piñiero. "I have confidence that your Federation Security will be able to authenticate it. This is not some elaborate ruse. Understand that I do not know the content of the praetor's message. It could be that she is issuing a declaration of war. But I do not believe that is what you will find when you play it."

Slask stood up and regarded Bacco again. "Whatever the praetor's message, I only hope that it is something you wish to hear." He paused, then said, "Actually, I hope that the praetor's message is something that you are *able* to hear." He bowed to Bacco, far more stiffly than when he first entered, then turned to Piñiero and did the same. Then he started toward the door.

"Slask," Bacco called after him. He stopped and turned around. "Thank you," she said, holding up the chip. "On behalf of my government and my people, thank you." She closed the distance between them and looked directly up into his face. "And *I* personally thank you, Slask."

Slask's silence drew out, and Bacco thought that he would leave without responding. But at last he said, "You are welcome, Nan." Then he turned and left. Agent Wexler followed him out.

Bacco peered over at Piñiero, not knowing what to think. But she knew of only one way to find out what the praetor wanted. She held up the chip. "Take this," she told Piñiero.

"Find me a Romulan interface so we can watch it, then meet me in the Ra-ghoratreii Room."

"Yes, ma'am." She stood up, crossed the room, and took the chip.

"And Esperanza," Bacco said. "Do it quickly."

Bacco sat in a comfortable chair in the Ra-ghoratreii Room, feeling anything but comfortable. She would listen to what Gell Kamemor had to say in her message, but she could not imagine liking what she would hear. Worse than that, she knew that she could in no way *trust* anything that the Romulan praetor would say. Bacco had done that before, and the results had been a lost space station and more than a thousand dead.

Piñiero occupied the chair to the president's right, an end table sitting between them. Together, they waited for the assistant chief of staff, Zachary Manzanillo, to return to Paris with a Romulan interface for the chip Slask had brought to Bacco. The Federation Security Agency possessed one, and Piñiero had sent Manzanillo transporting to Stockholm to retrieve it.

It had been only thirty minutes or so since Slask had departed the president's office, but it felt far longer than that. Bacco didn't particularly want to hear what Gell Kamemor had to say, but because the message had been delivered to her, she had a responsibility to listen to it. She wanted to review the message as soon as possible, though, and be done with it.

Quiet prevailed for a few more minutes, until Piñiero said, "I'm still concerned about the chain of custody." The chief of staff sat forward in her chair. Bacco saw a padd on her lap. "I know that you trust Slask's judgment, but we don't know who passed him the message. Simply because he believes in the person who gave it to him doesn't mean that we—"

"Kamemor gave the chip to Slask," Bacco said. She did not turn to Piñiero, but gazed directly ahead, at the large mirror adorning the opposite wall. She spoke with certainty, though she had only just worked out her conclusion.

"What?" Piñiero said. "That seems unlikely to me. I know

Slask has spent plenty of time in Romulan space, but under what circumstances would he be allowed anywhere near the praetor, much less be introduced to her?"

"Gell Kamemor has not always been the praetor," Bacco said, still gazing straight ahead at the mirror. Long and narrow, it reflected the top of the wall behind her. "She's been a senator, a governor, a diplomat, and a teacher. And for a time, she was nothing at all but a grieving widow." *A grieving widow who also lost her only child,* Bacco reminded herself. *Is that why I trusted her? Because I sympathized with her, thinking how difficult it would be for any woman to lose her only child?*

"That's true," Piñiero said. "But even if Kamemor had met Slask before, how would she know she could pass a back-channel message to you through him? As he noted himself, he is exceedingly discreet."

Bacco shrugged. "How do *I* know that *he* knows *her*?"

"Pardon me, ma'am, but it's not clear to me that you do know that," Piñiero said. "You've never mentioned before that we had a direct contact with Gell Kamemor, other than Ambassador Spock, and there have been times when I think you would have, since having such a contact would've made our lives a great deal easier."

Bacco stared at the mirror a moment more, then turned to Piñiero. "I've never mentioned it because I never knew it," she said. "Not until this morning. Not until Slask told us himself."

"I'm sorry, ma'am," said the chief of staff. "Did I miss the part of our meeting where the human and the Gorn communicated by way of a Vulcan mind-meld?"

As uneasy as she felt about what Kamemor's message would contain, Bacco still managed to laugh. "I think you just missed the language of politicians," she said. "Slask may never have run for office, but he knows how to converse as though he had." Bacco paused to consider the point she'd made, then added, "Or maybe I heard it just because Slask and I have known each other for so long."

"Heard what?"

"When you asked him how he received the message,"

Bacco explained, "he told you that he'd rather not reveal his contacts."

"That's right," Piñiero said. "And it's the reliability of those contacts that concerns me."

"But Slask didn't tell you *precisely* that," Bacco said. "He told you that he'd rather not reveal . . ." The president elongated the pause to make her point, then finished, ". . . his contacts."

"That's it?" Piñiero asked, her skepticism evident. "He hesitated, and between his words, you heard the name of Gell Kamemor? That seems like a small and unclear detail on which to base your inference."

"It's not only that," Bacco said, though she felt confident that Slask had revealed to her in that pause his direct contact with the praetor. "He also stated categorically that we could be sure of the message's authenticity. He would only say that if he could be sure himself, and there's only one way he could know definitely."

"You sound very definite yourself, Madam President."

"I know Slask well enough to realize that those are not small details," Bacco said.

Piñiero leaned back in her chair and peered up at the ceiling, as though she might find answers there. She seemed to consider what the president had told her. Bacco welcomed an examination of her argument, but as she'd made it, she'd convinced herself of its veracity.

When Piñiero looked back over at Bacco, the chief of staff said, "I think we still need Federation Security to authenticate the recording."

"Yes, I agree," Bacco said. "Just because—"

The intercom atop the end table chirped. Piñiero reached for it, thumbed its control surface, and identified herself.

"Ms. Piñiero, it's Zachary Manzanillo," said the assistant chief of staff. *"We have the interface you requested. We can play the contents of the chip whenever you're ready."*

Piñiero glanced at Bacco, who nodded once. "Go ahead, Zachary," said Piñiero. "We're ready."

"Yes, ma'am." Piñiero closed the intercom channel.

Bacco turned back to face the large mirror across the room. It immediately lost its reflective sheen, revealing a display screen beyond it. After only a second, the emblem of the Romulan Star Empire appeared—or at least what looked like the Empire's emblem. As always, it consisted of an artistically rendered representation of a raptor. But where previously it had been colored blue on one side and pale green on the other, only a single hue—a dark, grayish green—embellished it. Of even seemingly greater significance, the two four-clawed talons came together to hold a single orb, presumably meant to represent Romulus. In the past, each of the raptor's talons had held a sphere, one to symbolize Romulus, the other, Remus.

"Well, that's new," Piñiero noted.

"I guess the Romulan government is taking the independence of the Remans seriously," Bacco said. Though it could easily be considered unimportant, the modification to the Empire's crest impressed the president. Pride consumed the Romulans, and so Bacco would never have expected such a change, which some could view as a sign of weakness, an admission that the Reman slaves had fought and won their freedom from the Empire. That battle *had* taken place, but Bacco never expected the Romulans to acknowledge it so publicly.

On-screen, the revised emblem faded away, and Gell Kamemor appeared. She wore a gray blouse beneath a lavender suit jacket. She sat at a desk in what looked like an office. Hardbound books lined a series of shelves behind her. She began speaking without any sort of salutation. *"I have learned of the loss of the Romulan vessel* Eletrix *in the Bajoran star system, located within Federation space,"* she said. *"I also understand that the vessel was commanded by a woman named Orventa T'Jul."*

Bacco noticed movement, and she looked over to see Piñiero making notes on her padd.

"Commander T'Jul for a long time showed signs of a promising military career," the praetor continued. *"She rose through the ranks steadily, even quickly. Five hundred days ago, the success of a sensitive mission pushed T'Jul from the rank of subcommander to commander, and she was given her own starship: the* Eletrix.*"*

Bacco furrowed her brow as confusion overcame her. The message, no matter its source, did not seem intended for the president of the Federation. Bacco considered stopping it, but she supposed that whatever the praetor wanted to say to her could be buried within the message, with extraneous material placed at the beginning to confuse anybody who might have intercepted it.

"*Clearly,*" Kamemor went on, "*that promotion should never have happened. T'Jul's failure at Bajor demonstrates that. And while no one can know the mind of another—not even in the case of a commanding officer and his subordinate—and no one can predict the future actions of another, Fleet Admiral Devix has taken responsibility for the loss of the* Eletrix *and its crew.*"

Once again, Bacco saw Piñiero working over her padd.

"*Admiral Devix has served in the Imperial Fleet for a long time,*" said Kamemor. "*As its leader, he has commanded ably. But he believes it is time for him to step down. I have accepted his resignation. He will naturally stay on until a suitable replacement has been selected.*"

As the praetor paused, Bacco saw her move slightly forward in her chair. Kamemor also fastened her gaze forward, as though attempting to peer through time and space and connect with the Federation president—or with whomever the praetor had intended to receive her message. Kamemor's gray eyes held steady as she continued.

"*The choice of a successor to Admiral Devix is an important one. I already have a number of candidates in mind, but I would also appreciate hearing your opinion. To that end, we should meet. You know how to reach me.*"

The redesigned Romulan emblem appeared again on the screen. Bacco looked to her chief of staff. "Is that it?" she asked.

Piñiero finished operating her padd and then peered up. "I think so, but let's check." She tapped at the intercom control. "Zachary, the playback has ended. Can we tell whether or not there's anything else on the chip? Perhaps something embedded or hidden. Something difficult but not impossible to find?"

"*We've scanned the chip, Ms. Piñiero,*" said Manzanillo. "*As best we can tell, it contains one and only one audiovisual file, with a length of one minute, thirteen seconds. It is preceded and succeeded by a single image file."*

"Could there be anything secreted away in either file, or elsewhere on the chip?" Piñiero asked.

"Federation Security believes not," Manzanillo said, *"but they do intend to subject the chip to more rigorous testing."*

Piñiero peered up at Bacco with raised eyebrows. The president nodded, then said, "Mister Manzanillo, Federation Security may test the chip, but for the moment, I'm designating its contents as classified, to be viewed only with my direct authorization."

"Understood, Madam President."

"Do we need to see it again?" Piñiero asked Bacco.

"I don't think so."

Into the intercom, Piñiero said, "Thank you, Zachary," and she switched it off.

"So much for worrying about the provenance of the message," Bacco said, rising from her chair. Across the room, the mirror regained its silvered surface. Standing, the president could see her reflection. *Is it possible for white hair to get whiter?* she asked herself. It pleased her that she at least did not look quite as tired as she felt. "Even if the message did come from the praetor, she didn't mean for me to see it."

"Actually, ma'am," Piñiero said, "I think this message did come directly from the praetor, and I think she *did* send it to you."

"What are you talking about?" Bacco asked. She pointed toward the hidden display. "Kamemor starts with no preamble, and doesn't address me or anybody else by name or even by position."

"And don't you find that odd?" Piñiero asked. "That the praetor would go to the trouble of recording a message about a sensitive issue—Romulan fleet admirals don't just willingly resign—but that she wouldn't even hint at the identity of her intended recipient?"

Bacco considered that. "It did seem peculiar," she said.

"But I can't pretend to you that I've ever truly understood the Romulan mind."

"I think the praetor intentionally avoided mentioning you or your office explicitly," Piñiero said, "specifically so that she would retain plausible deniability should the chip be intercepted en route to you."

"You just said that she avoided mentioning me *explicitly*," Bacco said. "Do you think she referred to me *implicitly*?"

"Yes, ma'am," Piñiero said. "The praetor mentioned Bajor and the Federation in her very first sentence."

Bacco thought about that. *Maybe Esperanza's right.* The president sat back down in her chair. "Is there anything else that leads you to believe that the message was meant for me?"

"Yes," Piñiero said. "Kamemor spoke about T'Jul's *failure* at Bajor. I think she's implying that the attack itself was the failure, and not the loss of the ship. There is no question that the *Eletrix*'s abandonment of its mission with the *Enterprise* and its battle at the mouth of the wormhole are completely inconsistent with the praetor's declared policies toward the Federation."

"If we are to believe those declarations to be true," Bacco said. "I think you may be reading too much into this."

Piñiero consulted her padd for a moment. "Kamemor mentioned a mission in which T'Jul participated five hundred days ago," she said. "Do you know what happened at that time?"

Bacco didn't bother to count back on the calendar. She knew that Piñiero would tell her.

"The Breen, likely with the help of the Romulans, stole the schematics for the slipstream drive from Utopia Planitia," Piñiero said.

Bacco's mouth opened of its own accord, but she didn't say anything. She had to admit that such a reference by Kamemor to that time seemed like too much of a coincidence to have no meaning. She said so to Piñiero.

"I think it's also worth noting that when the praetor refers to that incident," the chief of staff said, "she states that, following it, T'Jul's promotion should never have happened."

"But what does that mean?" Bacco asked, trying to follow

the thread of Piñiero's argument. "Was Kamemor trying to disavow knowledge of the theft?"

"I think so," Piñiero said. "At that point, she'd only been in office a couple of months. It could be that the plans to steal the schematics had been left over from Tal'Aura's reign, perhaps had even already been put in motion. In fact, given the length of time the spy had been at Utopia Planitia before the theft, it's a certainty that the Breen portion of the plan had begun prior to Kamemor's being elevated to the praetorship. My feeling is that she didn't know about it until after the fact, and that she didn't know about the attack at Bajor either, so now she's decided to force out Admiral Devix."

"That's a dangerous game to play on Romulus," Bacco said. "When Tal'Aura set herself against Admiral Braeg and Commander Donatra, she ended up with a divided empire."

"Which is why Kamemor says that choosing a replacement for Devix is crucial," Piñiero said. "She may genuinely want your advice, but I think it's far more likely that she's signaling her intentions by providing us with a valuable piece of intelligence. I don't know how long it would be before we learned of a change at the top in the Imperial Fleet."

"And what do you think her intentions are?"

"I think they're in the last lines of her message," Piñiero said. "She says she wants your opinion. She says you know how to reach her. Most important, she says she wants to meet with you."

"That's a shrewd analysis, Esperanza," Bacco said. "And you may be right. But if Kamemor wanted to convey the message you think she did, why not just tell Slask so that he could tell me?" But Bacco already knew before Piñiero answered.

"Because she didn't want anybody but you to know," said the chief of staff. "And maybe she didn't fully trust Slask."

"It doesn't matter," Bacco said, and she stood up again. "I already met with the praetor. We negotiated for days, and I came away from the summit on Cort thinking that we'd actually accomplished something, that we'd taken the first steps on the road to peace. But look what's happened since then."

"Madam President," Piñiero said, "I think Praetor Kamemor

wants the same things you do: to forge peace and prosperity for the people you lead. I think she's reiterating that to you, letting you know that she opposes what took place at Utopia Planitia and Bajor. But I think she may be in trouble."

"Yes," Bacco said. "But whether Kamemor duped me the first time around, or whether she was sincere but lacked the control of her own government, we cannot deal with her again. Whether she's lying to us, or whether she's not strong enough to enforce the agreements we reach, there's no point in negotiating with her."

Piñiero rose from her chair, clearly disappointed. "So you're not going to respond to the praetor's message?"

"Actually, I am," Bacco said. "But not through Slask or any other covert conduit. Get the Typhon Pact ambassador into my office before noon. I want Praetor Kamemor to know that we have her former proconsul under arrest, and that we intend to try him for his crimes. Let's see what kind of a reaction that gets."

9

Sisko sat on the sofa in the front room of the house that he had designed in what now seemed like another lifetime. He peered out through the picture windows at the blossoming morning, the Bajoran sun shining on the land all the way to the Kendra Mountains in the distance. His gaze found the Yolja River and traced along its winding path. The quiet moment delivered to him a measure of peace, something that he'd found in short supply in recent years. In some ways, it felt as though he'd been gasping for air, and at last he'd been able to catch his breath.

"I think I'm going to have some tea," Kasidy called out to him from the kitchen. "Would you like some? I've got a new Vulcan blend I think you'd like."

"No, thanks," Sisko said. "Nothing for me." He'd come directly from Adarak after he and Jasmine Tey had taken Rebecca to school. Just turned seven, Rebecca seemed remarkably happy and well adjusted. Though she remembered her abduction at the age of three—she'd made reference to it a few months earlier—she showed no signs of any continuing trauma from that experience.

Likewise, although Sisko had not lived in Kendra Province with Kasidy and Rebecca in the past two and a half years, and even though, at one point, he'd gone nearly a year and a half without seeing or speaking to his daughter, she did not appear much affected by that either. Sisko did not lie to himself that his absence had not had an impact on Rebecca; he knew that it had, and that he must do everything he possibly could—short of compromising her safety—to make up for it. Their frequent subspace messages to each other between *Robinson* and Bajor helped, he thought, but nothing compared to the two of them spending time together. He relished every leave, when he would return to Kendra specifically to see her. Even with everything that had happened before his arrival, the previous two weeks had been no exception; they had been among the very best days of his life since his return to Starfleet.

It hurt him that those days had to end.

Depending on the repairs to his ship, he would have about two more weeks before being recalled to duty. He felt conflicted about returning to *Robinson*. Initially a refuge for him, a place he had escaped to after abandoning his family, the ship had become a great deal more than that to him. In some ways, it actually felt like a home. After a year of holding himself apart from his crew, he thawed, grew closer to the people with whom he served, and even made some genuine friends. And the recent mission to the Gamma Quadrant demonstrated unequivocally to him that his spirit had turned toward exploration.

But even with all of that, Sisko understood that the ship could never truly be a home to him. No place could, not without his family by his side. But he understood too well why that could never happen.

Thinking of the well-being of Kasidy and Rebecca brought to mind the terrible events at Deep Space 9. Seeing his wife's ship demolished before his eyes had hurt him badly, and even though she hadn't been on the ship, even though she had survived, the incident had left him scarred. So too did witnessing the destruction of the station, which for so long actually had been his home.

Sisko had not yet read through the casualty list from the station, but he had no doubt that people he had known, probably even some he'd considered friends, had perished. Such had been the case aboard *Robinson,* where a Tzenkethi attack had left thirty-two of his crew dead. He had also known most of Kasidy's crew aboard *Xhosa,* although many of them had also survived; so that the freighter could carry as many people as possible from DS9 to safety, most of Kasidy's crew had stayed behind on Bajor after bringing their first group of evacuees there. But her chief engineer, Luis García Márquez, had died, and crew members Brathaw and Pardshay as well.

The losses had hit Kasidy hard, and Sisko had spent time helping her through it. He contacted families with her to explain what had happened, though Starfleet and the Federation president's office also provided a great deal of assistance with that. Kasidy cried a lot, though never in front of Rebecca. It amazed Sisko how she could compartmentalize her grief, tucking it away when she needed to in order to provide a continuous, steady presence for their daughter.

After the disaster, Admiral Akaar had contacted Sisko aboard *Robinson.* Starfleet's commander-in-chief informed him of the concern that the Typhon Pact might be seeking to ally with the Dominion. Starfleet intended to send *Defiant* into the Gamma Quadrant to ascertain whether or not the Federation faced an impending threat from the Founders or the devoted soldiers they bred, the Jem'Hadar. The admiral wanted to know, if such a threat should materialize, whether Sisko possessed either the ability or the knowledge to collapse the Alpha Quadrant terminus to the wormhole. Akaar knew that Sisko had a relationship with the Prophets—the admiral called them aliens—and that he had spent time himself within the wormhole after the Dominion War. Sisko explained that, despite his experiences, he had no means or understanding of how to do such a thing.

Akaar had appeared to sense something during their conversation, and near its end, he asked a question. He wanted to know if Sisko remained in contact with the wormhole aliens, even on a sporadic basis. Sisko told him the truth: that he'd had no contact with them at all in years, and further, he never expected to again. The response seemed simultaneously to please and disappoint the admiral. Sisko felt that same mix of positive and negative emotions about the absence of the Prophets from his life.

For two days after the Typhon Pact attack, Sisko had dealt with the repercussions to his crew. As he would later with Kasidy for her crew, he contacted the families of those aboard *Robinson* who had lost their lives in the Tzenkethi attack. He worked with his first officer, Anxo Rogeiro, and his chief engineer, Relkdahz, on a repair plan for the ship. His crew had been scheduled for shore leave after their return from the Gamma Quadrant, and since the ship would require weeks at Starbase 310 to fix the damaged primary hull, Starfleet Command extended the crew's leave and released them from their duties. Sisko headed for Bajor.

"You sure I can't get you anything?" Kasidy called from the kitchen.

"No, thanks."

Kasidy had expected Sisko later in the day, after their daughter returned home that afternoon, but he'd acted spontaneously on an urge to see his wife without any of the family around. She invited him in with an ease and acceptance that, given the pain he'd caused her in recent years, seemed startling. The two weeks since the destruction of Deep Space 9, since he believed Kasidy dead, represented the greatest amount of time they'd spent together since he'd left Bajor and taken command of *Robinson*. They saw each other when he visited Rebecca during his leaves from Starfleet, but on those trips, he typically spent most of that time alone with their daughter.

Since Sisko had arrived back on Bajor after the attack on DS9, though, Kasidy had chosen to stay around when he came over to the house. Although the warning of the Prophets never strayed far from Sisko's mind, he could not object. Kasidy had endured—and continued to endure—a terrible emotional strain; she'd lost members of her crew, her ship had been destroyed, and she'd faced her own mortality when the station had exploded. He knew he would soon enough head back to *Robinson,* and so he opted to provide whatever solace he could for her. For some reason, the usual underlying tensions between them never appeared, and he felt no pressure from her to ignore the Prophets' warning and stay home with his wife and daughter for good.

Sisko also had to admit that he found comfort in Kasidy's company. That scared him to a degree too, worrying him that he would fail to find the strength to leave when the time came. For that reason, he focused often on his understanding that spending his life with Kasidy would put both her and their daughter in grave danger.

As he waited for Kasidy, Sisko heard the insistent tones of a companel. The kitchen contained a small interface, and he heard it react when Kasidy worked its controls. Footsteps followed, and his wife stepped out of the kitchen. He turned to regard her.

"It's Starfleet," she said, her voice a monotone, her face a frozen mask. That quickly, everything good they'd recently experienced seemed to fall away, as though all of the positive emotions and effortless interactions had been merely a façade.

"Oh," Sisko said. His scheduled return to duty remained days, if not weeks, away, but he surmised that somebody might want to update him on the status of the repairs to *Robinson.* He stood up and began to walk around the sofa. "I guess I'll use the companel in the office."

Kasidy said nothing more, but she also didn't head back into the kitchen. Rather, she watched him make his way across the living room, past the dining table, and into the hall that led to the rooms at the back of the house. When Sisko ducked into the home office—which also doubled as a guest room when needed—he glanced to his right and saw Kasidy still standing in place, staring after him.

Inside, Sisko moved to the companel mounted on the inside wall. He sat down and tapped at the controls. The Starfleet insignia blinked onto the screen, above the words INCOMING TRANSMISSION—ENTER SECURITY VERIFICATION. Sisko keyed in his lengthy access code, expecting to see the image of Admiral LaChance, who commanded Starbase 310, where Commander Rogeiro had taken *Robinson* for repairs. Instead, the imposing form of Starfleet's commander-in-chief appeared.

"Captain Sisko, this is Admiral Akaar," he said in his deep, resonant voice. *"I am contacting you for two reasons. First, to inform you that the* Defiant *crew's reconnaissance of the Gamma Quadrant has revealed no Dominion activity outside of their space. More specifically, there are no Jem'Hadar squadrons on their way toward the Bajoran wormhole."*

The news relieved Sisko, though he had in no way anticipated anything different. During the nearly eight years that followed the devastating war that had battered the inhabitants of the Alpha and Beta Quadrants, the Dominion had shown no signs of returning to the battlefield. Though he did not necessarily agree with their general policy of isolationism, he understood why the Founders would want to withdraw into themselves and close their borders.

"Additionally," Akaar continued, *"the* Defiant *crew located and disabled a cloaked communications drone near the Idran system. Of Romulan origin, the device was responsible for hindering your ability, and that of the* Enterprise *crew, to contact Deep Space Nine from the Gamma Quadrant."*

Sisko grasped why the Romulans had elected to block such transmissions: so that they could prevent Captain Picard from informing Starfleet Command of the apparent loss of *Eletrix*. Had the *Enterprise* crew succeeded in reporting that incident to Starfleet, a state of high alert might have compelled the crew of DS9 to search for cloaked vessels traveling through the wormhole. Perhaps ironically—since they seemed to have been a part of the same assault on the station—the four bombs planted aboard Deep Space 9 had provoked a high alert anyway, which had resulted in the discovery of the cloaked *Eletrix* returning to the Alpha Quadrant.

"Second, we now know that the Typhon Pact did have contact

with one or more Changelings in the Gamma Quadrant," Akaar went on. *"We do not know to what end, but we are understandably concerned about such an interaction. President Bacco therefore believes, and I agree with her, that we must find out the nature of the relationship between the Pact and the Dominion."*

Sisko knew from bitter experience the formidable nature of the Founders. If they joined forces with the Typhon Pact and launched an offensive, he saw no chance of victory for the Federation and its allies.

"Captain Sisko," Akaar said, *"in all of Starfleet, you have by far the most experience with the Founders. Because of that, I want you to travel to the Dominion and speak with them. We need to find out the reason for their meeting with the Typhon Pact, but we must also impress upon them that we have no desire at all to go back to war.*

"I know that the Robinson *is currently undergoing repairs at Starbase Three-Ten and that your crew are on leave. But Captain Ro is presently relocating her crew to a temporary facility on the surface of Bajor, so you will lead your mission aboard the* Defiant. *Lieutenant Commander Wheeler Stinson will beam you up to the ship from the Adarak transporter facility at fifteen hundred hours, local time. You will take command from Stinson, who will serve as your exec during your time aboard. You will find a detailed mission profile waiting for you, but I am giving you wide latitude to do what you deem necessary to keep the peace with the Dominion. Akaar out."*

The Starfleet emblem replaced the admiral's visage. Sisko reached forward and shut the companel down, then let himself fall against the back of the chair. He had just come from the Gamma Quadrant a couple of weeks ago after nearly six months there. Now he would have to return, not on a mission of exploration, but in an attempt to avert yet another war.

He didn't entirely know if he could face that.

Kasidy stood like a statue just outside the kitchen. She felt hollow and fragile, as though if she attempted to move, she might break into a thousand tiny pieces. So she didn't move as she watched her husband march down the hall and into the office, where, she had no doubt, he would hear from Starfleet that he had been recalled to duty.

And he's going to go, she thought. *Of course he's going to go.* A rage burgeoned within her, but not just at Ben. She railed at herself for foolishly believing that things had changed. But they hadn't. Yes, she and Ben had spent more time together than they had in a while, but they had never spoken of the future—a joint future that she'd simply assumed lay ahead of them.

Why? she asked herself. *Why didn't I bring it up?*

It wouldn't have mattered, she knew. It wouldn't have mattered because Kasidy wouldn't have been able to convince Ben to stay.

But if I had . . .

If she had, Kasidy knew that it still wouldn't have mattered, because when Starfleet—or anything or anybody else— eventually came calling, she would have had to let him go. She would have had to let him go because . . . because . . .

Kasidy didn't want to think about it. *Couldn't* think about it.

When finally she moved, Kasidy simply leaned back against the wall that divided the living room and the kitchen. Then, slowly, as though air gradually leaked out of her, she slid down the wall to the floor. She didn't break, but she felt broken.

She didn't want to think about why she would have to let Ben go. She couldn't think about it. About what she'd experienced when she and Nerys had been trapped aboard the piece of wreckage from Deep Space 9's docking ring. About what she'd experienced in the wormhole.

But then Kasidy closed her eyes, and she did.

Cassie Johnson stood in the front room of the police station, wringing her hands. Her feet scuffed on the shabby green tiles that covered the floor. Scared down to her marrow, she felt like running back through the big, heavy doors, down the stone stairs, and off down the street. Determined, Cassie held her ground, eyeing the doors in the side walls, each with frosted glass covered by a grille, and understanding that they led deeper into the precinct house. She watched as the woman in front of her looked up to the top of the tall desk and addressed the police officer Cassie herself had just tried to speak to, without success. But Cassie stopped seeing the woman and the policeman and the desk, instead picturing herself running from one side door to another, throwing them wide and calling out to Benny.

Benny.

Cassie wanted to help the man she loved. A good man, a kind man, a *deep* man, he loved her like no one else ever had. For so long, she'd just wanted him to get better, and she still wanted that, but she had the sense that everything had changed that day.

That morning, Cassie had gone in to work the breakfast and lunch shifts at Fatty's, but on Wednesdays, she had the afternoon off after two. That gave her just enough time to get to Riverdale and visit Benny for a couple of hours before she needed to pick up Becky from Mr. Tayman's niece, Jessie, across the hall. She had to take a subway and then a bus to get to the asylum.

For months, Cassie had seen a great deal of improvement in Benny, to the point where she had begun to believe that he might actually leave Riverdale sometime soon. He always agreed to see her when she came—in the past, he hadn't always—and he looked good, looked *healthier,* whenever an orderly escorted him to the visitors' lounge. And Benny smiled so much more often. That smile, filled with his gleaming white teeth that looked so vibrant in his dark, handsome face. That smile, so wide that it drove his cheeks up and wrinkled the corners of his eyes. That smile that had won Cassie over back in the day. She loved seeing it again.

Except that she hadn't seen his smile that afternoon. When she'd arrived at Riverdale, she'd been informed that Benny had tried to escape that morning, and that he'd fought with a couple of orderlies when they'd caught him. As a result, the asylum's administrator had turned Benny over to the police.

Cassie had raced through the city to the police station. She ran until she could run no more, a stitch in her side and her breath rasping in her throat. But she kept walking, making her way through the streets until she stood in front of the precinct house where they'd taken Benny. The building loomed before her like a fortress. Wide stone steps led up to a landing with a pair of large wooden doors. She saw that the paint had rubbed away around the knobs.

Cassie placed her foot on the first step, intending to climb them and go inside so that she could find out what had happened to Benny. She wanted to know what *would* happen to him. She wanted to know if she could see him. Cassie saw herself asking all of those questions. She could not see herself receiving any answers.

She stood like that for minutes, like a statue. She felt hollow and fragile, as though if she attempted to move, she might break into a thousand tiny pieces. So she didn't move.

Several police officers came and went. They traveled in pairs, she saw. Most of them looked strong and powerful. All of them were white.

Cassie wanted to help Benny, but she realized that she would need help herself. And nobody she knew would be able to do so. Nobody she knew was the right color.

But then Cassie thought of the people Benny knew, the people over in the office where he used to work. She tried to remember their names, if she even ever knew them, and then she worked hard to recall their faces. Like Benny, they wrote stories . . . and it struck her that one of them was a woman.

A woman will understand, Cassie thought. *A woman will be willing to help.*

So she'd taken her foot from the first step of the police station and made her way to that old office, the Trill Building, where Benny had once worked. The afternoon wore on, past five o'clock, the time she'd been supposed to pick up Becky from Jessie Tayman. It didn't matter. The young woman would try to make Cassie feel bad about it, but Cassie would explain what had happened. And she'd have to try to find some way to make it up to Mr. Tayman, who would also surely get an earful from his niece.

When the red-haired woman eventually came out of the building, Cassie recognized her at once—and also remembered her name: K. C. Hunter. She ran up behind Miss Hunter and reached out to take her arm. It took a moment to get her to stop, and a little longer for Cassie to explain who she was and what she needed.

But Cassie had been right: Miss Hunter was willing to help.

So while Cassie stood in the middle of the front room of the police station, envisioning opening the side doors and calling out to Benny, Miss Kay Eaton—she used *K. C. Hunter* as a pen name—looked up at the officer behind the desk and asked, "With whom am I speaking?"

Cassie watched the policeman raise his head and regard her from his elevated position. "I'm Sergeant La Dotio," he said. "What can I do for you, ma'am?"

Suddenly, a chunk of plaster fell from the ceiling and crashed to the floor, just a few feet to the left of Miss Eaton. Cassie stared at it in disbelief. A second later, she saw an even larger piece land beside it.

Cassie looked back up and saw two ragged holes in the ceiling. And then another piece of plaster broke loose and smashed down beside the others. Cassie let out a yip. Then she stepped forward and pulled on the sleeve of Miss Eaton's coat. "Come on," she said, having to raise her voice as the room around them grew loud. The building seemed to groan under its own weight, as though it might collapse at any minute. "We have to go."

Then the entire left side of the ceiling dropped to the floor with a thunderous sound.

Cassie stared up in disbelief. Through the gaping hole in the ceiling, she did not see the second story of the building, but the night sky. Even though she and Miss Eaton had walked into the police station just a few minutes ago, with the sun an hour or more away from setting, stars sparkled down on them.

"Come on," Cassie screamed, for the roar around them had not abated. The rest of the ceiling would come down soon. "We have to go now."

Above them, the remainder of the ceiling began to bow. Miss Eaton calmly looked from there down to the broken plaster on the floor, and finally over at Cassie. Oddly, she did not appear at all worried.

Cassie tugged at her arm. "Come on, Miss Eaton!" she yelled. "We have to go!" She could barely hear the sound of her own voice.

Miss Eaton blinked. "No," she said. The word didn't reach Cassie's ears, but she could see it on Miss Eaton's lips. "No," she said again.

Cassie froze, unsure what she could possibly do. She wanted to rush from the danger threatening them—she had a little girl to take care of—but she could not leave Miss Eaton. She started to try to pull her away, but then Miss Eaton took hold of Cassie's arm.

"Benny still needs our help," she said.

That stopped Cassie. She heard a tremendous cracking sound, like a frozen lake splitting as spring caught up with winter. She peered up again, and saw a web of fractures across the ceiling. More chunks began to fall, one after another, raining down all around them.

She looked at Miss Eaton and cried, "I can't help Benny if we stay here."

"Yes, you can," Miss Eaton said, staring deeply into Cassie's eyes. "And everything will be all right. I promise." Cassie hesitated. "Benny needs our help."

"Okay," Cassie said, not really knowing how she could stay in a building that might crush her in the next second, but knowing that she wanted to help the man she loved, the father of her child.

Around them, huge masses of the ceiling plunged to the floor. Cassie clung to Miss Eaton, waiting for one of the pieces to squash them flat. She closed her eyes.

Behind Cassie's lids twisted a curl of bright blue light, the sort of shape a person saw when they rubbed their eyes too hard. It wound like a corkscrew, its center a concentrated patch of white. It seemed familiar to Cassie, in a way she could not name.

The thunder of the collapsing ceiling surrounded her. As she clung to Miss Eaton's arm, Cassie cringed. She worried about her own well-being, and about who would take care of Becky, but mostly, she feared that the entire building would fall and bury Benny.

Cassie didn't know how long it took the ceiling to cave in, but she suddenly became aware that she could hear again. She expected a sound like light rain as plaster dust settled on the wreckage. Instead, she heard nothing.

Cassie opened her eyes.

The police station stood just as it had when she and Miss Eaton had entered. Cassie looked wide-eyed at the floor, its flat green surface free of any debris. She gazed up at the ceiling, the unbroken expanse of plaster a shock.

Cassie peered at Miss Eaton, who regarded her calmly. "What . . . what happened?" Cassie asked, then thought that she really meant to ask what *hadn't* happened.

"Everything will be all right," Miss Eaton repeated. She'd said that earlier, when the ceiling had seemed to be collapsing, and somehow she'd been right. It felt to Cassie almost like black magic, but in the short time since she'd enlisted Miss Eaton to help her, the woman had proven willing, able, and perhaps most important, trustworthy.

"Okay," Cassie said, though she didn't feel okay. What had she experienced? A hallucination brought on by fear? A premonition? Or was she losing her mind?

"Okay." Miss Eaton let go of Cassie's arm and turned back to the policeman sitting at the tall desk. "Do you have a record of a Mister Benny Russell being arrested and brought into the station this morning?"

The sergeant stared down with a blank face, then offered an annoyed sigh as he shuffled through a sheaf of papers. "No, I don't see any Benny Russell here," he said. "You sure you got the right precinct?" Cassie herself started to respond, but then the sergeant held up a sheet of paper. "Oh, wait. Russell, Benny," he said, reading. "Already been arraigned. Gotta bail ticket for him here." He gazed down at Miss Eaton. "Bail's set at fifty dollars." He pronounced the amount *fitty*. "You got dat much?"

Cassie's momentary elation at having found Benny crumbled beneath the weight of what his freedom would cost. "I don't have fifty dollars," she told Miss Eaton.

"Yes, Sergeant, we do," Miss Eaton said, reaching up and taking the bail ticket. Once more, a wave of gratitude washed over Cassie.

"Second door on your left, pay the officer," said the sergeant.

Miss Eaton turned to Cassie and took her by the arm again. "I'll pay you back," Cassie promised. "I'll get another job, I'll—"

"It's all right," Miss Eaton said. "Let's just worry about getting Benny out."

Cassie nodded. She wanted nothing more than for Benny to be all right, for him to be out of jail, out of the asylum, and back in her life again. *Really* back in her life, and not just for short visits on Wednesday afternoons. Back in her life . . . and in *Becky's* life.

Miss Eaton guided Cassie to the door that the sergeant had indicated. They opened it and went inside, into a long, narrow room. At its front end stood another desk, of regular height. An older, uniformed woman sat there. She had a wide, flat nose and slanted eyes; she looked Chinese to Cassie.

Peering up from where she wrote on a ledger, the woman said, "Can I help you?"

"We have a bail ticket for Benny Russell," Miss Eaton said. Cassie realized that the writer—a virtual stranger to her—had not only agreed to help, but had taken the lead in doing so. As Miss Eaton handed the piece of paper to the officer, Cassie reached for the small pocket hidden in the waist of her dress. From it, she extracted the only money she had with her: four dollars and change. She reached out to give it to her newfound friend, but Miss Eaton held up her hand.

"That's all right," she said. "I'll just write a check." Then she looked to the officer again. "I can write a check, can't I?"

"Cash or check," the policewoman said. "Fifty dollars." She took the bail ticket and wrote something on it.

Miss Eaton opened her handbag and pulled out a checkbook. She took a pen clipped to it and asked, "Do I make it out to the New York Police Department?"

"To the New York City Department of Corrections," said the policewoman. Miss Eaton filled out her check, then handed it over to the officer. The policewoman made a notation on it, then opened another ledger and began entering information. Once she'd finished doing so, the officer pulled two forms from a pile beside the ledger, placed a piece of black carbon paper between them, and rolled them into a typewriter on the side of her desk. Cassie had seen Benny do the same thing—position carbon paper between blank sheets—when he wrote his stories.

The policewoman asked Miss Eaton for several personal details, including her relationship to Benny. Cassie thought she would say *coworker,* but she answered *friend*—something she had demonstrated beyond doubt that afternoon. She also had to provide her home address and place of employment.

Once the officer finished filling out the forms, she pulled them from the typewriter and set aside the carbon between them. Then she handed the copy to Miss Eaton and told her the details of when and where Benny would have to appear in court to face charges of assault and battery. The idea horrified Cassie, and made her realize that, no matter what she and Miss Eaton accomplished at the police station, Benny's ordeal would not end that day. But she pushed such thoughts aside, focusing instead on freeing the man she loved from jail.

The policewoman pointed at the door through which Cassie and Miss Eaton had just come. "If you'll go back out front and wait, an officer will escort Mister Russell out shortly," she said. "Show the officer the release form."

"Thank you, ma'am," Miss Eaton said, and Cassie echoed her. They headed back through the door.

In the precinct's entry, Miss Eaton walked over to the chairs beneath the front windows, and Cassie followed. As they sat, Cassie said, "Thank you for everything you've done. I can't even believe you've helped so much. It's wonderful."

"I'm happy I could help," Miss Eaton said. "Benny's a good man. He doesn't belong in here any more than he belonged in an . . . in a hospital."

"Well," Cassie said, looking away, "I think Benny did need some help." The admission felt almost like a betrayal. Peering back at Miss Eaton, she added, "But he's faced a lot of difficult times in his life . . . a lot of hard situations."

Miss Eaton nodded. "I saw a few of them," she said. "It's an unfair world, and I think that finally got to Benny." Just as Cassie had done a few seconds earlier, Miss Eaton looked away. Shaking her head, she said, "Sometimes I feel this unfair world getting to *me*." Miss Eaton seemed to drift off into her own thoughts, and Cassie let her.

They sat quietly for a few minutes, and then a door on the left side of the room opened. Cassie looked over, hopeful. A policeman walked through the door by himself, but then he reached back and pulled somebody through after him.

"Benny!" Cassie called out. She jumped up and ran toward him. The policeman put up a hand though, stopping her.

"Miss Kay Eaton?" the officer asked Cassie. He blocked the way to Benny with his body.

"That's me," Miss Eaton said, coming over to join the group.

"You have his release form?" the policeman asked. Miss Eaton handed it over. The officer examined it, then handed it back. "We're releasing Benny Russell into your custody." He directed Benny toward Miss Eaton, then disappeared back through the door, pulling it closed behind him.

Benny gazed at Miss Eaton. Cassie saw that he had a deepening bruise on the left side of his face, but otherwise he looked good—tired, but good. "Hi, Benny," Miss Eaton said. "Been a long time."

Cassie watched him regard her, alarmed that she saw no hint of recognition in his eyes. "Benny," she said, her voice dropped down to a whisper.

He turned to her. "Cassie," he said, and her heart soared. Whatever else might be wrong, at least he knew who *she* was. She stepped forward and threw her arms around him.

"Oh, Benny, I've missed you," she said, hugging him tightly. She felt his arms come up around her back, and if he didn't hug her quite as tightly, she chalked it up to all that he'd been through that day. Cassie buried her face against Benny's shoulder, feeling the warmth of his body, its strength.

As she held him, Cassie closed her eyes tightly, and the blue and white whorl appeared again, reminding her of what she'd earlier imagined inside the precinct. At once, she wanted to take Benny and Miss Eaton and leave the police station. She opened her eyes, stepped back, and looked at Benny. "Come on, let's get out of here," she said.

"Yes," Benny agreed. "I have to get out of here." He didn't look at Cassie as he spoke, but past her.

Cassie turned and followed his gaze to the front door. Before she could turn back, Benny rushed past her, nearly knocking her from her feet. She stumbled to the side, bracing herself against the front of the tall desk to prevent herself from falling.

As she straightened back up, Benny reached the front door and opened it with enough force to cause the doorknob to thud loudly against the wall. Then he ran outside. He didn't wait for Cassie, and he didn't look back.

"Benny!" Cassie called after him, shocked. "Benny!" She started across the room, toward the front door, but a grip around her upper arm stopped her. Cassie tried to pull free, but the hold only tightened. She turned, expecting to see a police officer restraining her.

Instead, she saw Miss Eaton. She stared at the woman who had done so much to help her that day, but who now held her back. They looked at each other for only a fleeting moment, and then Miss Eaton suddenly peered back over her shoulder—back over her shoulder, and *up*.

Up to where I thought I saw the ceiling falling, Cassie thought. *But what does that mean? What does any of it mean?*

Miss Eaton turned back to look at Cassie. "You have to let Benny go," she said.

"Why?" Cassie wanted to know. Again, she tried to pull her arm free of Miss Eaton's grasp. "We can be together." After all that Benny had been through—after all they had both been through—she wanted nothing more than for them to be together with their daughter.

"No," Miss Eaton said, her tone adamant. "You have to let him go."

Cassie wanted to argue. *No, I don't want to argue,* she thought. *I want to go after Benny.* But she didn't. Something had driven her to Miss Eaton, who had completely proven herself, and Cassie knew that whatever the woman writer said, she would believe—even if she didn't want to believe it.

But Cassie saw Miss Eaton hesitate. In that brief interval, she hoped that her new friend and guide would change her mind, would let go of her arm, and implore her to run after Benny.

Miss Eaton did none of those things. "You have to let him walk his own path," she said, "or you'll lose him. You'll lose him forever."

And though she didn't understand it, though it hurt her deeply, Cassie knew that Miss Eaton had spoken the truth.

Sisko walked out of the home office and back toward the front of the house. Ahead of him, past the dining area, he saw that Kasidy hadn't returned to the kitchen. When he reached the end of the hall, he didn't see her in the living room either. "Kasidy?" He glanced behind him, toward the back of the house, but he'd been facing the open doorway of the office when he'd watched Akaar's message on the companel, so he would have seen his wife if she'd headed to one of the bedrooms or the 'fresher.

Sisko crossed the sitting area before the stone hearth and opened the front door. He stepped outside into the spring morning, raising a hand to shield his eyes until he acclimated to the bright outside light. Kasidy sat in one of the rockers at the end of the porch, peering out at the Kendra Valley, a light shawl wrapped around her shoulders. The curved runners beneath her ground against the wooden boards as she moved slowly forward and back. She did not look over at the sound of Sisko's voice.

She knows I'm leaving, he thought. *Or she at least suspects.* "Kas?"

"It's a lovely day, isn't it?" she said, with no trace of irony or artifice. She continued to rock in her chair, staring off toward the mountains as though mesmerized.

"Yes, it is beautiful," Sisko said, gazing out at the moba trees. He heard the gentle trickle of the rill that danced across the property. "This land called out to me from the moment I first saw it." Uncertain about his wife's state of mind, he immediately regretted saying something that evoked the past—not just his past, but *their* past.

Sisko considered heading back inside, but he knew that he had to tell Kasidy—even if she already suspected it—that he would be leaving. He pulled the front door closed behind him and walked down the porch toward her. It felt like stepping into a minefield.

"When do you have to go?" Kasidy asked.

Sisko froze in midstride, as though he'd heard the telltale click of a pressure plate beneath his foot. "I have to be at the Adarak transporter by two this afternoon," he said. He waited for the explosion.

It never came.

Kasidy kept rocking in her chair, but she turned and looked up at him. "Two. That's good," she said. "Then you still have time to go out to the hospice and say your good-byes to Elias."

"Yes," Sisko said, working to keep the surprise from his voice, even in the single word. He had anticipated a much different reaction from Kasidy about his departure, especially since the amount and quality of their time together over the previous two weeks had been unexpected. Out at the wormhole, and then aboard *Robinson,* their emotions had swung to extremes and back again, and that had driven them together. Sisko realized that he'd allowed his guard to drop, and as much as he knew that he could not share his life with Kasidy—for both her sake and Rebecca's—he saw that he had reentered his wife's life in a manner that promised more.

Sisko had always known that he would leave again, that he would return to Starfleet, and yet he understood that he had not behaved that way. Devastated when he'd believed her dead, he'd *needed* to be with her afterward, but by doing so, in the way that he had, he'd set her up for more disappointment. As he thought about it, it seemed cruel.

And maybe I wanted a different reaction, Sisko thought. *Maybe I wanted Kasidy to be angry or upset or sad.* That idea frightened him, because he *could* ignore the warning of the Prophets—he'd done it before—and return to the woman he loved. Had he spent the previous two weeks in her company not just because he'd wanted to and needed to, but because he *hoped* that she would fight for them to stay together, that she would make it even more difficult for him to leave again?

"Ben?" He saw that she had stopped rocking. As he watched, she withdrew one arm from beneath her shawl and held up an isolinear chip. "I wanted to give this to you before you leave."

Sisko walked the rest of the way to Kasidy and took the chip from her. "What is it?"

"It's a signed petition for the dissolution of our marriage," she said.

Her declaration sliced through him like a hot phaser beam. He sat down in the rocker beside Kasidy. "Are . . . are you sure?" he asked.

"I guess I am," she said. "It's what you want."

It's not what I want, he thought. *It's what has to be.* But he didn't say that, because Kasidy already knew the reasons he'd left, and would leave again. He looked down at the translucent green chip, with its embedded silver circuitry. "What changed your mind?" he asked.

Kasidy shrugged, then peered back out toward the mountains. "I don't know," she said. "I've been thinking for a while that maybe we need to move on with our lives. I mean, we'll always be parents together, but . . ." She leaned over toward him and gently placed her hand on his forearm. "I understand why you believe we can't be together," she said. "So it just seems as though I need to let you go."

"Kasidy . . ." He wanted to say so many things to her. He wanted to tell her that he still loved her, that he would *always* love her. He wanted to make sure that she knew he didn't *want* to leave her, that his heart had broken when he had, and that it had never mended.

"Ben, I still love you," she said, "but I understand."

"I still love you," Sisko said, grateful for the opportunity to say the words to her again.

Kasidy squeezed his arm, then sat back in her chair. Somewhere overhead, a bird screeched out its call. A soft breeze floated past, and on it, Sisko thought he detected a hint of *nerak* blossoms, though it had to be too early in the season for that.

"Are you all right?" Kasidy asked.

"Yeah," Sisko said, although he felt anything but all right. "Yeah. I just . . . I just need to think of everything I need to do."

"Really?" Kasidy said. "Things you need to do before you leave Bajor?"

"Um . . . no. No, I guess not," he said. "After I get back from seeing Elias, I just need to pack my duffel over at Jake and Korena's."

"Well, that should take only a couple of minutes," Kasidy said. "So you still have a little time. Why don't you sit back and enjoy some of the morning with me before you go?"

Sisko tried to read his wife's expression. He searched for anger and frustration, disappointment and sadness. Instead, he saw only love and acceptance.

And that hurt him. No matter the reasons, he had been the one to leave, and the one to stay away. But did he believe all along, somewhere deep in his heart, that someday he might find a way that they could be together again? But if Kasidy had given up . . .

Sisko pushed himself back in the rocking chair beside Kasidy. She smiled at him, then turned back toward the vernal landscape. He watched her for a while, his mind racing over all the complications in their lives, and thinking how simple love *should* be.

And so he decided to make it simple. He wanted to reach for Kasidy's hand and hold it one more time, feel their fingers entwined in the same way that their lives had entwined, but he knew that would complicate matters further. So he sat back and turned his gaze to the Kendra Valley, past the moba trees, across the land to the Yolja River, and beyond, to the mountains.

They stayed that way for a while, idling on the front porch

of a house that they had at some point come to call home. They sat together long into the morning, quietly, easily, until at last, Sisko had to go.

The Vanadwan Monastery spread across the crest of Angorseer Mountain, the tallest peak in the Releketh Range. Meandering staircases and long walkways connected the great complex of ancient structures that clung to the lofty slopes. At its highest point, its circular Inner Sanctuary reached farther skyward, its nine spired towers representing the Orbs of the Prophets, earning the site the sobriquet "The Crown of Bajor."

Vedek Kira Nerys gazed up at the majestic edifice, noting the jagged line near the top of the wall where the towers had been rebuilt a dozen years earlier. Far from any major settlements on Bajor, the monastery had survived intact throughout much of the Occupation, but when the Cardassians had begun running barges along the upper reaches of the Senha River, from which the Crown of Bajor could be seen, the Vanadwan monks feared for the safety of the venerable complex and its residents. In one night, seeking to avoid drawing unwanted attention to the monastery, the monks toppled first the spires, and then the bases, all the way down to the top of the wall. From the upper Senha, Vanadwan became invisible.

The Inner Sanctuary, first raised more than a millennium ago, had originally comprised seven towers, since, to that point, only that many Orbs had been discovered. When the monks rebuilt after the Occupation, they chose to include two additional towers, to symbolize the later discoveries of the Orb of Destiny and the Orb of Wisdom. Recently, the Vedek Assembly had relocated the Eighth Orb to Vanadwan.

Kira stood on the monastery's primary transporter plaza, the one given over to beaming residents and visitors to and from the site. A round courtyard surrounded by flowering bushes, the area looked nothing like a travel hub. A knee-high stone wall at its center enclosed the de facto transport stage, though all of the targeting scanners and most of the other equipment lay underground. Formerly intended to provide shelter for sentries, a small stone shack off to one side accommodated the transporter console and an operator.

A light breeze whispered through the courtyard, sending Kira's golden robes aflutter. She adjusted the mauve sash she wore over her right shoulder and brushed her hair from her face. She'd let her locks grow longer recently—they reached down past her shoulders—something she hadn't done since her time in the Resistance, and which she'd never felt comfortable doing while in uniform. Kira liked the way her longer tresses looked, but she hadn't quite grown accustomed to the weight of them again, or to how they could fall across her eyes.

As the breeze settled, Kira heard the familiar whine of the transporter. Behind the low wall, bright rays of white light appeared and then coalesced into the form of Benjamin, clad in his Starfleet uniform. He carried a small cloth bag in one hand. Kira waited for him to exit the transporter stage through the gap in the wall, and then she approached him, her hands outstretched. "Captain Sisko," she said, very pleased to be seeing her old friend.

Benjamin saw her and took her hand with his free one, giving her fingers a light squeeze. "Nerys," he said. "It's good to see you."

"And you," Kira said. "I know how busy the life of a starship captain can be, so I'm glad you could make it."

"I'm even busier today," he said. "The *Robinson* will be under repairs for at least another couple of weeks, but I drew duty aboard the *Defiant* this afternoon."

"The *Defiant*?" Kira said. "That ought to bring back memories."

"I'm sure it will," he said. "I'm sorry to rush you, Nerys, but I've got to be back in Adarak by fifteen hundred, so we should probably get going."

"Of course," Kira said. "It's a bit of a walk, so if you'd prefer, there's a site-to-site transporter just on the other side of the Sanctuary." She pointed, and Benjamin looked in that direction. When he saw the building, he lifted his gaze to its spires.

"Is that the Crown of Bajor?" he said, awe shading his voice. "It's magnificent."

"It is," Kira said. "And that's how most people react when they see it."

"I can't believe I've never been to Vanadwan before."

"Not even to visit your former first officer," Kira said, then regretted the words at once.

Sisko looked away from the Sanctuary and back at Kira. "I'm sorry, Nerys," he said. "I really should have come to see you before now."

"No, I'm sorry," she said. "I didn't mean to sound critical. I was just trying to be funny and not doing a very good job of it."

"I understand, but . . . it's been too long," Benjamin said. "I know we've spoken via subspace a few times, but we haven't seen each other since you visited me at Starbase Thirty-Nine-Sierra." A year and a half earlier, she had tracked him down at the Starfleet facility at Kasidy's behest, delivering the message that, even though he'd left his wife, he should still spend time with his daughter—a sentiment with which Kira agreed. She opened her mouth to reply, but Benjamin held up a hand to stop her. "I know I've said it to you since then, but not in person, so I just want to apologize for the way I acted back then—especially since you were right, both as a friend *and* as an interpreter of Bajoran prophecy."

"The latter can be a bit tricky," Kira said with a chuckle.

Sisko nodded. "But the more important thing is your friendship," he said. "And it's easy to see in hindsight that you had not only Kasidy and Rebecca's best interests at heart, but also mine."

"I'm just glad it worked out," Kira said. "So, do you want to walk or beam?"

"Why don't we walk?" Benjamin said. "At least that'll give us a little time to talk."

"Good, I'd like that." She pointed to a covered walkway that ran from left to right along the mountain's crest, connecting the Inner Sanctuary with the monastery's library. "We go through there," she said. They started forward together.

"I wanted to ask you, Nerys: how are you feeling?" Benjamin said. "Kasidy told me what happened." Deep Space 9 had been destroyed only fourteen days earlier.

"It was quite an experience," Kira said. "It reminded me a lot of the Occupation: working frantically to move people out of danger."

"Everybody but yourself."

Kira noticed that he did not say, or even seem to imply, that she had also failed to get his wife out of danger. She wondered if Kasidy had told him that it had been Kira who insisted they remain on the station. From the way he spoke, she doubted it.

"Do you remember any of it?" Benjamin asked.

"Everything up until the emergency bulkheads slammed closed," Kira said. "After that, the next thing I remember is waking up in a bio-bed on the *Enterprise*."

"I understand they pulled your section of the station out of the wormhole."

"That's what they told me," Kira said. "It's all a blank to me, but I have to think that the Prophets were looking out for us."

Benjamin didn't react at all, and Kira recalled that he hadn't acted publicly in the role of Emissary for quite some time. The Bajoran population observed this, but fortunately seemed to endure it equably; with Benjamin spending most of his time offworld, aboard *Robinson*, acceptance came easier. But Kira also remembered their last encounter in person, when he'd loudly proclaimed to her that he was no longer the Emissary. Among the people of Bajor, only Kira knew that.

They reached the walkway, crossed beneath its cover, and started down an incline along a wide path that curled around to the right. "How is life here at the monastery?" Sisko asked.

"Fulfilling," Kira said. "After living so much of my life in complete turmoil, I've found a serenity I never even really knew existed, much less thought I could achieve. And I've discovered that I love teaching. It's very satisfying to clarify the canonical— and even the noncanonical—texts for young acolytes and novices, to share the history and beliefs of our people."

"You sound happy."

"I am," Kira said. "I'm where I feel I belong. I don't regret my past—at least not most of it. My path took me through the Occupation and onto Deep Space Nine, and even to being the Hand of the Prophets. But what happened with the Ascendants . . . it just illuminated everything for me in a way I'd never seen before that."

"How is Raiq?" Benjamin asked.

Kira felt herself deflate. She fought her reaction, throwing her shoulders back and keeping her head high. "Still troubled," she said. "But better. She's learned a lot, mostly about herself, I think."

"She's recuperated from her wounds, though?" Benjamin asked. "She looked well the one, brief time I saw her."

"Her physical wounds?" Kira said. "I've stopped asking. She never wanted to discuss her condition, and I eventually realized that it hurt her for me to even bring it up. I think there are still some lasting effects from her injuries, and I'm not even sure if she'll ever fully recover. But she seems to be bearing up well. I'm always more concerned about her emotional well-being. Overall, though, she's made a long journey, and I'm very proud of her."

"That's good to hear," Benjamin said. "I'm sure she has you to thank for—" He stopped walking and talking, and Kira turned to see his mouth agape. She turned to look where he looked.

"This place has that effect on people," she told him.

The tree-lined northeastern slope of Angorseer Mountain dropped precipitously away from its soaring summit and the aerie atop it. It plunged to the floor of the Elestan Valley, through which flowed the Elestan River, a tributary of the Senha. Free of settlements, the landscape had changed little in the centuries since the first stones had been laid down at Vanadwan.

"I always think this view is why the hospice is on this side of the mountain," Kira said. "It might not have magical healing powers, but it has a remarkable ability to bring peace to the dying, and to the people they love who come here to say good-bye."

Benjamin nodded, but didn't say anything. He stood there for a few moments, peering at the vista. At last, he started walking again, and Kira went with him, pointing their way around to the right, to an uncovered pathway.

"How is Rebecca?" Kira asked. "She just turned seven, didn't she?"

"She did," Benjamin said, "and she's terrific. Smart like her mother, very determined . . . she loves to read . . . loves to be outside. You can never get her to stop running or jumping or skipping, unless you put a book or a starship model in her hands."

"The last time I was out to the house, she was up in one of the moba trees, pretending to survey the inhabitants of the planet below her," Kira said. "Those inhabitants included two snowmen, Kasidy, Jasmine, and me."

Sisko chuckled. "That sounds about right."

"And how is Kasidy?" Kira worried about asking, but it pleased her that Benjamin did not hesitate to respond.

"She's well," he said, but then he seemed to reconsider. "I think she's well, anyway. We've actually been talking a lot, and she seems very centered to me. I'm not sure, but what the two of you experienced on Deep Space Nine . . . your close call . . . I think that might have given her a new perspective about things."

"That sounds like a good thing."

"I think so," Benjamin said. "She agreed today to dissolve our marriage." It seemed to Kira that he said the words as though trying them on for the first time.

"Oh," she said. "Is *that* a good thing?"

Benjamin stopped and faced her. "I don't really know anymore, Nerys," he said. "I know that we can't be together . . . that I can't endanger her life and Rebecca's life like that . . . but I have never stopped loving her."

"I don't think she's ever stopped loving you either," Kira said. "But I do know your separation has been hard on her. She has Jake and Korena, and Jasmine, and friends, but still, she's really raising Rebecca by herself. And I know she misses you."

Benjamin nodded.

"I know you probably don't want to hear this," Kira said, "but the Prophets will guide you along the right path."

Benjamin sighed heavily, his features molding into a mien of great sadness. "I'm on my path alone. I think I have to be. And that path has led me into the wilderness."

Kira shrugged. "I have faith in the Prophets," she said. "But I also have faith in you."

Benjamin smiled, though he did not lose his look of sadness. "Thank you, Nerys. That means a lot to me."

They started walking again, until they came to the end of the walkway. To the right, a wide wooden door led into the mountainside. In front of them, terraces hung from the slope, from where the hospice facilities had been carved out of the rock. Kira reached forward and leaned into the heavy door, pushing it open.

Inside, the temperature dropped by several degrees. Lighting panels illuminated the corridor indirectly, lending it a soft, graceful air. Carpeting muted their footsteps. They walked forward into a reception area, where several people waited, and two women and one man sat behind a large semicircular desk. Kira approached one of the women. "Hello, Sulan," she said. A nurse for many years at the hospice, Ransel Sulan shared her given name with one of the most influential people in Kira's life, and a former kai, Opaka. Kira hadn't spent much time at the hospice until a month earlier, when Prynn Tenmei had moved her father there from Deep Space 9's infirmary, but she had immediately struck up a friendly relationship with the nurse, who had worked at the hospice for many years. Since then, Kira had begun practicing some of her good works there, offering spiritual aid to those who sought it.

"Good afternoon, Nerys," Sulan said. "You're here for Prynn and Elias, yes?" She spoke with a calmness and surety that Kira found somehow both condoling and hopeful.

"Yes, we are," Kira said, then gestured toward Benjamin. "This is Captain Benjamin Sisko." Kira typically did not need to introduce the Emissary anywhere on Bajor, but if Sulan recognized him, she gave no indication.

"How do you do, Captain Sisko," she said. "I'm Ransel Sulan, a nurse here at Vanadwan Hospice." Looking back to Kira, she said, "Doctor Bashir is already here. Would you like an escort to the room?"

"No, I know the way, Sulan, thank you," Kira said.

"May you know peace today," Sulan said, "and going forward."

They thanked the nurse, and then Kira led Benjamin down another corridor. Doors lined the walls, small signs printed in Bajoran identifying the rooms. More than halfway along the lengthy corridor, Kira stopped at a door and knocked lightly. It opened to reveal Prynn.

"Please come in," she said. Kira could see that she'd been crying, although she seemed relatively composed. Prynn closed the door after Kira and Benjamin. "Thank you both so much for coming."

Doctor Bashir came out from the other side of the bed and greeted them, hugging Kira and shaking Benjamin's hand. Vaughn lay in the bed, really no more than a memory of his former self. He had lost much of his body weight. His face, clean-shaven, looked gaunt, his cheeks hollow almost to the point of collapse. Several machines hovered over him, with a number of tubes reaching from them and down beneath the sheets. The equipment emitted no noises, as they usually did; they clearly still functioned—Kira could see that by the changing readouts—but they had been silenced.

Kira peered past the bed, to the glass doors that led out onto the terrace. They stood open, and the breeze she felt earlier had returned, carrying with it the fresh scents of the outdoors. She felt sure that, if Vaughn had been capable, he would have appreciated the beautiful view.

Benjamin stepped up to the bed, reached down, and rested his hand atop Vaughn's. Kira noticed that the cloth bag he'd brought with him still dangled from his other hand. "Have a lot of people come?" he asked Prynn.

"Oh, yes," she said. "It seems that my father touched many lives."

"I certainly think that's true of everyone in this room," offered Julian. Kira nodded her agreement, and she saw Benjamin do the same.

"Word has apparently gotten around Starfleet and beyond, because even though some people my father knew were too busy and too far to come, they still sent word," Prynn said. "Admiral Akaar, Admiral Nechayev, Captain Picard, Captain Dax . . . John Harriman and Amina Sasine . . . even a Klingon named Lorgh. And so many people have come by. A woman named Drysi Gravenor, who mentored my father back in their Starfleet Intelligence days, came all the way from Alpha Centauri. I've also seen just about everybody from the station . . ." Kira saw her choke up for a moment, and knew that, on top of dealing with her father's demise, she also had to face the loss of so many of her crewmates aboard DS9. "Captain Ro visited, and Colonel Cenn . . . even Quark."

"Quark?" Benjamin said. "I hope he wasn't somehow looking to turn a profit from this."

To Kira's surprise, Prynn actually chuckled. "He did mention something about auctioning off vacuum-desiccated body parts, but Captain Ro shut him down pretty quickly. Before they left, Quark left a bottle for my father." She pointed to a small table in the corner beside her, on which a number of items had been placed, including a clear, squarish bottle filled with a fierce red liquid. "It's Berengarian whiskey. My father never ordered any in his bar, according to Quark, but since he knew that my father was born on Berengaria Seven, he decided that it was somehow appropriate."

"How much did he charge you for it?" Julian asked.

Prynn didn't just chuckle, but laughed. "That's how much of an impression my father made even on Quark," she said. "It was a *gift*."

"In a lot of ways, Prynn," Kira said, "your father was a gift to all of us."

Prynn's eyes became misty. "Thank you, Nerys," she said. She reached to the foot of the bed and picked up a padd resting there. "Captain, as people have come by, I've asked them to bring something with them to read aloud. Some have brought poems, others have read passages from novels, and a couple of people even wrote something themselves. I hope you don't mind that I picked out something for you, specially for today."

"That's perfectly fine, Prynn," Benjamin said. "But before I read what you've selected, I have one more gift to add to your collection." He lifted the cloth bag he'd brought, opened it, and pulled out an object about the size of one of his old baseballs. Kira recognized it, because Vaughn had brought one back from the Gamma Quadrant. Benjamin stepped forward and handed it to Prynn, exchanging it for her padd. The object's rumpled surface shimmered, almost alive with the movement of a silvery layer of liquid.

"I know this," Prynn said. "My father has one of these."

"Yes," Benjamin said. "It was a gift to him from the Vahni Vahltupali."

"Yes, that's right," Prynn said.

"I visited their world not that long ago," Benjamin said, "and they asked about your father."

"Of course they did," Prynn said quietly. "He helped save their world."

"And they haven't forgotten that," Benjamin said. He reached forward and plucked at a narrow strip Kira hadn't even seen, which came loose with a snap. The object unfolded in an instant into a flat sheet, measuring about the size of a companel display. One side showed a beautiful holographic image of a tower, and beyond it, a gleaming city of gentle colors and steel shapes. "This tower," Benjamin explained, "stands at the center of their capital city. Your father was on it the day it collapsed, when the Vahni moon was destroyed." Prynn nodded. Kira knew that she'd been aboard *Defiant,* in orbit of the planet, when that had happened. "They've rebuilt, obviously, and there's a plaque on top of the tower telling the story of how your father and his crew saved their world. When they heard about your father's condition, they wanted you to have this."

"Captain, thank you so much for bringing this to me," Prynn said. "I'll treasure it." She studied it a few moments longer, then set it down among the other gifts.

Benjamin held up the padd. "Would you like me to begin reading?"

Prynn turned to Julian. "Doctor?"

"I've already begun administering an anodyne," he said, "which will make your father's final days painless."

Prynn nodded, her eyes once more becoming moist. "Whenever you're ready, Captain."

Benjamin moved to the foot of the bed, facing Vaughn. Prynn and Julian and Kira all watched him as he lifted the padd and read from it.

"This is 'Ulysses,' by Alfred, Lord Tennyson." He began to recite the work, a poem written in blank verse. His voice, deep and somber, carried the words with import.

Kira peered at Vaughn as she listened to the first-person narrative of an old king, idled and restless, recalling the many travels of his life. In remembrance, he celebrates both the good times and the ill, spent both among loved ones and in isolation. In all his experiences, the king internalizes what he sees, what he learns, and still hungers for more.

We're all a part of everything we experience, Kira thought. *But it takes a person of . . . what? Strength? Introspection? Honesty?* She didn't quite know. But she thought that it required a man of Vaughn's particular mix of traits to carry with him all that he'd encountered, to process it, to embrace it, to make it a visible and *conscious* part of his essential self. Kira did not understand all the literary references, but she thought that the tone of the piece beautifully evoked Vaughn's spirit.

As Benjamin continued reading, Kira noted the word that the king chose to describe the end of his life: *dull.* Many people— perhaps most, she thought—would choose a different adjective: *sad,* or *heartbreaking,* or *tragic.* But for Elias Vaughn, a man of great wisdom and of great flaws, an explorer of unrelenting passion, the word the poet had chosen—*Dull!*—seemed absolutely fitting, as if he had penned his work specifically for the captain.

The poem went on to describe what the king would leave behind, and how he would strive to continue a life of note until the very end. Though inevitable, death seemed like one more destination, one more opportunity for exploration. Benjamin read on, and the words flowed with an elegiac beauty.

Kira's gaze drifted from Vaughn to the man eulogizing him, and she saw tears gliding silently down Benjamin's cheeks. She peered over at Prynn, and saw her crying as well, and only then did Kira realize that her own eyes no longer remained dry. When she looked at Julian, she saw his tears threatening, but he also concentrated on the task he had been asked to perform. Carefully, he shut down the equipment that, for too long a time, had saved Vaughn's body from the fate that his mind had already suffered.

Benjamin read the final few lines of the poem.

> ". . . . . and tho'
> We are not now that strength which in old days
> Mov'd earth and heaven, that which we are, we are:
> One equal temper of heroic hearts,
> Made weak by time and fate, but strong in will
> To strive, to seek, to find, and not to yield."

Benjamin lowered the padd. Julian deactivated the last medical device, so that machines would no longer force sustenance upon Prynn's father. With that, whether it took five days, or ten, or fifteen, Elias Vaughn began his final journey.

10

The vase flew across the room and smashed into the wall, bursting in a spray of ceramic fragments, long-stemmed flowers, and water. It felt good to throw it, to physically act out her anger and frustration, and to look upon the results of her small-scale violence. But it solved nothing.

Praetor Gell Kamemor stood on one side of her office, her back bent and her left arm still out before her after grabbing up the vase from her desk and hurling it against the far wall. Slowly, she stood back up, straightening the cut of her modern, deep-blue jacket as she did so. She watched as her grandnephew, Proconsul Anlikar Ventel, turned to face her from halfway across the room, the data tablet in his hand dropping to his side, both of his eyebrows raised in an unmistakable expression of surprise.

"I concur," Ventel said. "And I'm not sure if any other response is possible."

Kamemor brought the meaty side of her fist down on her desk, her rage unslaked. "Tomalak," she said, pointing at the display mounted in the room's long side wall, tucked in among the full, neatly arranged bookshelves that ran from floor to ceiling. On the screen appeared the frozen image, not of Tomalak, but of Tezrene, the Typhon Pact's ambassador to the Federation. Earlier that day, Kamemor had received the Tholian's dispatch, transmitted from the UFP's capital city and carrying an unsettling message to the praetor from President Bacco. Watching it for the fourth time, studying it for nuance, meaning, and clarity, Kamemor had finally snapped.

"We still don't really know why or how Tomalak ended up on the Breen freighter," Ventel said. "Is it at all feasible that there is an explanation that does not implicate him as complicit in what happened in the Bajoran system?"

"I admire your optimism, Anlikar," Kamemor said, moving out from behind her desk and padding over to him across the shallow, light-gray carpet that covered her office floor. "And I welcome any explanation that would not paint Tomalak as a traitorous warmonger and me as a fool, but I don't see how that's possible. According to what you learned from Admiral Devix, your former fellow proconsul *requested* the assignment as the liaison aboard the *Eletrix*." After initially receiving Tezrene's dispatch, Kamemor had charged Ventel with gathering together whatever information he could about Tomalak's presence on the joint Romulan-Federation exploratory mission to the Gamma Quadrant. The proconsul had subsequently spoken via subspace with the Imperial Fleet's leader, Fleet Admiral Devix.

"Actually," Ventel said, consulting his data tablet, "Admiral Devix told me that Tomalak requested to be placed in *command* of whatever vessel was selected to join the *Enterprise,* but that his separation from the Imperial Fleet for roughly a thousand days disqualified him for such a responsibility. After that, he asked to take on the liaison position."

"Regardless, it's clear that he wanted to be on that mission," Kamemor said. "And it seems impossible to me that he was not involved."

"Considering his position aboard the ship, and the actions we know he took, I don't see another possibility," Ventel said. "But if Tomalak was involved, what does that mean? Has he been working at cross-purposes to us all along?"

Kamemor shook her head, thinking of all the policy decisions she had argued over with her two proconsuls. "It's difficult to know," she said. "It seemed as though we often enough found positions in common. And when we didn't . . . well, you know how I try to govern. I *like* to be persuaded by people with whom I disagree."

"What we do know," Ventel said, "is that Tomalak resigned as proconsul and rejoined the Imperial Fleet, where the first action he took was to request an assignment to command the Romulan half of the joint mission with the Federation." The proconsul absently tapped at the surface of his tablet. "But being on that mission was important enough to him that, when he couldn't command, he asked for and accepted a lesser position. It therefore seems clear that he must have had an agenda."

Kamemor considered that, walking across the narrow width of the room and perching herself on the square arm of her violet sofa. "We've been told that the likely architect of the *Eletrix*'s actions in the Gamma Quadrant and in the Bajoran system was the ship's commander, Orventa T'Jul," she said. "Could Tomalak have been conspiring with her? Chairwoman Sela's report not only didn't place any blame on him; it didn't even mention him at all."

"That's true," Ventel said, walking over to the sofa and taking a seat. "But as good as they are, the Tal Shiar aren't perfect."

"No," Kamemor said, looking down at Ventel. "But they also aren't always completely honest."

Ventel raised one eyebrow. "No, but . . . what does that mean in this context?"

"I don't know," Kamemor said. With an arch grin tugging up one side of her mouth, she said, "I certainly don't want to have to suspect my Tal Shiar chairwoman too. It's bad enough I have to remove Devix from duty." Fatigue washed over her, and she pushed herself from the arm of the sofa and down onto its main body. "I actually respect the admiral," she told Ventel. "He's been a soldier all his life. He's fought when he's been commanded to, and he's ordered troops into battle, but he has no history of fomenting war, so I really don't think he's involved in all this. But he is fleet admiral, so he must be held accountable; the incident at the Utopia Planitia Shipyards happened under his leadership, and now what's happened out at Bajor."

"If he's not involved," Ventel said, "it could be that there are forces working against him."

"I'm sure that's right, just as there are obviously forces working against us," Kamemor said. "That's why we're attempting to scour my government and rid it of traitors." When she heard herself employ the word *traitors,* it triggered an uncomfortable association in her mind. "I'm sure that's probably just what Tal'Aura and Shinzon and Dralath and all my predecessors back to Pontilus used as an excuse to purge themselves of political opposition. 'They disagree with me, so they must be traitors; execute them.'"

"You're probably right," Ventel said. "But we both know that's not what this is about. Tomalak is actually proof of that. He served as proconsul to Tal'Aura, with whom you almost never agreed politically. Yet after you became praetor, you asked Tomalak to continue in his advisory role. That demonstrates that you're not averse to—or afraid of—opposing viewpoints."

"No, I'm not," Kamemor said. "But look where Tomalak is now. I've been the leader of the Romulan Star Empire for less than six hundred days, and the incident in the Bajoran system is the second rogue military action that's taken place in that time." She paused, not wanting to utter aloud what she knew to be true, but knowing she had to face it. "Anlikar, my government is in trouble."

Ventel did not respond right away, and an uneasy silence

rose in the praetor's office. Finally, the proconsul stood from the sofa and walked toward the screen on the opposite wall, which still displayed the Typhon Pact ambassador to the Federation. Gesturing toward the screen, and obviously making reference to the message that Tezrene had conveyed, he said, "I really thought President Bacco would understand."

"I *hoped* she would."

Ventel turned to face the praetor. "Maybe your message was too subtle," he suggested. "Maybe she just didn't understand what you were really saying to her."

"She understood," Kamemor said. "Nanietta Bacco is an intelligent woman, with intelligent people around her." She peered over at the display, at the still-motionless image of Tezrene: her angular, crystalline head, her glowing triangular eyes, the angry-red color of her carapace. President Bacco's message stated that Tomalak had been captured after being present during the immoral and criminal actions perpetrated by the Typhon Pact in the Bajoran system, and the Tholian ambassador had relayed that to Kamemor in a scream that had all but demanded that Romulus immediately declare war.

Rising to her feet, Kamemor said, "Computer, screen off." The display faded to black. "I was tired of looking at her," she told Ventel. "And I'm tired of hearing hysterical voices."

"There do seem to be a lot of them lately."

The praetor walked to the end of the room and back behind her desk. Not overly large, more functional than ornamental, she enjoyed working at the modest space, which she kept well organized. "Anlikar, we have such a historic opportunity here," she said. "For so long, the Empire has been beset by powerful people advocating for war: selfish, egotistical people bent on utilizing force to elevate themselves; avaricious people who would gladly risk the lives of others to pursue their own self-interests; jingoists who fight for the sake of fighting and call it patriotism. But so many of those people are gone now."

"Many of them are," Ventel said. "Most of them, but there are still those who would choose war over peace."

"There always will be, I suppose," Kamemor said. "But for

now, for right now, where there's a Senator Durjik spouting bellicose rhetoric on the chamber floor, there's also a Senator Eleret, calling for calm and measured responses to interstellar problems. Where there are still old allies of Pardek like Mathon Tenv, there are also those like T'Jen, who rose to power alongside Tal'Aura, but then broke from her policies. The numbers are turning in our favor. We just have to endure long enough to let everybody see that there is a better way."

Ventel walked over to stand opposite Kamemor across the desk. "Inspiring words, Praetor," he said. "Truthful words. But somebody in the Empire orchestrated the events in the Gamma Quadrant and the Bajoran system, and before that, at Utopia Planitia. Maybe it was Tomalak."

"Maybe," Kamemor said. "In which case, with him now in the hands of the Federation, maybe our problems have been solved. But I don't honestly see Tomalak masterminding such operations. I know he commanded a starship for a long time, but he always struck me as somebody more inclined to take orders than to give them."

"Who, then?" Ventel asked. "Admiral Devix?"

Kamemor had already thought about such a possibility. As she sat down in the chair behind her desk, she said, "I don't think so. For one thing, if Devix was involved, wouldn't he simply have given Tomalak command of a ship for the joint mission when he requested it?"

Ventel turned his head quickly to one side, as though straining to identify a strange noise he'd heard in a far corner. He stood that way for a moment, then peered back at the praetor. "Somebody *did* support Tomalak's being given that command, even though Admiral Devix ultimately denied the request." Ventel looked at his empty hands, and then around the office. Then he bolted to the sofa and picked up his tablet, where he'd apparently set it down. He worked its controls as he hurried back to the desk. "Tomalak's support came from . . ." He gazed up at Kamemor, his expression grim. "It came from Admiral Vellon."

"Vellon?" The praetor slowly stood up. "*Enellis* Vellon?"

For more than two decades, Enellis Vellon had unabashedly championed the need for, and the patriotism of, the Tal Shiar. Nobody within the government doubted his deep connections to the secretive agency. Kamemor herself supported a strong intelligence community on Romulus, one with the capacity to extend its reach effectively throughout the Alpha and Beta Quadrants. But she also opposed terrorizing the Romulan citizenry, the invasion of privacy, and the use of intimidation and torture, all sins of which the Tal Shiar had so often been guilty.

"Which points us to the chairwoman," Ventel said quietly.

Kamemor glanced at the empty corner of her desk, where her flower-filled vase had sat just moments earlier. She thought that if it had still been there, she would at that moment have snatched it up and sent it flying again. "I *am* a fool, Anlikar," she said. "I trusted Sela. I read all of the files on her . . . spoke with people who knew her . . . who worked with her. It seemed as though she'd escaped her petty hatreds and elected to redirect her efforts toward the common good."

"The chairwoman probably believes that she *is* doing that," Ventel said. "And you can't possibly know everything about everybody. You were thrust unexpectedly into the praetorship. You had to form your government from the ground up, and that meant you had to trust some people who were already in place." He clearly tried to mitigate what Kamemor considered her own poor judgment.

"Irrespective of my mistakes, it doesn't change where we are now," she said. "This calls into question every piece of information Sela ever provided me." The reality of that induced Kamemor to think about what the chairwoman had told her about the attack on the Federation space station and starships. "She blamed the battle in the Bajoran system on Commander T'Jul . . . and the bombing at the Utopia Planitia Shipyards as well."

"But it was Sela behind those operations," Ventel said. "And she probably directed Tomalak."

"Why, though?" Kamemor asked. "What were her goals?"

"At Utopia Planitia, it was the acquisition of the quantum slipstream drive."

"Right," Kamemor said. "Fears still exist about Starfleet's advanced engines providing the Federation with a first-strike capability." In her memory, the praetor heard echoes of the past. "We used to say that about transwarp drive and the supposed *Universe* metaweapon."

"That's true," Ventel said. "But neither of those technologies ever proved out. Slipstream is a reality."

"Are you saying that we *should* be concerned?"

"I don't know," Ventel said. "Should we be?"

The conclusion seemed clear to Kamemor. She shook her head. "Contrary to what some senators might claim, I'm not an apologist for the United Federation of Planets. They have imperialistic tendencies, and a propensity for thinking there can be no way better than theirs." She circled around her desk to face Ventel at close range. "But I've worked with them, I've negotiated with them, I've even *befriended* a few of them. From all of those experiences, I'm sure of one thing: the Federation will *never* launch a first strike against the Romulan Empire or any other power. They didn't do so against the Dominion, and they didn't do it against the Borg. There is no chance that they would ever attack Romulus unprovoked. I can't say the same thing about the Klingons or the Kinshaya or the Graymel."

For an instant, a rush of memory overwhelmed Kamemor. She remembered vividly hearing, as a young woman, of the battle between a Romulan bird-of-prey and a Graymel scourge vessel. She recalled the news that while fighting a losing battle, the crew of the scourge ship had unleashed an isolytic subspace weapon. The resulting fracture in the structure of space-time shredded the nearby world of Algeron III, visiting a horrible death on its millions of inhabitants.

"Praetor?"

Shaking off her sudden melancholy, Kamemor completed her thought. "I can't even say that the Romulan Empire would never strike first against a perceived enemy," she said, "because we both know that the Empire has done that many times."

"But whether or not the Federation would actually do the same," Ventel pointed out, "Sela is apparently working to avoid even the possibility that they could."

Kamemor nodded. "She's trying to tip the balance of power in favor of Romulus . . . or in favor of the Typhon Pact."

"But there's no slipstream drive in the Gamma Quadrant."

"Not that we know of," Kamemor said, but then a terrible thought occurred to her. "But there is the Dominion."

Ventel's eyes narrowed. "Oh, no."

Kamemor walked the length of her office, attempting to puzzle out not just Sela's aims, but what had actually transpired aboard *Eletrix*. Pacing back toward Ventel, she said, "They failed. Their ships were destroyed, everybody but Tomalak killed. Even if they reached some sort of agreement with the Founders, they don't have the backing of their own governments. I don't support war, and neither do most of the other Pact leaders."

"Not right now," Ventel said. "For some of them, it's because they're afraid of the advantage that slipstream provides the Federation."

"Right," Kamemor said, reaching the desk again. "But that advantage is real. Maybe . . . maybe Sela sent Tomalak to secure some piece of technology that would negate it." She reached a decision. She circled her desk and sat down behind it again. "It's all speculation at this point," she told Ventel. "It may be important to determine what Sela and her followers were trying to accomplish in the Gamma Quadrant and at Bajor, but it's more important to figure out what comes next. Because I can promise you that this failure won't stop them. They are *zealots*."

"Are you going to have Sela arrested?"

"Not yet," Kamemor said. "We need her to lead us to her next action, and to her compatriots."

"That's a risk where the Tal Shiar is involved," Ventel warned.

"I know," Kamemor said. "But we do have people there we can trust. We'll use them if we have to, but even if we don't, we need to start preparing for somebody to take over the chairmanship. I want you to work on that."

"Yes, Praetor," Ventel said. "And what about Tomalak?"

"I'm inclined to let the Federation keep him for now," Kamemor said. "Even if I wasn't, I'm not sure they'd agree to surrender him anyway."

"No, probably not."

"What about the Senate?" Kamemor asked, thinking ahead, past the time when they could bring down Sela. "I thought that our most significant opposition came from there, but if it's strictly Sela and Tomalak . . ."

"We do have growing numbers of senators disinclined to go to war, though there are many who still distrust the Federation," Ventel said. "The bigger problem is the number who distrust you and the people you've surrounded yourself with. As praetor, though, you have shown strength through decisiveness, and that helps, even when you support ideas unpopular among the senators, such as removing restrictions on the public debate of policy."

"Those ideas might be unpopular in the Imperial Senate," Kamemor said, "but there's a great deal of support for them outside of Ki Baratan."

"So what's next?"

"You concentrate on the Tal Shiar," Kamemor said. "I need to figure out how we can determine what Sela and her followers intend to do next." Once more, the praetor rose from her chair. Her fingertips brushing the top of her desk, she set herself on a necessary path. "Then I need to stop them."

11

"So are we clear?" Ro asked.

"Yes, sir," said Blackmer. "But I have to ask: are you sure?"

Ro sighed, then stood up from her chair. When she did, her workspace—it measured far too small to call it an office—seemed to shrink by half its size. She faced her security chief across a short distance, and she thought if he'd had a chair to sit in, the entire room would be completely filled. "Honestly, Jeff, no, I'm not sure," she said. "We considered three people possible threats to commit sabotage on the station even before sabotage was committed, but we cleared those people."

"Thank goodness for that," Blackmer said with a wry smile, obviously acknowledging that Ro had suspected him, along with Lieutenant Commander Sarina Douglas and Ensign Rahendervakell th'Shant.

"Sorry about that," Ro said. Happy to have been wrong about Blackmer, she still felt justified in having questioned his loyalties, though she should have addressed her concerns far sooner than she had. "The point I'm making is that we don't know who placed the bombs on the station, and whatever physical evidence might have existed was destroyed along with Deep Space Nine. The only things we really know are the relatively small window of time when the bombs could have been placed and—because of the tight security we had with all the civilian Typhon Pact vessels traveling to and from the Gamma Quadrant—that there's a good chance a member of the crew was involved."

"But for all we know, the perpetrator might have died in the explosion."

Ro sighed again. "It's possible," she said. "You were of the opinion that the bombs hadn't been set to destroy the station, but to cause an evacuation. It could be that whoever planted them thought that they didn't have to worry about their safety."

Blackmer nodded. "I guess there's only one other thing we know with certainty," he said, "and that's who your original three suspects were."

"Exactly," Ro said.

"So I'll wait for your word," Blackmer said. "Is there anything else, Captain?"

Ro looked around her workspace. In addition to the small desk that occupied perhaps a third of the area, a replicator had been crowded into one corner, and a companel took up most of one wall. "Not unless you can find me nine or ten extra square meters somewhere."

"You should see the space Colonel Cenn assigned me," Blackmer said, throwing a thumb back over his shoulder toward the room's only door. "I'd have more room working in a holding cell."

Ro smiled. "So much for rank having its privileges," she said.

"At least when we get back to the *Defiant*," Blackmer said with a shrug, "the ship will feel like a palace." The security chief turned and waited for the door, then obviously realized it wouldn't open on its own. He reached forward and turned the knob. "Newfangled technology," he muttered.

Ro followed Blackmer out, and the chief headed to the tiny area Cenn had doled out to him. Buffeted by the confused noise of construction and renovation, the captain stopped and surveyed what until recently had been the abandoned Wyntara Mas Control Center. She had taken one of the rooms tucked into the front corners of the building for herself, a space that had previously been utilized for simple storage. The other front room contained control panels for the building's infrastructure, all of which had been overhauled by her engineers. She saw that the gate between the two rooms stood open, allowing bright sunlight to shine inside.

The transformation of the old transportation control facility had progressed well, but Kifal Illior's estimate that Ro's crew could begin working there within ten days had proven overly optimistic. In part, that had been because Ro still lacked a chief engineer to oversee the modifications, but the scope of the changes required had also grown beyond the specifications initially supplied to the Bajoran transportation minister.

Ro regarded what would eventually be her crew's temporary new workplace. The sounds of activity came from every direction, and she saw many of her engineering crew busily upgrading the center. Abutting the right-hand wall, directly in front of her, stretched a six-person transporter pad. Though it hardly projected an air of permanence, it certainly improved upon the emergency two-person unit to which she'd beamed on her first visit there. An even larger cargo transporter sat against the left wall.

Straight ahead, beyond the transporters, where rows of

outmoded equipment had once lined the floor, new companels, computer interfaces, and other gear gleamed, most of it still awaiting installation. Halfway up the walls, which rose ten meters to the building's ceiling, a second floor neared completion, as did two basic, unenclosed turbolifts, one on either side. In order to have enough room for her crew, Ro had insisted on the additional story. It would be difficult enough to have several dozen personnel continuously away on *Defiant*; she didn't need to have the rest of her people in two different locations on Bajor.

Ro walked to the nearer wall, to where a built-in ladder reached up to the ceiling. She climbed high enough so that she could survey the entirety of the new floor. It remained empty of equipment, but she could see in the lighted crawlspace below it a menagerie of optronic cabling, power distribution nodes, router circuits, and numerous other items she hadn't taken enough engineering courses at Starfleet Academy to recognize.

"Captain?"

Ro looked down and saw a man wearing a Starfleet uniform with the gold collar of the operations division. Ro recognized him at once, though she'd seen him only a few times since they'd served together aboard *Enterprise*. She hoped that he brought with him the salvation of her engineering team.

Ro descended the ladder, her boots ringing against each rung. When she reached the floor, she turned to see her old crewmate approaching. He had light brown hair, thinning and curly; a pale, doughy face; and a physique that, while not exactly overweight, suggested that he hadn't missed too many meals recently.

"Captain Ro," he said. "Chief Engineer Miles O'Brien reporting for duty." His Irish accent softened his vowels, hardened his consonants, and lent an almost lyrical quality to his voice.

"Chief," Ro said, "it's good to see you." She held out her hand in the human tradition, and O'Brien accepted it with a firm grip. Ro then waved toward the bustle of the renovations just as a sound like a phaser beam slicing through metal filled the area. "Not a moment too soon," she said, raising her voice to be heard.

O'Brien regarded the scene with a look of mild confusion. "What is this place?" he asked, raising his own voice.

The phaser-on-metal noise faded. "You mean Starfleet didn't tell you?"

"Tell me what?" O'Brien asked. "Starfleet Command issued me new orders last week assigning me to Bajor, and I just assumed that meant the *Defiant*. They said that you needed a new chief engineer—" O'Brien abruptly stopped speaking as he seemed to realize something. "I heard about what happened on Deep Space Nine," he said. "I'm sorry. I know you lost a lot of people."

"Thank you," Ro said, as always deeply saddened when she thought about the members of her crew and the civilians who hadn't made it safely off the station. "One of our losses was our chief engineer."

"Jeannette Chao," O'Brien said.

"That's right. Did you know her?"

"Met her a couple of times over the years," O'Brien said. "Same circles, you know. I've been detached to the Starfleet Corps of Engineers for a while, so I tend to meet a lot of engineering types. Chao seemed very capable."

"She was," Ro said. "Not everybody could keep our hulking Cardassian ore-processing station functional."

O'Brien grunted in amusement. "Tell me about it."

"Remind me," Ro said, recalling that O'Brien had transferred from *Enterprise* to Deep Space 9 to become the station's chief engineer. "How long did you stay on DS-Nine?"

"Seven years."

Ro calculated backward on the calendar. "I guess you left just before I got there."

"That would have been the end of twenty-three-seventy-five."

"I arrived shortly after that," Ro said, trying to remember that period. "Now that I think about it, I used to hear your name mentioned quite a lot back then—I think because you were such good friends with Doctor Bashir."

"Depends which one of us you ask," O'Brien said, but his

smile confirmed Ro's statement. "We've kept in touch, but it's been a while since we've gotten together. It'll be good to see him again." Another blast of clamorous noise erupted. O'Brien looked over at all the uninstalled equipment scattered about and the work being done, then up at the new second story. "So, you still haven't told me what this is," he yelled.

"Let's head to my office, where it's a little quieter," Ro yelled back. She led him over to the corner and allowed O'Brien to precede her inside. She closed the door behind her, mercifully cutting off the racket from the rest of the facility. When she looked past O'Brien, she saw that the room must've shrunk while she'd been out of it. "I said it would be quieter in here," she told the chief, "not more comfortable."

"I think you might need to add a few square meters just to get to 'not more comfortable.'"

"Take the chair," Ro told him. "I've been sitting all day." O'Brien settled himself at the captain's desk, which stood facing the wall, though the chair faced outward. Ro leaned against the replicator in the corner, to which she then pointed. "Would you like something to drink?"

"No, thanks."

"Where are you coming from, Chief?" Ro asked. "Were you still on Cardassia?"

"Yeah, I've been based there for quite a while now," O'Brien said. "Did a lot of work on reconstruction after the war. Lately, though, since the Union joined the Khitomer Accords, I've been helping the Cardassian Guard, upgrading ships' systems, retrofitting spacedocks, things like that. I also get a fair amount of assignments with the SCE that take me offworld."

"Sounds like they've kept you busy."

O'Brien grunted his agreement for a second time. "I'm *always* busy," he said. "And you haven't even mentioned my fifteen-year-old daughter and my ten-year-old son."

"Are they that old already?" Ro asked, surprised. "So you're not just busy, but frantic."

"That's probably a better description," O'Brien said. "Keiko says nobody in the family stops moving except to sleep."

"How is Keiko?" Ro asked. "What's she been doing?"

"She's great," O'Brien said. "She's a botanist with the IAAC."

"I'm not sure what that is."

"Oh, it's the Interstellar Agricultural Aid Commission," O'Brien explained. "It's a private organization, but they work closely with the Federation. We first went to Cardassia so that Keiko could be the project leader for the planet's agricultural renewal efforts."

"Wow," Ro said. "Sounds impressive."

"You know Keiko," O'Brien said. "She's definitely that."

"How does she feel about leaving her position?" Ro asked.

"For right now, we're just considering moving the family," O'Brien said. "Most of the heavy lifting's been done on Cardassia's agricultural renewal, so Keiko's going to see what else is available, both there and on Bajor. I mean, we know Bajor— Keiko once worked for six months here as the chief botanist on an agrobiology expedition—but Cardassia's actually become home. It's close to Bajor, though, so until we figure out exactly what we're going to do, we'll still get to see each other regularly."

"Sounds like you've got it worked out," Ro said. She stepped away from the replicator and placed her hand on the door. "So you asked about this place," she said. "What we have out there is the new Deep Space Nine."

"Pardon?"

"Since the loss of the station, Starfleet has assigned several starships to patrol the entrance to the wormhole," Ro said. "But as you know, that's only a portion of the duties that the crew of Deep Space Nine performed. We don't have a space station anymore, obviously, but we're going to try as best we can to mimic its functions from here."

"From a *ground*-based facility?" O'Brien said. "That seems awfully ambitious. Bajor doesn't even have any orbital facilities to speak of."

"We plan on bringing in some tenders to lock in geo-synchronous orbit," Ro said. "We know it's ambitious, but the alternative to trying to substitute for the functions of the station is to eliminate them until there's a *new* station in place."

"*Is* there going to be a new station?" O'Brien asked. "I'd heard that some councilors considered it too costly a use of resources at this point."

"Some apparently do feel that way," Ro said, "but fortunately, the full Council voted with Starfleet."

"Good. I think it's necessary." O'Brien paused, then said, "It'd be pretty interesting to work on constructing a brand-new space station from the beginning."

"I'm glad you feel that way," Ro said, amused but not surprised that Starfleet Command hadn't provided Chief O'Brien with all the details of his new billet. After all, they hadn't even bothered to inform her of his name or arrival date. Ro pointed at the door of her office and said, "In addition to transforming a decades-old Bajoran transportation center—" Then she pointed skyward. "—you're also going to be one of the engineers in charge of building the new station."

"Really?" O'Brien said, a big smile forming on his face. "Now *that's* a project."

"I'm sure it is, and I'm sure you'll enjoy working on it," Ro said. "But don't get any ideas. You're not stepping foot off this planet until you help us remake this place."

"You drive a hard bargain, Captain."

"Welcome aboard," Ro said. "Have you been assigned quarters yet?"

"Not yet," O'Brien said. "I came directly here from the shuttle that brought me. I've got my duffel just outside."

"We've taken over some old government housing in Aljuli, which is a town just south of here," Ro said. "We won't be living in luxury, but it's also not a Cardassian ore-processing facility either."

O'Brien chuckled at that. "Good point."

Ro reached up and activated her combadge. "Ro to Cenn."

"Cenn here, Captain."

"Desca, where are you?" Ro said. "I've got our new chief engineer over here at the control center."

"I'm in Aljuli," Desca said. *"I'm working on our living arrangements."*

"Perfect," Ro said. "I'm going to send Chief O'Brien over so you can help him get settled. We need him well rested so he can get this place operational as soon as possible."

"I'll meet him at the local transporter."

"Very good, Desca. Ro out." She opened the door, then exited with O'Brien to the main floor of the control center. Fortunately, a wall of noise didn't greet them. "Colonel Cenn Desca is my first officer," Ro said.

"*Colonel* Cenn?" O'Brien said. "I thought that Starfleet absorbed the Bajoran Militia."

"Only the branch not based on the planet," Ro said. "Colonel Cenn almost never worked offworld—almost never even left Bajor—until I recommended him for the position of Bajoran liaison officer on the station. He agreed, on the condition that he remain attached to the Militia. That was under Captain Kira. When I took command of the station, he agreed to become my first officer."

"Captain?" came a voice from beside Ro. She turned to see Lieutenant Commander Douglas. "You wanted to see me?"

"I did," Ro said. "Wait for me in my office and I'll be right in."

"Yes, sir," Douglas said. She headed into the captain's office.

To O'Brien, Ro said, "So retrieve your duffel and contact the local transporter in Aljuli. They'll beam you there, and Colonel Cenn will get you situated."

"Yes, sir," O'Brien said. "Thank you, Captain."

Ro watched him for a moment as he headed toward the open gate, pleased that her new chief engineer had finally arrived. Then she started back toward her office. At the door, she stopped and took a deep breath. She didn't expect that the next few minutes would be particularly easy.

Then she opened the door and went in to meet with Sarina Douglas.

12

It felt strange for Sisko to be back on *Defiant*. He had spent so much time on the compact powerhouse of a starship—and its predecessor—when he commanded Deep Space 9, but he had set foot on it on only a handful of occasions since his return from the Celestial Temple seven years earlier. As he peered from the command chair around the bridge, he saw not a single familiar face from his tenure on the station. Of course, he'd gotten accustomed to a new set of faces on a different starship anyway.

"Captain, long-range scanners are reading two more Jem'Hadar fighters," reported Lieutenant Commander Wheeler Stinson from his station on the port side of the bridge. The dim, red-tinged lighting confirmed the continued operation of *Defiant*'s cloak. "Traveling at warp five. On our present course, they'll pass within seventy-five thousand kilometers of us." The young officer did not sound concerned about an encounter with a pair of Jem'Hadar heavies, but resigned, even bored.

"Dalin Slaine, go to red alert," Sisko ordered.

"Yes, sir," said Slaine. She crewed the tactical station off to starboard. Around the bridge, lighting bars began to pulse red.

"Lieutenant Tenmei, drop us out of warp," Sisko said.

"Slowing to sublight speed," replied Tenmei from in front of Sisko, where she sat at the arced console that combined the ship's conn and ops functions. The thrum of the main engines faded. "We have dropped out of warp."

"Very good," Sisko said. "Commander Stinson, cut main power."

Stinson let out a rush of breath, a quick sigh that unmistakably conveyed his frustration with a procedure Sisko had ordered several times since *Defiant* had entered Dominion space. For the moment, the captain ignored the inappropriate response. "Cutting main power," Stinson said.

Again, the sounds of the ship changed, the usual background drone growing fainter. Secondary power kept the bridge consoles, life support, and the ship's cloak operational, but Sisko knew that *Defiant*'s power signature, extremely high for a vessel of its relatively small size, had been cut by half. The two measures—reducing the ship's velocity and slashing its power output—would prevent the Jem'Hadar from locating *Defiant*.

Or at least it would keep them from finding it *easily*.

Tense moments passed.

"They're nearing their closest approach to us," said Stinson. "Like the others, they're actively sweeping surrounding space with antiproton beams."

"On-screen," Sisko said. On the main viewer, two Jem'Hadar fighters appeared, their warp nacelles glowing a purplish white, the undersides of their beetlelike hulls a deeper purple.

Sisko knew that antiproton scans could, under certain circumstances, aid the Jem'Hadar in detecting cloaked vessels. The captain therefore avoided those circumstances. But it had also been a long time since anybody in Starfleet had needed to evade the Jem'Hadar, and Sisko didn't know what sort of advances they'd made in their cloak-penetrating technology.

Sisko waited. Around him, the *Defiant* crew did too. Most of them appeared anxious, though not scared. The captain imagined that their successful avoidance of the Jem'Hadar to this point had eased their fears of a confrontation.

Stinson, though, did not look anxious. He glanced around the bridge and shifted in his chair, as though time couldn't pass quickly enough for him. More than anything, he appeared impatient.

"They're passing us," Stinson said. "No change in their heading."

Sisko waited a few seconds to ensure their safety, then stood up. "Well done, everybody," he said. "Lieutenant Tenmei, resume course and speed to the Omarion Nebula."

"Aye, sir."

"Viewer ahead," Sisko said. "Mister Stinson, I'd like you to join me in the ready room." He started toward the portside aft exit.

"Sir?" Stinson said from his station.

Sisko didn't bother to look around, but continued on toward the door. "You heard me," the captain said, and for the first time, he hardened his voice.

Without checking to see if Stinson followed—though he assumed he did—Sisko exited the bridge into one of the side halls behind it. He crossed the main port corridor and entered the ship's ready room. He went to the desk, swung around it, and sat down. When he did, he saw Lieutenant Commander Stinson stepping inside.

Sisko waited for the door to close. Stinson approached the desk and took a seat in one of the chairs before it. He wore a harried expression. Sisko said nothing at first, allowing the young man's emotions time to marinate.

"Sir?" Stinson finally asked, the look on his face changing to one of annoyance.

"I didn't give you permission to speak, Mister Stinson," Sisko said, his tone cold. "And I don't recall asking you to have a seat."

Stinson stared at the captain, nonplussed. "Sir?" he said again.

"On your feet, Commander," Sisko barked.

For just a moment, Sisko thought that Stinson wouldn't comply. Considering the substantial risks of entering Dominion space, the captain had no interest in wasting his time and attention on having to discipline his own crew. *But then it's not my crew, is it?* He knew that it didn't matter. The men and women aboard *Defiant* had a job to perform, and Sisko would see that it got done, even if it meant locking up his first officer in the brig.

Stinson appeared to realize that the captain truly meant for him to stand, and so he did. He did not mask his irritation.

Neither did Sisko.

"Am I bothering you, Commander?" Sisko said.

Stinson raised his chin and said nothing.

Sisko rose and came out from behind the desk to stand beside the man serving as his exec. "That wasn't a rhetorical question."

"Sir?"

"Stop saying 'sir,'" Sisko said loudly. "Am . . . I . . . bothering you?"

Stinson turned his head toward the captain. "Permission to speak freely," he said.

"No, you do not have permission to speak freely," Sisko told him. "You have permission only to answer the questions I put to you. Now: am I bothering you?"

"Sir . . . Captain, I—"

"That's a yes-or-no question."

Sisko expected Stinson to say no, but the lieutenant commander surprised him: "Yes."

The answer also impressed Sisko. Stinson had the courage and confidence of his youthful inexperience. During their journey through the Gamma Quadrant, as the captain had registered the young man's displeasure with some orders, Sisko had checked his background. Stinson graduated third in his class at the Academy, where he excelled across Starfleet's disciplines. As a cadet, he showed a penchant for piloting, and in his first spaceborne assignments, aboard *Victoria Falls* and then *Viriya Parami,* he spent time working in both engineering and the sciences, and even briefly in security. His aspirations, though, had always been in command, and he'd found a supporter in Ro Laren when Starfleet had assigned him to Deep Space 9. But then, Sisko suspected that Stinson had never displayed insolence toward Captain Ro.

"Commander, I happen not to care whether I'm bothering you," Sisko said. "Because the fulfillment of your emotional state is not the reason we're in the Gamma Quadrant. We have a job to do. The Typhon Pact had contact with the Founders, and we need to know why. Because it's entirely possible that if the two have formed an alliance, the Federation and its allies might be facing a war that would all but obliterate each and every world in the Alpha and Beta Quadrants."

Sisko paced around Stinson, behind his back, until he faced him from the other side. Stinson turned his head to look at the captain. "Eyes front, mister," Sisko snapped. "You're at attention." Stinson obeyed, and for the first time since they'd entered the ready room, the emotion had gone out of his face.

"I understand that, with Captain Ro busy on Bajor and Starfleet assigning the *Defiant* to this mission, you probably think that you should have been given the chance to command—because, after all, during the normal course of your duties, when Captain Ro is unavailable, you *do* command the *Defiant.* Why, you might wonder, did Starfleet send this old man to take this opportunity from you?

"But this *isn't* an opportunity," Sisko continued, building up a head of steam. "It's a mission that could be critical to the lives of literally *trillions* of people. I graduated Starfleet Academy twenty-nine years ago. I served during the last Federation-Tzenkethi War, the Dominion War, and the Borg invasion. I'm an honest-to-goodness war hero *and* a religious icon. I've logged more hours in the Gamma Quadrant than anybody in Federation history, and I had a Changeling serve under my command for seven years."

Once more, Sisko circled behind Stinson. No trace of the lieutenant commander's annoyance remained visible. "I also happen to know that a cloaked starship radiates a minor subspace variance when traveling at warp, that the *Defiant* has an outsized power signature, and that the Jem'Hadar are capable of detecting both those things."

Sisko stepped away from Stinson and moved back behind the desk, where he sat down again. "While my calls to bring the ship out of warp and to reduce its power output might irritate you in your quest to log star-hours, they might also have saved this crew so that we can accomplish what we set out to do. So tell me . . . Lieutenant . . . Commander . . . Stinson . . . which one of us do you think is better equipped to be leading this mission?"

Stinson stared straight ahead, his face pallid. "You, sir," he said, his voice coming out in a whisper.

"I didn't hear you," Sisko said.

Stinson swallowed, then said, "Sir, you, sir."

"Good," Sisko said. "That's good."

"Permission to speak freely so that I might apologize, sir," Stinson said.

Sisko resisted the impulse to smile. *The kid's got perseverance,* he thought. *And nerve.* "Commander," he said, pulling his tone back to a flat, professional level, "I don't need an apology. What I need is for you to conduct yourself as a senior member of my staff. Do you think you can do that?"

"Sir, yes, absolutely, sir."

"Then we won't need to talk about this again," Sisko said.

"That being the case, I won't need to mention this incident in my log."

Stinson glanced quickly down at Sisko, then resumed his stationary stare directly ahead. "Thank you, sir."

"You're welcome, Commander," Sisko said. "Dismissed."

Stinson turned crisply on his heel and exited the ready room. When Sisko had been the lieutenant commander's age—Stinson would turn twenty-eight the following month—he'd been stationed aboard *Okinawa* under Captain Leyton, happily ensconced down in engineering. He'd had neither Stinson's ambitions nor his drive. Sisko saw ability there—Captain Ro must have as well—but the question would be whether Stinson could temper his confidence with humility, his desire with patience, and his instinct with experience. *He'll probably end up as Starfleet commander-in-chief one day,* Sisko thought. *Either that or as just so much dust floating among the stars.*

Sisko reached forward and activated the interface on the desk. He'd been about to order the computer to play some of the messages he'd received from Rebecca while he'd been on his previous mission in the Gamma Quadrant, when he realized that those messages remained aboard *Robinson. Just as well.* He didn't need any distractions.

But he did feel distracted. Although he'd passed through Adarak on his way to the Vanadwan Monastery, then back to Jake and Korena's to grab his duffel and say good-bye, and finally up to *Defiant,* he hadn't stopped at the courthouse to file the signed dissolution of marriage documents that Kasidy had given him. He would, it had been what he'd sought for all this time he'd been away from her, but he just hadn't been able to do it that day.

Sitting back in his chair, Sisko thought about that, about Kasidy and Rebecca, and about all the many things that had happened since he'd first encountered the Prophets. He knew—he could *feel*—that they had no further use for him, and yet still they held sway over his life. For unless he could figure out some way around their warning, or they released him from it, his life could not be what he wished it to be.

Sisko sat in *Defiant*'s ready room for a while, trying to think his way around everything. He'd done so many times before, without result, but that didn't stop him from trying again. Finally, though, his mission interrupted his thoughts.

"Bridge to Captain Sisko," came Stinson's voice across the intercom. Sisko heard no undue emotion in his voice.

"Sisko here. Go ahead, Commander."

"Captain, we are approaching our destination."

"How many Jem'Hadar vessels in orbit?" Sisko asked. If they protected the planet in large numbers, it could make it difficult for him to do what he'd come to the Dominion to do.

"None, sir."

"Say again." Sisko could not believe what he'd heard, but even as Stinson confirmed the absence of any Jem'Hadar vessels in orbit of the planet, the captain realized that the success of his mission had likely been jeopardized—perhaps even been made impossible. "Assume standard orbit," he said as he stood and headed for the door. "I'll be right there. Sisko out."

"Long-range sensors," Sisko said as soon as he entered the bridge. "There have to be Jem'Hadar ships nearby."

"Scanning," Stinson said.

On the main viewscreen, a brown orb hung in space, the gas and dust of the Omarion Nebula a hazy backdrop. The rocky world looked dull and lifeless, as it always had to Sisko—but somehow it looked different too. His concern about his mission increased. He reached the command chair, but did not sit.

"I'm reading at least a dozen Jem'Hadar vessels within the Omarion Nebula," Stinson said. "There may be more, though. The nebula is disrupting the sensors. None of the Jem'Hadar ships are in the immediate vicinity, though."

"Can you read any life signs on the planet?" Sisko asked.

"Indeterminate," Stinson said. "There's a significant ionization effect in the upper atmosphere."

"Caused by what?" Sisko asked.

Stinson worked his controls. "Unknown, sir. I've never seen readings quite like these."

"Will that have any effect on the transporter?" Sisko wanted to know.

"It wouldn't be safe to beam down, sir," Stinson said.

"Then prepare a shuttlecraft for launch," Sisko ordered. He saw Stinson point to Lieutenant Aleco, who set to work at his station, presumably contacting the shuttlebay. "Lieutenant Tenmei, you're with me. Commander Stinson, you have the bridge." As Tenmei secured her station, Sisko waited for his first officer to approach him. "Commander, will communications be possible from the surface?"

"Possibly," Stinson said. "It'll be problematic."

"All right," Sisko said. "I intend to be back aboard ship within the hour, two at the outside, but just in case that doesn't happen: Under no circumstances are you to engage in battle with the Jem'Hadar. You can stay cloaked, you can run, but you cannot fire your weapons. Is that understood?"

"Yes, sir."

"If for some reason I don't make it back to the ship, you are to head back to the Alpha Quadrant, contact Starfleet Command, and inform them of what happened," Sisko said. "If you are captured by the Jem'Hadar or encounter a Vorta, explain who you are and ask to speak with a Founder. If you meet a Founder, explain our presence in Dominion space and try to find out about their recent contact with the Typhon Pact. Whatever information you learn, take it back to Starfleet."

"Yes, sir."

As Ensign th'Shant took over at the conn, Sisko headed for the door, Lieutenant Tenmei falling in behind him. The captain believed in Stinson's abilities, in his raw potential, but he hoped that those abilities would not be put to the test by the Dominion.

Sisko stood outside *Sagan,* where the shuttlecraft sat on a high patch of ground that overlooked the Great Link.

Except that there was no Great Link.

As Lieutenant Tenmei had piloted *Sagan* down through the planet's atmosphere, Sisko had seen through the forward viewports the barren orb that the Founders had left behind.

Beneath the ionization effect, the shuttle's sensors functioned, confirming the complete dearth of life on the surface. Sisko and Tenmei circled the globe, but they found nothing.

The captain had ordered the lieutenant to land the shuttle anyway. *Because when a Changeling takes the form of something else,* Sisko told himself, *sensors no longer detect it as a Changeling.* If the entire Great Link had formed themselves into a layer of rock on the planet's surface, scans would identify the rock, but not the Founders.

Sisko stood beside *Sagan,* cupped his hands to his mouth, and called out: "Odo!" The single word echoed across the land. He waited, then tried again. And again. Nobody answered.

Sisko knew that the Founders had gone. They had done so once before, he remembered, abandoning their world for another just before the Obsidian Order and the Tal Shiar had attempted to wipe them out. Instead, the Founders had destroyed the entire force of twenty Cardassian and Romulan starships.

The captain wondered what had triggered the Founders' latest relocation. *Perhaps another attack.* The ionization in the upper atmosphere could have been an artifact of weapons fire leveled at the planet.

It occurred to Sisko that such an attack could actually have eradicated the Great Link. Or perhaps the morphogenic virus that Section 31 had infected them with during the war had recurred. But if the entire population of Founders had been destroyed or had died out, how would the Vorta and the Jem'Hadar have reacted? Might they have forged an alliance with the Typhon Pact, intending to wreak vengeance upon the Federation?

Sisko needed more information. He had to learn what had become of the Founders, and if they lived, he had to find them. If not, it would become vital to determine who controlled the Dominion, and whether or not they had negotiated with the Pact.

The captain tapped his combadge. "Sisko to *Defiant.*" He had tried to contact the ship several times from the shuttle, without result. "Sisko to—"

The hum of a transporter filled the air—but not the hum of a Federation transporter. Dominion technology evidently had no trouble negotiating the ionization of the planet's upper atmosphere.

Sisko turned to see multicolored streaks of light coalescing. He didn't even bother to draw his phaser. Three Jem'Hadar soldiers materialized in a triangular formation, two in front, one behind. All of them held phased polaron rifles trained in his direction.

Sisko raised his empty hands, palms out. "I'm not here to fight." It surprised him that he remained both alive and conscious long enough to utter those words. He glanced up at the forward ports in the shuttle and saw that three Jem'Hadar surrounded Lieutenant Tenmei.

The Jem'Hadar stood there and said nothing. Then the soldier in the rear of the triad moved to one side, revealing a fourth member of the group. She stepped forward, between the front two Jem'Hadar, and up to Sisko. A rawboned Vorta, she had a pale complexion and vivid indigo eyes. Dark hair fell past her shoulders and framed her face, her long, ridged ears just visible among the strands. "Starfleet," she said. "I recognize the uniform."

"I'm Captain Benjamin Sisko. And you are?"

"I am Vannis," the woman said. "So if you're not here to fight, Captain Benjamin Sisko, then why have you come?"

"To speak with the Founders."

Vannis's eyes darted for a moment, but the captain didn't know why. He knew that the Vorta both revered and feared the Founders—the Founders had bred the Vorta that way—but Sisko thought he saw something other than that in the woman's fleeting expression. Has *something happened to the Great Link?*

"The Dominion's borders are closed," Vannis said. "The Founders do not wish to speak with you or anybody else from beyond our territory."

"So *you* are speaking for them?" Sisko asked.

"I carry out the will of the Founders," Vannis said. "You have violated our borders and are trespassing in Dominion space. I will see to it that you and whatever ship brought you here are escorted away. If you return, you will be killed."

Sisko understood that the Vorta's reference to the ship meant that *Defiant* had not been captured, though Vannis clearly distinguished *Sagan* as an auxiliary craft. He also recognized that, despite shrouding their society in a veil of isolationism, the Dominion did not have a standing policy of slaughtering intruders. Perhaps Odo had managed to influence his people.

Or maybe the Founders have been killed, Sisko thought again, *and so the Vorta and the Jem'Hadar aren't executing trespassers because they aren't sure what they should do.*

"Actually, I came here to talk to the Founders because somebody else violated the Dominion's borders," Sisko said. "I want to find out what happened when they did, and I want to help the Founders ensure that it doesn't happen again."

Vannis offered Sisko a smile devoid of warmth and humor. Sisko had seen the same oily expression many times on the faces of the Weyoun clones. "I thank you for your obviously genuine desire to aid the Founders, but that is the purpose for which They created the Vorta and the Jem'Hadar. As you can plainly see—" She waved her arms about to include everybody present in and around the shuttle. "—we are perfectly capable of dealing with trespassers."

"I'm sure you are," Sisko said. "But I must speak with a Founder. The safety of my people, and of the Dominion itself, may be at stake." He allowed himself the prevarication on the basis that if the Founders did ally with the Typhon Pact, any war that followed would be devastating to all sides.

"The Founders are perfectly capable of protecting Themselves, and as I told you, They have no wish to speak with outsiders," Vannis said. "I do not question Their will; I carry it out. If you are disinclined to permit me and the Jem'Hadar to accompany you out of Dominion space, I'm afraid that we will have to kill you." She paused expectantly, as though awaiting a response to a most reasonable proposition. Holding her hands together in front of her, she added, "I leave it to you, Captain Sisko."

Sisko knew he didn't have much time to make a decision. He also realized that, dead, he would be unable to speak to the Founders. He didn't know if Vannis truly intended to allow him and his crew safe passage out of the Dominion, or if she just wanted to unmask *Defiant* so that she could order the Jem'Hadar to destroy it. At the moment, though, Sisko needed more time to convince the Vorta of his intentions. "I guess we'll leave."

Vannis smiled again. "Excellent," she said. "Now that wasn't terribly difficult or painful, was it?" She motioned toward the shuttle. "Shall we take your vessel into orbit and to the ship that must surely be orbiting there? Then you and your entire crew can leave together."

Sisko didn't argue. He headed for *Sagan* and boarded it, and Vannis followed. When she saw the close quarters within—the shuttle had a normal crew capacity of four— she dismissed the Jem'Hadar outside, who transported away. Keeping Sisko at the back of the shuttle, the Vorta told him to instruct his pilot to return to their ship in orbit, with weapons and shields powered down. The captain did so, and he specifically instructed Tenmei not to attempt either to overpower their captors or to flee.

"We don't want to fight," he told the lieutenant. "Remember that we came here to talk." He peered at Vannis. "If you will just contact the Founders and ask them—"

Vannis nodded to one of the Jem'Hadar soldiers, who jammed the butt of his rifle into Sisko's gut. The captain doubled over, then dropped to his knees, pain searing through his midsection. One idea after another for escaping occurred to him, but the captain knew that he had to avoid violence at any cost.

"You may have come here to talk, Captain," Vannis said, "but I'm not in a chatty mood."

Even through his pain, Sisko thought, *Just my luck: I run across the only Vorta in the universe not in love with the sound of her own voice.*

Tenmei took the shuttle back into orbit. As *Sagan* cleared the atmosphere, Sisko saw a trio of Jem'Hadar fighters hovering above the planet. He didn't know if Tenmei had brought the shuttle into space near *Defiant,* but if she did, the ship remained cloaked.

"Contact your vessel, Captain," Vannis ordered. "Tell your crew to show themselves."

Still on his knees, Sisko reached up and activated his combadge. "Sisko to *Defiant.*" He received no response.

"Try again," Vannis said. "Your lives, and those of your crew, depend on it."

"Then I'm going to tell them our situation," Sisko said, "if that's acceptable."

"Go ahead."

The captain climbed to his feet. "Sisko to *Defiant.* Commander Stinson, I need you to decloak the ship. Lieutenant Tenmei and I are carrying three Jem'Hadar soldiers and a Vorta aboard the *Sagan.* They wish to escort us safely out of Dominion space."

Defiant did not appear.

The captain didn't blame Stinson. In his place, deep in Dominion territory, with three Jem'Hadar ships in close proximity, Sisko doubted if he would have trusted orders issued by a captive commanding officer. Stinson had his orders, and so Sisko expected him to take the ship back to the Federation and report what had taken place.

"Captain, if your crew don't show themselves," said Vannis, "the Jem'Hadar are going to shoot your pilot. If your ship doesn't appear at that point, they are going to kill you. Once that's done, I will call in every Jem'Hadar fighter near the Omarion Nebula and have them blanket the space around this planet with polaron fire. Without your help, we will find your crew, and they will die. With your help, we will find your crew, and they will live."

"How do I know you're telling the truth?" Sisko asked, still playing for time, still trying to figure out what to say to convince Vannis to allow him to speak with a Founder.

"I didn't claim to be telling the truth," Vannis said. "But what does it matter? If I'm lying, you will die anyway. Your only opportunity for survival is to help me and hope that I'm being honest."

Under most circumstances, Sisko would never have considered risking the lives of the forty men and women aboard *Defiant*. But Akaar's orders had been clear: He considered the ship and crew expendable in the interests of keeping the peace. Fighting their way out was not an option.

The captain tapped his combadge again. "Sisko to *Defiant*." He hesitated, but then realized something: He actually *did* believe Vannis. If her orders had been to kill trespassers on sight, she already would have done so, and then she would have ordered the Jem'Hadar to search for *Defiant*. "Stand by," he said into his combadge.

"Captain—" the Vorta started.

"Vannis, I know that you find meaning in your life by serving the Founders," Sisko said. "But if you kill me, if you murder my crew, you will *upset* a Founder, you will *offend* him."

"My orders are *from* the Founders."

"But I am friends with one of them," Sisko said. "Have you heard of Odo?"

"Odo," Vannis said. All of the Jem'Hadar turned toward Sisko at the mention of the name.

"Yes," Sisko said. "Do you know him?"

"Yes," Vannis said. "Of course I know Odo."

"Then you must know that he lived in the Alpha Quadrant for many years," Sisko said. "The space station on the other side of the wormhole . . . we served together there for seven years."

"You're lying," Vannis said.

"I'm not," Sisko said. "But even if you think I am, are you willing to chance displeasing Odo? Are you willing to risk disappointing a Founder?"

The Vorta smiled, and Sisko suspected that she wanted to have one of the Jem'Hadar snap his neck. But she said, "Contact your ship, Captain, and tell them to remain where they are. Tell them that this craft will remain where it is while I go check your story."

"Please tell Odo that I need to speak with him about an

urgent matter," Sisko said, hoping that Vannis would actually do as he asked.

"Captain—"

"Yes, I know, if I'm lying, then the Jem'Hadar will kill me and my crew," Sisko said, anxious for the Vorta to be on her way.

To the Jem'Hadar, Vannis said, "If they try to escape, kill them." Then she touched a device on her wrist, and a transporter beam whisked her away.

13

In his cramped cabin, Denison Morad worked his padd to confirm the vessel's location: it had just entered the Nivoch system, on course for the second planet, which supported a midsized Cardassian colony. Then he sent a signal to the other three of his associates on board. Renest Kener and Govar Hekt replied at once, confirming their preparedness, but valuable time passed without a third response. Just as Morad thought he would have to leave his cabin, skulk along the crew deck, and quietly knock on a door, Koler Trang finally transmitted his readiness.

Morad quickly bent to his travel case and extracted from it the disruptor pistol that Kener had assembled during their journey. Needing to pass through security scans, Morad and his True Way sympathizers had each carried component pieces of the tools they would need to accomplish their task. Once under way, Kener, their tech expert, had constructed two disruptors, two explosive devices, and a computer-override interface.

The group of four had all separately signed on to work aboard the tow vessel *Formek* after half of its eight-member crew failed to arrive for duty prior to its departure from Olmerak. Hardly uncommon, such defections from crews on for-hire vessels occurred for a variety of reasons, among them illness, an overindulgence in *kanar,* a pretty woman, a handsome man, arrest, death, and even, on rare occasions, a better opportunity on another ship. In this case, the missing crew had suffered from encounters with Hekt and Trang. Desperate to deliver their cargo on time, *Formek*'s master had taken on the first four qualified individuals who'd happened by looking to work for a berth—although Morad suspected that the master's requirements included only the abilities to walk, draw breath, and pull an antigrav sled.

After tucking the disruptor into his waistband, Morad pulled on a jacket to cover it. Not by nature a violent man, he would nevertheless do whatever he needed to do in order to push Cardassia back to its days of greatness. Ready to continue that pursuit, he touched a control on his padd that would signal the others to take action.

Morad tossed the padd onto the cot—he'd have time enough to retrieve it later—then slapped at the button beside the door. The single panel slid halfway open, then ground to a halt. "Worthless scow," he grumbled, though he knew well how valuable the old tug would be. He threw a shoulder against the door jamb, then lifted his leg to the panel and pushed. The door moved a finger's length, then another, and at last withdrew completely into the bulkhead.

Stepping into the corridor, Morad glanced to his left, where he saw Trang standing several doors down, outside his own cabin. Peering in the other direction, he spotted Kener, and ahead of her, Hekt. All three looked to Morad, who raised his hand above his head and pointed one finger to his right, toward the center of the ship.

A vessel designed to tow large objects, *Formek* more or less resembled the wings of a bird. Tractor beam generators occupied the tips and midpoints of those wings, and focusing emitters lined the aft hull. The bridge, which served as the pilothouse and the towing control room, filled a superstructure set above the intersection of the ship's two wings.

The group moved quickly forward, leaving the crew deck and making their way through cargo holds that they had themselves loaded. When they reached the center of the ship, they chose not to board the turbolift there, thinking that it could alert the two officers working the bridge. Instead, Hekt started up a ladder set into the bulkhead. Morad expected his associate to find the hatch locked when he reached the overhead, but it opened with just a push, its locking mechanism apparently not working. Morad didn't know if the ship's master had grown careless over time, or if perhaps he lacked sufficient resources to repair and secure his old vessel, but whatever the case, Morad appreciated anything that made his task easier.

Once Hekt had climbed to the deck above, the others followed. They quietly approached the door to the bridge. Making a show of drawing his disruptor, Hekt then reached for the button beside the door. Standing beside him, Kener grabbed his forearm and held it still. Then she looked over at Morad and pointed to a boxy, handheld device that hung at her hip. He recognized the computer-override interface she had fashioned, and so he nodded.

Kener pushed Hekt's arm down before releasing it. She examined the bulkheads around them, then dropped to her knees and pulled off an access plate. She spent a few moments surveying the equipment inside, then crawled forward and hauled off another plate. Again, she peered inside, and almost immediately, she reached to detach the interface from her hip. She placed it on the deck, then pushed at the boxy device, causing one side to spring open. From within, she selected two leads, which she attached to something inside the bulkhead.

When she finished, Kener looked up at Morad and nodded. He pointed at Hekt and Trang, then at the door to the bridge. The two men braced themselves, ready to rush inside. Morad peered back down at Kener and nodded. She pressed a control on her device, and the bridge door slipped open.

As the two Cardassian men at the controls turned in their chairs, Morad recognized the ship's master and his second officer. The first officer and the relief pilot doubtless slept down in their cabins. Before either of the two men could even say anything, their eyes grew wide as they faced the emitter end of Hekt's disruptor.

"What—?" the master started to say, but the shrill blare of Hekt's weapon filled the bridge, its brilliant golden beam blinding in the small space. The master collapsed in a heap to the deck. Morad saw smoke rising from the charred hole in his chest.

The second officer raised his hands high above his head. "Don't shoot," he said. "You can have whatever you want."

"We want your ship," Hekt said, and fired again. The disruptor beam threw the second officer back against the forward port, where he slid down the control panel and joined the master on the floor.

Morad felt numb. He hadn't intended to harm anybody— and particularly not Cardassians—unless absolutely necessary. He didn't know what to say, but then Kener said it for him: "You didn't have to kill them."

"We don't need any hostages or witnesses," Hekt snarled back.

Kener shook her head in apparent disgust, but she said nothing more. She stood from the deck and pushed past Hekt and Trang. With her foot, she tried to move the bodies of the two men from where they blocked the chairs. "Help me," she said, looking over at Hekt. "This is your doing."

Hekt grunted, but he moved forward and dragged away first one body, then the other. Kener sat down and began studying the console. "Morad," she said, "we need to find the controls for the tractor beams."

As Morad headed toward the bridge, Hekt hurried by him and punched at the call button for the turbolift. "Where are you going?" Morad asked.

"We still have two potential liabilities aboard," he said, brandishing his disruptor. The door to the lift glided open, and Hekt disappeared into the car. Trang followed.

Morad entered the bridge and sat down beside Kener. As he did, he saw a bank of monitors in the port bulkhead beside him, all of them trained from different angles on the tug's primary cargo. Out behind the ship, a web of a dozen or more tractor beams connected to an enormous solar collector, obviously intended for orbit above the Nivoch colony.

"I've got impulse engines and warp drive over here," Kener told him. "I'll start programming our course."

"Good," Morad said as he searched his console for the tractor controls. When he found them, he threw one switch after another. As he did so, he watched the monitors, where the beams began to wink off in sequence. The solar collector shifted menacingly with the uneven forces applied to it, but once the last tractor vanished, it fell behind *Formek,* set adrift.

"We're ready to go to warp," Kener said.

Morad turned to her. "Do you have a comm system over there?"

Kener looked. "Yes," she said. "Why?"

"Send a message to the Nivoch colony," he said. "Send them the coordinates where they can find their solar collector."

"Are you sure?" Kener asked.

"It's a Cardassian colony," Morad said. "And we've got sympathizers there."

"I know, but sympathetic or not, we don't need anybody coming after us."

"Do you think Nivoch has enough ships that they can send a squadron out to corral their runaway solar collector *and* chase after us?" Morad asked. "Besides, as long as they get their cargo, they're not going to care about what happens to this ship."

"What about the other cargo we loaded?"

"Didn't you look at the manifest?" he asked. Kener shook her head. "*Yamok* sauce and *rokassa* relish. I think the colonists are going to care a lot more about getting their solar collector into orbit."

Kener offered him a smile. "I think you're right."

"Good," Morad said. "Then let's get this ship moving. Once you clear the ecliptic, take us to the highest warp factor you can manage without making this crate fall apart."

"I think we should be able to make warp five."

"Excellent," Morad said. "That should get us there in time. I don't want to leave the Tzenkethi waiting."

Standing with her colleagues on the lateral floor of their lab, Nelzik Tek Lom-A saw activity begin on her sensor interface. She watched the readings march across her display, marked in particular by extremely high proton counts and rapidly increasing wave intensities. Recognizing their meaning, she turned her gaze skyward, peering out past the transparent superior floor, out into the space above the Vir-Akzelen asteroid. The awful openness that the extent of the stars threatened normally would have set her on edge, but her excitement at completing the final phase of project testing mitigated her anxiety.

Out past the superior floor and against the backdrop of stars, space unfurled, creating a great hole in the firmament. Lightning-white at its center, it spun blistering red at its edges. It reeled around almost like a living thing.

Then, at its heart, the faintest speck appeared. Nelzik could see no detail on the object, but she knew its identity. Not long ago, she and her colleagues had sent the probe *into* the wormhole they had created. They programmed it to make its journey through the cosmic tunnel until it emerged in a new locale. They had set it the task of surveying its new surroundings for a specific length of time, then reversing course and heading back through the wormhole.

In just days, Nelzik and her colleagues had prepared and launched more than a dozen such probes, each encoded to attempt their voyage with different timing. Some remained at the far end of the wormhole longer, some shorter. Not all of them had returned, but the scientists had expected that; their calculations had predicted it.

Out in space, the rolling flurry of radiance pulled in on itself, disappearing with a pinpoint flash of light, as though it had never been. *But it definitely exists,* Nelzik told herself with pride. With the last probe, they would know with certainty the precise parameters of that existence. Nelzik and her colleagues had initially calculated those values according to theory, but although their mathematical results had been close, they had not proven completely accurate. A slight variance in the density of subspace had decreased the values of both the length of the wormhole and the time it remained stable. Still, the actual figures would suffice for their purposes.

"We are receiving telemetry," announced Vendez Tek Lom-A from where he stood at his own computer station. Nelzik walked over to him and peered at his screen.

"Do the numbers reflect our latest calculations?" she asked.

Vendez reached up and pointed to a series of equations and a table of numbers. The glow of his greenish-yellow flesh reflected in the display. "They are exact," he said, the chiming sound of his voice tolling with the thrill of their accomplishment. Nelzik shared his satisfaction.

Crossing back to her own workstation, Nelzik initiated a link to Vendez's interface and collected the fresh data he'd received. She then used those numbers as input for the program she had written to extract the final parameters of their creation. In just moments, a table of information appeared on her display.

Nelzik read through the results. She saw that the machinery she and her colleagues had crafted could generate a wormhole anywhere from 1.2 to 5.3 light-years in length. Anything shorter and the gravitational stresses within would not allow it to open into normal space-time; anything longer, the structure would not be strong enough to support itself. They could target the far end to a precise location, but that terminus would remain there only for a brief period, equating to four times the interval required to traverse the wormhole; after that, the far terminus would fluctuate, moving in an unpredictable direction and settling elsewhere.

When Nelzik had originally been assigned to lead the project, not long after the discovery of the Bajoran wormhole, the objective she'd been given had been to develop identical technology. It had taken some time and numerous failures to determine that Tzenkethi science—and Romulan science, and Breen and Klingon and even Federation science—lacked the technical sophistication required to achieve such a goal, and would fall short into the foreseeable future. But Nelzik perceived something else beyond inevitable failure. She saw another way, a less complex way, to realize a form of the project's aim—a less useful form, but not a use*less* one.

As she and her colleagues had neared the end of their work,

she'd been informed by a representative of the autarch himself that the Coalition and other elements within the Typhon Pact urgently needed the product of their labor. They needed it, she understood, for the purpose of neutralizing the military superiority of Starfleet, which the UFP enjoyed by virtue of its quantum slipstream drive technology. As a zealous Tzenkethi patriot who had matured under the shadow of continued Federation imperialism and aggression, she would take great pride in helping to keep her people safe from that evil empire.

Nelzik knew that her colleagues felt the same way, as did their contact with the True Way. It pleased her to know that the Coalition did not wage its ongoing battle with the immorally, foolishly republican Federation alone. With the aid of Denison Morad and his True Way partisans, as well as the assistance of the Breen and the Romulans, Nelzik would soon provide the Tzenkethi and all the Typhon Pact worlds with the tools they needed to combat the UFP and its Khitomer Accords allies.

For even though Nelzik could not provide the Coalition and the Pact something exactly like the Bajoran wormhole, negotiating tens of thousands of light-years and remaining stable across millennia, she could, in a very real way, give them the Bajoran wormhole itself.

14

As evening neared, Julian Bashir walked hand-in-hand with Sarina Douglas down the main thoroughfare of Aljuli, a stretch of interlocking brick pavers only marginally wider than the other lanes in the town. Situated just a few kilometers due south of the Wyntara Mas Control Center—soon to be Starfleet's ad hoc Bajoran Space Central—the town of Aljuli had, according to what Bashir had read, sprung up decades ago, when construction had first begun on the transportation control hub. At the time, transporter technology had been in regular, if not widespread, use across Bajor, but the cultural imperatives of the era supported people residing close to wherever they plied their vocation. Bashir knew that mentality still existed on Bajor, instilled by a society more inclined to walk to their destination than to beam there. Hardly Luddites, the Bajorans nevertheless tended to prefer life in pastoral settings; much of their world continued to be dominated by an agrarian lifestyle, with only a small number of large cities.

"I like it," Bashir told Sarina as they walked along. They'd been on and off the planet since the destruction of Deep Space 9, but had spent most of their time aboard the ships patrolling the system. Unfortunately, Bashir had been assigned to *Canterbury*, while Sarina had ended up on *Venture*. But the day before, Captain Ro had recalled Sarina to Bajor so that she could assist Chief Blackmer in identifying and implementing the security needs of their refurbished control center. And just an hour earlier, the captain had ordered Bashir to the planet in order to help configure a medical facility for the crew in Wyntara Mas.

"Really? You like it?" Sarina said, making a show of looking around at the town. "When you talked about the excitement of being posted on the Federation's frontier, I didn't think this was what you had in mind."

Bashir peered around as well, and saw a few other people out strolling. The walkway ran between a couple of restaurants, an inn, and a number of storefronts—several of which appeared to specialize in farm products and equipment, others in local arts and crafts. Bashir thought that the inn looked more like a private home than a public house, and he doubted that it had seen many guests in the years since the control center had last closed down.

"I think it's quaint," Bashir said.

"You mean it's old," Sarina said.

"It's cozy."

"You mean it's small."

Bashir could see the playful look in her eyes, but did he see something else too? As much as he knew she intended her comments only in a joking manner, he perceived something in her tone that suggested that she genuinely didn't want to be there. Of course, all of the surviving crew continued to deal with the emotional repercussions of what had happened at DS9. He almost asked Sarina about how she felt, but then opted to try a different tack. "Would you prefer to be on different ships?" he asked.

"No, of course not," she said with a sigh, swatting him gently on the shoulder as they walked. "But that doesn't mean I have to like this."

"I know there's not much to the town, but at least we're together," Bashir said, though even he had to admit that their accommodations could have been more satisfying. To house the crew, the Bajorans had provided them access to the largest building in Aljuli, a three-story, multi-unit brick building on the edge of town. Bashir and Sarina had just come from there, after he'd been assigned a place to stay. It had been constructed at the same time as the control center, specifically for the purpose of housing the people who would serve there. Small, with just a bed, a computer station, and no cooking facilities—the complex contained its own mess hall—each room had been designed for an individual, not for a couple or a family. Captain Ro had temporarily assigned people like Phillipa Matthias, DS9's lead counselor, to one of the starships in the system, simply so that she could live with her husband and two children.

"We're not even in the same room," Sarina complained.

"But we're right next to each other," Bashir said, donning his optimist's hat. "And you can come visit me any time you like." He leaned in and playfully nuzzled her neck. Sarina smiled, but again, Bashir sensed something amiss—something different, he thought, than post-traumatic stress. Trying to lighten her mood, he said, "Come on, where's your spirit of adventure?"

"Adventure?" Sarina said, and again, she exaggerated her movements as she craned her neck to look around. "Kind of slow for an adventure, wouldn't you say?"

Bashir shrugged. "It'll get us rested up for our brand-new space station."

"We'll have to rest for . . . what? Two years?" Sarina said. "Living here, I'll grow old in that time."

"Ah, but with each gray hair, you will become a very handsome old woman."

"Handsome!" Sarina said, her voice rising. Instead of a swat, she punched him in the shoulder. "How dare you," she went on, and even though she protested, whatever she'd been holding on to seemed to disappear. "That's like me saying that you're a *lovely* man."

Bashir stopped and turned to face Sarina, adopting an air of offense. "I'll thank you to know that I *am* a lovely man."

"Oh, brother." Sarina rolled her eyes and resumed walking. Her lightheartedness pleased Bashir, who trotted to catch up with her. He took her hand again as they approached an intersection.

Arranged more or less on a grid, Aljuli comprised six streets running east to west, and four north to south. A park filled the southwestern block of the city, a pond at its center. Beyond the paved streets, farmland decorated the landscape in tones of green and brown and gold. The town and the surrounding areas, before the influx of Starfleet, supported a population of about two thousand.

As they reached the intersection, the Bajoran sun dipped below the horizon, sending a vibrant pink and orange glow against the clouds. "Now that's lovely," Bashir said. They stopped to admire the sunset.

As they stood gazing at the sky, Bashir heard a loud voice in the distance, though he could make out no words. He turned his head and strained to hear. Other voices reached him, swelled, fell away. Then a familiar chirp played through the gathering dusk. "I think *that's* where we're headed," he said.

"I think so," Sarina agreed. "Maybe that—and you—will make this place bearable."

They made their way down the side street. They passed a number of professional buildings—the town hall, constabulary, transporter station, the office of public works—most of which sat dark. Halfway to the next street, light shined onto the walkway from two sets of double doors, both flung open to the evening, as well as from a large window between them. As they neared, the light from within fluttered, throwing a series of colors onto the brick pavers. A rowdy chorus of voices followed a moment later: *"Dabo!"*

Bashir led Sarina through the first set of doors into a place they'd never been, but that seemed familiar. What might once have been a theater had been transformed into something different. On the far side of the large space, a stage marched along the wall, and it amused Bashir to see two women and a man—each of them scantily clad, all of them members of Quark's waitstaff—swaying to jazzy music playing in the background. Where seats might once have been anchored to the floor facing the stage, dozens of circular tables sat, all filled to capacity. In the very center, Hetik and M'Pella—one of the rare Bajorans born with no rhinal ridges—worked the dabo wheel, surrounded by a noisy throng. A stairway ran up the wall to the left, though it had been roped off. On the right-hand wall stretched a massive mahogany bar, in no way resembling any style Bashir had ever seen on Bajor; more than anything, he thought it belonged in a nineteenth-century pub in the United Kingdom. Quark, Treir, and Aluura worked behind the bar, making and passing drinks to customers, as well as to a waitstaff that, at first glance, included more than a few faces Bashir did not know.

"Seems like this is the place," Sarina said, loudly enough to be heard over the clink of gold-pressed latinum, the whir of the dabo wheel, the music, and the chatter of two hundred or more people.

"Would you like a drink?" Bashir asked, leaning in toward Sarina.

"At least," she said.

Bashir pointed, and they headed for the bar. They waded through a sea of customers—only about half of them in Starfleet uniforms—and dodged around Frool carrying an overloaded tray. When they reached the bar, the green-skinned Treir looked up from mixing a cocktail and spotted them.

"Doctor, Lieutenant," she said with a generous smile. "You made it."

Bashir understood that Treir had intended her remark lightly, referring only to his and Sarina's first visit there, but he saw a shadow pass over Sarina's face. He felt the emotion too.

Treir saying that they'd made it could have been interpreted in a serious vein to mean that they'd managed to escape the destruction of Deep Space 9—something so many others had not. Bashir forced himself to say, "Yes, we're here."

Treir must have realized her inadvertent indiscretion, because she suddenly looked stricken. She leaned forward on the bar and said, "I mean, it's good to see you two here in our new place."

While Bashir tried to figure out how to respond in a way that would allow them all to escape the terrible undertones that had developed, Sarina bent toward the bar. "It's good to be here," she said, "and it's good to see you." She reached forward to the inside edge of the bar and patted Treir's hand. Treir looked sad and grateful at the same time, her eyes beginning to gleam.

Before tears could run down her face, though, a boisterous voice proclaimed, "Well, if it isn't the most charming couple in Wyntara Mas." Quark, dressed in a patchwork jacket that might have contained more colors than actually existed, sidled up beside Treir and threw an arm around her. "Chatting it up with my most charming employee."

"Try *partner*," Treir said, jabbing her fist softly into Quark's stomach.

Quark lowered his voice, as though speaking conspiratorially, to tell Bashir and Sarina, "Look what happens when you take the *slave* out of *Orion slave girl*."

Treir scoffed and pinched the back of Quark's ear. "Fine," she told him, then said to Bashir and Sarina, "I'll see you two later."

As Quark reached up to massage his ear, Bashir pondered his sudden appearance before them. Some people who knew the barkeep—a *lot* of people who knew the barkeep—often considered him a fool, but not only a fool. Many judged him crass, ill-mannered, and insensitive. Oftentimes, Quark took no action to dispel such views, and Bashir wondered—not for the first time—if perhaps the Ferengi cultivated such an image for some reason. Over the nearly fifteen years that the doctor had known him, Quark had certainly behaved in all sorts of boorish ways, in all sorts of circumstances. But then he'd also done things that people either didn't know about—such as selflessly helping Bajoran orphans during the Occupation—or didn't notice—such as what he'd just done.

Strangely, people often seemed to forget about the superiority of Quark's hearing, despite the very noticeable size of his ears. Bashir had no doubt that the barkeep had heard Treir's comment and the muted reaction it had elicited. And *his* reaction had been to swoop in to free the three of them from an awkward situation. But Bashir suspected that if he shared that observation, plenty of people would characterize Quark's behavior either as coincidentally helpful or as driven by an ulterior motive. Bashir believed neither of those things.

"So: welcome to Quark's Bar, Grill, Gaming House, and Ferengi Embassy to Bajor," he said. "Wyntara Mas branch."

"I didn't hear holosuite in there," said Bashir, disappointed but not surprised.

"Not yet," Quark said, his grin filled with sharp, misaligned teeth. "But there's room upstairs. I'm working on it."

Something suddenly occurred to Bashir, something he hadn't thought about since the attack on the station. "I guess having a holosuite wouldn't matter anyway," he said, "considering that we lost Vic."

Beside him, Sarina gave a small nod in agreement; since transferring to the station, she too had enjoyed spending time at Vic's Las Vegas lounge. Bashir considered contacting his friend Felix—who had created the self-aware, 1960s-era Vic Fontaine hologram—to see if he might be willing to design a replacement. The thought immediately soured. *That would be like trying to have a friend replaced,* he realized. *And it's not like I can replace Jeannette Chao or Jason Senkowski or Jang Si Naran.*

"Actually, Doctor," Quark said, "I have something to show you." He bent behind the bar and disappeared from view.

"Quark, whatever it is, I'm not really interested in—" Bashir began, but then the barkeep popped back up, holding a *device.* "What is that?" Quark set the object down on the bar. A gray metal cube standing elegantly on one corner atop a black base, it had chaser lights along several edges, and what looked like input slots for isolinear optical rods. Bashir felt a thread of hope.

"This, my good doctor," Quark said, waving his hand over the device with a flourish, "is Vic."

Bashir saw Sarina brighten, and knew that the expression on her face mirrored his own. "You saved him?"

Quark shrugged. "What can I say? He was good for business, and I plan on making that true again."

"What is this machine, though?" Sarina asked. "I thought Vic's program was on an isolinear rod."

"It is," Quark said, and he turned the device around. On the newly visible side, Bashir saw a rod sticking out of a slot.

"Is that . . . ?" Bashir asked, pointing.

"That's Vic," Quark said. "This is a holosuite simulation tester. I usually use it to run new holoprograms to check them for bugs and to make sure they don't crash. Before we left the station, I figured that, if I just stuck Vic's program in here, he'd keep singing."

"So Vic is still—" Bashir had been about to say *alive,* but even as strongly as he felt about the lounge singer, as much as he'd interacted with him through the years, and even as much as he considered him a friend, it seemed wrong to use that word after everything that had happened. "—still running?"

"He's still running," Quark said. "Of course, I don't have a functioning holosuite yet, but I've got my lobes to the wind."

"Quark, if you don't mind my asking," Sarina said, "how did you get this off Deep Space Nine? When we were evacuating, we didn't allow people to take their belongings. That would have increased the amount of time to get people off the station, and we needed as much room as possible so that we could rescue as many people as we could."

"I didn't take any extra time," Quark said. "I loaded Vic into my carryall as soon as I heard about the bombs, which was before the evacuation started." Bashir realized that, with the Ferengi's connections on the station—both living and technological—he'd probably known about the sabotage before most of the crew. "As for taking up extra room . . ." Quark picked up the simulator and held it above his head. "You see this? I'm taking up exactly as much space as somebody who's tall. *Less* space, even."

"Are you trying to tell me that you held a carryall over your head during the entire evacuation?" Sarina asked, her tone disbelieving.

"Don't be ridiculous," Quark said. "I paid Morn to hold it over *his* head." He nodded to one side, and Bashir glanced in that direction. It did not surprise him in the slightest to see the loquacious Lurian at the end of the bar, a tankard raised to his shriveled lips.

"You *paid* Morn?" Bashir asked suspiciously.

"Well, I took a few slips of latinum off his tab," Quark said. He crouched down and set the simulator back behind the bar. When he reappeared, Sarina apparently chose to let him off the hook.

"So did I hear you say 'Quark's Bar and *Grill*'?"

"There's a kitchen in back," Quark said. "Not a large one . . . I should really think about knocking out a wall and expanding—"

"'Expand or die,'" Bashir quoted.

"The Ninety-fifth Rule of Acquisition," Quark said. "Very good, Doctor. So what can I get you two lovebirds?"

"How about something local in honor of our new home?" Sarina said.

"I've got a nice springwine from the Ovarani Valley," Quark said. "That's in northeastern Wyntara Mas."

"Perfect," Sarina said.

"And for you, Doctor?"

"I'll have a Finagle's Folly."

"Both fine choices," Quark said as he settled a pair of glasses on the bar before them, then turned toward the bottles on the wall. He pulled a tall, curvy bottle from where it lay horizontally on a shelf, then poured its pale blue contents for Sarina. As he restocked the bottle and retrieved ingredients for Bashir's drink, the doctor asked him a question.

"How did you manage to get this place together so quickly?"

Quark set a couple of bottles down behind the bar, then

began preparing Bashir's drink. "The Fifty-fourth Rule of Acquisition," he said.

The doctor had read through the Rules years ago, but he knew that one, though he didn't see how it applied as an answer to his question. "'Never trust anybody taller than you'?"

"That's the Fifty-*third* Rule." Quark finished pouring, then dunked a silver stirrer in the glass and swirled it around until the Finagle's Folly achieved a deep green color.

Bashir tried again. "'Take joy from profit, and profit from joy'?"

"That's the Fifty-*fifth* Rule," Quark said. As he returned the bottles to their places, he said, "The Fifty-fourth Rule is, 'Rate divided by time equals profit.'"

Bashir nodded. "Also known as the 'velocity of wealth.'"

"That's right," Quark said. "I lost everything on the station, notwithstanding Vic Fontaine. Fortunately, since I run the Ferengi Embassy to Bajor, the Congress of Economic Advisors automatically insures me."

"So this is all from an insurance disbursement?" Sarina asked.

"This?" Quark said, looking around. "No. This came from a little account I have at the Bank of Luria. I'm still waiting for the insurance payoff. I'll need it if I'm ever going to be able to install those holosuites . . . which I'm definitely going to need."

"I don't know," Bashir said, turning to observe the place. "You look pretty busy to me."

Quark waved the idea away. "A lot of these people are locals."

"I didn't even know the town had this many people in it," Sarina said, and she gave Bashir a playful push.

"The problem is that there are already a few places to eat and drink in Aljuli, so once the newness of my place wears off, I'll need the holosuites to keep them coming back."

"That's okay, Quark," said another voice. "I have faith in you to turn a profit."

Bashir recognized the voice, and he turned toward the speaker. For a moment, he felt incapable of identifying the man because of the context, and because he hadn't seen him in so long. Finally, he managed to say, "Miles?"

"How are you, Julian?" O'Brien asked, slapping his hands down on Bashir's shoulders.

"Miles!" the doctor repeated. He reached out and the two men hugged. When they stepped back, Bashir asked, "What are you doing here?"

"Say hello to your new chief engineer," O'Brien said.

"Miles, that's fantastic," Bashir said. "That calls for a drink."

"Quark," O'Brien said, "I don't suppose you have any Irish whiskey back there?"

The Ferengi reached down and held up a bottle.

"That's amazing," Sarina said.

Quark shrugged. "I knew he was coming three days ago."

"That's impossible," O'Brien said. "*I* didn't even know I was coming three days ago."

"Whatever you say, Chief." Quark pulled the stopper from the bottle, poured O'Brien his drink, then headed to the other end of the bar.

Bashir turned so that he faced both O'Brien and Sarina. "Miles, you remember Sarina Douglas, don't you?"

"Of course," O'Brien said, but as he reached to shake her hand, he stopped. "Wait. I saw you yesterday at the control center, didn't I? Captain Ro wanted to talk with you in her office."

"That was me," Sarina said.

"I'm sorry," O'Brien said. "I didn't recognize you. I guess with the uniform . . . I mean, Julian told me that you joined Starfleet, and that you transferred to Deep Space Nine, but . . ."

"It's okay, Chief," Sarina said. "Obviously, I didn't recognize you either."

"Well, who ever remembers a mug like this one?" O'Brien said.

"I don't want to sound like I'm not happy to see you," Bashir said, "but what *are* you doing here? What'll you be doing, since we don't have a space station anymore? I can't imagine that the control center's going to keep you all that busy."

"Probably not," O'Brien said, "but somebody's got to build you a new station."

"Of course," Bashir said.

"How's your family?" Sarina asked. "Julian told me that Keiko's been working on the agricultural renewal of Cardassia."

"That's right," O'Brien said. "She's—"

A Starfleet security officer stepped between Bashir and Sarina, while another walked up behind her. "Sarina Douglas?" said one of them, a human woman called Patrycja, but whose surname Bashir could not remember. He recognized the male Andorian officer as Deskel ch'Larn.

"Yes?" Sarina said.

"Is there a problem?" Bashir asked, trying to push his way between ch'Larn and Sarina.

"Doctor, please step back," ch'Larn said, opening the flat of his palm in front of Bashir.

"Tell us what's going on here," Bashir insisted.

"Sarina Douglas," said Patrycja, "we are taking you into custody."

"Wait, what?" Bashir said. He tried again to get past ch'Larn, but the security officer took hold of his arm, pushed him back, and did not let go.

Patrycja held up a set of hand restraints. "Please raise your forearms out in front of you."

"Wait! Don't—" Bashir said, and he felt O'Brien behind him, reaching to hold him back, telling him he shouldn't interfere.

The security officer clamped the restraints onto Sarina's wrists. Bashir couldn't believe what he was seeing. "You have to stop this," he said. "There's clearly been a mistake."

"There's no mistake, Doctor," ch'Larn said quietly.

"What are you charging her with?" Bashir demanded.

Patrycja glanced over at ch'Larn, as if trying to decide whether she should answer the question. But then Sarina said, "Tell me. What am I charged with?"

"You're not charged with anything," Patrycja said. "You're wanted for questioning about the destruction of Deep Space Nine."

"What?!" Bashir said. He couldn't believe what he'd heard.

It seemed like a living nightmare. "That's absurd. You have to know she had nothing to do with—"

"Julian," Sarina said. "It's all right." He looked at her, and as he had earlier, he saw something wrong, something troubling in her expression, though he could not say precisely what.

"No," he told her. "It's not all right."

They looked at each other for a long moment, and then Sarina turned away. "Let's go," she told Patrycja.

The two security officers each took one of Sarina's arms and guided her through the closest set of double doors and out into the evening. Bashir watched them go, and then his knees suddenly felt weak. He wobbled. O'Brien steadied him, then helped him onto a barstool.

"Quark," O'Brien called out, "I need a glass of water over here."

He said other things after that, but the words came to Bashir as though from a distance. The doctor looked down at the floor, but didn't see it. He could see only the woman he loved being led away in restraints, facing interrogation about the destruction of DS9 and the deaths of more than a thousand people . . . civilians . . . children. It made no sense. Sarina could never have put the lives of almost seven thousand people—including her own and his own—at risk. She could never kill a thousand people. She could never kill *one* person. That's not who she was. None of it made sense.

And then another number rose in Bashir's mind, a number beyond one, beyond one thousand, beyond seven thousand . . . a number that he suddenly thought would plague him for the rest of his life: 31.

15

Sisko awoke with his head throbbing and his back aching. His eyelids blinked open, and for a moment he could make no sense of what he saw: a flat surface, boots, chair bases. But then it all came back to him, and he pushed himself up to a sitting position on the *Sagan* deck, leaning against the aft bulkhead.

He saw Lieutenant Tenmei sitting at the shuttle's main console. Between them stood the three Jem'Hadar. One of them held his polaron rifle aimed at Sisko, the other at Tenmei, while the third stood at ease—or whatever passed for ease in a creature created and bred to live his life as a ferocious soldier.

"Lieutenant, are you all right?" Sisko asked.

Tenmei jumped, obviously startled. "Yes, sir," she said, turning in her chair to look at the captain. "How are you?"

Sisko pushed off the deck and got his feet under him. "Stiff," he said, "but otherwise all right. Did you sleep?"

"I dozed," Tenmei said. "I put my head down on the panel."

"How long has it been?"

Tenmei checked her console. "Twenty-seven hours, thirteen minutes," she said.

Sisko propped himself against the bulkhead, exhausted. His slumber had not been restful. He wondered if the Jem'Hadar had slept and doubted it. He also wondered when the soldiers would require their next dose of ketracel-white, the drug they required to live, but which the Founders had engineered their bodies to be unable to produce. "No word from the *Defiant* or Vannis, I take it?"

"No, sir."

Sisko shook his head. The delay frustrated him, but he also took it as a positive sign. It could mean that Vannis had indeed contacted Odo—or at least some Founder. If whoever the Vorta communicated with had been on the other side of the Dominion, it could take him some time to reach the former world of the Founders.

Sisko gazed out the forward ports, where he could see an arc of the dirt-brown planet below. It really did look lifeless, and while he'd thought a day earlier that had always been the case, he suddenly remembered that, when the Founders had been there, the surface took on a slightly shimmering effect from space. He'd seen no indication of that the day before, and he did not see it at that moment. It troubled him that the Founders might have needed a reason to relocate again, but he thought it even more disturbing that they might have been eradicated either in an attack or by the morphogenic virus. He wanted to question the Jem'Hadar, ask them when they had actually last seen one of their gods in person, ask them if—

The sound of a transporter rose in the cabin. Sisko saw recognition in the eyes of the Jem'Hadar, and he thought that the two aiming their weapons might fire, but they didn't. The captain had just enough time to wonder if Lieutenant Commander Stinson had taken the initiative to attempt a peaceful resolution to the situation, but then he saw the multiple hues of a Dominion transporter beam. The Jem'Hadar soldiers disappeared within the glimmer of the variegated light.

Sisko moved forward to join Tenmei at the main console. "Lieutenant," he said, intending to have her scan for the Jem'Hadar vessels while he contacted *Defiant*—if Stinson hadn't taken the ship back to the Federation—but then the hum of the transporter returned. Sisko turned to look aft, where he saw two sets of beams. When they at last faded, they left behind Vannis and a Changeling. Odo looked to Sisko as he always had, wearing—or pretending to wear—his old Bajoran constable's uniform.

"Odo," Sisko said. It pleased him simply on a personal basis to see his old friend alive and seemingly well, but the captain also hoped that the Changeling's presence would allow him to complete his mission.

"Captain," Odo said, his voice sounding as gruff and stern as it always had. Sisko motioned toward Tenmei and introduced her. "We've met," Odo said, "although at the time, I believe she held the rank of ensign."

Sisko suddenly thought of a potentially troubling possibility, and he voiced it. "Is that really you, Odo?" Though the Changeling recognized the captain, and even Tenmei, Sisko knew that such knowledge could have passed from Odo to other Founders via the Great Link.

"It's me, Captain," the Changeling said. "But is that really you? The last I knew, you'd left Starfleet."

Sisko smiled, amused by Odo's dry wit, and thinking that a sense of humor might be as good a way as any to confirm somebody's identity. "I did step away for a while," the captain said. He spread his arms, showing off his uniform. "But I'm back." With no foolproof way of knowing whether the real Odo actually stood before him, or if some other Founder had assumed his form, Sisko decided to proceed as though he fully accepted the Changeling's claim. It would not alter what the captain needed to say or what he needed to find out.

"You may be back in Starfleet," Odo said, "but you're also back in Dominion territory." The Changeling stepped forward until he stood directly in front of Sisko. "It's not that I'm not pleased to see you, Captain, but I thought you understood that the Dominion has, at least for the present, closed its borders to outsiders. I'm afraid that includes Federation vessels and citizens."

"We've respected that for seven years," Sisko said. "And we'll continue to respect it going forward. But something has happened that concerns us greatly, and it involves the Founders. I only came here so that I could talk to them."

"You can talk to me, Captain," Odo said. "But I believe I know what it is you're going to say."

That gave Sisko pause. "Then I'll just come right out and tell you," he said. "We are worried about the possibility that the Dominion has allied with the Typhon Pact."

"The Typhon Pact?" If Odo did not actually stand in front of Sisko, if another Founder only imitated his identity, he did an excellent job. The Changeling's not recognizing the name of the Typhon Pact also came off as convincing.

"It's an alliance among six of the Federation's—" Sisko chose not to use the first word that came to him to describe the members of the Pact: *enemies*. "—neighbors. It includes the Breen, the Romulans, and the Tzenkethi." The captain specifically named those powers because they had been the ones involved in the attack on Deep Space 9.

Odo nodded slowly, then paced away. He brought one arm horizontally up to his waist and rested his opposite elbow atop it. As he moved slowly through the shuttle's small cabin, he touched a hand to his chin. Sisko recognized the gesture as one he'd seen Odo make on numerous occasions. "Yes," Odo said. "That makes more sense now."

"What does?" Sisko asked.

"That a Breen freighter and a Romulan warbird ended up traveling together inside Dominion space."

Sisko stood up straighter. "When did this happen?"

"I'm not entirely sure," said Odo. "But weeks ago, at least. I only just learned about it."

"You didn't know?" Sisko said. That could be troubling. If the Founders had negotiated with the Pact, but Odo didn't know about it . . . "Did any of the Founders know?"

Odo simulated a sigh in his convincing humanoid imitation. Sisko wondered if he even knew anymore that he did it. Though the Changeling had often had difficulties mimicking so-called solids, he had perfectly effected the look and feel of one particular emotion: exasperation. "One Founder knew," he said. "Laas."

"Laas?" Sisko said. "The Changeling who visited you on the station before you went back to the Great Link."

"Yes," Odo said.

"Do you know . . . did he talk with them?" Sisko recalled that Laas did not like solids, believing them inferior to Changelings, and a threat. The captain could imagine more than one scenario in which Laas's dealing with members of the Typhon Pact would not end well for the Federation.

"Laas *always* talks," Odo said. "Not always with a humanoid mouth, but in or out of the Link, he's always communicating something. But yes, he did speak with the crews of those ships."

A jolt ran through Sisko's body. He lowered his head and shook it, feeling defeated. *How can we be heading into another war?* He had grown so tired, not just of putting himself in situations where others tried to kill him, but of trying to kill others himself. *Whatever happened to Starfleet's mission to explore the galaxy, its quest for knowledge?* Though he dreaded the answer, he asked the question anyway. "Did the Pact seek an alliance? Do they want to join forces with the Dominion to attack the Federation and its allies—which, by the way, now include the Cardassians and the Ferengi?" He'd mentioned the addition of the latest signatories to the Khitomer Accords in the desperate hope that doing so might somehow deter the Founders from teaming with the Typhon Pact.

"The Cardassians and the Ferengi?" Odo said. He grunted in what Sisko knew to be his approximation of a laugh. "I'm not sure which of those is more of a surprise."

Despite the seriousness of the situation—or perhaps even because of it—Sisko actually laughed. "I'm not sure either," he said. "But, Odo, that's the only reason I've come. I need to know if the Federation is facing another war. The Typhon Pact is powerful, but they're not all belligerent, and there even seems to be some belief on some of their worlds that maintaining peace with the Federation is preferable to the alternative. But if the Pact can gain a lopsided advantage, such as allying with the Dominion, then the war hawks could win out."

"War," Odo said with disdain. "Why should I be surprised? Humanoid history is filled with it."

"I agree," Sisko said. "And I'm sick of it. Which is why I'm here trying to *avoid* war."

"And how are you doing that, Captain?" Odo asked. "By violating our borders?"

"By seeking out the Founders to talk with them," Sisko said, the tone of his voice almost pleading. "To find out if you've allied with the Typhon Pact, and if you have, then by asking you to reconsider. And to tell you this: we do not want war, with the Dominion or anybody else."

Odo gazed at Sisko for a moment in silence. Finally, he said, "No, the Dominion has not joined with the Typhon Pact, nor will we. But when the Breen and the Romulans were here, they did not seek any such alliance; they came to steal."

"To steal?" Sisko asked, surprised. "Steal what?"

"I don't know," Odo said. "As I mentioned, I only just became aware of this incident. When I got word of your presence here, I was on my way to investigate. If you would like, you may come with me."

"Yes, please," Sisko said. Though it satisfied his orders to learn that the Typhon Pact had not successfully entreated the

Founders to their cause, it seemed important to know just why the Breen and the Romulans had visited the Dominion. "The *Defiant* is here in orbit, cloaked," he said, hoping that Lieutenant Commander Stinson hadn't already headed the ship back to the Alpha Quadrant.

"Then let's go aboard," Odo said. "We can take the *Defiant* to the site of the theft, and from there, you can return to Deep Space Nine."

"Odo," Sisko said, "there is no more Deep Space Nine. The Typhon Pact destroyed it."

"What?!" Odo appeared stunned. "Is . . . is Nerys—?"

"No, no," Sisko hurried to say. "She's fine. She's actually no longer on the station, or even in Starfleet. She's become a vedek."

"A vedek?" Odo seemed almost as surprised about that as he had been about the destruction of DS9. "Vedek Kira," he mused. "Is she happy?"

"I saw her on Bajor just before coming on this mission," Sisko said. "I don't think I've ever seen her more at peace, both with the universe at large and with herself."

Something close to a smile pushed at Odo's features. "I'm glad," he said. "After everything she's been through, she deserves peace."

"We *all* deserve peace," Sisko said. He turned and looked through the forward ports. "I don't think I can convince my first officer to decloak the *Defiant* as long as there are Jem'Hadar fighters here."

Odo looked at Vannis. "Dispatch them," he told her. "Have them return to their patrol duties."

"Yes, Founder, right away," said Vannis. She padded to the aft bulkhead and spoke quietly into a device wrapped around her wrist.

Sisko glanced at Tenmei, and she immediately set to checking the shuttle's sensors. Then the captain reached out and took Odo by the shoulders, something he couldn't recall ever doing. "It really is good to see you," he told the Changeling. "I hope that you're doing well here, that your life back among your people has been satisfying."

Odo said nothing at first. Sisko heard the taps of Tenmei's

fingers on her console and the tones that answered her movements. Aft, Vannis stood mutely waiting for the next orders from her god. At last, Odo said, "It's been . . . an education."

"I hope that's a good thing," Sisko told him.

"That remains to be seen."

Sisko didn't like the sound of that, but before he could say anything more, Tenmei looked up and said, "Captain, the Jem'Hadar ships are breaking orbit."

Sisko reached up and tapped his combadge, which responded with a chirp. "Sisko to *Defiant*." He received no reply but silence. "Sisko to *Defiant*."

More silence. And then, finally: "*Defiant. Stinson here, sir. We were just waiting for the Jem'Hadar to leave the area.*"

"Noted," Sisko said. "Commander, transmit your location and an entry path for the shuttle to Lieutenant Tenmei. Prepare to go to warp as soon as we're aboard."

"*Yes, sir,*" Stinson replied.

"Sisko out." To Odo, he said, "Thank you."

"Don't thank me yet," Odo said. "I'm not sure what we're going to find."

Sisko stood with Odo in the massive building. The captain thought that *Defiant* would have fit inside it easily, perhaps several times over. The roof soared above them, the walls rose in the distance like great, imposing boundaries to a secret place. *And that's what this is,* Sisko thought. *One of the Founders' secret places.*

Industrial lighting panels two-thirds of the way up on the walls shined brightly enough to provide more illumination than the Overne sun. Around the periphery at the far side of the structure, huge complexes of machinery sat inert. They looked to Sisko like automated predators lying in wait; he could imagine them thundering to life and devouring anybody who made the mistake of wandering too near.

But closer to Sisko, near the center of the great building and all around where he stood, absence marked his surroundings. The lighter color of the concrete floor across long stretches pointed to machinery once there, but now gone. Remnants of connections reached out from the walls and up from the floor, as though the place had striven to hold on to the equipment that had ultimately been taken.

"I'm sorry this happened," Sisko told Odo. "Not just because of what it could mean for the Federation, but because it is a violation of your sovereignty and your security. But it won't happen again. Starfleet is guarding the entrance to the wormhole with multiple starships; the Typhon Pact will not be back."

"That's good to know," Odo said.

Sisko heard two sets of footsteps behind him, but one of them had a strange cadence that sounded wrong; instead of a two-part rhythm—*heel-toe, heel-toe*—three beats defined the steps—*heel-middle-toe, heel-middle-toe*. The captain turned to see Vannis escorting a being that belonged to a species the captain had never before seen. They had entered through an open doorway in the wall nearest Sisko, beyond which he could see the pale gray light of the overcast Overne day.

Sisko waited with Odo as Vannis and the being approached. A golden fur covered the being's visible, basically humanoid body, though a complicated-looking piece of clothing covered its torso. At least a head taller than the captain, it possessed legs that moved in a manner Sisko had trouble making sense of, until he realized that the joint that approximated a human knee could bend in both directions, forward and backward, and did so as the being walked. Each leg intersected with a foot not at its heel, but in the center, which explained the three-way tempo of its steps: *first heel–middle–second heel*. Sisko saw that it also had two arms on one side of its body, and two on the other. Likewise, it had two pairs of eyes on its round head. Sisko saw nothing he could identify as ears, nose, or mouth. The one being almost looked like two standing back-to-back, sharing a set of legs.

"Founder," Vannis said as she and the being reached the group, "this is Vildish Senra-Nesk. When this particular installation is in production, he works as its supervisor."

"All right," Odo said. "Can you tell us the purpose of the equipment that was stolen?" He pointed around to where machinery had obviously been removed.

Senra-Nesk looked at Odo without saying anything. Then he swiveled his head on his neck to look at the Changeling with his other set of eyes. It fascinated Sisko to see one pair of eyes colored yellow, the other blue.

"Founder, my apologies," Vannis said. "Our translators have problems with the Overne language. If I may assist?"

"Go ahead," Odo told her.

Vannis opened her mouth and emitted a series of noises ranging from clicks and snaps, to chirps and twitters, to hums and drones. It sounded nothing like language to Sisko. That the Vorta could even speak in such a fashion impressed him.

Senra-Nesk stared—with his blue eyes—at Vannis. When she finished, he clicked and chirped and hummed in response, though Sisko could not tell from where on his body the sounds emanated. "Senra-Nesk says that the machinery utilized to manufacture structural integrity field generators and deflector generators has been taken. The corresponding equipment used in full-scale testing of those systems has been removed as well."

Odo looked from Vannis to Sisko. "Does that mean anything to you, Captain?"

"I'm not sure," he said. He looked around at the empty spaces where the missing machinery once stood, then padded away from Odo and Vannis and Senra-Nesk. The Typhon Pact had clearly had an important purpose in making their way into the Dominion and stealing what they had. Odo had explained that the Romulans had abducted Laas and then faced down a Jem'Hadar squadron in order to acquire what they sought, which meant they hadn't been averse to taking considerable risks. They'd also demonstrated that at Deep Space 9, where they'd chanced all-out war to bring the purloined gear back to their people.

Sisko turned and made his way back to Odo and the others. "You may be unaware of this," he told the Changeling, "but over the last few years, Starfleet has outfitted some of its vessels with a new type of technology called quantum slipstream drive. It allows a starship to travel at significantly increased effective velocities."

Odo arched an eyebrow at Sisko with a knowing expression. "And the Breen and the Romulans and their allies have taken exception to the Federation employing such an advanced engine system."

"Yes," Sisko said. "That's true, even though we've only installed the new drive on a small number of starships."

"So what?" Odo said. "Your enemies can't know with certainty how many ships you've reconfigured with this slipstream. And from the way you describe it—'significantly increased effective velocities'—it sounds as though they have reason to fear that the Federation could use it to great tactical advantage."

"I think that's probably true," Sisko admitted.

"So are you saying that what they've stolen from here might allow them to match that technology?" Odo asked.

"I don't know," Sisko said. "But I think it's a possibility."

"Then I'm not sure what the problem is," Odo said. "You have the technology, so why shouldn't they? I'm not saying that they had a right to steal it from the Dominion or anybody else, but if this Typhon Pact feels that there's an imbalance in the relative might of their alliance and that of the Khitomer Accords, why wouldn't they want to even that out?"

"That's one thing in theory," Sisko said. "It's another in practice. We know that we will never use the quantum slipstream drive, or any other technology, to strike first at our enemies. We can't be as sure of the Breen and the Romulans and the Tzenkethi."

"What about the Klingons?" Odo said. "Or the Cardassians? Will they be as disinclined as the Federation to commencing such an attack? And what of the Federation itself? Leadership changes. New people can bring new ideas—even *bad* ideas."

"Starfleet hasn't provided the slipstream drive to any of its allies," Sisko said. "Odo, I didn't come here to debate this with you. Some of what you say may be right, but you know the Federation. You know who we are as a people. You fought by our side against your own people. That has to say something about how you feel about us, about our motives, about our *hearts*."

"It's not your hearts I'm concerned about," Odo said. "It's your trigger fingers."

Sisko sighed heavily. He felt frustrated and angry and sad—and even resigned to the fact that Odo had a valid perspective.

"All I know is that I am trying to avoid another war," he said. "I think maybe you've helped me do that."

"I'm not sure how."

"Knowing that the Founders have not allied with the Typhon Pact will keep the Federation from militarizing more, which could go a long way to preventing the outbreak of hostilities. Knowing that the Typhon Pact might once again be trying to obtain the ability to produce slipstream drive could help us in negotiating with them. And it absolutely will help us in *understanding* them."

"I hope so," Odo said. "The Dominion has closed its borders specifically so we can take an inventory of who we are—not just the Founders, but all of us." He looked first to Vannis, and then to Senra-Nesk. "We are striving to find a way to survive together in peace and harmony." He peered around the building. "That's why this place and so many others like it are no longer in operation. We have enough starships and weaponry to protect the Dominion, and we employ them to do so, mostly at the borders these days. If we're not going to expand, if we're not going to battle others, we have no need to continue assembling the tools of war."

"I can appreciate that," Sisko said. "I genuinely hope that the Dominion finds itself, and is able to achieve your vision for it."

"Thank you, Captain," Odo said. "Is there anything else I can help you with?"

"No," Sisko said. "But thank you for what you have done." He looked in turn at Vannis and Senra-Nesk, and thanked both of them as well. Vannis translated his words for the Overne. Then the captain started toward the open door. Once outside, beyond the sensor scattering field of the building, he would be able to transport up to *Defiant* and head back to the Federation.

When he had almost reached the door, Odo called after him. "Captain, please tell Nerys . . . just tell her that I asked after her."

"I will."

"I wish you luck, Captain."

"Good luck to you, Odo," Sisko said. "When you're ready . . . when the Founders are ready . . . we'd welcome another opportunity to get to know them, and for them to get to know us, as friends."

"I'll bear that in mind."

Sisko left the building and walked out into the cloudy afternoon on Overne III. Several dozen meters from the building, he activated his combadge. "Sisko to *Defiant.*"

"*Defiant. Stinson here, sir.*"

"Beam me up, Commander," Sisko said. "As soon as I'm aboard, head us back to the wormhole and take us to maximum warp."

"*Yes, sir.*"

Sisko turned to peer up at the enormous manufacturing plant, which had once been used in the construction of Dominion starships. An instant later, a hum enveloped the captain, and the building faded from his view.

16

When Gell Kamemor entered the audience chamber from her office, she saw that Fleet Admiral Devix had already been escorted inside. Proconsul Ventel stood with him across the room, between a pair of tall pillars, their backs to her as they apparently studied one of the many pieces of traditional art adorning the space. Uhlans Preget and T'Lesk stood beside the closed entry doors, ready to protect the praetor.

Kamemor crossed the chamber quietly, her soft-soled footwear making little noise on the gleaming black floor. Before she drew too near the men without making her presence known—an impoliteness she would not permit herself—she said, "Gentlemen, I'm so sorry to have kept you waiting."

Both Devix and Ventel turned toward Kamemor and greeted her as she arrived in front of them. Anlikar looked as though he'd aged a decade over the past twenty or so days. Although his hair had begun graying in his youth and had completely lost its color before he'd lived his first full century, his face seemed more deeply lined than ever. Kamemor understood that the demands of their jobs had begun weighing heavily on him. It had been relatively easy, less than a hundred days into her praetorship, for the two of them eventually to discount the attack on the Federation's Utopia Planitia Shipyards as an isolated rogue incident, as a holdover action planned by her predecessor and carried out by a zealot already in place to do so. With Tal'Aura dead and Commander Marius—the man who had taken his Romulan warbird to Utopia Planitia—in a military prison, such an episode seemed unlikely to recur.

But what had taken place not even two dozen days earlier could not as readily be dismissed. Their realization that the chairwoman of the Tal Shiar had been involved in the recent rogue action had shocked them. Although numerous heads of the elite intelligence agency had earned deserved reputations for hardness, cunning, and treachery, they had always performed in service *to* the praetor. The women and men who led the Tal Shiar had typically achieved their ultimate goal; few ever aspired to any other role in government, and none had ever been subsequently elevated to the praetorship.

For his part, Admiral Devix appeared even older, but then he'd already made it beyond his sesquicentennial. Yet Devix did not carry his age in the color of his hair—still black—or in the creases of his face—still relatively unlined for so mature a man— but in his eyes. His gaze looked like that of a man who had seen too many defeats, and who knew that, as his losses mounted, his time passed. In the last half-decade, he had suffered ignominies too great for even his vaunted, oft-decorated career to overcome. There had been the coup by Shinzon, Reman independence, and the schism wrought by Donatra, and though many others shared far more blame for those events than Devix, he had been the man standing at the head of the Imperial Fleet. During Kamemor's tenure as praetor, the two rogue military actions threatened to undermine her government, even as she had begun to draw more support in the Senate and among the people. Even though Kamemor believed that nobody in the admiral's position could have prevented almost any of the failures over which he had presided, she needed to demonstrate her strength. In truth, though she considered Devix a loyalist, a true patriot, and a man not given to battle for battle's sake, she wanted somebody more vigorous as fleet admiral, with an unblemished record on which to begin leading the Romulan military.

But the praetor had not called the admiral to her chamber; earlier that morning, he had requested an audience. "What is it that I can do for you today?" she asked.

While Ventel had been sure that Devix would withdraw the resignation she had demanded of him, or appeal her decision to replace him, Kamemor had disagreed. The admiral did not have just as much pride as most Romulans; in her opinion, he had *more*—more pride and less arrogance, a rare combination in the Empire. He might not have chosen to step down had the praetor not insisted he do so, but since that determination had been made, the proud Devix wanted to ensure that a worthy successor be named to his post. Kamemor assumed that he had asked for a meeting to further discuss that.

"Would you care for some tea while we talk?" she asked the admiral, pointing to a small table off to the side, on which a tea service sat.

"Thank you, no, Praetor," Devix said. "I did not come for discussion, but to inform you of an issue of great concern."

"That sounds rather ominous," Kamemor said.

"It may not be," Devix said. "Under normal circumstances, I would categorize it as likely a temporary situation, at worst a loss or perhaps even a tragedy, but given what has happened recently, I am alarmed to think it could be something far greater than all of that."

Kamemor could see that the admiral's visit cost him. Whatever he had to tell her, he did not want to; he would, though, because his duty demanded it. "Please tell me what is troubling you, Admiral."

"One of our warbirds has failed to report."

A chill ran through Kamemor. "Is that unusual?" she wanted to know. She already understood where her questions would lead, but she had to ask them.

"It's not uncommon," Devix said. "Ships encounter interstellar phenomena that interfere with communications, commanders order subspace silence when belligerents are near, ships remain cloaked for lengthy periods of time while on patrol . . ."

"And starships can be destroyed," Ventel suggested. "Either accidentally or at the hands of an aggressor."

"That is sometimes the case," Devix said.

"But none of the legitimate reasons for the disappearance of this particular warbird satisfy you," Kamemor said, more statement than question.

"No, Praetor," said the admiral.

"Tell me why."

"The warbird in question, the *Vetruvis*, was part of a detachment included in a military exchange with the Tzenkethi," the admiral said. "Even with that assignment, its crew made regular daily reports to the Imperial Fleet. Three days ago, we stopped receiving those reports."

"Did you contact the Tzenkethi?" Ventel asked. Kamemor felt sure that Devix had done everything he possibly could to locate the missing starship. Had he not, he would not have stood in the praetor's audience chamber, admitting to another possible failure under his leadership.

"We did contact the Coalition," Devix said. "Their military claims that the *Vetruvis* never arrived as part of the exchange."

"Do you believe them?" Ventel asked.

"It doesn't matter," Kamemor said before the admiral could respond. "If the Tzenkethi are being truthful, then the reports from the *Vetruvis* have either been fabricated or are themselves lies. And if the Tzenkethi are lying, then we have an additional problem, possibly one much bigger than the crew of a single ship conducting another rogue action—which is of course the concern that drove you to come here today, Admiral, is it not?"

"Yes, Praetor," Devix said. "After the attack on the Federation space station, and keeping in mind what happened at Utopia Planitia, that is precisely my concern."

"If the Tzenkethi are lying, we must learn why," Kamemor said. "It could be something unfortunate, but in the end forgivable, such as the accidental loss of our ship in their territory, under their aegis. But it could also be that they support whatever rogue action the *Vetruvis* crew might be undertaking."

"Where was the warbird at last contact?" Ventel asked.

"Near Lamemda," Devix said. "It's a star on the border of Tzenkethi space, on the edge of the Badlands."

"The Badlands," Ventel said. "Then not far from the Cardassian Union."

"Which means not far from Bajor and the wormhole," Kamemor said.

"You can understand my concern," said the admiral.

"Yes," Kamemor said. "You were right to come to me with this, and I'm grateful for it."

"There's more, Praetor," Devix said. "The commander of the *Vetruvis* is Kozik."

"Should I know that name?" Kamemor asked.

"During the unauthorized action at Utopia Planitia by Commander Marius aboard the *Dekkona, Centurion* Kozik served as the ship's tactical officer. Later, when the *Dekkona* crew engaged the Federation vessel *Aventine* near Breen space, he had been promoted to executive officer, though he still held the rank of centurion. After we removed Marius from the ship, we distributed the crew throughout the Fleet. Promoted to subcommander, Kozik served as second-in-command aboard *Vetruvis* until fifteen days ago, when his commanding officer suffered a fatal brain aneurysm on the bridge."

"And he succeeded to command of the ship?" Ventel asked. "That seems like a rapid ascent, from centurion to commander, from tactical officer to ship commander, in that period of time."

"All of his promotions and transfers have been handled by Admiral Vellon," Devix said.

Vellon! The puppet of the Tal Shiar. Kamemor knew that she would have to neutralize the admiral along with Chairwoman Sela.

"You're saying that Kozik is a part of this rogue element in the Imperial Fleet?" Ventel asked.

"There seem to be too many connections to disregard it as a possibility," Devix said.

"I agree," said Kamemor. "The question is: What can we do about it? How do we find the *Vetruvis*?"

"Short of sending a wing of Imperial warbirds into Tzenkethi space—and possibly into Cardassian space—I'm not sure we can," Devix said.

Kamemor imagined the response that a squadron of Romulan vessels would draw from the Cardassians. Even the Federation, in answer to the awful events in Bajoran space, had increased their military presence at their borders. But while Starfleet often showed admirable restraint in reacting to provocative actions, Central Command could not be accused of such self-discipline. And once a Khitomer Accords ally had engaged in military action against a member of the Typhon Pact, others—the Tzenkethi, the Breen, the Klingons—would surely follow. The Federation would have little choice but to enter the fray as well.

"Rather than searching for a single, probably cloaked vessel in potentially hostile space," Kamemor said, "we need to know what action Kozik intends to take, and then prevent him from doing so."

"Sela?" Ventel said. "If you intend to interrogate the chairwoman, I don't see that netting us actionable information. I believe she would rather take her own life than give up the cause to which she has put so much time and energy. She has long sought vengeance against the Federation."

"I agree with you, Anlikar," Kamemor said. "But there is somebody else from whom we might pry what we need to know." She stared into Admiral Devix's tired eyes and saw the pride and determination that had brought him so far in his Imperial Fleet career. Or perhaps Kamemor imagined all that. Even after all that had happened, though, she trusted the admiral's professionalism, his loyalty, and most of all, his reluctance to send his troops into battle as anything but a last resort. "Admiral," she told him, "I'm going to need you back on the bridge of a warbird."

17

Somebody walking through the atrium in the opposite direction said something to Bashir, but he only vaguely registered the sound of her voice. Her words did not penetrate the daze that had been enveloping him ever since Sarina had been seized by Starfleet security three days earlier. The doctor offered no reply to the woman, but just kept walking.

The dim lighting in the building's entry hall, reflecting the lateness of the hour, matched Bashir's state of mind. He felt as though he'd existed in a fog since that terrible evening in Quark's new place. He escaped the miasma just once, to bluster at Captain Ro about the injustice of taking into custody an innocent woman. But even then, his own doubts about Sarina circled him like vultures waiting for a wounded animal to finally die. He knew what he wanted to believe, pushed himself in that direction, toward the brilliant light of his love, attempted to hold his ground, but he continued to feel himself slipping closer to the darkness.

Bashir reached the bank of turbolifts in the housing facility that Starfleet had taken over in Aljuli. The center of the three doors opened and he entered the cab. As the door slid closed behind him, he absently announced his destination—"Third floor"—before falling back into the seemingly endless loop of thoughts that had filled his mind during Sarina's detainment.

She worked for Section Thirty-one, he thought. He hated the simplicity of that fact, but he knew that he could count on the reality of it because Sarina had admitted it to him. *She didn't just admit it,* he thought. *She declared it to me.*

When the door to the lift didn't open in a reasonable amount of time, Bashir realized that he'd tried to activate the cab via voice command, though it only had a manual interface. He reached out to the control panel and pressed the number *3,* which lighted at his touch. The lift began to rise.

During the year that he and Sarina had been together on DS9, only once, at the very beginning, had Section 31 contacted either of them. *At least, only once as far as I know,* Bashir thought. An operative named L'Haan appeared in his quarters while he'd been asleep—and lightly drugged, it turned out—and spoke to Sarina. In that conversation, L'Haan confirmed Sarina's mission: to make Bashir fall in love with her, for the ultimate purpose of finally pulling him into Section 31 as a full-time operative.

That's what Sarina told *me,* Bashir thought. He'd believed it at the time, and he believed it still. But he'd come to doubt her reasons for telling him about L'Haan's visit. Sarina avowed that she no longer wanted to be a part of the organization, and she didn't want Bashir joining them either. Together, they conspired to try to develop a means of bringing them down. Deeply concerned about revealing their intentions to the ever-watchful organization, they discussed their plans only occasionally, utilizing a coded shorthand of their own devising. Of course, their precautions about plotting the demise of the organization would have meant nothing if Sarina had turned around and divulged them herself. But with no additional contacts—again, none that Bashir knew about—they began worrying about Section 31 less and less.

The turbolift reached the third floor and its door glided open. Bashir stepped into the long corridor that ran the length of the building, and started toward his quarters. His footsteps thudded dully on the new carpeting that had been put down since Starfleet had taken possession of the facility. His head also thudded.

Sarina told me about Section 31, Bashir thought, *and about how they intended to seduce me to join them.* But could her revealing that information, while accurate, also have been a part of the organization's plan to lure him in . . . a part of *Sarina's* plan? His mind spun when he considered the circles-within-circles machinations of the covert group.

Bashir reached his quarters and tapped his access code into the panel beside it. The door withdrew into the wall, and he stepped inside the compact room that would be his home whenever he served at the updated control center in Wyntara Mas. He knew that he would also spend time aboard *Defiant,* and possibly aboard the other ships patrolling the system.

As the door closed behind him, Bashir smelled the slightly sour air inside and decided to open the room's one small window. He walked between the bed on one side and the computer interface on the other, over to the outer wall. He tugged at the window, but it seemed stuck. He gave up and moved to the bed—barely more than a cot—and dropped onto his back atop it. He wanted—he *needed*—rest, but he knew that he would have to slow down his thoughts for any hope of sleep. He closed his eyes and tried to blank his mind.

Instead, more questions presented themselves. If he assumed that Sarina had been lying to him, that she worked willingly and completely as an operative of Section 31, and not, as she maintained, as a double agent working to bring them down, did it then follow that she had planted the bombs on Deep Space 9? He didn't think so. What possible motive could Section 31 have for wanting the station destroyed? In their twisted way, they worked to *protect* the Federation, not to put it at risk, which the loss of DS9 surely did. And while they showed no reluctance about doing what needed to be done to achieve a particular aim, Bashir could not imagine that they would willingly cause the deaths of more than a thousand Federation citizens.

Except that Bashir also recalled that Chief Blackmer believed the bombs hadn't been set to destroy DS9, but to compel its evacuation. An empty station would have weakened the Federation's defenses at the wormhole, and therefore created a more open path for the cloaked Romulan warbird to sneak back into the Alpha Quadrant. That sounded more like something the Typhon Pact would do than Section 31. But whoever had planted the bombs, could the results—with the crew unable to eject one of the failing reactors—have been accidental? If so, did that mean—*could* that mean—that Section 31 or Sarina might have been responsible, since the intended goal would have fallen far short of killing so many people?

Bashir rubbed at his eyes. The pain in his head had progressed from a mere thudding to an unrelenting pounding. He hadn't brought any of his medical gear from the infirmary he'd set up at the rear of the control center, but he always left a medkit in his residence. He slowly stood from the bed and made his way past the computer interface and into the 'fresher.

Inside the tiny compartment, Bashir ran cold water in the sink, put his hands beneath the spout, then slapped his face. He didn't want to wake himself up, but to escape the haze surrounding his mind, which would not let him rest. He considered taking something to help him sleep, but settled for a simple analgesic. He found his medkit in the cabinet above the sink, pulled out a hypospray, found a vial of the palliative he sought, and administered the medication to the base of his neck.

Bashir returned his medkit to the cabinet, which he then closed. Seeing himself in the mirror mounted on the cabinet door, he thought again about his contention that Sarina would never kill, and particularly not innocent people. But hadn't he done that himself, during their mission to Salavat? Hadn't he made the choice to kill—to *murder*—civilian engineers in his attempt to keep the slipstream drive out of the hands of the Typhon Pact? He'd rationalized his actions at the time, telling himself that he worked to prevent many more deaths than that— that if the Pact acquired slipstream, then the chances of war erupting became that much more likely. He didn't know if he still believed his justification, because how could you quantify life? It seemed a simple matter to claim one death is better than two, but does that truly justify causing the one death?

Bashir grabbed a hand towel and wiped his face dry, then exited the 'fresher, still drying his hands. He froze when he saw somebody in his room, sitting in the chair in front of the computer interface. Dressed wholly in black, the woman would not have to declare her affiliation. She had straight black hair that she wore down to her shoulders. He could not see her ears, but he knew that they tapered up to a point.

"Good evening, Doctor."

"Don't you people tire of this?" Bashir said in disgust. "Don't *you* tire of it? All this cloak-and-dagger window dressing? Don't you look stylish in your mysterious dark clothing, and aren't you so terribly clever to have infiltrated my little cubicle of a room." He threw the towel back into the 'fresher, then crossed to stand by the bed, opposite the woman in black. After he'd spent so much time thinking about Section 31 in recent days, it seemed uncanny that a member of the organization would suddenly appear before him. But his anger trumped his wonder. "Am I supposed to be impressed because you have a silent transporter?

Or maybe it was something far more basic than that?" He pointed to the door on the other side of the computer interface than the 'fresher. "Maybe you had to crouch in my closet among the worn shoes and dirty laundry I haven't gotten around to recycling in the replicator downstairs. Oh, my, yes, how very glamorous."

"My name is L'Haan," the woman said.

"I know who you are."

"Do you?" L'Haan said. "Then Ms. Douglas has mentioned me."

"I only meant that I know where you're from, who your associates are," Bashir said. "You're L'Haan, fine, but you're also Sloan and Cole and Ethan Locken. Because you're all the same."

"All of us?" L'Haan said. "Including Ms. Douglas?"

Bashir shook his head, then sat down on the bed. "Say what you like," he told L'Haan. "I don't care." He harbored his own doubts about Sarina, but he wouldn't allow somebody like this woman to contribute to them.

"But you *do* care for Ms. Douglas," L'Haan said. "Quite a lot, I'm given to understand."

"What do you want?"

"She's not guilty."

"Don't you think I know that?" Bashir spat, launching himself off the bed and over to the outer door. "Of course she's not guilty." He'd reacted too quickly, he knew, too vociferously to hide his uncertainty. He also noted that he'd said *not guilty*; he hadn't said *innocent*.

"Well," L'Haan said, "I'm glad that you do know that." Her tone told Bashir that she saw through his declaration of support for Sarina, all the way to his fears. "The question I have to ask then is, why are you allowing her to wallow in custody?"

"She hasn't been charged with anything," Bashir said. *Not yet.* "She's being detained so she can answer questions about what happened on the station."

"Have you seen her?" L'Haan asked.

"You mean you don't know?" Bashir said. He walked back over to the bed.

"Let's just say I want to hear your version of things."

"I saw her briefly the night they took her in," Bashir said.

"And what did she tell you?"

"What do you think she told me?" Bashir said. "'Yes, of course I did it, Julian, I murdered a thousand people and I'd do it again.'" What Sarina had done had been to look deeply into his eyes and tell him that she had nothing to do with the destruction of Deep Space 9. And for a time—perhaps too short a time—that had been enough for him.

"Really, Doctor Bashir, you must learn to govern your passions," L'Haan said. "They will be your undoing."

"I like my passions."

"Have you spoken with Captain Ro?" L'Haan asked. "Have you tried to make her understand that she's made a mistake?"

"Of course I have," Bashir said. "And the captain's not convinced that Sarina's guilty."

"So Ro thinks that the investigation may clear her of any wrongdoing."

Bashir nodded.

L'Haan shrugged. "Maybe that would happen. But we can't take that chance. Because the Federation and Bajor took more than just a bloody nose on this one, and people are crying out for justice. It won't be sufficient for President Bacco to say, yes, somebody destroyed one of our vital assets and killed a thousand people in the process, and no, we don't know who it was, but let's not worry about it, they probably won't do it again. That would make everybody feel too vulnerable, and after the Dominion, after Tezwa, after the Borg, after the formation of the Typhon Pact, the Federation can't have that. Bacco can't have that. Akaar can't.

"And even you can't."

"What are you saying?" Bashir asked. "That because these people *need* to blame somebody for what happened, they're going to find Sarina guilty even if she's innocent?"

"'*If* she's innocent,' Doctor?" L'Haan said quietly, her eyes boring into his. "How quickly we lose trust."

Bashir said nothing.

"Here's what's going to happen, Doctor," L'Haan said. "Federation Security will hold on to Sarina for questioning as long as they legally can. When that time runs out, as it soon will, they'll indict her. They'll indict her because they won't want to let her go, and then public sentiment and everybody's need for a villain will be enough to see her convicted."

"They can't convict anybody without evidence."

"But there is evidence, Doctor," L'Haan said. "There is her position in security, which allowed her access to the very locations on Deep Space Nine where the bombs were found. There is her unsubstantiated, and even refuted, accusation that Rahendervakell th'Shant made threats against the station. There is her survival of the disaster.

"And then there would be the revelation of her illegal mission to Salavat, her violation of Breen borders, her abetting the murder of Breen civilians, all of which can establish Ms. Douglas's character. There's also the matter of her having been genetically engineered. The general public doesn't like that."

Bashir's legs suddenly felt as if they could no longer support him, and he sat back down again on the bed. "At least half of that is immaterial to what happened on Deep Space Nine," he said. "And the rest is at best circumstantial."

"But *circumstantial* doesn't mean *not convincing*, Doctor," L'Haan said. "You understand the way most humanoid brains operate, and so you must know how thoroughly unreliable eyewitness testimony is. In many crimes, particularly sophisticated ones, physical evidence is completely lacking. That leaves only circumstantial evidence, and it's what puts most criminals in prison."

"If they truly are criminals," Bashir said.

"Because they need her to be," L'Haan said, "they will make Ms. Douglas a criminal."

"That might be the way your version of justice works," Bashir said, "but that's not Federation justice."

"How naïve, Doctor," L'Haan said. "But as I said, Ms. Douglas is not guilty, and she is far too valuable an asset for us to lose."

"So why don't *you* do something about it?" Bashir asked, although he absolutely did not want Section 31 to come to Sarina's rescue.

"What do you think I'm doing by speaking with you?"

"I mean, why don't you just break her out of custody?"

"We could do that," L'Haan said. "You know that we could. But then what? She wouldn't be as useful an agent because she'd be a fugitive. She'd lose all her value as an undercover operative. She'd have to stay in the shadows, and really, I'm not sure how satisfying that would be for her . . . or for you. Because then your choices would be to join us, or never to see Ms. Douglas again. No, it's better that she keep an identity that people know and trust. But that means her name needs to be cleared. As the man who loves her, everybody would expect you to try."

"How am I supposed to do that?" Bashir said.

"By finding the actual culprit, of course," L'Haan said.

"And who is that?"

"I don't know," L'Haan said. "If I did, I wouldn't be here right now."

"So if you don't know who planted the bombs, how the hell am I supposed to find out?" Bashir said. "Deep Space Nine is gone, and along with it, whatever physical evidence that might have existed."

"All of the physical evidence is gone?" L'Haan asked. "Did you know that revitrite, the Andorian explosive used in making the bombs, leaves behind a radioactive signature in cellular material?"

"I don't think that's true," Bashir said.

"Really?" L'Haan said. "Even under certain circumstances, such as when it's in the vicinity of a fusion reactor core?"

"That doesn't sound quite right either."

"Maybe not," L'Haan said, her tone oddly nonchalant. "But what difference does that really make? Not everybody will know that, and I'm sure you would be able to produce some experimental results to reinforce such an assertion."

"Am I hearing you correctly?" Bashir asked. "Are you suggesting that I substitute another innocent person to take the blame instead of Sarina?"

"I'm suggesting only that Ms. Douglas is not guilty of the crimes for which she will be charged," L'Haan said, "and that you therefore need to do everything within your power to see her freed."

"*Everything* within my power?" Bashir said. "Sarina wouldn't want me to do that."

"Even if she's guilty?"

"She's not guilty!"

L'Haan smiled, which, on a Vulcan, looked peculiar to Bashir. "I know she's not, Doctor. After all, that's why I'm here."

"Even if she were guilty, you'd be here."

"No," L'Haan said. "If she were guilty, we would have killed her by now."

Bashir looked away, revolted by L'Haan, revolted by Section 31. "Get out."

"Of course," L'Haan said, and she stood from the chair. "It's almost time for me to be going anyway. But before I do, tell me, hasn't Captain Ro ordered a new round of physicals for the crew?"

The question seemed like a non sequitur. "She has," Bashir said.

"Interesting," L'Haan said. She walked over to the door and reached toward the activation touchpad beside it. Before pressing her finger to it, she turned back to Bashir and said, "Don't you think that performing physical examinations of the crew would be a reasonable time to check for radioactive signatures?"

"Get out," Bashir said again. Suddenly, he began to feel dizzy. He tried to rise, but he slipped and thumped back down onto the edge of the bed.

L'Haan twirled a finger in the air in front of her. "A mild anesthetic gas to which I've developed an immunity. Be glad for it; you'll sleep well."

Bashir pushed up from the bed again and managed to get to his feet.

L'Haan triggered the door, which opened behind her. "Listen, Doctor, see that you free Ms. Douglas. Don't do it for us, or even just for yourself; do it for her." Then she turned and left.

Bashir staggered after her. He fell against the jamb as he got to the door. He looked out into the corridor, but of course, L'Haan was gone.

Bashir lurched back to the bed and sat down again. He thought to activate his combadge and call security, but he knew that it would be useless.

A moment later, Bashir fell back on the bed, unconscious.

18

"**C**aptain, we're receiving a message from Starfleet Command."

Sisko peered over to the port side of the *Defiant* bridge, to where Lieutenant Aleco worked the communications console. The captain had hoped to receive a response to the message he'd sent to Starfleet, but he hadn't anticipated one so quickly. The ship still had several hours to travel before it would reach the Idran system and the wormhole.

"It's encrypted and marked 'captain's eyes only,'" Aleco said.

While the message Sisko had transmitted to Starfleet Command had been likewise coded and sent directly to Admiral Akaar, he hadn't expected a similarly configured reply. He'd already received an uncoded, unrestricted response from Captain Euler, who had simply confirmed that Sisko's message had made it through the wormhole to *Canterbury,* via the communications relay in the Gamma Quadrant. Euler had routed the captain's message directly to Command.

Sisko had no idea what Starfleet wanted so urgently to tell him, but he grew immediately concerned. He expected only verification that the information he'd transmitted to the commander-in-chief—a report detailing his experiences in the Dominion and what he'd learned from Odo—had reached its destination. He hoped that something else hadn't happened at the wormhole, leaving *Defiant* as some final measure of defense.

"Transfer it to the ready room, Lieutenant," Sisko said. "Commander Stinson, you have the bridge." As his first officer acknowledged the order, the captain stood, straightened his uniform overshirt, and headed for the portside aft exit.

As he made his way to the ship's ready room, Sisko thought about the Bajoran wormhole. He realized that, as important as it had been since he and Jadzia had discovered it—or *re*discovered it—it had just become *critically* important. Whatever the reason for the Typhon Pact's theft of equipment from the Dominion—whether to aid them in developing their own version of the quantum slipstream drive, or in the creation of some new type of weapon system, or something else entirely—they had failed in their quest. They had risked a great deal in their attempt, though, and that suggested to Sisko that they would likely try again. Unless the members of the Pact intended to travel at warp nine for a century-long round trip to the Gamma Quadrant, they'd have to make another run into Bajoran space. That meant that it would become absolutely vital for Starfleet to prevent cloaked vessels from entering the wormhole.

Sisko entered the ready room and made his way behind the desk. He saw the Starfleet emblem on the screen of the computer interface there, meaning that Lieutenant Aleco had already routed the message. "Computer, this is Captain Benjamin Sisko. Play eyes-only message from Starfleet Command." On the display, the image of the commander-in-chief appeared.

"Captain Sisko, this is Admiral Akaar." Sisko could see the iconic Golden Gate Bridge in the background, through the windows of the admiral's office. *"I received your report from the Gamma Quadrant, and I immediately consulted with the Starfleet Corps of Engineers regarding the stolen equipment you identified. Without a functioning Jem'Hadar vessel, it's not possible for them to positively conclude that the Typhon Pact could utilize that machinery to construct a working slipstream drive, as you suggested. It is their opinion, though, that the equipment* might *provide the Pact such a solution. Further, they believe that it's possible that such a solution might not be confined to installation on specially designed hulls, but on virtually any starship."*

Sisko closed his eyes and dropped his head. Starfleet had a small number of slipstream equipped vessels, which it utilized primarily for the purposes of exploration. If the Typhon Pact could develop entire fleets of slipstream starships, though, they could overrun the Federation with relative ease. The captain looked back up at the screen as Akaar's message continued.

"Considering the great lengths to which the Pact went in order to attempt both the acquisition of this equipment and the return of it to their territory, it seems clear that it must be crucially important to them. Having the ability to convert any of their vessels to utilize slipstream drive would fall into that category, and it certainly is consistent

with what we know of their rhetoric about Starfleet's own slipstream. We are therefore proceeding on the basis that this is what the Pact sought with their actions in the Gamma Quadrant and at Deep Space Nine."

Sisko took no pleasure in having been right in his assessment of the use to which the Pact would put the purloined equipment. He could only hope that he would be wrong about their making another attempt to acquire it from the Dominion.

"This means that the Typhon Pact began planning this action at least five months ago, when they proposed at the summit on Cort that civilian Pact ships be permitted into the Gamma Quadrant, and that a joint Starfleet–Imperial Fleet mission also take place there. Given that, it is my opinion that the Pact will not give up on attempting to acquire such technology. Obviously, the only place they know where they can find it is in the Dominion.

"Captain Sisko, you reported the continued policy of the Founders to keep the borders of the Dominion closed to outsiders. That would appear to redound to our benefit, and yet it did not prevent the Typhon Pact from succeeding in their first attempt to steal the equipment. President Bacco believes, as do I, that the Federation will benefit from opening and maintaining a new dialogue with the Founders—or at least with the Dominion. I am therefore tasking you with figuring out how best to accomplish this."

Sisko did not know what he or anybody else could say or do to convince the Founders to accede to such a request. Odo, who could readily be considered a friend of the Federation, had made the stance of the Founders quite clear. Sisko believed that any messages transmitted to the Dominion would likely go unanswered, and that additional attempts to visit would lead not to rapprochement, but to confrontation.

The admiral looked off to the side, then reached to retrieve a padd from his desk. He glanced at the device's display, then said, *"I also have a report here that says repairs to the* Robinson *will be completed in twelve days. With Captain Ro working to establish her crew on the surface of Bajor, you will remain in command of the* Defiant *until you can return to your own ship."*

The admiral set the padd down on his desk, then added, *"Good work out in the Gamma Quadrant, Captain. Akaar out."*

The Starfleet emblem reappeared on the screen. Sisko stabbed at the controls of the computer interface to deactivate it. He considered responding to the commander-in-chief to explain the dangers in pushing the Dominion, even in the area of simple diplomacy, but he didn't think it would do any good. If anything, he would have to have a real-time conversation with the admiral—and Sisko didn't think even that would do much good. *After two years of bloody war with the Dominion,* Sisko thought, exasperated, *how can anybody in the Federation not know that it's a bad idea to act in opposition to what the Founders want?*

"Especially if all they want is to be left alone," Sisko said aloud.

He sat back in the chair and sighed. He thought about the wormhole, about the Typhon Pact, about the Dominion, but just then, none of those things seemed important to him. He closed his eyes and saw his little girl, whom he wanted to grow up in peacetime. "Every child should grow up in peace," he told the empty room.

Sisko had gone into battle often during his Starfleet career, and he would doubtless do so again if called upon, but he felt sick of it. He remembered Elias Vaughn, so late in his life, diving into the exploration of the universe, and how much joy he found in doing that. At that moment, Sisko thought, nothing would have fulfilled him more than charting stars.

"Charting stars," he said, "and hugging my daughter."

On the main viewscreen, the luminous blue gyre rotated open, revealing the stars of the Alpha Quadrant. Sisko watched from the command chair as *Defiant* navigated through the end of the wormhole and back into Bajoran space. The ship emerged facing phaser banks and quantum torpedo tubes aimed in its direction.

"Full stop," Sisko ordered, part of the new procedures Starfleet had put in place with respect to the wormhole.

"Full stop, aye," said Tenmei.

Directly ahead of *Defiant,* Starfleet's flagship patrolled near to where Deep Space 9 had once kept station. Off to port, the *Galaxy*-class *Venture* approached, firing blue beams from its forward emitters. Sisko knew that the deployment of a multiphase tachyon detection grid across the mouth of the wormhole had become standard procedure whenever a ship came through it, to ensure that no cloaked vessels entered or exited after it. He envisioned a more automated approach, and resolved to speak with Starfleet Command about it.

"Viewer astern," Sisko said. If some cloaked vessel had followed *Defiant* in an attempt to sneak into the Alpha Quadrant, he wanted to know about it at once. Lieutenant Aleco reversed the angle on the screen, revealing *Venture*'s tachyon beams searching the space in front of the wormhole's entrance and finding nothing. Sisko felt himself relax. He hadn't anticipated any ships trailing *Defiant* from the Gamma Quadrant, but then, nobody had expected the Romulan warbird behind the Breen freighter.

"Captain," said Aleco. "We're being hailed by the *Enterprise*."

"On-screen."

Just as the wormhole closed with a sparkle of light and *Venture* soared past where it had been, the viewer blinked and the image of Captain Picard appeared. Worf, his first officer, sat beside him, as did a Bajoran man, likely the ship's counselor. *"Captain Sisko,"* Picard said from the command chair. *"Welcome home."*

"Thank you, Captain," Sisko said. He understood Picard's sentiment, but he couldn't help but think that he no longer considered Bajor home.

"Have you anything to report from the Gamma Quadrant?" Picard asked. *"Anything that the 'guardians of the wormhole' need to know about?"*

"No, nothing," Sisko said. "We detected no activity anywhere near the Idran system, and the Dominion remains, by their own choice, sequestered within their own borders."

"That's good to hear," Picard said. *"As must be obvious, the* Enterprise *has joined the* Brisbane, *the* Canterbury, *and the* Venture *on patrol in the system. With* Defiant, *that will complete the set of sentries, according to Starfleet Command."*

"That's a considerable force," Sisko noted.

"At the moment," Picard said, *"Starfleet considers the Bajoran system and the wormhole considerable vulnerabilities."*

"Understood," Sisko said. "My orders are to contact Starfleet Command and meet with Captain Ro on Bajor."

Picard stood from his chair and walked to the center of the *Enterprise* bridge. *"Before you do, Captain,"* he said, *"I think there's something that you might want to see."*

"Captain?" Sisko said.

Picard turned and gestured to one side, to a woman stationed at a freestanding console on the bridge's upper level. *"Transmitting,"* the woman said.

"We've just sent you local coordinates, Captain," Picard said. *"Have a look on your viewscreen."*

"All right," Sisko said. "*Defiant* out."

Picard nodded his acknowledgment as an empty field of stars returned to the screen.

"Coordinates received," said Aleco.

"All right, then," Sisko said. "Put it on-screen."

Aleco operated his controls, and the image on the viewer shifted. A different set of stars appeared, with something barely visible at the center of the screen. Sisko stood up and took a step forward. "What is that?" he said. It looked to him like a small ship, possibly two, but it made no sense to him why Picard would want him to see other Starfleet vessels. *You can't turn around in the Bajoran system without bumping into a Starfleet vessel.*

"Magnifying," said Aleco.

The viewer blinked again, and when it did, the unknown objects resolved themselves into a ship and something not immediately identifiable. Sisko recognized the vessel as a *Hercules*-class tug. It had a roughly triangular primary hull, with a *C*-shaped secondary structure trailing out from the base of the triangle; a warp nacelle rose from each side of the rear structure. A series of white beams emanated from the inside of the *C,* all of them connecting to a boxlike object even larger than the ship that towed it. The object looked essentially like a hemisphere with its peak truncated.

"What is it, Captain?" asked Stinson.

"I'm not sure precisely what it is," Sisko said. "It could be a docking module, a cargo bay, crew quarters, or maybe it's just a work module. But whatever it is, it appears to be the first piece to arrive for the construction of Starfleet's new Bajoran space station."

II

The Abjuration
of Rough Magic

Prospero: . . . . I have be-dimm'd
The noontide sun, call'd forth the mutinous winds,
And 'twixt the green sea and the azur'd vault
Set roaring war . . .
. . . . But this rough magic
I here abjure; and, when I have requir'd
Some heavenly music—which even now I do—
To work mine end upon their senses that
This airy charm is for, I'll break my staff,
Bury it certain fathoms in the earth,
And deeper than did ever plummet sound
I'll drown my book.

—William Shakespeare,
The Tempest, Act V, Scene 1

19

Morad had never before boarded a Romulan starship, and he doubted that many Cardassians ever had. He recalled hearing, years earlier, about a united Cardassian-Romulan task force that had attempted to engage the Dominion in battle, but which had been obliterated in an ambush. Fortunately, the charge he and his compatriots in the True Way had set for themselves would not require them to confront the Dominion—at least not directly, if the information that Chairwoman Sela had supplied proved accurate.

As the final preparations continued for the mission to come, Morad stood beside the command chair on the warbird's bridge. The Romulan commander sat there and surveyed his crew in the dim green glow that apparently signified the operation of the ship's cloak. At the moment, Morad heard few voices, and those that he did came in low, faraway tones over the communications system. The responsive notes of control panels provided most of the ambient sound, joined together by the droning undercurrent of the ship's impulse drive, which waited to take the warbird and its passengers on an impossibly long voyage.

Morad glanced past the Romulan commander at the other man who stood beside him. At least, Morad assumed Keln, the Breen engineer, was male. With the opaque, constantly worn environmental suit, though, as well as the harsh electronic rendering of his—or her—speech, who could tell? As he considered the matter, Morad realized that he not only didn't know what Breen looked like outside of their suits, but whether or not they even had two distinct genders. For all he knew, their people came in *more* sexes than that, just as those bizarre Andorians did.

In many ways, it saddened Morad that the True Way, a fundamental pro-Cardassian movement, needed to ally with aliens in order to help bring about the Union's return to glory. But the last decade and a half had been beyond difficult for Cardassia. In large part, Morad's people had brought about their problems by not assuming their natural superiority, not asserting their inherent dominance over other races. Central

Command had given up on Bajor, allowing the weak to escape their duty to serve the stronger. After that, there had been negotiations—*Negotiations!*—with the usurping Federation, who coddled and protected the Bajorans. Then finally, when the righteous war had come, Cardassia's own people, members of its own military, had turned into traitors and handed victory to the UFP and its allies.

And now we don't just negotiate with the Federation, Morad thought bitterly, *we* ally *with them.* Castellan Garan had committed the entire population of the Union to an association that included more than the sanctimonious UFP, more than the brutish Klingons, more than the avaricious Ferengi; it included the *Bajorans.* Just the thought brought Morad to the threshold of apoplexy.

On the main viewscreen, the Vir-Akzelen asteroid sat in position in open space, the science complex based there clinging to its rough surface. Morad and his True Way compatriots had used *Formek,* the tug they'd acquired, to tow the entire Tzenkethi facility to its new location precisely 3.2 light-years from Bajor. Nelzik had specified that her equipment would function from as far away as 5.3 light-years, but even she agreed that it would be wiser not to tax the new technology.

The first officer of *Vetruvis,* Subcommander Analest, paced over to stand before Commander Kozik. For a Romulan, Morad thought, even with the pointed ears and the wavy forehead, Analest looked appealing. "Commander," she said, "the crew reports that all systems are ready. The cloak is functioning at optimal levels. The impulse engines are on standby, the singularity drive ready for faster-than-light travel at your command. Our course for the Bronis star system has been calculated from our point of egress and entered into the navigational computer."

Bronis II, Morad knew, would stand in for Overne III, the site to which the Breen and the Romulans had proceeded in their first attempt to acquire the needed equipment. That mission had failed because the Typhon Pact lacked a direct route to the Gamma Quadrant other than through Federation space. But circumstances had changed.

Like Overne III, Bronis II hosted an enormous starship manufacturing complex in the Dominion. Once they arrived there, the Breen engineer, Keln, would identify and extract the equipment that the Typhon Pact required in order to develop quantum slipstream drive. With that capability, the Pact would be able to attack the Federation and its allies—though not Cardassia, per the True Way's agreement with Sela. Castellan Garan would have little choice but to withdraw from the Khitomer Accords, and once Cardassia's ties with the UFP and Bajor had been cut, its people could finally begin their journey back to greatness.

"Are you ready, Keln?" Kozik asked the Breen.

Keln replied with a short burst of electronic distortion. The commander appeared to accept that as an affirmative response.

"And you, Morad?" Kozik asked.

"I am," Morad said.

Kozik nodded to Analest, who stepped to the center of the bridge. "Centurion Rentin," she said, "open a channel to the laboratory."

At a console to Morad's left, Rentin worked her controls. "Channel open," she said.

"Go ahead, Morad," Kozik told him.

Morad took a breath, then carefully enunciated, "*Vetruvis* to Vir-Akzelen."

The image of the Tzenkethi facility replaced that of the asteroid on the main viewscreen. Morad saw the lightly shining—*And lovely*—form of Nelzik, the project's lead scientist. When she spoke, he could not hear the chimelike quality of her voice, its sound obviously swallowed up by the Romulan ship's translation software and spit out as a feminine but distinctly not Tzenkethi voice. "*Vetruvis, this is Nelzik,*" she said.

"Nelzik, this is Morad," he said. "We are ready for you to begin."

"*I understand, Morad,*" Nelzik said. On the screen, she gestured to her colleagues, who set to work on their control panels. Then, to Morad, she said, "*Prepare to commence insertion.*"

Morad turned to Kozik. "We should also watch the asteroid, Commander."

Kozik nodded to his first officer, who ordered Rentin to display Vir-Akzelen on the screen. The view of Nelzik shrank to fill half of the display, while the other half showed the asteroid hanging in space. After a moment, a ray of vibrant blue light hurtled from the far side of the complex and up into space. As Morad watched, the light fractured into other beams that formed a conic shape. He waited with a mixture of anticipation and anxiety.

When the beams vanished, Morad could feel Kozik's gaze turn to him, no doubt skeptical and accusing. But then a grand whorl of blazing red light coiled into existence. It curved around a radiantly white core. A probe launched from the asteroid and soared directly into the center of the vermilion whirlpool.

On the other half of the screen, Nelzik consulted a display. *"The wormhole is generating . . . and has reached a length of one light-year . . . two light-years . . . three."* Morad knew that the critical juncture of the Tzenkethi's scientific and engineering marvel lay just ahead, the final part of the process that had been borne out in theory and in simulations, but that they hadn't been able to test in practice. *"Three-point-one light-years,"* Nelzik reported. *"Three-point-two."*

Morad waited for the essential piece of information. And then waited too long. He felt his expectations sink into a morass of disappointment.

And then Nelzik announced, *"We have contact with the Bajoran wormhole."* She paused again—maddeningly so for Morad—and studied her screens. *"We have a solid connection,"* she said at last. *"Our wormhole is stable, and its far terminus is clear into the Bajoran wormhole."*

Morad looked to Kozik. "Let's go," he said to the commander.

"Ahead one-quarter impulse," Kozik ordered. "Give me a whole-screen image."

Nelzik blinked off the viewer, and the flame-red wormhole resized to fill much of the display. It grew larger as *Vetruvis* drew nearer. The white light at its center became almost blinding.

"Wave intensities are increasing swiftly," somebody reported, obviously from the sensor station. "And I'm detecting very high proton counts."

On-screen, the colored sides of the wormhole fell away, leaving its dazzling white heart. For a terrifying moment, it seemed to Morad as though they headed directly into a star. He feared that all his hopes would end in the fiery destruction of *Vetruvis*.

But then a tunnellike formation appeared on the viewer. Luminous streams of red light flowed around the ship. The warbird passed through enormous circles that seemed either to constitute or support the outer structure of the wormhole. Sets of concentric circles lined its periphery.

The ship began to quiver, like a boat entering the rough water of a river. Morad heard a whine develop in the sound of the impulse drive. The ship bucked, and he had to quickly adjust the position of his feet to prevent himself from toppling to the deck.

"Instruments show a change in the readings ahead," said the officer at sensors.

"Is the wormhole destabilizing?" Kozik demanded.

"No, sir, it doesn't appear so. I think that—"

The shapes and contours on the screen suddenly changed, their colors going from scorching red to a cooler blue, the outlines of everything visible becoming clearer and better defined. The motion of the ship settled, though it did not calm completely. The bleat of the impulse drive eased back to a steady hum.

All of the differences forced Morad to wonder about the actual stability of Nelzik's wormhole. She and her colleagues hadn't been able to make any wormhole they created maintain its far end in a single location for very long, but their theory had told them that they could change that by anchoring their wormhole to something established and constant—the only known choice for such an anchor being the Bajoran wormhole. Morad could only hope that Nelzik's theories proved true in practice. Otherwise, he would spend the rest of his life seventy thousand light-years from home . . . or he would have to chance that Kozik could successfully run *Vetruvis* through what must surely be a Federation gauntlet in the Bajoran system.

Suddenly, another turning flux of color swam into view up ahead, opening from the inside out. Like the lights of a city to a traveler lost in the desert, stars appeared and promised salvation. *Vetruvis* raced forward and into their midst.

Analest strode to a console and glanced over another officer's shoulder, then said, "Confirming that we have reached the Gamma Quadrant."

Morad felt exhilarated. It took considerable willpower for him not to call out in triumph. All of his careful planning—his reaching out beyond the True Way to the Tzenkethi, to the Romulans, his willingness to accept their assistance when his goals coincided with theirs, his desire for Cardassia to have power over a wormhole of its own, his realization that the Typhon Pact's failure at the Bajoran wormhole could be surmounted—all of it had started moving rapidly toward fruition. In just days, once they collected the equipment they needed, they would be heading back to the Alpha Quadrant with the means to defeat the Federation. And with that, the Cardassian Union could reclaim both Bajor and its rightful place in the galaxy.

Beside Morad, Commander Kozik said, "Set course for the Dominion."

20

The turbolift climbed along the outer wall, carrying Ro toward the second level of what had once been the Wyntara Mas Control Center, a management hub to oversee transportation within the province. Over the previous few weeks, it had transformed into something much different: Bajoran Space Central, a ground-based substitute for the lost Deep Space 9. With a much smaller crew capacity, no facilities for visitors, and only a limited presence in space—if that presence ever arrived—the new complex would fall well short of providing a complete replacement for all of DS9's capabilities and services. But with the transfer of security for the wormhole to a squadron of Starfleet vessels, BSC would at least allow the resumption of transport and trade through Bajoran space. The rate and volume of traffic through the system and—once Starfleet Command approved it—to and from the Gamma Quadrant would necessarily have to drop, but the center would still supply a significant degree of continuity while the Corps of Engineers constructed another space station.

The lift alighted at the second level, the addition of which had doubled the number of personnel who could work in the complex on a single shift. Ro stepped out onto the new story at its open front side, where a transparent-aluminum barrier rose a meter and a half to a padded rail that ran across its top edge. The captain walked to the center of the floor, leaned on the railing, and peered out at the forward end of the building. No exterior alterations had been made to the two enclosed rooms that sat in the corners, though the plans called for an eventual expansion of her office.

Where the name of the control center had once emblazoned the forward wall above the two rooms, a large viewscreen had been hung. At present, it showed a view from orbit, from a runabout, *Yolja*. Stars mostly filled the display, but a verdant, cloudless arc of Bajor cut across the bottom right-hand corner, and one of the planet's five moons, Derna, peeked out from just beyond the horizon. Ro hoped that *Yolja* would not remain alone in orbit much longer.

The captain turned and surveyed the expanse of the second level. Half-walls had been raised to divide the area into workspaces, some larger than others, depending on the use to which they would be put. She heard the agglomeration of many voices as her crew prepared to resume operations as best they could.

Ro turned and made her way to the nearest pathway between the workspaces. She walked along toward the rear of the building, swinging her head left and right as she did so, taking in the sight of her crew discharging their duties. A number of personnel saw her and offered a smile or a nod or a verbal greeting.

The captain reached the rear of the building and turned into the pathway there. Huddled together over a padd, security officers Cardok and Shul Torem carried on an animated conversation. As she recalled, Shul had spent more years on Deep Space 9 than just about anybody else, living there with his wife, Aba, a civilian. After the destruction of the station, Aba had relocated to Bajor to stay with family she and her husband had there, and so Ro had made sure to post Shul planetside.

Reaching the next pathway, the captain headed back toward the front of the second level. She passed by one workspace, where she saw Lieutenant Merimark busy at her computer interface, and an odd memory recurred to her. Ro recalled that, for some reason nobody had ever been able to adequately explain to her, Captain Vaughn had at some point taken to calling her *Stefka*, despite her first name being *Kaitlin*.

Thinking of Vaughn brought a sadness to Ro, but also a sense of hope. Not long after she had first arrived on Bajor to resettle her crew and plan for the future, she had visited the Vanadwan Monastery. On the heels of so much loss, Ro hadn't particularly wanted to pay a final visit to an old friend with his still-mourning daughter, but she considered Prynn a friend too, and so felt that she needed to support her.

At Prynn's request, Ro had selected something to read at Vaughn's bedside. She intended to bring the actual book she owned that contained the piece, but it had been lost with the station. She found a soft copy of it and carried it with her to Vanadwan on her padd. An old tale she'd first heard as a child and which had always stayed with her, "Song of the Traveler" seemed a particularly apt story for Vaughn. Prynn seemed to appreciate it, and by the time Ro finished reading, they both had tears in their eyes.

The experience had been sad, but also uplifting in a way Ro hadn't anticipated. It felt like an affirmation of life to pay tribute to Vaughn, but also a kindness to finally let him go—because, after all, he had truly been gone for a long time. Ro also found a deeper connection with Prynn, and believed that the closure she had at last decided to experience would free her to return to a normal, healthy, fulfilling life.

Ro arrived back at the front of the second story and turned

right, toward the other side wall. When she reached it, she entered
the other turbolift that had been installed and descended back
to the first level. Once there, she did as she had above, taking
a brief stroll among her crew. Later that afternoon, just before
the center would officially go on line, she would address them,
tell them of the tremendous pride she had in them, let them
know how much they impressed her with their stalwart efforts
in such a time of adversity, and thank them for making the BSC
operational.

When Ro had first seen the erstwhile Wyntara Mas Control
Center, she'd had serious doubts about whether it could really
be converted into a workable replacement for DS9, and not
just because of the station's massive size, abundant facilities,
and location in space. The control center did not seem ideally
suited—or at all suited, really—to providing a base for her crew.
But with no other better options, she forged ahead anyway. And
while Transportation Minister Kifal's original estimate of only
ten days to transition the complex to a minimally functioning
Starfleet facility had proven unworkable, Ro's engineering staff
had ultimately made the transition happen. The addition of
Chief O'Brien helped enormously, although, with the design
and construction of the new station beginning, the captain
knew that she could use even more additions to her engineering
crew—a need she had already taken steps to address.

Minister Kifal had also calculated that, on top of the ten
days he'd allotted for the initial adaptation of the center, it would
require another thirty days to complete all necessary upgrades.
Chief O'Brien believed that it would take at least twice as
long to bring the BSC to an optimal level. Still, they would
go operational later that day, and Ro felt grateful for that. She
and her crew needed something better to do than replacing old,
outdated equipment with modern but temporary equipment.

Ro reached the rear of the building, where the two rooms
in the corners there afforded 'fresher facilities. Between them
stretched the largest single space that had been set aside by
itself—though it had been subdivided within—and the only
area contained by full walls; it housed the infirmary. The

captain approached its entryway and looked inside. She could see the main examination table off to the left, as well as several bio-beds along the far wall. Nurse Edgardo Juarez and Forensics Specialist Michael Strang stood talking together over a computer interface, while Doctor Pascal Boudreaux worked at a bank of medical displays.

Ro didn't see Doctor Bashir, which might have been for the best. He'd been furious when she'd had Lieutenant Commander Douglas taken in for questioning about the bombs planted on Deep Space 9, though the captain had emphasized to him that Sarina hadn't been charged with any crimes. Ro's subsequent discussion with Bashir, after the doctor's visit from the Section 31 operative, had unfolded even more uncomfortably, although the captain thought it might actually end up yielding a positive result.

Moving on, Ro walked up the next pathway, headed to the front of the building. She left the workspace and continued on toward her office. As she passed between the two transporter platforms, she gazed up at the viewscreen, where she saw essentially the same orbital vista she'd seen a few minutes earlier. When she looked back down, she noticed that her office door stood open.

Ro stepped up to the doorway and peered inside. Apparently studying one of the early architectural renderings of the new space station, which the captain had printed out and hung on her wall, her latest crew transfer stood with his back to her. Even by the back of his head, though, she recognized him. "Lieutenant *Commander*," she said, emphasizing his promotion in rank since last she'd seen him.

Nog turned to face her. "*Captain* Ro," he said. He stuck out his hand, and she took it in her own, but then they both added their free hands. "How soon before it's *Admiral* Ro?"

"Not until the Fire Caves freeze over," she said with a snicker. "I'll actually be lucky if I can manage to hold on to the rank of captain for very long."

"Oh, I don't know about that," Nog said, his expression turning serious. "Word is that you saved more than fifty-five hundred lives in an almost impossible situation."

"Thanks for saying so, Nog," Ro told him, "but, you know . . ." She left unfinished her thought about all those who'd perished aboard DS9.

"Yeah, I know," Nog said quietly.

Seeking to move the subject away from Deep Space 9, Ro stepped inside and closed the door behind her. She pointed to a chair in the corner—she'd had the replicator removed and placed just outside—and both she and Nog sat down. "I have to tell you how pleased I am that you accepted my request to transfer here."

"Well, I appreciate your making it a request and not an order," Nog said.

"I was surprised to learn that you went back to security," Ro said. "I wasn't sure you still wanted to be an engineer, but I thought if you did, then this might be a good opportunity for you to get back into it."

"Actually, I only accepted a position in security to get aboard the *Challenger*," Nog said. "I was hoping that the chief engineer position would become available."

Ro didn't mention that Nog had already achieved the same position on the station. "I guess you'd had enough of Deep Space Nine," she said, remembering when Nog had come to her to request a transfer. She started to wonder if perhaps Nog had no longer wanted to work under her command. *But then why would he agree to come back?*

Nog shrugged. "At the time I decided to leave, it was an easy choice," he said. "Don't get me wrong; I loved my time there. I mean, I grew up there."

"And maybe that was part of it?" Ro asked. "You weren't really clear about why you wanted to leave."

"Maybe that had something to do with it," Nog said. "I'd been there as a boy, and so as a man, I suppose I wanted to get out and see more of the galaxy." He paused and seemed to consider this. "I think I also wanted to be more than an engineer . . . not something *else,* like in security, but something . . . I don't know . . . *more.*"

"You mean like command?" Ro asked.

"You're joking, right?"

"Not at all," Ro said. "I mean, I'm not offering you my job."

Nog smiled. His skewed, pointed teeth reminded Ro of Quark. "Why would I want your job?" he said. "Commanding a space station without a space station."

"There are plenty of land-based starbases throughout the Federation," Ro said.

"Yeah, but none that have no orbital facilities and are housed in a barn," Nog joked.

Ro laughed. "It does kind of look like that, doesn't it?" she said. "Still, I'm convinced we can be effective here, at least in the short term."

"I have no doubt of it," Nog said. "Which I guess is the real reason I'm here. I'm happy to face the small challenges that this place will offer, but I understand that there are some leadership positions available for the engineers working on the new station."

"When you accepted the transfer," Ro told him, "I also assigned you to work with the Corps of Engineers. You and Chief O'Brien will be part of the lead design team."

"That's fantastic," Nog said. "Thank you, Captain."

"You've earned it," Ro said. "You're a good engineer, and you've shown . . . well, *more.* I know you can do this."

"I'm looking forward to it," Nog said. He lapsed into silence for a moment, then said, "You know, I think the main reason I transferred away from here was the station."

Ro's brow creased in confusion. "You mean the actual station?" she said. "Deep Space Nine itself?"

"I mean Terok Nor," Nog said. "The *Cardassian* space station. I'm a Starfleet engineer. I wanted to work on Federation technology."

"Well, you'll definitely get the chance now," Ro said. "We're supposed to be getting a state-of-the-art facility."

"I'll make sure we do," Nog said. "It'll be great to work with Chief O'Brien again too."

"He wasn't here for more than two days before he started suggesting that he could use a few more engineers," Ro said.

"Particularly experienced engineers. I'm sure he'll be thrilled to find out you've transferred."

"You mean he doesn't know?"

"I just told him that I picked up another engineer," Ro said.

"Thank you, Captain."

"You already said that."

"I know, but . . . we don't even have a station yet and I already feel like I'm home," Nog said. "I enjoyed my experience on the *Challenger*, and I liked the people I served with, but it never really felt like it did here. I think I like the idea of roaming around the galaxy, but there's something about staying in one place for the long term. You can always travel, but it's good to have a place to come back to . . . someplace . . . I don't know . . . I guess, permanent."

A shadow darkened Ro's thoughts for a moment as she considered the *im*permanence of DS9, but she forced her way past it. "You're going to be helping design and build a completely new space station," she said, "so I'm sure that you can include a dedicated room for yourself."

"And an extra holosuite or two for Uncle Quark," Nog said.

"Don't even suggest that to him," Ro said. "It'll be all he ever talks about until I promise to try and get that for him."

"I won't need to tell him," Nog said. "He'll think of it on his own."

Ro nodded, thinking that Quark would probably mention it any day. She started to ask if Nog had spoken with his uncle lately when somebody knocked on the door. "Come in," Ro called.

The door opened and Chief O'Brien poked his head inside. "Pardon me, Captain, but I thought you might—" He stopped when he spied Nog sitting in the corner. "Hey, Nog!" Turning back to Ro, he asked, "Is *this* the new engineer who's transferring in?"

"He is," Ro said. "Assistant chief engineer here, and co-foreman on the new station, along with you and the SCE representative."

"That's fantastic," O'Brien said, and the echo of Nog's own

words underscored for Ro that she'd made the right choice. But then the chief voiced the major concern that she'd had when requesting Nog's reassignment. "Of course, you were a chief engineer yourself. I hope that's not going to be a problem."

"That's fine," Nog said, waving a hand before him. "I just want to get back to engineering, and having the chance to help design and build a new space station . . . it's a great opportunity."

"Oh, I know," O'Brien agreed.

"Besides, when I was your assistant before," Nog said, "I always did all the hard work anyway."

"If by 'hard work,' you mean hunkering down in an access conduit and eating tube grubs, I agree," O'Brien said.

"That happened *one* time," Nog protested. "And I hadn't had any breakfast."

O'Brien looked over at Ro, pointed a thumb in Nog's direction, and said, "Next thing you know, he'll be in the tool locker chowing down on a slug steak."

"Better than that . . . what was it . . . potato casserole you had that time," Nog said.

"Hey, that casserole was my mother's very own recipe," O'Brien said.

"You used a recipe?" Nog said. "I just assumed it was trial and error . . . mostly error."

"Listen—"

"Boys, boys," Ro said, putting an end to the playful interaction. "You two can do this when you're in a Jefferies tube somewhere." She enjoyed seeing the byplay between the two friends, but she still had a lot of work to do before the afternoon. "Was there something you wanted to see me about, Chief?"

"Yes, sir," O'Brien said. "I thought you might want to see what's going on." He pointed outside her office.

Ro rose and followed O'Brien out of her office, as did Nog. When they all stood in the main section of the building, the chief turned and gestured up at the viewscreen. Where before there had been empty space, a half dozen ships now floated. They each had a long, flat platform, with a superstructure perched at one end. Four of the six had been maneuvered together in pairs and connected with access tubes, and runabouts currently worked to bring the remaining two tenders into position. As they watched, another runabout swept in and landed on one of the platforms, filling about a quarter of its surface area.

"Excellent," Ro said. She turned to O'Brien. "Chief, would you show our new engineer around? We've only got about three hours until we open for business."

"'Open for business'?" Nog said. "Captain, I think you've been spending too much time around my uncle."

"Maybe so," Ro said with a smile. "Chief, find Desca and make sure that we're still on schedule. I need to contact Captain Euler on the *Canterbury* to talk with him about getting some of her crew onto the tenders."

"Yes, sir," O'Brien said, and he and Nog started toward the workspaces.

Ro turned back to her office so that she could contact the *Canterbury,* but before she reentered her office, she glanced back up at the viewscreen. She watched as a pair of runabouts—*Brahmaputra and . . . Is that the* Rubicon?—guided one of the free tenders toward the other. Then she headed back into her office, energized about the prospect of really getting back to work.

21

"It is beautiful up here," Kasidy said.

Kira sat with her friend beneath a broad umbrella on one of the many terraces at the Vanadwan Monastery. The afternoon had turned misty, and a light fog had begun to drift across the lower elevations. From their lofty vantage, it looked almost as though they had taken a trip to the legendary cloud city of Stratos.

On the glass-topped table between the two women spread the remains of the lunch they'd shared. Amid the mostly empty plates, Kasidy had her hand wrapped around a mug of *deka* tea, while Kira sipped at a *raktajino*. A piece of half-eaten *tuwaly* pie sat in front of Kasidy.

Kira followed her friend's gaze out over the encroaching haze. "This place always seems to inspire tranquillity," Kira said. "That, and a lot of daydreaming."

"We're at a monastery," Kasidy said. "Aren't you supposed to call it 'meditation'?"

"Oh, right," Kira said, smiling. She felt a bit of a chill in the air, and thought she'd been right to don her traditional vedek's robe, with its heavier, russet-colored material. She looked over to check on Kasidy, but she also seemed comfortable, wearing a dark blue jacket over her gold blouse. Kira hadn't seen Kasidy since they'd been rescued by the *Enterprise* crew, and it felt good to just relax and talk. "I'm really glad to hear that Rebecca's doing so well in school."

"She loves it," Kasidy said. "And at least so far, she's a much better student than her mother ever was."

"Is she still insisting that she's going to be a 'space captain'?" Kira asked.

"Oh, absolutely," Kasidy said. "She loves all those spaceship models that Ben and I got for her, but at this point, I think the thing she's most enamored of is being able to order people around." Kasidy leaned forward across the table, as if about to reveal something in confidence. "Rebecca had a few friends over at the house the other day, and I couldn't help doing a little eavesdropping. They were playing 'spaceship,' and Rebecca was Captain Sisko, while the others were all just crewwomen. When she gave them orders, there was no name, it was just 'Crewwoman, do this' and 'Crewwoman, do that.'"

"Thank goodness she hasn't found out about admirals yet," Kira said. Kasidy opened her eyes wide in mock horror, and then laughed. Kira took a swallow of her raktajino, then asked, "So how about you, Kasidy? You haven't said much about yourself. How are you doing these days?"

"I'm all right," Kasidy said, in a manner that sounded far from convincing. "Life's certainly been . . . interesting."

"Is that good?" Kira wanted to know.

"I don't know," Kasidy said. "It may be 'interesting' as in the old human curse, 'May you live in interesting times.'"

Kira tried to process that, because at first, the statement didn't seem like an expression of ill will. "You mean . . . 'interesting' like the Occupation was 'interesting'?"

Kasidy nodded. "Like the destruction of Deep Space Nine was 'interesting.'"

The station, Kira thought. "How are you handling all of that? It was all pretty traumatic." Kira knew, because her life had for so long been defined by such events.

"It was difficult," Kasidy agreed. "I'm all right, I guess. I mean, I'm not waking up screaming in the middle of the night or anything. I've seen a counselor a few times . . . mostly dealing with my grief about losing my friends on the *Xhosa*. But overall, I'm doing well. I have Rebecca to keep me grounded and focus my attention."

"She does do that," Kira said.

Kasidy drank some of her tea, then asked, "What about you, Nerys? How have you handled what happened to us?"

Mindful that Kasidy, given her history with Benjamin, didn't much like hearing about the Prophets, Kira said, "I just feel grateful that we survived."

"You don't feel that maybe the Prophets had something to do with that?" Kasidy asked, surprising Kira.

"I didn't say that," she told Kasidy. "I think the Prophets have to do with a great many things." Kira paused, and then in an attempt to provide a little lightness, she said, "I mean . . . look at me." She ran a hand down the front of her vedek's robe.

Kasidy smiled, but only thinly. "Right," she said, "but . . . we ended up in the wormhole."

Kira held up her open hands, palms skyward. "Sometimes the intervention of the Prophets is more obvious than at other times."

"I guess so," Kasidy said, a response that also surprised Kira. "So do you remember anything while we were in there?"

"No," Kira said. "The last thing I recall is being in the docking ring with you when the emergency bulkheads closed." She recalled telling Benjamin the same thing not that long ago. "The next thing I knew, I was waking up in the sickbay aboard the *Enterprise*."

Kasidy nodded, but her eyes looked faraway. Kira gave her a moment. When she didn't continue, Kira asked, "Why? Do you remember being in the—" Naturally inclined to say *Celestial Temple*, she didn't, for Kasidy's sake. "—wormhole?"

"Me?" Kasidy asked, almost as though shocked out of a trance. "I was just asking about you because . . . you know, because of your beliefs and all."

"Oh, okay," Kira said, though she noted that Kasidy hadn't actually answered her question. "So how are things with Benjamin?"

"He's on the *Defiant* at the moment, waiting for the *Robinson* to be repaired," Kasidy said. "He plans on spending some time with Rebecca here on Bajor next week."

"Good," Kira said. "That's good." She knew that Kasidy thought it very important that Rebecca grow up knowing her father and having his influence in her life, even if he couldn't stay with them. Kira believed the same thing, and so it pleased her that Benjamin made sure he spent time with his daughter.

With a slight lull in the conversation, Kira once again drank from her raktajino. She finished it and set her cup down on the table. The mist had stopped, she saw, leaving everything covered with just a thin layer of moisture.

Suddenly Kasidy looked over at her with a very serious expression. Kira suspected what she would say. "I signed the petition to dissolve our marriage."

"I didn't want to say anything," Kira told her, "but Benjamin mentioned it to me. He was here just before he headed up to the *Defiant*."

"Right, I remember," Kasidy said. "How *is* Elias?"

"As of this morning, his body was still breathing," Kira said. She hesitated to use the word *alive*. "He may last a few more days, maybe even a week, but it'll be soon now."

"Ben thought a lot of him," Kasidy said.

"Quite a few people did," Kira said. "But I'm glad his daughter's finally able to let go. For his sake, but mostly for hers."

Again, Kasidy fell silent, obviously with her own thoughts,

perhaps about Vaughn. Kira recalled the first time she'd met him. He'd come aboard from *Enterprise* just after a renegade Jem'Hadar force had attacked the station. Strong, intelligent, and confident, Vaughn later ended up helping save Deep Space 9 and its crew from those same Jem'Hadar, and then asked if he could stay on as her executive officer. For all his self-assuredness, though, he also possessed a vulnerability that—

"He hasn't filed the petition," Kasidy said. "I checked the courthouse in Adarak on my way here."

Kira didn't know what to say. "I know Benjamin's been busy aboard the *Defiant* . . ." A statement without much value, she chided herself. As she thought about it, though, she didn't understand why Benjamin would delay in making official something he'd been seeking for quite some time.

"I don't even know why I checked, or why I'm thinking about it," Kasidy said, but plainly it had been on her mind. "Ben's been very clear about why he can't be with me."

"I know," Kira said. "I'm sorry."

Kasidy peered over at Kira. She looked sad, but Kira saw no tears in her eyes. "I know you are," Kasidy said. "But you agree with him, don't you?"

"It's not my place to agree or disagree," Kira said. She did not want to discuss the prophecy upon which Benjamin acted. Kira felt bad enough that, at the time he'd decided against going through with his marriage, she'd told him that he was doing the right thing.

"No, it might not be your place," Kasidy said, "but that doesn't mean you don't have an opinion."

"My opinion really doesn't matter," Kira insisted. "I just wish that the situation were different."

"So do I," Kasidy said. "In fact, I'm thinking of making things different myself."

"I'm not sure what you mean," Kira said. *But I don't like the sound of it.*

"I mean that I'm thinking of leaving Bajor."

"Oh," Kira said. She immediately reacted negatively. She wanted to tell her friend that she couldn't run away from her problems, that she shouldn't uproot her daughter from her home, that she had friends on Bajor who loved her . . . but Kira didn't. Because how could she presume to know what would be best for Kasidy and Rebecca?

"This place . . . Bajor . . . and Kendra . . . especially Adarak . . . this place has been mostly good for Rebecca and me," Kasidy said. "And for Ben, when he was here, and when he comes around now. And the people have been too . . . except . . ."

"I know," Kira said, perceiving that Kasidy didn't want to talk about Rebecca's abduction, and that she'd come to consider it an aberration. "You built a home for yourselves here. Literally, yes, but I mean figuratively too."

"We did," Kasidy said. "But with Ben gone, it's not the same. You're here, Nerys, and there's Jake and Rena, and Jasmine, and Rozahn Kit and my other friends, but . . . the last couple of years here without Ben . . ." She paused, obviously searching for the right words to express herself. "It was different when Jake and I were building the house, and afterward, when I moved in. Back then, I was waiting for Ben to come back. Now I'm not waiting for anything."

Kasidy quieted, and Kira didn't want to say anything that would interrupt her thoughts. After a moment, Kasidy went on. "And even with the Prophets and the prophecies and the Emissary and the Avatar, even with all of that, the Bajoran people have been respectful and very kind. But without Ben, it's beginning to be too much . . . too much, and at the same time, not enough. With the *Xhosa* and some of my crew gone, with Jake and Rena headed for Earth, and Ben off on the *Robinson* or the *Defiant* or some other starship . . . you know I love you, Nerys, but I really don't have all that much keeping me here anymore."

"I love you too," Kira said. "Does Rebecca know you're thinking about this?"

"No, not yet," Kasidy said. "She loves it here, and that's important, of course, but Bajor's all she's ever known. I'm sure she can be happy elsewhere too. And it might be better to relocate now while she's still so young."

"I'll miss you," Kira said.

"I'll miss you too," Kasidy said. "But you know, even if Ben suddenly decided to come back, and even if I could find a way to trust him again, I think I still might be considering this move." She looked earnestly at Kira. "Do you think I'm being selfish?"

"I think you're trying to figure out what's best for you and your family," Kira said. "Whatever you decide to do, I'll support you."

"Thank you, Nerys," Kasidy said. "That means a lot."

Kira smiled. "Any ideas where you might go?"

"A few," Kasidy said. "Earth, maybe. My brother's on Cestus Three. Oh, and I've been hearing some very good things about the colony on Allamegras."

"Is that the planet with the 'rainbow moon' effect?" Kira asked.

"Yes, that's the one." Kasidy sounded genuinely excited about it.

"I bet that must be quite a sight," Kira said. When Kasidy didn't respond, Kira asked, "Are you close to making a decision?"

"I don't know," Kasidy said. "Obviously, there's no real rush, but if we're going to do it, I'd rather do it and get on with our lives."

"That makes sense," Kira said.

"So, yeah, I guess I am close to—"

A series of tones warbled out an insistent call. Kasidy reached down to the pocket of her jacket and withdrew a timepiece. "Oh, it's already time for me to go and get Rebecca from school. She's learning about volcanism, so I told her we could visit Volcano Park in the Southern Islands."

"She'll love that," Kira said. "It looks like the surface of an alien world down there."

"Well, if she could take a spaceship to get there, it would be perfect," Kasidy said. "But since I want to get home in time for dinner, she's going to have to settle for the transporter."

Kasidy rose and started to collect up her dishes, but Kira told her not to bother, that she would take care of it. "Thanks," Kasidy said. "And thanks for listening."

"Anytime," Kira said. She stood up and hugged her friend.

Kasidy started up a sloping walkway that led to the transporter plaza, and Kira watched her go. Once Kasidy had passed out of sight around a curve, Kira sat back down. She picked up her raktajino, but saw that she'd already finished it, so she set the cup back down.

Over the course of their time together, Kasidy had talked about many things—things important to her and to her family—but Kira found herself thinking most about something that she hadn't said. When asked if she remembered being inside the wormhole after Deep Space 9 had been destroyed, she evaded answering—which of course managed to answer the question without the need for words. Since Kasidy had suddenly begun to consider leaving Bajor, Kira wondered if something *had* happened inside the Celestial Temple, something that had perhaps scared her enough to chase her from the system.

I hope not, Kira thought. She wished she could find out just what Kasidy had experienced without having to press Kasidy herself about it. Maybe then Kira would know how best to help her friend.

As she sat thinking, it began to rain.

Esperanza Piñiero, chief of staff for President Bacco, stood in a VIP passenger lounge on Spacedock and peered out through a port at Earth. Below her—she didn't know how many kilometers away—lay the immense sweep of Europe. She saw the Americas in darkness, spied the day-night terminator tracing across western Africa, and knew that morning had come to Paris and the Palais de la Concorde not long before.

Of course, she thought. *I'm here feeling like it's after midnight*—long *after midnight.*

As though to underscore her thoughts, Piñiero yawned widely. Alone in the lounge—her Federation Security escort, Magdalena Ferson, waited just outside—she didn't even bother to cover her mouth. She only wanted to get back to her apartment and crawl into bed.

It had been an exhausting three days. Months ago, she

had scheduled the president on a whirlwind "tour of the solar system," something of a glad-handing trip in preparation for her reelection campaign the following year. *Of course, I can't even get her to tell me* if *she's going to run for office again.* President Bacco had done such a fine job as the Federation's chief executive that Piñiero desperately hoped—for the sake of two quadrants, scores of worlds, and trillions of sentient beings—that she would place her name on the ballot.

Piñiero hoped that most of the time, anyway. But after the past three days, she fantasized about arriving back in Paris to discover that the president had tendered her resignation and returned to her home on Cestus III. After a good night's sleep—*Or two!*—Piñiero would follow right behind her into retirement.

The trip would not have taken the president all that far from Earth. With the Federation still on high alert after the events at Deep Space 9 and the Bajoran wormhole, though, President Bacco had felt that she shouldn't leave Paris—and certainly not for something as scurrilous as a political tour. Starfleet had reinforced its presence along its borders near the Typhon Pact worlds, as had the Klingons, Cardassians, and Ferengi; not unexpectedly, the Breen, Tholians, and Tzenkethi had followed suit. The Federation had also rebuffed a clandestine appeal from the Romulans for a one-on-one summit of some kind. The president wanted peace above all, but believed that she should be in the capital, with her cabinet and the Federation Council, in case hostilities should erupt. With so many adversarial starship crews in such close proximity to one another, it would take just one errant phaser blast or disruptor bolt, or perhaps even merely a miscalculated navigational plan, to ignite the fuse in a room full of explosives.

But that didn't mean there was any reason for the chief of staff to stay close to home, Piñiero thought, even as she recognized the absurdity of her complaint. President Bacco had wanted simply to cancel the trip, but Piñiero had argued that she should go, that if anything did happen, Admiral Akaar and his staff at Starfleet Headquarters could handle it until a fast ship carried her on a quick jaunt back to Earth. The chief of staff also tried to impress upon the president the political importance of her paying a visit to New Berlin and Tycho City on Luna, of pressing the flesh in Bradbury Township and Utopia Planitia on Mars, of putting some face time in at Jupiter Station and Christopher's Landing out at the gas giants.

And I convinced her, all right.

As soon as President Bacco agreed about the political value of such a tour, Piñiero realized that she'd made a mistake in pushing so hard. The president opted not to cancel the trip, but to send the chief of staff in her stead. At that point, Piñiero suggested *postponing* the entire affair, but too late; her fate had been sealed.

I really need to learn when to keep my mouth shut, she thought, even as another yawn overcame her.

So she had filled in for President Bacco, an a priori impossible task. After three days of little or no sleep, scores of holovids, hundreds of hands shaken, and several billion kilometers of travel, Piñiero made the penultimate leg of her journey, taking a shuttle from the moon to Earth Spacedock. From there, she intended to transport down to the Palais, where she would make a quick report to the president about the trip, then head home for a couple of hours' sleep before going to her office to address all the issues that had surely piled up on her desk in her absence.

But it's never that easy, is it?

Piñiero's shuttle had arrived at Spacedock on time, but when she showed up with a transport pass to the Palais de la Concorde, the operator informed her that he did not see her name on the schedule. Under normal circumstances, she could just beam down to some other location and fix the issue when she got home, but once she attempted to get into the Palais without proper authorization, she became a security risk. So she would have to wait until they verified her identity, her transport pass, and the fact that a simple mistake had been made—probably by Zachary Manzanillo, the assistant chief of staff, with whom she would have to have a talk.

He'll probably tell me that the president put him up to it, she thought. *An object lesson about how hard I'm allowed to push on certain things.*

"Well," Piñiero said, her voice sounding loud in the empty room, "at least they put me in the VIP lounge instead of a holding cell." She realized that Magdalena probably had company outside the room of at least one or two Spacedock security guards, and that Piñiero wouldn't be allowed to leave until she'd been cleared.

Tired and frustrated, she turned from the port and examined the lounge. Not all that large, it had been appointed beautifully, with dark, elegant furniture, rich wall coverings, striking pieces of art, and just enough perfectly manicured plants. In her weariness, though, Piñiero hadn't noticed earlier that she saw no access points to companel compartments, sleeping modules, or even replicators. "Okay, so it *is* a holding cell," she said. "Just a *VIP* holding cell." Rather than fret about it, she decided that she should be thankful that she saw a door to a 'fresher tucked discreetly into a corner.

"And at least I have a beautiful view," she said, turning back to the port. Piñiero reached out a hand and leaned against the smooth, transparent surface. She felt wistful as she looked at Europe, where her bed waited for her.

And then something moved outside the port. The space before her eyes shimmered, as though she were seeing Earth through running water. Suddenly, where there had been nothing, there was something—something that should not have been there.

Piñiero turned and raced for the door as an alarm began to blare. The door didn't open when she reached it, and so she punched the activation panel beside it. The door slid open, and she saw that two Spacedock security guards did indeed stand with her personal agent.

"Maggie," Piñiero said, yelling to make herself heard over the sound of the alarm, "I need to speak with somebody in the Palais *right now*!" She looked not only at Magdalena, but at the other two guards as well. "I don't care what you have to do, but get me to a companel."

"Yes, ma'am," Magdalena said, and she turned and bolted down the corridor.

No doubt trained to do their jobs even in an emergency, the two Spacedock guards moved to block Piñiero's path, apparently just in case she chose to make a run for it. Instead, the chief of staff turned and walked back into the lounge. She paced back to the port.

Piñiero could feel her heart pounding in her chest as she stared out at the Romulan starship.

22

Fleet Admiral Devix stood on the bridge of the Imperial Fleet scout vessel *Enderavat* and gazed at the image of Earth filling the main viewscreen. Mostly a collection of deep blue, brown, and white patches, it really didn't look all that much different from Romulus. Devix's homeworld appeared a little more blue-green, perhaps a little paler, but from orbit, not much distinguished the two planets.

Once, long ago, Devix had envisioned himself taking in that view of Earth, as though from on high, just before he rained plasma torpedoes and disruptor bolts down on its surface. In his youth, as a newly minted uhlan, dreams of glory played through his mind: he saw himself materializing in the Federation capital to find it toppled and in flames. He wanted to revel in stilling the beating hearts of the Empire's enemies.

Back then, Devix had known destruction and death in concept alone. In his military career, though, he would come to witness both—far too much of both—and to understand that the cold universe did not care which lives it devoured with its entropic appetite. He came to realize that survival and death, good and evil, joy and pain, did not divide people, but united them: a dead Romulan, a dead human, what difference did it make, what difference *was* there?

In his advanced years, Devix had become, much to the chagrin of those with hatred in their hearts, a lover of peace. He ruled the men and women of the Imperial Fleet, saw them trained to attack and kill, but in the end, sought only to have them return safely to their starships or their bases at the end of each day—and when possible, not to carry the blood of others back with them. People like Senator Durjik and Chairwoman Sela, who jockeyed and argued and pushed for war, did so from the safety of the Hall of State or Tal Shiar headquarters, perfectly content to tell others whom to fight and why, or to maneuver them to it, but unlikely to take up arms themselves. Cowards masquerading as heroes, fools asserting their thoughtless plots as wisdom and patriotism. In a career that had taken him from the lowest foot soldier to the supreme commander of all Romulan military forces, the admiral had learned to identify most of the real enemies in the galaxy: ego, arrogance, self-righteousness, a hunger for power, a lack of compassion and perspective, an unwillingness to understand. In his experience, such enemies could just as easily be found within as without.

The events of the last half-decade had worn Devix down, in a way that had left him drained. He took some solace that nobody in his position could have either foreseen or contended with some of those incidents, such as when the madman Shinzon emerged from the shadows on Remus to assassinate the praetor and most of the Senate. But what had occurred more recently, the two attempts to obtain the quantum slipstream drive technology from the Federation, involved rogue actions by his own people. Looking back, he could easily distinguish Admiral Enellis Vellon, sympathizer and puppet of the Tal Shiar, as a villain, but perhaps too late—though he knew that the praetor would deal with him in an appropriate manner. Devix himself would step down soon, once his replacement had been chosen and evaluated, but until then, he would do what he had to do to lead the Imperial Fleet *and* keep the peace.

"Admiral," said Subcommander D'Voral from his sensor board off to port, "two Federation starships are approaching us from orbit, and I read multiple vessels exiting the docking facility." He spoke with utter calm, plainly not flustered by the circumstances. By order of the praetor, Devix had handpicked his crew.

"We're being hailed on multiple channels," said Lieutenant Terrin from her position at communications.

Devix spoke without raising his voice. "Select the one we need, Lieutenant," he said. "Take your time to verify both the physical source of the transmission and the identity of its sender."

"Yes, sir," said Terrin. "We're getting many signals from nearby starships, several from ground-based defensive emplacements . . ." When she paused, Devix glanced over to see her place a small, silver receiver in one ear. She listened for a moment, then said, "We're hearing repeated orders to acknowledge the hails . . . more than a few threats . . . demands for an explanation of our presence."

On the screen, Devix saw two Starfleet vessels approaching across the top of the planet. He recognized the closer one as *Akira*-class, the farther as a *Sovereign*.

"Subcommander D'Voral," the admiral said, "confirm our offensive and defensive status."

"Weapons are completely powered down, Admiral," said D'Voral, "as are the shields. Additionally, the cloak has been taken off line."

"Very good," Devix said. "Anything, Lieutenant Terrin?" It bothered him that he felt compelled to ask the question, since his crew knew their jobs and would keep him appropriately informed.

"Working on it, sir," Terrin said. "The amount of chatter is considerable and . . ." Devix looked over when she paused, and the lieutenant peered up from her console at him. "I have it, Admiral." She operated her controls. "Isolating the channel now."

"On-screen, Lieutenant."

The view of Earth and of Starfleet's reaction to the sudden appearance of an interloper fled the display, replaced by the image of a large, powerful-looking human. He wore his gray hair pulled back from his head, and he had a dark, penetrating gaze. Devix knew his Starfleet counterpart on sight, but then recalled that the commander-in-chief hailed not from Earth or any of its colonies, but from Capella IV. They had met once, a long time ago, both of them so far—in so many ways—from the ranks they would ultimately achieve.

"Commander-in-Chief Akaar," Devix said. "This is Fleet Admiral Devix, aboard the Imperial scout vessel *Enderavat*. Please forgive our sudden appearance. If we did not travel under cloak, we obviously would not have been able to reach Earth." He saw a long suspension bridge in the distance beyond Akaar, identifying his location as Starfleet Headquarters in San Francisco.

"*Admiral,*" Akaar said, his features as quiet as though they had been hewn from wood, "*you have ten seconds to explain your presence in Federation space before I order a dozen ships to close on your position and open fire.*"

Devix doubted that Starfleet had twelve starships available at Earth to support such a threat, but he took Akaar's meaning. "Commander-in-Chief, I have little desire to see my crew and my vessel reduced to cinders, and even less to launch any attack of our own. If you will check your sensors, you will find that this vessel possesses only light weaponry, and with its systems powered down, has no immediate ability to fire its weapons, to protect itself with shields, or to hide itself with a cloak."

Akaar peered off to one side, and Devix assumed somebody provided him corroboration of the *Enderavat*'s status. When the commander-in-chief looked back, he said, "*You've earned yourself another five seconds to explain why the head of the Imperial Fleet has brought a Romulan vessel to the very heart of the Federation.*"

Devix drew himself up in an attempt to project his seriousness of purpose. "I have come because we need to talk."

"*Then talk,*" Akaar said.

"This is something we must do in person, Commander-in-Chief," Devix said.

Akaar did not reply at once. His jaw set and his eyes fixed, he could have been a statue. Before he began speaking again, Devix said, "You will have preparations to make, of course. You will want to isolate me once I transport down, to ensure that I am who I say I am, and that I am bringing no weapons—no explosives, no biological agents, no threats of any kind—to your shores. I will travel alone. I will provide coordinates so that you may use your own transporter to retrieve me."

The narrowing of Akaar's eyes provided the only indication that he even registered the words Devix spoke.

"While I am on Earth, my ship will remain undefended and unprepared to launch an attack," Devix continued. "I ask that you refrain from boarding the *Enderavat*. My crew have their orders and will not deviate from them. When our meeting has concluded, I will take my ship—weapons, shields, and cloak still off line—directly to the Neutral Zone, preferably with a Starfleet escort."

When Akaar finally broke his silence, he uttered just one word: "*Why?*"

"Commander-in-Chief," Devix said, "I trust that, in your position, you will understand this better than anybody else possibly could. As *the* military leader of my people, I despise war. I am therefore here to discuss something very different."

"*Is there any reason at all for us to trust you?*" Akaar wanted to know.

Considering the situation, Devix felt it best to admit the truth. "From your perspective, there is no reason whatsoever," he said. "But I implore you, Leonard James Akaar. There is everything to gain from simple talking."

Again, Akaar slipped into silence. Devix could see the effort in the Starfleet admiral's eyes, could see him weighing competing judgments, calculating the danger each potential course of action might hold. Finally, he said, "*I will order every ship in Earth orbit to hold station and refrain from opening fire on the* Enderavat. *Will you stand by while a decision is made on your request?*"

"I will," Devix said. "But time may be a critical component of our conversation."

"*I understand,*" Akaar said. "*Stand by. Starfleet out.*"

The view of Earth returned to the screen. On it, the two Starfleet vessels Devix had seen a few moments earlier had drawn very close, both taking up positions off to starboard—obviously so that they would not risk striking the nearby space station if called upon to fire their weapons. The ships floated in such proximity to *Enderavat* that the admiral could read their names: *Susquehanna* and *First Minister*.

Nobody on the bridge said anything. Devix turned and walked over to sit down in the command chair. He and his crew could do nothing more but wait.

Via the dedicated transporter just outside his office, Akaar made it from Starfleet Headquarters in San Francisco to the Palais de la Concorde in Paris in less than three minutes. He entered the Monet Room—the situation room—at a run. He did not beat the president there. Jas Abrik, the Federation Security Advisor, had also arrived.

"How in the hell does a Romulan ship travel through light-years of Federation space into Earth orbit without Starfleet knowing about it?" Bacco demanded of the admiral even before he'd taken a seat. "I guess I should be happy it's not a warbird hovering a hundred meters above the Palais."

"Planetary defenses would have alerted us had the vessel entered the atmosphere," Akaar said. He regretted the defensive response even as he offered it.

"Thank you," Bacco said. "I feel so much safer now."

As Akaar sat down opposite the president at the round conference table, the door opened and a small Vulcan man— Undersecretary of Defense Vorent—entered at a brisk pace. He carried several padds with him, which he set down as he took a seat beside the security advisor. When Vorent glanced up and saw the president peering in his direction, he said, "Secretary Shostakova is presently out of the system, meeting with—"

"I know where the secretary is," said the president. "What I want to know right now from the Department of Defense is how a Romulan ship can cross—"

"Madam President," Akaar interjected quietly. Without the chief of staff present to keep Bacco properly focused, the admiral knew he would have to try to do so. "With a Romulan ship already in Earth orbit, I would suggest that the more important question is not *How did it get there?* but *What do we do about it now that it is?*"

The president took a breath and appeared to settle her emotions. "You spoke with the fleet admiral? What's his name?"

"Devix," Akaar said. "And yes, I did speak with him. He wants to meet with me to talk."

"About what?" asked Abrik.

"He didn't specify," Akaar said. "He only said that he wants to speak with me in person, that he despises war, and that our conversation may be time-sensitive."

"The praetor is forcing Devix to resign," Abrik said. "Could this be a defection?"

"Such an action would not be consistent with the admiral's character," Vorent said. "He is a staunch loyalist."

"He could be pretending to defect," Abrik said. "Then planning to function as a double agent."

"I don't think that makes much sense either," Vorent said. "He and the Romulans would know that we would treat any such defection cynically, if we even granted him political asylum."

"Wait," Bacco said. "Nobody's talking about giving asylum to the current and soon-to-be-former head of the Romulan Imperial Fleet. Relations with the Empire are at a low ebb, and I don't think antagonizing the praetor or the military is the way to win them over."

"But by providing asylum—" Abrik started, but Akaar cleared his throat, a sound like gravel being ground together, cutting off the security advisor.

"We do not know for what reason Admiral Devix has come to Earth," Akaar said. "He could be seeking political sanctuary, but I don't think so."

"Then what does he want?" Bacco asked.

"I think he wants exactly what he said he wants: to talk with me."

"But for what purpose?" Abrik asked again.

"I don't know," Akaar said. "But since the attack in the Bajoran system, this is the second time that the Romulans have sought discussion. I believe that it is in our best interests to hear them out."

"They have lied to us," Bacco said. "They caused the deaths of more than a thousand of our people and we don't know how many of their own. They destroyed a space station, along with whatever trust we had built up with them. Should we give them the opportunity to do so again?"

Akaar considered this, but then recalled the Ten Tribes of Capella. He thought about his people's bloody history, their tendency toward fast violence, and how far they still had to go before they would be worthy of joining the Federation. "The alternative to talking," Akaar said, "is not talking. And I do not believe that not talking with our adversaries has any chance of turning them into our friends."

The president sat back in her chair and regarded the admiral. "So you're suggesting that we should live up to our high-sounding principles, is that it?" The hint of a smile played at the edges of her lips.

"Yes, Madam President," Akaar said. "Something like that."

"And what if the admiral dies—by his own hand or otherwise—while he's on our soil?" Bacco asked. "What do you suppose that will do for interstellar relations?"

"That's a risk, of course," Akaar said. "But I don't believe that he came here to end his own life."

Bacco nodded. "All right, we'll talk to Fleet Admiral Devix," she said. "But I want it done safely. I don't want the last act of a disgraced military man to be a suicide bombing that attempts to prove his patriotism by killing Federation citizens."

"Understood," Akaar said.

"So then how will you speak with him?" Bacco wanted to know.

Akaar didn't quite have an answer. He wanted to volunteer to transport up to the Romulan ship, or to beam over to a Starfleet vessel *with* Devix, but he didn't believe that the president would find either choice palatable. He looked to Abrik and Vorent, hoping that they might offer a suggestion. Neither of them said anything for a few moments, until at last the security advisor spoke up.

"There's the penal colony in New Zealand," Abrik said. "The inmate processing section of the maximum-security division is set up to receive individuals considered dangerous and a possible threat to colony personnel. We can transport Devix there, verify his identity as best we can, check him for weapons, disarm him if necessary, execute a scan for disease."

Akaar looked over at the president. "I believe that would suffice for our needs," he told her.

Bacco stood up. "Then that's what we'll do," she said.

"I'll set it up," Abrik said. "Admiral, I'll let you know as soon as we're ready."

"Understood," Akaar said. He rose and made his way toward the door, headed for the office he kept in the Palais. From there, he would contact Admiral Devix.

"Admiral," Bacco said, stopping him as he reached the door. "Be safe. The praetor may be replacing the head of her military, but I don't want to have to replace mine."

"Yes, ma'am," Akaar said, and he proceeded to his office.

Devix stood again in the middle of the *Enderavat* bridge, speaking with his Federation counterpart. The admiral could see that Akaar had moved from his Starfleet Headquarters location, obviously to the secure facility they had set up for their discussion. Devix understood the precautions—had in fact suggested them—but the inability of his crew to perform a quick extraction did draw his concern, though he could say nothing about it.

"Admiral," Akaar said on the main viewscreen, *"we are ready to receive you."*

"I understand," Devix said. "I will head to the transporter pad for which we provided you coordinates. I will contact you from there, and you can beam me down."

"Acknowledged," Akaar said. *"Starfleet out."* The screen returned to a view of Earth and the two Starfleet vessels.

Devix turned to the sensor board. "D'Voral, the bridge is yours. Do you understand your orders?"

"Yes, sir."

"Very good," Devix said. "I'll be back shortly." He quickly exited the bridge into a turbolift and ordered it to take him to the nearest transporter room. As the lift began to move, he allowed himself a brief moment to wonder about his legacy. The last half-decade had seen failures in the Imperial Fleet under his leadership, but there had also been a time when he had collected one impressive military victory after another, beginning with the Klingon conflict at Nequencia. At this point in his career, Devix felt that neither category of engagement fairly represented the most important aspects of his time as fleet admiral. For decades—*Decades!*—he had kept Romulus fundamentally at peace. There had been some clashes during that period, but for the most part, he saved Romulan lives by not committing those lives to unnecessary military action.

But people often mistake an absence of action for in*action,* Devix thought. Some historians, he knew, would characterize the fleet admiral as untried during those times of peace, a military man not forced to fight, and therefore not proven. They would not see that he prevented conflict, that he eschewed battle whenever that would best serve the Empire and the Fleet.

But this, he thought. *If what I do here becomes known, how will I be remembered? How will I be* judged? At least part of the answer to that, he knew, would depend on the results of his actions while in orbit of Earth.

The turbolift eased to a stop and its doors opened. He paced out of the cab and into the corridor. Just a few strides took him to his destination.

Devix stepped inside the transporter room. He peered at the pad, at the precious cargo atop it, then moved to the control console. He tied into the communications system, knowing that Lieutenant Terrin had kept the channel open to the Starfleet commander-in-chief. "Devix to Akaar."

"Akaar here," came the immediate response. Although the admiral's voice remained even, the swiftness of his reply seemed to betray a level of anxiety. *"Are you in position?"*

The admiral took one final look at the transporter pad across the compartment, then said, "Yes, I am."

Fleet Admiral Devix heard the hum of the Federation transporter rise, then saw streaks of white light form. He watched the entire process, until the pad stood empty. Then he left the transporter room and headed back to the bridge, hoping that he had done the right thing.

Admiral Akaar stood in the main processing room in the maximum-security wing of the New Zealand Penal Colony, along with a transporter operator and a pair of security officers, all from Starfleet. They stood in a large room, divided into thirds by thick walls of transparent aluminum. Akaar and the others stood in the outer section of the room, while the inner section contained the transporter platform; the middle portion of the room remained devoid of any adornment beyond the phaser emitters that lined the two narrow side walls.

It had been explained to Akaar that authorities would transport the few inmates sentenced to serve in the maximum-security wing directly to the inner third of the main processing room. Immediately upon transport, shields automatically snapped into place to prevent beaming out of the room. Security sensors would automatically check for weapons and dangerous materials anywhere on—or inside—the inmate, and biological scans would search out diseases, particularly those intended for bacteriological warfare. Further, sensors would work with Federation security databases to confirm the inmate's identity.

Akaar stood beside the transporter console, while the two security officers positioned themselves on either side of their section of the room. When Devix hailed him, the admiral reached up and activated his combadge. "Akaar here," he said. He would know shortly whether or not the trust he'd shown his Romulan counterpart had been misplaced. "Are you in position?"

Devix paused for just a second, then said, *"Yes, I am."*

Akaar nodded to the transporter operator, who set to working the console. Because of the two walls of transparent aluminum separating the inner third of the room from the outer third, Akaar could not hear the familiar whine of the transporter, but he saw the white beams of light as they brightened and coalesced into a shape.

"Transport complete," the operator said, but she spoke her words in a whisper.

Akaar stared at the platform, then reached up and tapped his combadge again. "Akaar to Starfleet Headquarters," he said. He waited a moment as Starfleet's internal communications system routed his signal directly to his own office. He did not take his gaze from the platform.

"Starfleet Headquarters," said the voice of his first assistant. *"This is Lieutenant Reel. Go ahead, Admiral."*

"Reel, I need you to patch me through to the Palais de la Concorde immediately," he said. "To the president's office."

"Right away, sir," Reel said. *"It'll be just one moment."*

As Akaar waited, he glanced down at the console and activated the communications controls there, opening a channel to the inner third of the room. Then he looked back over at the transporter platform, drew in a breath, and said, "Welcome to Earth, Praetor."

Gell Kamemor sat in front of President Bacco's desk, feeling a mix of conflicting emotions: exhaustion and exhilaration, fear and anticipation. The trip from Romulus to Earth had been long and harrowing—harrowing not because she felt personally endangered, but because she believed that another rogue attack impended, that the commander of the missing vessel, *Vetruvis,* meant to commit an act of aggression against the Federation. If Kamemor failed to prevent that, then she knew that war would likely follow not far behind, and as Admiral Devix raced her toward Earth, she knew that failure could come in any number of ways. If the ship carrying her got turned back, stopped, or captured, or if she arrived too late, or if the president refused to speak with her, then the praetor's efforts would amount to nothing.

Kamemor had never been to Earth, although during her years as an ambassador, she'd thought that an opportunity would likely arise. But back then, the tensions among the Empire, the Federation, and the Klingons had been too great to overcome. While so many of her people had sought an alliance between

Romulus and Qo'noS—specifically to empower them to attack Earth and the Federation—she had contributed to a different effort, one that she'd hoped would force the Romulan Star Empire to accept peace, if only grudgingly. After the Tomed Incident, peace *had* come, but in the form of Romulan isolationism. As praetor, she wanted more than that—much more.

Kamemor looked around the office. Two men—clearly security officers—stood inside the room, silent and stoic. Although she understood the reasonable need for them, their presence somehow felt accusatory.

The praetor gazed through the wall of windows that looked out on Paris. Twilight embraced the city and would soon draw deeper into the clutches of night. Already lights had begun to twinkle throughout the landscape. Paris did not resemble Ki Baratan or Ra'tleihfi or Villera'trel or any other city on Romulus, but had a character all its own. The iconic tower by the river— she'd seen it before in holopics, though she couldn't recall its name—seemed to imbue its surroundings with a certain quality, a certain style that made it unique in her experience.

Behind her, Kamemor heard the door open. She turned in her chair to see the president of the Federation enter the office at a brisk clip. Her chief aide, whose name Kamemor did not recall, followed. The praetor rose as a matter of etiquette, but Nanietta Bacco offered no greetings and made no reintroductions. She began speaking as she made her way behind her desk, and as her aide moved toward the chair beside Kamemor.

"According to Admiral Akaar," the president said without even making eye contact, "you made quite an entrance."

After Bacco sat, so too did the praetor and the president's aide. "I hope you will excuse the subterfuge," Kamemor said. "But my previous attempt to engage you met with rejection."

Bacco peered across the desk, her face a mask, devoid of any sense of fellowship. "I'm afraid that I wasn't in the mood to talk with you after the crew of a Romulan warbird participated in an unprovoked attack on a Federation space station," she said, her voice cold. "To be frank, Praetor, I'm not really sure that I want to talk with you now."

Kamemor understood the anger she felt from the president, but it disappointed her. She knew that the two leaders wanted the same things for their people, and she'd hoped that they could quickly return to the common ground they'd trod at the summit on Cort. The praetor realized, though, that it would take a great deal of effort to reestablish, even minimally, their political relationship. "I understand your feelings, Madam President," Kamemor said. "I am very sorry for the loss of life in the Bajoran system."

"I'm afraid that your apology doesn't mean much to the men, women, and *children* who were killed on Deep Space Nine," Bacco said, her anger not abating, "or to the families and friends robbed of their loved ones."

Kamemor lowered her head, sincerely pained by the thought of Romulans taking such actions under her leadership, no matter that they'd done so without her knowledge or sanction. "It was a great tragedy," she said.

"No, it *wasn't* a tragedy," Bacco snapped back. "It was a crime. It was *murder*."

Kamemor raised her head and looked across the desk at the president. She saw eyes filled not just with the anguish of loss, but with venom. It hardened Kamemor. "Yes, apparently it was murder," she said.

"'Apparently'?" Bacco fired back.

It seemed to Kamemor that the conversation threatened to unravel even before it had really gotten started. She waited a beat, willing herself not to react to Bacco's heated emotions. "Madam President," she said, "when we met at the summit, when you and I and the other leaders negotiated to open the Typhon Expanse to Khitomer Accords vessels, and the Gamma Quadrant to Typhon Pact vessels, I did so with great hope. But I felt an even greater sense of accomplishment when you and I forged an agreement specifically between Romulus and Earth. The Federation has allies, and the Empire has allies, but we are the preeminent powers in the Alpha and Beta Quadrants. We lead not just our own people, and not even the alliances of which we are a part; we lead this entire section of the galaxy. In the end, peace and war are *our* responsibility. And with our agreement to launch a joint project . . . a mission of exploration . . . to me, that epitomized hope. For we would not simply be exploring the universe, but each other."

Bacco did not reply at once, and the praetor thought that perhaps she had reached her. But when the president finally did speak, she still seethed. "Fine words, Praetor," she said, "and yet the crew you sent on that mission of exploration faked the destruction of their own vessel."

"What?" Kamemor said, both surprised and confused by the president's assertion. "Do you mean that the crew of the *Eletrix* is still alive?"

Bacco blinked, as though she did not understand the praetor's question. "No," she said. "When the crew of the *Eletrix* was about to be captured by Starfleet, they destroyed themselves and their ship."

"But you said . . ." Kamemor tried to make sense of the president's statements, but couldn't. "I don't understand. You're saying that the *Eletrix* crew destroyed their ship *and* faked the destruction of their ship?"

Bacco stood up so quickly that her chair teetered and almost toppled to the carpet, but then it thumped back down onto the floor. She pointed at Kamemor, and it seemed as though the president could barely contain her rage. "Do . . . not . . . lie . . . to me."

"Madam President, I am not here to lie to you," Kamemor said, distraught that she could not better control the flow of the conversation, but suddenly aware that she lacked essential details about exactly what had taken place in the Bajoran system. "I am here to try to save both the Empire and the Federation, to save our people from destroying each other."

"Then you've got your work cut out for you," Bacco said, dropping her hand back to her side. "Do you know how many people here screamed for an armed response to your attack? Who wanted us to declare war right then and there?"

"Why didn't you?" Kamemor asked quietly.

"I keep asking myself that," Bacco said. "But believe me, there's still time."

Kamemor peered up at the president and attempted to imagine how she would feel in her place. She tried to gauge what her own response would have been if Federation, Klingon, and Cardassian starships had made their way into the Typhon Expanse and destroyed a space station there. She would have felt betrayed, of course, but also angry and distrustful. Wouldn't she have wanted to strike back? *Maybe. Probably.* But that could not be the answer. "The Romulan Empire does not want war."

Bacco raised her hand, and for a moment, the praetor thought she meant to strike her. She even heard at least one of the security officers behind her move, and realized that they thought the same thing. But then Bacco brought the flat of her hand down hard on her desk, making a loud slapping noise. "The Romulan Empire seems to do nothing but *incite* war," she said, her voice rising. Her fury evident, she stalked out from behind her desk and across the office. When she reached the far side, she turned and demanded, "Why are you here?"

Kamemor didn't know what she should say, concerned about angering the president further. But she had traveled to Earth—had *risked* coming to Earth—for a reason, and she would see it through. "I am here because I am concerned that another attack on the Federation may be about to take place."

Bacco stared silently from across the room. From beside her, the president's aide said, "Another attack? Where? When?" The aide had been so quiet that the praetor had forgotten that she was even there.

"I don't know," Kamemor admitted.

"You don't know?" Bacco said, marching back across the office. "Then why come here? So that when the attack occurs and more Federation citizens are killed, you can claim that you tried to warn me, and we therefore shouldn't retaliate?" She returned behind her desk, but did not sit. "That's not going to happen. If there's another Romulan attack, you can say good-bye to the Neutral Zone."

Kamemor said nothing. She sat motionless and looked

up at Bacco. The conversation had spun out of control. She had underestimated the president's anger, probably because Kamemor knew her own good intentions, while Bacco saw only treachery. The praetor had to make sure that the president understood all that had happened so that they could move forward together. "Utopia Planitia," she finally said.

"What?" Bacco asked.

"The plans for your quantum slipstream drive," Kamemor said, "were stolen from the Utopia Planitia facility and taken to the Breen Confederacy."

"Yes," Bacco said. She sat back down behind her desk. She looked tired to the praetor, as though her own anger had worn her down. Kamemor empathized; she knew the ire she felt for Sela, for Tomalak, for Admiral Vellon, and how much that had drained her energy and will. "Twenty-one Federation deaths in that attack," Bacco said. "An attack in which a Romulan vessel participated."

"You reported it as an industrial accident," Kamemor said.

The president's eyes burned. "Because if I had reported the truth," she said, "then we would have gone to war."

"But that's not the only reason," Kamemor said. "You did not reveal what happened so that you could, with impunity, send a covert team into the Confederacy to destroy what the Breen had stolen from you."

"What the Breen *and* the Romulans had stolen," Bacco said.

"Yes," Kamemor agreed. "But not on my order."

"You see, though, that doesn't matter much to me," the president said. "Because even if you didn't order the attack on Utopia Planitia, it still happened on your watch. Whether you are willfully bent on perpetrating violence against the Federation, or whether you're so weak and ineffective a leader that you can't prevent your own people from doing so, it doesn't really matter, does it? Because it all ends with the same result."

"I knew nothing of the assault on Utopia Planitia," Kamemor said. She found the admission difficult to make, probably because of the president's remark about her being an ineffectual leader—and more likely because, to some extent, that had been true. "When I learned about what happened, and about the likely use of a phasing cloak in the commission of the theft, I feared Romulan involvement. I had the matter investigated, and when I learned the identity of the starship commander who took part in the operation, he was removed from duty and sent to a military prison, where he still remains."

"That still doesn't bring back the people who died at Utopia Planitia," Bacco said.

"Nor those who died in Breen space when their slipstream prototype was destroyed," Kamemor said.

"Don't you dare try to turn this around," Bacco said, raising a finger toward the praetor. Kamemor knew that she had risked the president's wrath with her comment, but she needed to make a larger point. "I didn't order an unprovoked attack. I was reacting to one and protecting my people."

"There are those who feel that acquiring slipstream drive technology," Kamemor said, "is a means of protecting the people of the Typhon Pact worlds."

Bacco dropped her hand to the top of her desk with a thud. "They claim that the drive provides the Federation with a military advantage, is that the reasoning? Because you'll notice that the Federation hasn't used its 'superior technology' against the Typhon Pact."

"It is my understanding that in extracting your covert operatives from Breen space," Kamemor said, "a slipstream-enabled vessel was utilized." Bacco opened her mouth to reply, but the praetor pressed on. "But that is immaterial to me," she said. "I don't agree with those who see the Federation as a threat because of slipstream. I don't believe that your government will ever launch a preemptive strike against the Romulan Empire or any other of the Typhon Pact members."

"That's not who I am," Bacco agreed. "That's not who *we* in the Federation are."

"I believe that, Madam President," Kamemor said.

"All right," Bacco said. "So why are you telling me all this?"

"Because I want you to understand that I didn't know about the attack on Utopia Planitia," Kamemor said, "and that I took measures afterward to prevent something like it from happening again."

"By imprisoning the commander of the Romulan vessel," Bacco said.

"Yes," Kamemor said. "And it was a simple matter to characterize the entire operation as one orchestrated by my predecessor before her death, and set in motion well before I became praetor."

"That still doesn't absolve you of blame," Bacco said.

"No," Kamemor allowed. "But these are still relevant facts of which you should be aware."

"They're not that relevant," Bacco said, "considering what happened at the Bajoran wormhole."

"That was another attack by rogue elements," Kamemor said. "At least, rogue elements from the Empire. I have so far been unable to ascertain whether the crews of the Breen and Tzenkethi ships were acting as agents of their respective governments or on their own. But the attack was clearly meant to undermine the burgeoning détente among the worlds of the Typhon Pact and the Khitomer Accords."

Bacco squinted for a moment, as though attempting to better see the praetor. "That might be one reason for the attack," she said.

"You believe that there was another reason?" Kamemor asked.

"It's what we've been talking about," Bacco said. "It was another attempt to acquire technology to help develop slipstream."

"I didn't know that," Kamemor said. In a way, it pleased her that the attack had possessed a purpose—albeit a misguided one—other than just to sow terror and distrust. "I didn't know that Starfleet had a slipstream production operation at Deep Space Nine."

"There was no such operation at the station," Bacco said. "That's not what happened."

"Forgive me, Madam President," Kamemor said, frustrated, "but I don't know what happened. I came here to find that out, so that I can stop it from happening again."

"Why should I believe you?" Bacco asked.

"At this point, you probably shouldn't," Kamemor said. "But whether you do or not, would it make a difference to tell me what you know about the attack in the Bajoran system?"

The president looked to her aide. "I don't see any reason not to tell her," the woman said.

"All right," Bacco said. "When the *Enterprise* and the *Eletrix* were engaged on their mission in the Gamma Quadrant, the Romulan crew staged the crash of their vessel, with a complete loss of life. They did this so that they could then sneak into the Dominion and steal equipment that would allow the Breen to develop slipstream drive."

"How do you know this?" Kamemor asked.

"We know about the staged crash because the *Enterprise* crew found it when they responded to a counterfeit distress call," Bacco said. "And we know about the theft of the equipment from the Dominion because we spoke with a Founder after it happened. We believe that the crew of the *Eletrix* destroyed their ship so that Starfleet would not discover the equipment they'd stolen."

"Are you certain that the equipment was stolen from the Dominion," Kamemor asked, "and not *given* by them?"

Again, the president looked to her aide. "We're as sure as we can reasonably be," the woman said.

"That's good," Kamemor said, "because an alliance between the Dominion and the rogue elements of the Typhon Pact would be extremely dangerous."

"The possibility did concern us," said the aide.

Kamemor nodded. "Madam President," she said, "since the attack in the Bajoran system, we have identified the people in my government and in the Imperial Fleet responsible for plotting that action, as well as the theft at Utopia Planitia. I am taking steps to permanently remove their ability to mount additional such acts."

"Didn't you say you'd come here because you were concerned that there might be another attack?" Bacco asked.

"Yes," Kamemor said. "A Romulan warbird has disappeared

under suspicious circumstances. Its commander was an officer aboard the Romulan vessel at Utopia Planitia."

"So you believe that this commander will make another attempt to acquire the slipstream drive?" Bacco asked.

"No, I didn't, because I didn't know that the attack in the Bajoran system had anything to do with slipstream," Kamemor said. "But that seems like a logical conclusion."

"But you don't know where or when this commander might attack?" Bacco asked.

"No," Kamemor said. "But I believe that there is somebody on Earth who might know."

"Are you accusing somebody in my government of complicity?" Bacco asked.

"No," Kamemor said. "I am accusing somebody in your *custody*."

"Tomalak," Bacco said.

"Yes."

"Your former proconsul."

"I never agreed much with Tomalak," Kamemor said, "and I certainly didn't know of his hidden agenda, but I kept him on as proconsul because I value opposing perspectives."

Bacco leaned back in her chair. "So you want to speak with him?" she asked.

"What I *want*," Kamemor said, "is to place my hands around his neck and squeeze until he's breathed his last breath. But for the benefit of the Romulan Empire and the Federation, yes, I would speak with him."

"I still don't know that I can trust you," Bacco said, but Kamemor could see that the president *wanted* to trust her.

"Understand this," Kamemor said. "I am not trying to avoid a war between the Typhon Pact and the Khitomer Accords, or between the Romulan Empire and the Federation. I am trying to establish a relationship . . . a friendship. It's a big galaxy; there's no good reason we can't share it."

"I agree, Praetor," Bacco said, "but if you are losing control of your government, what difference do your efforts make?"

"I didn't have control, clearly," Kamemor said. "What's

worse is that I didn't know it. But I am taking control, wresting it from the usurpers. As I said, we've learned who the most powerful of them are, and we are stopping them. At the same time, there are fewer senators these days inclined to seek war with the Federation or anybody else. Individuals whom I know I can trust will soon be in major positions of authority within my government. And my people . . . most of them, anyway . . . only want what your people want . . . what *all* people want: to live their lives free of pain and sorrow and want. And while there will always be those things for all of us, the least we can do as leaders is to minimize them as best we can. Keeping us out of another war would be a good start."

"I can't argue with that," Bacco said. "But if you think that these rogue elements are going to go after the slipstream drive again, we may not have to worry. Our Starfleet installations have been re-fortified, and a strong force guards the wormhole."

"That is all good to know," Kamemor said, "but I would still feel better if we could learn the details of what is to come."

"Do you really believe that you can get that information from Tomalak?" Bacco asked.

"Yes," Kamemor said. "I know Tomalak. I worked with him. He's a small, self-important dullard who puffs out his chest and calls himself a patriot even as he undermines the collective good of the Empire. I know how to talk to him."

Turning to her aide, Bacco said, "Esperanza, what do you think?"

Esperanza, Kamemor thought. *Esperanza Piñiero.*

"I think it's something worth trying," Piñiero said.

Bacco stood up again, and then so did her aide. Kamemor rose as well. "Praetor, I will need to speak with my advisors," she said. "I can have Esperanza escort you to visitor's quarters."

"I would remind you that we may not have much time," Kamemor said.

"I understand."

Piñiero walked toward the door, and Kamemor followed, as did one of the security officers. As they left the president's office, the praetor didn't know whether or not she would be

permitted to speak with her former proconsul. She could only
hope that she had done a good enough job of making her case to
the Federation president.

23

Bashir leaned in over the primary examination table and
brought his hand up in front of his patient's face. "Breathe
into this, Ensign." He indicated the tube he held, to which he'd
attached a bulb containing a gelatinous red substrate. "Let's
check out your lung function."

Vakell th'Shant took hold of the tube, but he peered up at
the doctor with what seemed like a quizzical expression. The
Andorian's facial features didn't change, but his antennae bent
at an angle that betrayed his confusion. "I don't remember this
test," th'Shant said.

"That's because it's probably one you've never been given
before," Bashir said. "But the captain wanted it added to
everybody's physical." As part of establishing the new Bajoran
Space Central, and in light of some of the injuries suffered
during the destruction of Deep Space 9, Captain Ro had ordered
a fresh round of medical exams for every member of the crew.
She'd handed down the edict more than two weeks earlier, after
consulting with Bashir, but he and his staff hadn't been able to
begin until after the center had become operational. In three
full days, they'd managed about two dozen physicals, although
they would have finished a few more if not for the captain's late
and questionable addition to the regular set of tests.

"The captain's dictating medical policy?" th'Shant asked.
"That seems a little odd."

I couldn't agree more, thought Bashir. To the ensign, though,
he said, "It's not as though she randomly found the test in a
reference book and just decided to insist we do it. When the
medical staff spoke with her about all the injuries that the
crew suffered, we brought it to her attention that a number
of personnel had been trapped in small, pressurized sections
of wreckage for some time. Some of those sections didn't stay

completely pressurized, so there could have been some lung damage along the way." Bashir hoped that his explanation sounded more plausible to the ensign than it did to him.

"I was in a runabout," th'Shant said, "not a piece of the wreckage." He tried to hand the tube back to the doctor, but Bashir held up the palm of his hand in a halting motion.

"Physical exams for a crew have to be standardized," he said. "You know that." The doctor understood that th'Shant couldn't have known that, since it didn't happen to be true—and couldn't be, considering how many different species served in Starfleet—but he made the assertion authoritatively.

Even though the ensign's antennae adjusted from a confused attitude to one of mild suspicion, he brought the tube up to his thin, blue lips. He inhaled deeply, and Bashir stopped him with a hand to his shoulder. "Normal breaths, Ensign," he said. "About half a dozen." Th'Shant did as instructed, then handed the tube back over to the doctor.

Bashir took the tube and carried it over to the side of the room, to where Nurse Etana Kol worked at the main medical console. "Andorian *thaan*, lung function at rest," he said. Etana accepted the tube, removed the bulb at the end, then attached the bulb to a fitted, interchangeable receptacle on the console. She repeated the doctor's words, then tapped at a control panel, apparently to initiate an analysis.

Bashir paced back over to the foot of the exam table, reached down, and pulled the stair simulator up from below. The arced piece of metal glided up along its curved tracks until it locked into its vertical orientation with an audible click. Bashir reached above th'Shant's feet and released the two padded steps of the simulator, which worked in opposition to each other; when a patient depressed one, the other came up, and vice versa.

"Move down the table, Ensign," Bashir said, "so that you can put your feet up here." He patted the simulator. Th'Shant slid down the table, his knees rising as he bent his legs. Then he raised his feet and pushed them against the steps. The doctor pointed out the handholds for him to use on the sides of the bed, then asked, "Are you comfortable?"

"I'll be comfortable when I can go back to my station," th'Shant said.

"We both will be, Ensign," Bashir said, a little more sharply than he'd intended. The doctor didn't like what Captain Ro had asked him to do, for a variety of reasons—including that he thought it had no chance of success—but he needed to ensure that he didn't take it out on his patients. Being careful to moderate his tone, he said, "Give me an easy but consistent pace for one full minute."

"Yes, Doctor."

The Andorian began pumping his legs in a steady rhythm. Bashir worked a small control panel on the side of the exam table and set a timer for sixty seconds. Then he stepped back and observed th'Shant, but his mind immediately began to wander—as it often had over the previous ten days. Sarina had been taken into custody at the beginning of that time, and then placed under arrest and charged almost a week after that. Captain Ro's assurances to the contrary, the entire situation troubled Bashir greatly. While he didn't necessarily believe that the captain would lie to him—though she had shown no misgivings about having *him* lie to the crew—he found it difficult to countenance her claims that she believed fully in Sarina's innocence.

Maybe that's because I'm not sure that I *believe in Sarina's innocence,* Bashir thought.

On the night that Sarina had first been taken into custody at Quark's, the doctor had subsequently found Ro still in her office at the center. He closed the door behind him when he went in, then proceeded to offer her some heated words. She allowed him to continue for a while, until she reminded him that Sarina hadn't been arrested, but had voluntarily gone in for questioning—although the restraints Sarina had been led away in made her seizure seem far from voluntary. Then the captain suggested that the doctor not visit Sarina while she remained with security.

"Why not?" Bashir had asked. "Why shouldn't I see her?"

"For two reasons, Doctor," Ro said. "First, because she

asked me to keep you away. She thought that it would be easier for both of you that way."

"There's nothing easy about this," Bashir said.

"Second," Ro said, "we need the crew to see you not only upset, but having your own suspicions about Sarina."

For a moment, Bashir had thought that the captain somehow perceived the doubts he'd begun having about the woman he loved. But then she explained that Sarina had *volunteered* to be brought in for questioning, not because Ro considered her a real suspect, but so that the true saboteur would begin to feel comfortable, to believe that they had escaped detection and capture.

Bashir found the plan—if it could even be called that— absurd. Just because an innocent individual had been taken in for questioning, or even arrested, that would not cause the guilty party to suddenly start leaving clues or have a change of heart. But Ro insisted that Sarina wanted to try, so Bashir let it go. It bothered him not to see her, and to have to rely on the captain's confidence about what she and Sarina were attempting to accomplish.

At the examination table, a chirp indicated that a minute had passed. "That's enough, Ensign, thank you," the doctor said. Th'Shant dropped his feet back onto the table's surface, his knees up, then pushed himself back up so that he could lie completely flat. Bashir produced the tube again, but this time added a different bulb to it. "One more time, Ensign," he said.

Th'Shant took the tube and blew into it once more. An Andorian, he possessed considerable strength and stamina, and even after a minute's continuous exercise, he did not breathe much more heavily than he had at the start. Bashir relayed the tube and its bulb over to Nurse Etana.

As she set about processing the second bulb from Ensign th'Shant, Bashir thought about how, years earlier, Etana had served as a sergeant in the Bajoran Militia. She decided to try her hand at nursing, though, so that she could spend more time with Nurse Krissten Richter, the woman who would eventually become her wife. Etana, a field medic for her Resistance cell during the Occupation, made a relatively smooth transition from one career path to the other.

When some of DS9's surviving personnel had to be assigned elsewhere, before the BSC had become operational, the captain had sent Etana and Richter to *Brisbane,* so that they could be together. But then that changed. And it changed because L'Haan appeared in Bashir's room.

The doctor hadn't wanted to inform Ro about his visit from the Section 31 operative, primarily because he hadn't wanted to divulge Sarina's prior association with the organization. To his surprise, though, Ro already knew about Sarina's involvement with Section 31, and even her desire to put an end to the group. Bashir assumed that the captain's knowledge had come from her investigation of Sarina months earlier, but it turned out that, after Sarina had transferred to DS9, she'd gone to Ro and told her all about it herself.

As a result, the captain hadn't been surprised that L'Haan had shown up to speak with Bashir. Because Section 31 still believed Sarina to be one of their operatives, Ro had actually counted on one of their members appearing, hoping that they might provide valuable information about what had happened on DS9, something that had gone overlooked or misunderstood. But L'Haan revealed no such information to Bashir. When he recounted their conversation for the captain, though, Ro had still taken something away from it—something which she immediately acted upon by recalling Nurse Etana from *Brisbane,* wanting her to help conduct the upcoming physical examinations of the crew.

At the medical console, Etana finished working at her panel. "Transferring the test results to your padd, Doctor," she said.

"Thank you," he said. He picked up the padd from where it sat on the desk beside the console.

Bashir had almost refused the captain's orders regarding the physical exams. At a very basic level, he thought what she wanted him to do might violate medical ethics, although he also understood that, as members of Starfleet, the crew willingly relinquished some of their rights. But the doctor also didn't know if he could do what Ro wanted him to do convincingly and effectively. And even if he could, the entire plan would hinge on enlisting the crew, one member at a time, to keep the details of their physical to themselves.

The doctor carried the padd back over to where th'Shant still lay on the examination table. "Now, then, Ensign, let's take a look," he said. "You can sit up if you like." As th'Shant swung his legs over the side of the table, Bashir read through the display of all the measurements he'd taken and tests he'd performed on the Andorian. "Height and weight are consistent and healthy for your age and species," he said. "Although I've got your master file from Starfleet Medical here, and it looks as though you've lost some kilos since your last workup." He looked up across the padd at th'Shant. "Have your eating habits changed?"

Th'Shant shrugged. "With everything that's happened, maybe so," he admitted.

"Of course," Bashir said. "Have you been seeing one of the counselors?"

"Lieutenant Knezo," th'Shant said. With Counselor Matthias assigned to one of the ships in the system so that she could live with her family, the responsibility for the crew's emotional health had fallen to DS9's assistant counselors, Lieutenants Knezo and Collins. Starfleet had also sent another, Ensign Valinar, to Bajor to help with the workload.

"Good," Bashir said. He ran through th'Shant's results, all of which fell within expected ranges and spoke to the overall health of the ensign. Finally, he reached the last test. "Okay, then there's the lung function exam," he said. "Everything appears to be normal." He glanced up at th'Shant. "I guess it paid to be on a runabout instead of a piece of wreckage."

Th'Shant offered a thin smile. Bashir looked back down at the padd. He stared at it for a long moment, then furrowed his brow. "Is something the matter, Doctor?" th'Shant asked.

"It's probably nothing," Bashir said. "Oddly enough, it's on your 'lungs under exertion' test."

"But I told you, I was on the *Rio Grande* when the station . . ." He didn't finish his sentence.

"Yes, I'm aware of that," Bashir said. "And these results aren't showing any sign of damage caused by a loss of pressurization." Again, he looked up at the ensign. "When you breathe, you're obviously inhaling atmosphere. Within your lungs, there is a gas exchange through the pulmonary alveoli, allowing oxygen in the air to be taken into the blood, and carbon dioxide contained in the blood to be exhaled." Bashir saw that th'Shant's antennae curved, lowering the tips toward the top of his head. He didn't know what such a movement signified.

"I understand respiration," the ensign said, his tone registering obvious distress. "What's the problem?"

Bashir had been through this, or something like this, with the other two dozen of the crew on whom he'd performed physicals over the previous few days. He hated it. "There are certain substances that, if airborne, can be taken into the lungs and become lodged in the alveoli. I'm reading some microscopic fragments there."

"Is it something serious?" th'Shant asked, concerned. "Is it something you can treat?"

"It could be serious if we don't do anything about it," Bashir said. "The condition can be treated, but it depends primarily on what the substance is that's entered your lungs."

"And what is it?" th'Shant asked. Bashir could see that the blue flesh of his face had paled.

"I don't recognize this," Bashir said. He tapped at the controls of his padd, which emitted several tones in response. "I'm just running it through the substance database," he said. "It shouldn't take very—" Again, the padd chirped. "Here it is. The substance is . . ." The doctor peered back up at th'Shant, offering the ensign a suitably confused expression. ". . . revitrite?"

Bashir had only enough time to register the tensing of th'Shant's antennae before the Andorian sprang from the examination table. The doctor felt the heel of the ensign's hand slam into his chest. Bashir flew from his feet and rammed into the wall behind him. His head snapped back, and then he felt himself sliding down toward the floor. His vision swam. Everything suddenly seemed far away.

As he slipped toward unconsciousness, he heard a high, piercing sound. He dimly recognized it as a phaser blast, and recalled that Captain Ro had assigned Nurse Etana to the physical exams specifically because of her military training. He wondered if she'd been able to stun th'Shant, but then he could no longer keep his eyes open.

24

With Weyoun at his side, Odo materialized outside one of the production facilities on Bronis II. They stood in bright sunlight, beside a dark strip of shadow thrown by the massive building. Seeing nobody else there, Odo turned in place and regarded their surroundings. A vast plain reached in every direction, though he could see a long mountain range far off in the distance.

"Venetheris told me that she would greet us here," Weyoun said. Odo took note, as he often had of late, that the Vorta spoke to him without any hint of fear. In the past, Weyoun and the clones who had preceded him had revered Odo so much as one of their gods that they lived in a perpetual panic that they would disappoint him. But Weyoun had changed—had, in fact, grown.

"It's not a problem," Odo said. "I'm sure she'll be here soon." In the nearly eight years since his return to the Dominion—and to what at that time had been the Great Link—the Changeling had spent a great deal of time with Weyoun, as well as with Rotan'talag, a Jem'Hadar not reliant on ketracel-white. Initially, Odo sought to influence the two through his interactions with them, but that changed when the Founders, in the wake of the death of the Progenitor, had dispersed throughout the galaxy. Odo and Laas endeavored to chase down their fellow Changelings, to calm them and bring them back home. They managed to locate several individual Founders, as well as some who remained together in small links, but their efforts could not overcome the terrible despair that had infected their people. When Odo had finally abandoned his labors to restore the Great Link—though Laas had continued on his own—he'd focused on what remained of the Dominion. He aspired to drastically change the cultures of both the Vorta and the Jem'Hadar, the two species that kept order among the many others who served the interests of the Founders. But Odo quickly learned that, even in the guise of a god, he could not easily modify what genetics, time, and experience had wrought. Instead, he returned to his attempts to effect change in Weyoun and Rotan'talag as individuals, simply by way of his relationships with them.

With the Vorta and the Jem'Hadar by his side, Odo had also worked to keep the Dominion intact after the disappearance of the Great Link. Fortunately, few Dominion denizens ever saw a Founder in person, and so the Changelings' absence had little direct impact on day-to-day affairs. Through his instructions to the Vorta—and, to a lesser extent, to the Jem'Hadar—Odo strived to soften the entire civilization, to unite the separate societies within it into a more cohesive whole, to bring its component parts together in a way that benefited the most lives.

It had been a long road, and Odo traveled it still. Laas returned at some point, and though he did not share Odo's acceptance of solids or his ambitions for the Dominion, he stayed. Other Founders returned as well—twenty-seven so far, twenty-seven parts of a whole—and though they remained anguished and disconsolate, Odo believed that would change, especially as more of them came back and re-formed what might one day again be the Great Link.

Odo had kept the borders of the Dominion closed, hopeful that he would have enough time to accomplish his goals. It troubled him that the Breen and the Romulans had felt emboldened enough not only to violate the sovereignty of the Dominion, but to steal from it, and to do so by way of kidnapping and the threat of additional violence. Odo had liked seeing Sisko, but that too had been an infringement of Dominion space.

The sound of rattling metal broke the silence of the almost-empty plain. Odo and Weyoun turned toward the building, where a door rolled upward. A shape emerged from inside, low to the ground and moving quickly. It traveled in a sinuous motion, not side to side, but up and down. Its head remained steady as it snaked forward.

When the Bronis reached them, she stopped, drew herself up, and balanced on the end of her body, which separated into four small segments at the tip. She had mottled gray flesh and a flat, wide head, with a thin slit of a mouth and two dark eyes that functioned independently of each other. She hissed in Weyoun's direction, which the translator Odo had brought with him interpreted as, "Welcome, Vorta. I am Venetheris."

"Greetings, Venetheris, and thank you for meeting us," Weyoun said. Bowing his head toward Odo, he introduced the Changeling.

"We are honored to have you here, Founder," Venetheris said, her original words a sibilant whistle. "We are sorry that it must be under such circumstances."

"You're not at fault," Odo said, and meant it. When Weyoun had approached him with Venetheris's report of what had occurred on Bronis II, the Changeling had immediately cast the blame upon himself. He could have ordered different protections for the idle starship and weapons plants throughout the Dominion, but that would have required reassigning Vorta and Jem'Hadar from tasks he considered more necessary. Based on the information provided by Laas, and later by Sisko, Odo had treated the theft from Overne III as a singular event, unlikely to recur. That had evidently been a mistake. "Please show us," he told Venetheris.

The Bronis did not turn left or right, but swept her head backward over her body, then began to undulate toward the open door. Odo and Weyoun followed. When they entered the shadow cast by the building, Odo noted a significant drop in temperature.

Venetheris stopped just a couple of meters inside the doorway and once again rose up to her full height. Odo and Weyoun stepped up beside her. Around them spread vast amounts of machinery, taking up a large area of the floor and reaching up toward the roof. Farther on, though, at the other end of the structure, a peculiar emptiness bespoke what had happened. As with the facility on Overne III, equipment had been stripped from its place and removed.

"The machinery with which we manufacture deflector and structural integrity systems has been taken," Venetheris said. "So too has the equipment with which we test those systems."

"And nothing else is missing?" Odo asked. It likely wouldn't make a difference either way, but Odo wanted to be thorough.

"No, nothing else," Venetheris confirmed.

"Do you know when this happened?" Odo asked.

"Not with certainty," Venetheris said, "but no more than a day or so ago. It might even have taken place earlier today."

"There is no indication that the protections against transporters have been compromised?" Odo wanted to know. "And no signs of forced entry?"

"No," Venetheris said. "It defies explanation."

But Odo knew the explanation: a phase-cloaked vessel and transport enhancers. "Do you have other production facilities on the planet with similar equipment?" he asked.

"Yes, we do," Venetheris said.

Odo turned to Weyoun. "I want those plants protected from the inside," he told the Vorta. "Here, and on Overne Three, and wherever else we've got such facilities."

"Yes, Founder," Weyoun said. "I'll make the arrangements as soon as we return to the ship."

Odo asked several other questions of Venetheris, until satisfied that he had all the information he needed. He thanked the Bronis, then started for the door. Weyoun followed. Once they had made it outside and moved beyond the influence of the building's sensor-scrambling field, Weyoun contacted the ship for immediate transport. Within moments, the multihued lights of a transporter beam formed around them.

Odo and Weyoun materialized in an alcove on the bridge of Jem'Hadar Attack Vessel 971. When they stepped from the platform, Weyoun said, "I will take care of reassigning Vorta and Jem'Hadar resources at our starship production facilities."

"Thank you," Odo said. "I need to send a message myself." As Weyoun marched to a nearby console, Odo considered what to say in the communication he would transmit to Sisko. He would inform him of the theft, of course, and of the apparent use of a phasing cloak in doing so, but somehow, he thought he needed to say more.

But then he realized the flaw in sending a message to Sisko. If the vessel carrying the crew who had stolen the equipment from Bronis II had already made it back to the wormhole and successfully navigated past the Starfleet forces there, then Odo's warning would arrive too late. And if the vessel hadn't reached the wormhole—which seemed likely, since the theft had occurred so recently—if it still flew between Dominion space and the Idran system, then its crew would probably block any signal headed in that direction.

Odo realized that he didn't need to say more in his message. He needed to *do* more.

He crossed the bridge to one of the Jem'Hadar there. "Third Rotan'talag," he said, "set course for the Anomaly." Even if he could not successfully transmit a warning, and even if he could not stop a vessel he could not find because it concealed itself with a cloak, perhaps he could still outrun it. If so, then he could deliver his warning in person. To Rotan'talag, he said, "Highest possible speed."

25

The praetor of the Romulan Star Empire stood outside a detention cell that looked larger and far more comfortable to her than it really needed to be. Back on Romulus, she would have expected a bare, compact compartment, with the barest necessities of life provided for in the most minimal of ways. She wondered if the difference resided in the presumed innocence upon which the Federation based its judicial system. Would an individual awaiting trial receive gentler treatment than one already convicted? She didn't know, but the question interested her.

Kamemor had no idea where on Earth her escorts—Federation Security Advisor Jas Abrik and a pair of security officers—had taken her. When she had contacted Admiral Devix aboard *Enderavat* to tell him that she would be removed from Paris to an undisclosed location, he had voiced grave concerns. Perhaps foolishly—though she didn't think so—Kamemor felt no concern regarding her own safety while in the custody of President Bacco's government, but Devix insisted that one of his officers be permitted to accompany the praetor on her journey. The president left the decision to Abrik, whom she charged with the logistics of the trip. Consequently, Subcommander D'Voral had transported down to watch over Kamemor.

The group of five had beamed from the Palais de la Concorde in Paris to a secure, secondary location. There, they embarked on a self-contained, cylindrical shuttle and traveled at high velocity through subterranean tubes—at least, the tubes *seemed* subterranean, though Kamemor realized that she did not know for sure. When they arrived at a third site, they then boarded a lift and descended what seemed like a considerable distance, until they reached a detention facility.

While the security officers took Subcommander D'Voral to a room where they could all observe Kamemor on a display screen, Abrik ushered her to a door. He described in detail precisely what she would find on the other side, which didn't amount to much. He also told her that he would ensure that the door secured behind her, and then he would join the others so that he too could observe. Finally, Abrik allowed her to enter the room on her own.

Inside, she'd found exactly what Abrik had described to her. The small room possessed few features. The door through which she passed marked the only interruption in the wall around it. Directly across from her, a second door led to a 'fresher. Between the two doors, in the center of the space, sat a plain bench, with a padded seat and back. To her right, a huge display formed the entire wall, though it did not look like a display as much as it did a vista—a street-level view of Ki Baratan, the capital city of Romulus. And finally, to her left, a force field composed the fourth wall, containing the detention cell beyond it.

When Kamemor had first entered the room, Tomalak had been lying supine on the narrow mattress at the far end of his cell, his eyes open and staring toward the ceiling. He didn't bother to glance over when she stepped inside and sat down in the center of the bench, and so she did not say anything. Eventually, as he shifted his position on the bed, she saw his gaze dart briefly in her direction.

Had anybody else been in the room besides Kamemor, perhaps Tomalak would have pretended as though he hadn't stolen a glance, hadn't seen who had come to visit him—or, more likely, to interrogate him. But he did see her, and clearly her presence shocked him. When she thought about it herself— that she stood somewhere on the planet Earth—it shocked her too.

"Praetor," Tomalak had said, leaping to his feet and racing toward her. He wore a multi-toned brown jumpsuit, belted at the waist. "I can't believe that you're here."

"I can't really believe it either," she'd told him. "But I needed to find out for myself what happened in the Bajoran system, and why *you* are here."

Tomalak had lied to her almost from his first word. He claimed that he'd been unwilling to carry out Commander T'Jul's plan to attack the Federation, and so he'd been forced to escape to a civilian vessel. He said that he had no idea that the cloaked *Eletrix* had attempted to follow the Breen freighter through the wormhole. He and the crew of the freighter tried to flee because they did not wish to take part in the action against the Federation, and they feared their own destruction. The freighter crew, rather than be captured, chose to commit suicide.

For a while, Kamemor had listened. For a while, she even affected belief. But the more the two spoke, the more apparent Tomalak's fabrications became, and the more he realized that the praetor grasped his mendacity.

But all of that had been at least half a day earlier, perhaps longer. They hardly stopped speaking, one or the other of them finding things to say. At first, Tomalak acted forthcoming, but as their interaction wore on, the praetor saw behaviors and emotions she readily recognized in her former proconsul: derision, sarcasm, annoyance, anger.

Through it all, she had a sense that she should wait for his fatigue. Kamemor did not threaten Tomalak, nor did she promise him anything. She asked mostly indirect questions, but would from time to time approach an issue in a straightforward manner. She doled out bits of information, hinted about other things she knew—some of which she did, some of which she didn't. She understood from the beginning that she would not achieve instant success, but that if success came, it would be as the result of a process.

As she stood before the force field and peered into the cell, she watched Tomalak carefully. He sat on the edge of the bed, bent over, elbows on his knees, head bowed. He could have been feigning weariness, but Kamemor didn't see how. She felt exhausted herself.

"I'm going to try again, Tomalak," she said quietly. "And I'm going to keep trying until you give me what I need. But not only what I need—what the Romulan Empire needs."

Tomalak lifted his head and laughed. "You have no notion what the Empire needs," he said. "If you did, I wouldn't be sitting here, because I wouldn't have needed to save Romulus from its own leader."

"It's interesting you should characterize things in that way," Kamemor said, "because during my time as praetor, I keep finding myself having to extract the Empire from situations *you* caused—situations that, by your own estimation, put Romulus and the Typhon Pact at risk."

"You're blathering, old woman."

"You stole the plans for Starfleet's quantum slipstream drive from Utopia Planitia," Kamemor said. She hadn't mentioned the attack on Utopia Planitia during their long conversation, much less associated Tomalak with it. When she did, he flew to his feet, though he seemed to resist the impulse to charge across his cell toward her. "You succeeded in stealing the plans, but in doing so, you also blew up part of an orbital facility and killed

Federation citizens. You provided President Bacco justification to retaliate militarily against the Empire and the Pact, even to declare war. If that had happened, if the Federation and its allies had gone to war, Romulus would have been forced to fight *without* the slipstream drive. Yes, you'd stolen the plans for it, but how many hundreds of days would it have taken to make it operational?

"So you worried that the Federation enjoyed a military advantage," Kamemor continued, "then forced a potential situation for them to employ that advantage against us." She stared at Tomalak, then added, "You're not very bright, are you?"

This time, Tomalak did rush across his cell, so quickly that Kamemor thought he would strike the force field. He stopped just short of it, though it buzzed at his close approach. From very near, he looked at her with undisguised hatred. "I did not endanger the Empire," he said. "The Breen . . ." He shook his head and turned away. Perhaps he thought he'd told Kamemor too much.

"So I'm wrong?" she said, trying to keep the conversation alive and heading in the direction she needed it to go. "You didn't plan to kill Federation citizens, and thereby risk a war that even you believe the Empire was not equipped to win?"

"No, of course not," Tomalak said. "There were to be no deaths. Explosions, yes, but carefully timed and precisely placed."

"You speak of explosives as though they were exacting instruments," Kamemor said. "That seems . . . optimistic."

Tomalak shrugged. "A few dead Starfleeters," he said with disdain. "The Federation doesn't have the spine to go to war over so little a loss."

"So you thought you would see if you could provoke them by blowing up an *entire* space station?" Kamemor said.

Tomalak offered a guttural response, throwing up a hand and stalking away. He ended up across his cell, with his back to her. But Kamemor knew—and he must have known—that he could not escape.

"What you did at Utopia Planitia," she said, "you did again

in the Bajoran system. You so desperately wanted the slipstream drive for Romulus, and yet you again risked war without delivering it."

Tomalak turned and peered over at Kamemor. She had not revealed to him until that moment that she knew the goal he'd carried into the Gamma Quadrant with him. She thought she saw him reevaluating her, reevaluating what she knew. She seized the opportunity.

"Yes, I know that you stole equipment from the Dominion that would allow you to develop slipstream drive," Kamemor said. "And so in that action, you risked another war with the Founders, with the Jem'Hadar."

Tomalak hurried back over to stand opposite Kamemor. "A *minimal* risk," he said. "We killed no Changelings, no Jem'Hadar. We captured some in battle, but we let them go. We did not seek enemies; we sought strength for the Empire."

"So you took pains not to antagonize the Founders—at least not too much—but you still had no problem provoking the Federation, whom you believed had a tactical advantage?" Kamemor said. "It makes no sense."

Again, Tomalak shook his head. He appeared more tired than ever. Kamemor sensed defeat in him.

Very softly, she said, "If we go to war today, that—" She took a step to the side and pointed across the room to the display of Ki Baratan. "—gets destroyed."

Tomalak looked over at the image of the Empire's capital city, then back at the praetor. "There were supposed to be no deaths," he said. "We just wanted to travel back through the wormhole, cloaked, and slip back home, unseen."

"Really?" Kamemor said, her voice full of skepticism. "Is that why you also planted bombs on Deep Space Nine, and had Breen and Tzenkethi starships waiting cloaked nearby? So that you could 'slip back home, unseen'? That's not terribly convincing."

"The bombs were planted so that Starfleet would evacuate the station," Tomalak said. He sounded oddly desperate to convince the praetor. "I don't know if they were planted late, or not found in time, but the evacuation hadn't ended by the time we got there. And when they went off, they were supposed to disable the station, not destroy it."

"And the Breen and Tzenkethi ships?"

"A backup plan behind a backup plan," Tomalak said.

"Because no matter what, the most important thing was to acquire the capability of slipstream drive for the Empire and the Pact," Kamemor said. "And yet, instead of strengthening the Empire and the Typhon Pact, you've left it without slipstream and on the brink of war with the Federation and the Khitomer Accords."

Tomalak's eyes flashed. In that look, Kamemor saw all she needed to know about him. He used slipstream as a pretense, she realized, a patriotic rationalization to forward his own agenda—an agenda she had long ago come to understand had to do with the common good of the Romulan people only insofar as it would elevate him to a prominent status.

"Yes, we're on the brink of war," the praetor said. "Both sides—the Typhon Pact and the Khitomer Accords—massing at the borders, preparing to fight at the slightest provocation."

Tomalak jeered. "You see," he said, "even destroying a Federation space station is not cause enough to compel them to fight."

"What difference does it make to you?" Kamemor asked. "With the advantage of slipstream, the Federation and its allies will be victorious. And it won't affect you, because this is where you'll sit for the rest of your life."

One side of Tomalak's mouth edged up in a smirk. "We'll see," he said.

"Oh?" Kamemor asked. "Will we?" Kamemor had waited for such a statement. "We'll see, because you think that one of your powerful compatriots will find a way to bring you back to the Empire? Commander Marius of the *Dekkona* can't do it, because Admiral Devix threw him into a military prison. Commander T'Jul of the *Eletrix* can't do it, because she's dead. Perhaps Subcommander Kozik of the *Vetruvis,* who recently became *Commander* Kozik. But no, he's unavailable at the moment."

"I'm sure he is," Tomalak said. Kamemor noted the statement, which seemed to indicate that Tomalak knew the next plan Sela intended to put into action.

The praetor turned and walked away from Tomalak, away from his cell. She crossed the room all the way to the display of Ki Baratan, and she stood gazing at it for several moments. When she turned back, Tomalak stood looking at her from his cell.

"Do you think, I wonder, that your most powerful ally will find a way to bring you home?" Kamemor asked him. "That they will somehow infiltrate the Federation system and see you acquitted of your crimes? Or that they will see me deposed and my successor negotiate for your release, perhaps in some sort of prisoner exchange? Or that they will simply find you and break you out of this existence?" She walked slowly back toward the cell, made her way around the bench, and sat down at its center. "You are misguided, Tomalak," she said. "Sela gave you up."

She saw that he could not control the expression on his face, which showed both surprise at Kamemor's knowledge of Sela's duplicity, and rage that Sela had not protected him. But in the next instant, he attempted to cover. "I presume that you are speaking of Chairwoman Sela," he said. "I'm afraid that I don't—"

"Fine," Kamemor said, standing up. "I can leave now. And once I do, I think you'll have no trouble believing that I will never be back. Nor will anybody from my government—which, of course, no longer includes Chairwoman Sela." A lie, though not for long; Sela would remain free—though under surveillance—only until Commander Kozik and *Vetruvis* could be stopped. Once there could be no chance of Sela or any of her associates warning Kozik that people were searching for him, the chairwoman would face the inside of a cell in Ki Baratan, one far less comfortable than the Federation cell housing Tomalak.

"Please," Tomalak said, motioning toward the exit door. "I've been wanting you to leave for some time now."

"All right," Kamemor said. She took a few paces toward the exit, then said, "But rest assured, the Federation will convict you of your crimes, and they will imprison you for the rest of your life." She looked past him on one side, then on the other. "Your cell is nicely appointed . . . for a cell. And the image of Ki Baratan should keep you from being too homesick, I imagine."

"We'll see," Tomalak said again, but the praetor saw that the idea of remaining in a Federation cell for the rest of his days worried him.

"Yes, we will," Kamemor said. "We'll see testimony from Sela, former chairwoman of the Tal Shiar. Because once we arrested her, we gave her a choice. We promised her freedom in exchange for your captivity. She revealed you as the mastermind of all these operations, of the Utopia Planitia theft, of the Gamma Quadrant mission, of Kozik's mission."

Tomalak laughed, a short, hard sound.

"I feel the same way," Kamemor said. "But right now, Sela is our most important witness, so we have to believe her. If you have something different to tell me, then perhaps you can go free instead of Sela. Because one of you will end up imprisoned." Kamemor shrugged. "I'd prefer it to be the one who actually planned all of these rogue acts, but I'll settle for either one of you."

"It was Sela," Tomalak said. "These were her plans."

"So what?" Kamemor said. "She's no longer chairwoman of the Tal Shiar, no longer welcome in the Imperial Fleet or the government, and her movements will now be monitored continuously, but within one entire sector of the Empire, she is free to roam."

"But it *was* Sela who planned everything," Tomalak said.

Kamemor strolled back to the force field. "I believe you, Tomalak. Actually, I never believed her story. But it was all we had."

"I can tell you a different story," Tomalak said.

"I'm sure you can," Kamemor said. "But that's all it will be to me: a story. I need something more."

"What?"

"I don't need to know about your or Sela's involvement in the plans to steal slipstream from Utopia Planitia or the Dominion," Kamemor said. "I need to know the *next* plan."

"And if I tell you?" Tomalak asked.

The praetor raised her eyes and stared directly into Tomalak's own. "If you tell me, then you won't be in the Imperial Fleet and you won't be in the government, but you will be home. And although we will monitor your movements, you will be free."

Tomalak stared back into the praetor's eyes. He said nothing for a long time. He didn't move, and neither did she.

And then he started talking.

26

Kira regarded the form of her dying friend. Elias Vaughn looked nothing like his former self. The bedclothes—only a sheet and a thin blanket—seemed somehow too large for the body they covered. His skin looked like cheap paper, almost translucent. It pained Kira to see so substantial a man in so insubstantial a form.

And yet he continued to live. Yes, in the most significant way, he had perished two and a half years earlier, above the world of Alonis, aboard *U.S.S. James T. Kirk,* in a successful attempt to save the lives of people on the planet and the crew of his ship—but he hadn't saved his own life. He had died a hero's death, without fully dying.

At first, it had required a complex array of life-support equipment to sustain him. After a time, that changed, and he required machines only to breathe for him and to provide nutrition and hydration. Eventually, even the respirator became unnecessary. But though his body endured, it became clearer with each passing day that his mind would never return. Finally, none of the equipment employed to keep Vaughn alive remained. And though he would soon die—perhaps at any moment—he had already lasted longer than most in such circumstances.

Somehow, even in death, Vaughn seemed indefatigable. His

mind had gone, his spirit had flown, and yet his body fought on. A fragment of the poem Benjamin had read occurred to Kira:

> . . . that which we are, we are . . .

Kira knew that she would never forget Vaughn.

"Are you all right, Prynn?" Kira asked. Vaughn's daughter sat in a chair beside the bed, her hand resting atop her father's.

"Yeah, I am," she said. Even with Prynn's eyes rimmed in red from crying, Kira believed her. After Prynn had asked Doctor Bashir to remove Vaughn's feeding and hydration tubes, she'd reported to *Defiant* for a mission. She said what she believed would be her final farewells to her father, fully expecting to find him no longer alive when she returned. With so many of his friends having visited him, and the lovely words they'd brought and read aloud, she told Kira that it seemed fine for her to be away when her father finally passed.

But when Captain Sisko had brought back *Defiant,* Prynn had learned that Vaughn hadn't yet died. Because of that, she decided to spend the last few minutes or hours or days of her father's life with him. Granted a leave of absence from Starfleet, she essentially moved into the hospice. She slept in a visitor's room not far from her father's, spending as much time with him as she wished.

"I just wanted to stop in and see him again," Kira said. "And to check on you."

"I appreciate that, Nerys," Prynn said. "But I really am all right. This—" She looked down at her hand resting atop Vaughn's. "—feels right."

"I'm glad," Kira said. She walked over to Prynn and put a hand on her shoulder, squeezed it. "I'll see you soon."

Prynn smiled.

Kira left the room. On her way out of the hospice, she said good-bye to the people she had come to know there. Outside, she started back up the path that overlooked the Elestan Valley.

Kira had a rare free afternoon, and she almost didn't know how she should spend her time. That morning, she'd thought about transporting out to Ashalla, perhaps to visit the Shikina Monastery and walk the grounds, but it seemed redundant to leave one religious milieu for another. She considered visiting Opaka, but then hadn't been able to reach the former kai.

Kira had been intending at some point to beam out to Aljuli so that she could walk over to the new Bajoran Space Central—a name that struck her as rather grand for what the old Wyntara Mas Control Center looked like. She didn't doubt that Ro and her crew had improved it greatly, though, especially since she'd heard that Miles O'Brien and Nog had returned. But although Kira hadn't seen some of her friends from the station for a while, and even though she wanted to check on them after what had happened, she also didn't want to intrude on their grief, or interfere with their process of mourning. Really, she should contact Laren and confer with her about when would be the most appropriate time for her to visit.

Something else called to Kira, though, and in that moment, she decided to act on it. She followed the path around and up toward Vanadwan's primary transporter plaza. When she reached the crest of the mountain, she turned to her right and headed along the covered walkway toward the Inner Sanctuary.

Kira approached the temple as she always did, with a sense of reverence both spiritual and secular. She certainly understood—and *felt*—the religious significance of the Crown of Bajor, but the age of the place, its endurance, and its beauty also impressed her. As she neared it, she drifted out from beneath the cover above the walkway and gazed upward, along the lines of the Inner Sanctuary's structure, up to the spires that she could see from her location.

When she reached the old wooden doors, Kira pushed them open and entered. Inside, she waited as her eyes adjusted to the dimness. Small, colored windows near the circular roof provided scant illumination, bolstered only by the flicker of candlelight.

Kira saw only a few worshippers within the temple. A straight wall cut across the round space about three-quarters of the way across it. Seated before it, at a table that looked even older than the Sanctuary itself, sat Vedek Sorva, his face buried in the pages of a large tome spread open before him.

Kira approached him, her footfalls sounding hollow and small in the high-walled space. When the vedek looked up and saw her, he smiled. "Vedek Kira," he said. "How good to see you." He rose to greet her, and his slow, awkward movements made him seem older even than the dark, pitted table at which he sat.

"Please, please, don't get up," Kira told him, but he paid no attention. "Vedek Sorva," she said, reaching out to take both of his hands in hers. "It's good to see you too."

"Come by for some afternoon prayer?" Sorva asked.

"Actually, I was wondering if there was anybody in the Orb room," Kira said. "I was thinking of going in myself."

"Of course, of course," Sorva said. "The room is all yours. Let me take you." Kira could easily have made her way to the door that led to the Orb room, but as the administering vedek in the temple at that time, Sorva had the privilege of escorting the faithful inside. "Have you consulted the Eighth Orb before?"

"I never have," Kira said. The Eighth Orb had only been returned to Bajor from Cardassia seven years earlier, along with three other Orbs: Souls, Truth, and Unity. While many Bajorans flocked to the capital to see them, Kira had resisted. She did so not because she didn't want to experience more of the Prophets' love and guidance, but because she didn't want to force the issue. *Let everybody get out of the Orbs what they need,* she'd thought. *And when the time is right for me, I'll know it.*

"Well, we all walk our own paths in our own time," Sorva said, echoing Kira's own sentiment.

They reached the door at the end of the straight wall, and Sorva pushed it open. The ancient metal hinges creaked. Kira followed him into the room.

The curved outer wall led around to another straight one, which met the first straight wall at a right angle. The ark stood on a small table in the corner, a pair of candles burning on either side of it. "May you hear what the Prophets have to tell you," Sorva said.

"Thank you."

Sorva withdrew and pulled the door closed behind him. Kira regarded the ark. It looked rather plain to her, as they always did, but then how could any artisan hope to match the complex beauty of what the ark would contain? Kira stepped forward, feeling the anticipation of her experience as a flutter in her stomach.

When she reached the table, Kira slipped to her knees. She concentrated for a moment on her breathing, steadying herself, clearing her mind. Then she reached up to the ark, took hold of the wooden handles jutting out of its sides, and pulled it open.

The Orb of Destiny bathed her in its otherworldly light.

Kay Eaton watched as Benny Russell flung open the front door of the police station and raced out into the city.

"Benny!" Cassie Johnson called after him. "Benny!" She tried to follow, but Eaton wrapped her hands around Johnson's upper arm.

What am I doing? Eaton thought, uncertain why she felt so strongly about not allowing Johnson to chase after her boyfriend. But then something—a flicker of emotion, a flash of intuition—made her glance back over her shoulder. Where earlier Eaton thought she'd seen pieces of the ceiling fall to the floor, she once again saw the sky. She understood that she didn't *really* see it, that the plaster above the room remained intact, and even if it hadn't, if there had been holes there, the second story of the building might have been visible, but not the sky.

But in her mind, Eaton envisioned the ragged edges along the openings in the failed ceiling. Through the gaps, she imagined seeing not the second floor, but the pinpoint lights of distant stars. Among them, one of those lights moved.

It's the Temple, she thought. *It's the spaceship in my story.*

And though Eaton did not truly see the holes in the ceiling, or the stars, or the spaceship she'd written into existence, still she saw more. A vibrant blue pinwheel of light appeared and spun energetically in the night, and a moment later, a red one joined it. Somehow, all of that confirmed what Eaton had already decided: that Miss Johnson had to let Benny go, that if she didn't, then they could never be together again.

She looked back at Johnson. "You have to let him go," Eaton said.

"But why?" Johnson asked, still trying to tug her arm free of Eaton's grasp. "We can be together."

"No," Eaton said, surprised by the certainty in her voice, but also comfortable with it. "You have to let him go." She hesitated to say the rest of it, but knew that she must. "You have to let him walk his own path . . . or you'll lose him. You'll lose him forever."

Johnson stopped struggling at once. "What?" She stared into Eaton's eyes, as though searching for something. "What are you talking about?"

"I . . ." She almost said that she didn't know, but she did. "It's the way it has to be."

"Always?"

The question startled Eaton. It seemed so basic, and so obvious, and yet she hadn't expected it. *Always?* she repeated to herself. *Would Cassie Johnson* always *have to let Benny go?*

"Maybe not," Eaton said, and she felt the rightness of her answer, the reality of it. *Because what's true one day might not be true the next.* Events occurred and circumstances changed. "Maybe if—"

The front door suddenly burst open. Still standing beside each other, Eaton's hands still on Johnson's arm, the two women jumped, startled. They both peered over at the doorway. Benny stood there, his eyes wide. "Where's my friend?" he demanded.

"What?" Johnson said. "Benny, do you mean me?"

Benny looked around the room, but past Eaton and Johnson, as if they didn't exist.

"No," Eaton whispered, and she tightened her hold on Johnson's arm. "Let him go," she said. Johnson said nothing, but kept her gaze solidly on Benny. So did Eaton.

Benny bounded over to the high desk at the center of the back wall, where the sergeant on duty sat. "You there," Benny said, pointing up at him. "Constable, do you have a bail ticket for Eli Underwood?"

The police officer—*What was his name? La Dotio?*—looked up briefly from whatever had him so engrossed. *Probably a racing form,* Eaton thought. La Dotio peered down at Benny with a blank expression, then returned his attention to whatever he'd been doing.

"Benny, who . . . who is Eli?" Johnson wanted to know. She seemed confused. Her body slumped, as though she'd all at once lost the will to fight. She looked to Eaton, clearly in need of guidance.

"It's all right," Eaton whispered. "Stay right here." She released her hold on Johnson's arm, then walked over to where Benny stood in front of the tall desk. Eaton reached up and put a hand on his shoulder. He flinched, but when he looked at her, she saw recognition in his eyes. "It's me, Benny," she said. "It's me, Kay. I bailed you out."

"Kay," he said, taking her by the shoulders. "I have to get Eli out." He sounded desperate, his manner fraught.

"Who's Eli?" Kay asked.

"We came in together," Benny said. "We came in from . . . from . . ."

"From Riverdale?" Eaton asked. "From the asylum?"

"We came in together," Benny repeated.

"Okay," Eaton told him. She looked up at the officer. "Excuse me, Sergeant," she said, adopting her professional tone. "Has a Mister Eli Underwood been arraigned? Do you have a bail ticket for him?"

Begrudgingly, as though the effort somehow cost him, the officer shuffled through the papers on his desk. "Underwood . . . Underwood . . . yeah, here we go." He held out the same type of form he'd earlier handed Eaton for Benny. "Bail set at fifty dollars," he said as she took the form. "Second door on your left, pay the officer." He acted as though he delivered new information, as though he hadn't said the same words to her only moments earlier.

"Thank you, Sergeant," Eaton said. "Come on, Benny. Let's go get your friend." She pointed toward the door the officer had mentioned.

"Yes, thank you, Kay," Benny said. "I have to set Eli free."

"We both do," Eaton said. As she walked with Benny toward the proper door, Eaton looked over at Johnson and pointed to the chairs that stood against the front wall, underneath the tall windows. "Sit down," she said. "We'll be right back."

Eaton could tell that Johnson didn't want to let Benny out of her sight, but also that she trusted Eaton. *Why wouldn't she? I paid to get Benny out of jail, and now I'm doing the same thing for his friend, just to calm Benny down.* But Eaton also knew that it was more than all of that. Johnson had *faith* in her.

She and Benny reached the door, which featured a metal grille over a frosted glass insert. Eaton opened it and they went inside, to another desk, one of normal height. Oddly, a different woman sat there than when Eaton had bailed out Benny. Younger, she had exotic features and dark, almond-shaped eyes. "Can I help you?" she asked. She wore her long hair tucked up under her cap.

Eaton produced the bail ticket she'd acquired from the sergeant at the front desk, unslung the strap of her pocketbook from her shoulder, and dug out her checkbook again. Once she'd paid the New York City Department of Corrections another fifty dollars, the officer instructed her to wait out front, and that somebody would bring Mister Underwood out shortly.

Eaton and Benny returned to the front of the police station. Johnson looked up expectantly from where she sat, rising when she saw them. Eaton waved her back down, and she sat. Eaton guided Benny over to the corner to wait. "Are you all right?" she asked him gently.

"I have to free Eli," he said again. Even though she hadn't seen Benny recently, Eaton had known him for a few years. Although he was a good, sometimes brilliant writer, it hadn't completely surprised her when he'd become troubled. The world didn't always play fairly with people, and perhaps that applied to Benny more than most. But he seemed off in a different way at the moment, obsessed with freeing his friend. He had a wild look in his eyes, and he uttered his demand as though reciting words spoken by voices inside his head.

Isn't that what I've been doing? Eaton asked herself. She had behaved as if she knew Cassie Johnson, not just in passing, but as a good friend. Eaton felt she knew some of the things Johnson should and shouldn't do, but where had all that originated, if not from within her own mind? It occurred to her that she didn't even have enough money in her account to cover the two checks she'd written to the Department of Corrections that day.

As minutes ticked by, Eaton stood quietly with Benny. His breathing had calmed from when he'd frantically reentered the police station, and his eyes no longer appeared quite as stormy. "Everything's going to be all right," she told him, and she found that she actually believed that.

The far door finally opened, and another police officer entered with an old man who looked as though he could barely stand up. Pale and lifeless, he wore garments that might once have fit him, but hung on his body like outsized bedclothes. His skin resembled cheap paper, and Eaton thought that he probably suffered from consumption. His eyes seemed empty.

"Kay Eaton?" the officer said.

"I'm Kay Eaton."

"You have a release form?" the policeman asked. Eaton gave it to the officer, who studied it for a moment, then handed it back to her. "We're releasing Eli Underwood into your custody," he said.

Benny rushed over, as though he hadn't recognized his friend until he'd heard his name. When the officer released his grip on Underwood's arm, the old man would have collapsed to the precinct floor if Benny hadn't caught him. Benny threw an arm around his friend's waist and pulled one of Underwood's arms across his shoulders.

"Come on, Eli," Benny said. "We have to go." Holding his friend up, Benny headed for the door.

"Wait," Cassie Johnson said, leaping to her feet. "Where are you going?"

As Benny balanced Underwood's body against his own, he reached for the door and pulled it open. Then he took hold of his friend once more and started out into the city.

Eaton went over to Johnson. "It's all right," she said. "Remember, you have to let him walk his own path."

"What does that even mean?" Johnson asked, obviously frustrated. "I'm worried about Benny." She began to push past Eaton so that she could get to the front door.

"Wait," Eaton said, grabbing for Johnson's arm again, but Johnson pulled it away. Eaton wondered how she could possibly stop her, but then an idea came to her. "I'll go," she said. "I'll go after Benny. You go home and wait, and I'll follow Benny. I'll make sure . . ." *Make sure of what?* But the words rose in Eaton's mind, and so she said them. "I'll make sure he comes home to you."

A sequence of expressions passed over Johnson's face: anxiety, relief, fear, elation.

"Trust me," Eaton said.

Johnson nodded. "I have faith in you," she said.

"What's your address?"

Johnson told her, then said, "But you better hurry."

"Right," Eaton said, and she strode toward the front door and through it.

Outside, down on the sidewalk, Eaton immediately ran into trouble. She didn't see Benny anywhere. She looked left, trying to see past the many people crowding the street. Then she peered in the other direction. Thinking that she'd already failed, she wondered how she could possibly face Cassie Johnson.

But then she saw Benny in the distance, heaving himself forward as he continued to carry his friend at his side. *How far has he gotten already? One long block? Two?*

Eaton hurried down the sidewalk after Benny. She moved as quickly as she could, but her high-heeled shoes made it difficult. She thought about kicking them off, but running barefoot along a teeming New York City street didn't seem like a good idea. Her handbag flopped against her body, and she grabbed it to hold it steady.

Eaton reached an intersection and had to wait for the traffic signal to change. As she did, she looked behind her, hoping that she wouldn't espy Johnson following her, hoping that she had gone home. Fortunately, Eaton didn't see her.

She hastened on when the signal changed. She kept looking on either side of the people near Benny's location, to make sure that if he entered a building or turned onto another street, she would see him. Every few seconds, she would catch sight of him, though, and he kept moving forward, toward the direction of the setting sun.

The crowd thinned as Eaton pursued Benny, until at last she had an unimpeded view of him. From the way he hauled his friend along, she could not tell if Underwood even remained conscious. Up ahead, she saw, the Hudson River loomed, a natural impediment to Benny's westerly flight. She waited to see whether he would turn uptown or down, hoping he wouldn't head out onto one of the piers.

And then the light of the setting sun reflected off the river and into Eaton's eyes. She turned her head and put a hand up to protect herself against the glare, but she didn't slow her pace. When she looked ahead again, Benny and his friend had vanished.

Frantic, Eaton tried to increase her pace. By the time she reached the river, Benny had beaten her there by minutes. She stopped at the riverfront and, hands on hips, scanned the area, searching in every direction.

Dejected, perspiring, she turned and peered out over the water, again wondering what she could say to Cassie Johnson. The setting sun gleamed off the river, turning its surface into a vibrant blue that looked electric. But as she gazed out, she saw a dark spot on the water amid the glow of the day's last light.

It's a boat, she realized. She squinted into the sunset, trying to make out the figures on board. Then she saw Benny and his friend.

Where's he going? Eaton thought. *New Jersey? That doesn't make any sense.* Of course, it never made any sense to Eaton for people to go to New Jersey.

"Benny!" she called out, waving her arms. If she could get his attention, maybe she could talk to him, convince him to return. "Benny!"

But as she called out, she saw the water in front of the boat begin to swirl. At first, Eaton thought she imagined it, but as she looked on, she could definitely see it wheeling around in a circular motion. The water spiraled downward, creating what looked like a hole in the middle of the river.

And then it began to burn red.

"Benny!" she cried out, louder, worried that he didn't see the vortex. But then she realized that, even if he did, he wouldn't be able to escape it. Its currents had caught the boat.

I have to help him, Eaton thought. In desperation, she looked up and down the waterline for another small boat. When she spotted a man not too far away pulling one up onto shore, she ran for it.

As the man stepped away, Eaton threw her hands against the boat and pushed it as quickly as she could into the water. "Hey!" the man yelled after her, but she ignored him and leaped into the boat. She threw her handbag down, then seized one of the oars from where it lay and lifted it up into the curved metal piece that would hold it while she rowed; then she did the same with the second oar.

"Benny!" she cried out again as she began rowing. *He won't be able to escape,* she thought. *I have to get there. I have to—*

"—get to Benjamin."

Kira blinked, disconcerted for a moment. She realized that she'd spoken aloud, which had apparently interrupted her Orb experience. She reached up and closed the ark.

As she stood up, Kira felt a new awareness. Confused images swarmed through her mind. She knew from her own history that people never fully understood Orb experiences. Communing with the ancient, sacred artifacts reached beyond mere comprehension, and it sometimes took years to fully integrate an experience into oneself.

But in that moment, Kira knew what she had to do.

Lying on his back, Miles O'Brien reached up and closed the access panel beneath the runabout's main console. Then he gripped one of the forward chairs in the cabin and pulled himself up, considering it a moral victory when he groaned only once. He took a seat at the console and activated it with a touch. Earlier that day, one of the pilots had reported a problem with the shield monitoring display, and the captain had asked him to take a look at it.

O'Brien performed a quick diagnostic, which indicated that he had solved the issue. While the runabout crew believed a serious problem had arisen with the shield generators, the chief immediately suspected one of the relays between the shielding systems and the display. O'Brien had been right. Of course, he'd been a Starfleet engineer for a lot of years, so he expected to be right.

"Chief?"

O'Brien spun in the chair to see a woman peeking in through the open cockpit door. "Captain," he said, then realized his blunder and corrected himself. "I mean, Vedek."

Kira Nerys stepped inside the cockpit. "Actually, Chief, considering that we've known each other for almost fifteen years, and that I carried your and Keiko's son in my womb for six months, I think you should just call me *Nerys*."

One side of O'Brien's mouth rose in a half-smile. He stood up and crossed the cabin, his hand extended. Kira took it with a strong grip. "How are you?"

"I'm good, thanks," Kira said. "But don't stop on my account." As O'Brien retreated back to the chair, she asked, "So how about you?"

"Nothing to complain about here," he said. "Of course, that usually doesn't stop me."

Kira chuckled. "I've never known an engineer who didn't grumble about something," she said. "So how are Keiko and Molly and Kirayoshi?"

"Great, all great," O'Brien said. "So what brings you by?"

"I was hoping that you and I could talk about that," Kira said. "Do you have five minutes to take a walk?"

"Sure, I was almost done in here anyway," O'Brien said. "I just needed to check on the replicator. The crews say it's been acting up a bit."

"And you can't have an effective Starfleet crew if they can't get good raktajino," Kira said.

O'Brien rolled his eyes. "Isn't that the truth?"

Kira turned and quickly ducked out of the cabin. O'Brien rose from the chair, took a moment to survey the cockpit for anything out of place, then followed Kira outside. He stepped down onto the BSC's one makeshift runabout pad, which they'd constructed out of the thermoconcrete used to build emergency bunkers. O'Brien knew it wouldn't last, but it would at least provide a stopgap until they could complete the permanent pads.

"What do you think of our big barn?" O'Brien asked, pointing over at the center. "It's—" He realized that he didn't see Kira. He took a few steps toward the center, thinking that she must have gone inside already, though he didn't see how she could have made it that far so quickly.

That's when the runabout lifted off behind him.

27

Sisko sat in the ready room aboard *Defiant*, peering at the computer interface on the desk. There, a split-screen view displayed the images of Admiral Akaar and Captain Picard.

"The Typhon Pact—or elements within it—have apparently engineered their own version of an artificial wormhole," Akaar said.

"How is that even possible, sir?" Sisko asked. "There are certainly differences in technology between the Khitomer Accords and the Typhon Pact, but for the most part, we're on a relative par with each other. Yet Federation scientists are nowhere near being able to create a stable wormhole."

"That's the good news," Akaar said. *"According to our sources, the wormholes that the Pact can create are relatively short— crossing no more than five or so light-years of normal space-time— and they aren't stable. They can control the near terminus, but the far terminus does not remain in one place for very long."*

"That is good news," agreed Picard. *"Producing a wormhole*

without stable termini necessarily limits the Pact's use of such technology."

"*That would be the case,*" Akaar said, "*if the Pact hadn't discovered a means of anchoring the far terminus.*"

"Admiral, again, I don't see how that's possible," Sisko said. He'd read enough reports over the years about the Bajoran wormhole to have an idea of the tremendous gravitational stresses involved. "If you were to try to anchor a wormhole to a planet, even a massive planet, the gravity well wouldn't hold it. You could certainly use a black hole to do so, and perhaps even some less massive stars, but if that's where the journey through their wormhole ends, in the center of a star . . ." It suddenly occurred to Sisko that such technology could conceivably be employed as a weapon, as a delivery device with which to inject—

"*As far as we know, their technology cannot anchor their wormhole to a planet or to a star,*" Akaar said. "*They can only link it to an existing, stable wormhole.*"

"An existing, *stable* wormhole?" Sisko said. In all the exploration Starfleet had ever done, only one example of such an entity had ever been found. "You mean the Bajoran wormhole."

"*That's what we believe, yes,*" Akaar said.

"*Which means that the Typhon Pact would have access to the Gamma Quadrant without having to enter Federation space,*" Picard noted.

Sisko drew the final conclusion to which Akaar no doubt headed. "And since the Pact has demonstrated its almost obsessive desire to create their own quantum slipstream drive, and since we know that the Dominion has the equipment they need to make that happen, that gives us every reason to believe that they'll try again to acquire it."

"*That's what we believe their plan is,*" Akaar confirmed.

"*Do we have any notion when they might make this attempt?*" Picard asked.

"*No,*" Akaar said, "*but a Romulan warbird, the Vetruvis, is presently unaccounted for, and its commander is a suspected conspirator in one of the other attempts to acquire slipstream.*"

None of that sounded good to Sisko, but he also worried

about the nature of the solution the admiral would propose. "So what are your orders, sir?" he asked.

"*Our primary aim must be to prevent the Typhon Pact from acquiring slipstream,*" Akaar said. "*At the moment, it remains by far our best deterrent. In a couple of years, as Starfleet completes its recovery from the Borg invasion, that will likely no longer be the case. For right now, though, we need to keep it out of the Pact's hands. That means that we must either find a method of preventing them from anchoring their wormhole to the Bajoran wormhole or, if necessary, ensuring that they cannot acquire the equipment they need from the Dominion.*"

"My recent contact with the Founders was friendly," Sisko said, "but they also made it quite clear that they did not want contact with anybody outside the Dominion, including the Federation. I suspect we would find it virtually impossible to negotiate any sort of agreement with them about their equipment, and even warning them of the possibility of another attempted theft might not go over well."

"*All of that may work to our benefit, Captain,*" Akaar said, "*since the Dominion will clearly be averse to dealing with the Typhon Pact. But the Pact was successful in stealing the equipment they needed once, and although they evidently had the element of surprise then, we still cannot discount the possibility that they will succeed again.*"

"*Agreed,*" Picard said.

"*My choice, though, is not to have to rely on the Dominion for anything,*" Akaar said, "*which means that we need to take care of this ourselves if we can. Finding a way to fortify the Bajoran wormhole, to make it impossible for the Pact to anchor their wormhole to it, would be the ideal solution.*"

"We can have the scientists who were stationed at Deep Space Nine and who have studied the wormhole take a look at that, Admiral," Sisko said, "but from my own experience, if such a solution is even possible, it's unlikely to be developed any time soon."

"*Another alternative would be to find a way to disrupt the Pact's wormhole once it has been anchored,*" Akaar said. "*It might be as simple as firing a phaser blast or a quantum torpedo into it.*"

"With all due respect, Admiral," Sisko said, "we have no idea how firing weapons within the wormhole will affect the aliens who reside there. And in attempting to disrupt the Pact's wormhole, we could end up affecting the Bajoran wormhole." Sisko had some very strong feelings about the Prophets, some of them certainly not positive, but he did not wish to see their existence endangered.

"Captain Sisko, I already know the answer to this, but I have to ask," Akaar said. *"Is there any prospect of getting assistance from the aliens within the wormhole?"*

"No, Admiral," Sisko said. "Not as far as I know."

"Well, as I said before, I'd rather take care of this situation ourselves anyway, rather than relying on somebody else," Akaar said. *"Captain Sisko, because of your long experience with the wormhole, as well as with the Dominion, I'm placing you in charge of this mission. You've got five starships out there at Bajor. Use them as you see fit, but under no circumstances are you to leave the Bajoran system and the Alpha Quadrant terminus of the wormhole undefended."*

"Understood, sir," Sisko said.

"Keep me informed. Akaar out."

The admiral signed off, leaving Sisko's display showing the visage of Captain Picard. *"So what do you think our first action should be, Captain?"* Picard asked.

"I think I'd like to take a look at the wormhole," Sisko said. "Make sure that it hasn't been compromised yet."

"I think that would be the prudent course," Picard said. *"Once we do that, perhaps we can station one of our ships in the Gamma Quadrant to make continuous checks for cloaked vessels emerging from the wormhole."*

"That's a possibility," Sisko said, "although if the Pact sends a stronger force, it could leave a single Starfleet vessel vulnerable."

"It is a thorny situation," Picard said.

"Let's do a recon first," Sisko said. "Then we'll go from there."

"Understood," Picard said.

"Please brief the other captains on what the admiral had to say."

"At once," Picard said.

"Thank you, Captain. Sisko out."

Even before the display went blank, Sisko rose and headed for the *Defiant* bridge. As he exited the ready room and crossed the main portside corridor, he wondered about the Prophets. Would an attempt to anchor another wormhole to theirs put them at risk? Would they be able to prevent such a thing from occurring, or combat it if it did? He didn't know. He had never been able to answer many questions about the Prophets, and it had been a long time since he'd been able to answer any at all.

The door to the bridge opened before him. Inside, the crew waited at their stations. Sisko had lost Lieutenant Tenmei to an understandable leave of absence, and Ensign th'Shant to an arrest for an unfathomable crime. The first officer, Wheeler Stinson, had taken over at the conn, and Zivan Slaine, a Cardassian officer, at tactical.

"Commander Stinson," Sisko said. "Take us into the wormhole."

Transitus

The anticipation of success filled Denison Morad when he heard Lieutenant Reval's report.

"We are approaching the Idran system," she'd announced an instant earlier from her station on the port side of the *Vetruvis* bridge.

Morad stood beside Commander Kozik, who sat in the command chair with a satisfied look on his face. The Gamma Quadrant terminus of the wormhole, Morad knew, opened into the Idran system, which put the Romulan vessel and its valuable cargo only moments away from the fulfillment of their mission. When he thought about the odds he had overcome to make his achievement possible, Morad felt a powerful pride. His triumph provided a perfect example of Cardassian superiority, the very reason that had compelled him to embark on his long journey. The True Way may have had to utilize the assets of others to achieve their victory, but they had done so as leaders.

"Commander," Reval said, "sensors are picking up another vessel entering the system."

Morad felt a flutter of unease at the unwelcome news.

"Identify," Kozik said. "Is it Starfleet?"

"Scanning now," Reval said. Morad glanced over to the sensor console. As Reval operated her controls, the pale glow of the panel reflected across her features. "It's not Starfleet," she finally said. "It's Jem'Hadar, and they're headed for the wormhole."

Morad turned back to Kozik in time to see his jaw clench. "It's probably the ship transmitting the message," the Romulan commander said.

Almost as soon as the warbird had departed Bronis II with the slipstream-related equipment, Centurion Rentin, the ship's communications officer, had intercepted a message that had originated in the Dominion, and that had been intended to inform the Federation of the Typhon Pact's theft. Kozik had tasked Rentin with jamming the transmission.

"Commander, I can confirm that the Jem'Hadar ship *is* the source of the message," Rentin said. "Even now, its crew is continuing to transmit."

The executive officer, Subcommander Analest, looked up from where she crewed the ship's weapons and defensive systems. "Will we reach the wormhole before the Jem'Hadar do?" she asked. Morad wondered the same thing, knowing that the success of the mission might depend on the answer.

"Calculating," Reval said, again working her controls. When she peered over at Kozik, Morad knew what she would say even before she uttered the single word: "No."

"Commander," Rentin said, "once the Jem'Hadar vessel passes us, I'll no longer be able to block their transmission."

The news unsettled Morad, but he attempted to maintain his confidence. He reasoned that, even if the message reached the Bajoran system before *Vetruvis* made it into the wormhole, it seemed unlikely that any Starfleet crews stationed there would have time enough to react. He thought that the greater concern came from the Jem'Hadar vessel and what it might do once it reached the wormhole.

Commander Kozik looked to his first officer. "Analest?" he said, clearly soliciting her opinion.

"I don't think we have much choice," said the subcommander.

"I agree," Kozik said.

At once, Analest acted on the commander's implied order. "Lieutenant Natrel, give me an attack vector," she told the pilot. "We need to stay ahead of the Jem'Hadar vessel and move in fast." Morad watched as Analest's hands flew across her console. "We'll drop the cloak as late as possible on our attack run, and hit them hard. I'll target engines and communications."

"The Federation's communications relay is on the edge of the system," reported Rentin. "Once we strike the Jem'Hadar vessel, it would be a simple matter to destroy the relay as well." Morad saw Kozik nod to Analest, who told the pilot to prepare for such a maneuver.

"Bringing us about," said Natrel.

"On-screen," ordered Kozik.

On the main viewer, the image shifted, and the Jem'Hadar fighter appeared. Morad could see that *Vetruvis* would come in from below and strike the ship's glowing purple underbelly. At the sensor station, Reval began counting down the distance between the two ships. Morad found himself holding his breath, and he forced himself to breathe as normally as he could.

"Now," Reval said. The dim green lighting on the bridge brightened, which Morad knew signified to the crew that the warbird no longer flew under cloak. At the same time, he saw a disruptor barrage pound into the Jem'Hadar vessel, accompanied by a fusillade of plasma torpedoes. The enemy vessel's shields flared brightly beneath the onslaught, which continued until *Vetruvis* soared past. As it did, the ship quaked.

"Polaron blasts," announced Reval. "Shields down to ninety-three percent, but otherwise a minimal effect."

"Adjusting course to the communications relay," said Natrel.

Morad continued to watch the viewer, and he saw a vague shape appear in the center of the screen, the object barely visible. It grew larger as *Vetruvis* approached, but before the Cardassian could make out any detail, disruptors seared through space in front of the ship. The relay exploded in a fiery flash, its destruction confirmed by Analest.

"Status of the Jem'Hadar ship?" Kozik asked, looking for the answer that Morad also wanted to know.

"Considerably damaged," Reval said. "Their communications are down, their shields are below fifty percent, and their warp engines appear to be off line."

"They won't need warp speed to reach the wormhole," Kozik noted. "Are their sublight engines still operational?"

"Scanning," Reval said. "They are, Commander, and the ship *is* still headed for the wormhole."

"Stop them," Kozik ordered.

Morad kept his gaze on the main screen as the starscape swam across it. The Jem'Hadar vessel hove into view, and *Vetruvis* headed directly for it. Morad saw a flash of light an instant before the Romulan warbird shook violently. His hand flew out to the arm of the command chair in order to brace himself and keep from falling.

"Direct hit with polaron cannon," Reval called out over the clamor. "Shields down to seventy-nine percent."

On the viewer, bright green streaks of disruptor fire leaped forth from *Vetruvis* and slammed into the Jem'Hadar vessel. Plasma torpedoes provided a staccato accompaniment. The enemy vessel's shields flared again and again, and then a jet of atmosphere burst into space from its wounded form. "Their shields are down to thirty-one percent," Reval said as *Vetruvis* swept past the fighter. "Their impulse engines are off line and their hull has been breached."

"Well done," Kozik said. "Cloak us and take us to the wormhole."

Morad waited for the lighting to dim, the visual signal to the crew that their ship once more traveled invisibly through space. But the illumination didn't change. Morad peered about the bridge, as though he could distinguish the problem with just a glance.

"Commander," Analest said, "the cloak is down."

Concern rose immediately in Morad's mind, but Kozik

quickly dismissed the failure of the ship's cloaking device. "It doesn't matter," the commander said. "Take us into the wormhole."

Analest peered up from the weapons and defense console and over at the pilot. "Natrel, best possible speed to the wormhole," she said. "Take us home."

On the viewer, Morad saw the field of stars reorient once more as the ship's pilot pointed *Vetruvis* onto its new heading— onto its *original* heading. The encounter with the Jem'Hadar vessel had momentarily shaken the Cardassian, but he suddenly felt a renewed sense of assurance as they began the last major leg of their journey. He kept his gaze on the viewscreen.

When the brilliant blue whorl of light appeared, Morad silently rejoiced as *Vetruvis* dived into its star-bright center.

Sisko sat in the command chair of *Defiant,* his eyes locked on the main viewer. Before the ship, the Bajoran wormhole reached through subspace toward the Gamma Quadrant. Great blue streamers of energy rippled as they always had, and the familiar white rings edging the perimeter flowed past. Raindrop-like concentric circles dappled the inner surface of the artificial tunnel, lending an additional sense of movement to the ship's surroundings. Nothing seemed out of the ordinary.

But then, in the distance, Sisko spotted a fearsome red glow. The hue marked a departure from the norm within the wormhole, the palette of which the captain had through the years come to know well. Sisko felt a hollow sensation grow in the pit of his stomach. Even at a distance, even unidentified, the irregularity seemed like a violation. "What the hell?" Sisko said, though he already knew what the crew would find. He stood up, as though doing so would afford him a better view.

"I'm getting confused readings," said Lieutenant Commander Candlewood from the sensor station. "Some excessively high proton counts, but not uniformly. It scans as a rent in the fabric of the wormhole."

"Commander Stinson, slow us down," Sisko said. "Bring us to a stop in front of it. I want to get a good look." In truth, the captain would have preferred to avert his gaze from what struck him as a defilement of the Celestial Temple.

"Aye, sir," replied Stinson.

On the viewscreen, as *Defiant* neared it, the scarlet spot resolved into a blemish on the side of the wormhole. As the ship drew closer, though, Sisko discerned the area's edges, and realized that the color came not from the circumference of the Bajoran wormhole, but from the walls of what had been attached to it.

"I'm seeing the attributes of a wormhole within the opening," Candlewood said, "but there's also some variability."

The rim of the aperture did not appear smooth, Sisko saw, but ragged. The coupling also appeared to affect some of the Bajoran wormhole's regular characteristics. Around the region of intersection, the normally graceful motion of the energy streamers became irregular and disjointed. A trio of the outer white circles had wrinkled.

As *Defiant* came to a halt before the opening, the ship bucked. "Steady," Sisko said.

"I'm encountering some gravimetric disturbances, Captain," Stinson said.

"It scans almost like a tidal force," explained Candlewood. "There's an ebb and flow of space-time through the opening." The science officer worked the sensors, obviously attempting to puzzle out the unusual readings. "It's almost as though the new wormhole is trying to tear itself free." Sisko imagined a whip with its tip fixed, but the rest of its length still in motion.

"Is there any way to help that process along?" Sisko asked. "To make it tear away?"

"Possibly," Candlewood said, "but we're going to need to collect detailed readings and take some time to analyze them. Even if we can figure out a means of dislodging it, there's the question of how that would impact the Bajoran wormhole. It could cause its structural integrity to fail around the opening, which could result in a cascade collapse."

Sisko could not help but think of the Prophets, and wonder how such an event would affect them. Could they even survive if the Celestial Temple fell in on itself? "Gather all the information you need for an analysis," he told Candlewood. "Lieutenant Aleco, open a channel to the *Enterprise*."

"Yes, sir," said Aleco from where he sat at the communications console.

Sisko set his hands on his hips and regarded the bright red abnormality. It filled him with revulsion. *It looks like a scar,* he thought. *No, not a scar, because the Bajoran wormhole hasn't healed . . . it's a wound . . . a mutilation.* To the man whom many still considered the Emissary of the Prophets, the attached wormhole felt like an abuse . . . even an atrocity.

"Sir, I can't raise the *Enterprise* or any of the other ships," Aleco said. "The communications relay must be down." Starfleet's continuous comlink that ran from the Gamma Quadrant into the Alpha Quadrant provided the only means of transmitting messages through, or from within, the Bajoran wormhole.

"We can't leave this site unguarded," Sisko said, more to himself than to the crew. Since the Typhon Pact had constructed their artificial wormhole in a way that provided them access to the Gamma Quadrant, they might already have sent ships on their way to the Dominion. And if the communications relay *had* gone down, Sisko could easily envision its destruction at the hands of the Pact—which would confirm that at least one of their vessels had already navigated through the two wormholes. If so, the captain could not allow any of those ships back through.

Stepping forward, the captain leaned in beside Stinson at the integrated conn and ops station. "Commander, would it be possible to position the *Defiant* within the intersection in order to form a blockade?"

Stinson tapped at his controls, which chirped in response. "We can obstruct a portion of the opening," he said. "Maybe as much as half of it if we extend our shield envelope, but that would still leave enough space for another vessel to slip past us."

Damn! Sisko thought, understanding that, in order to fully protect against the Typhon Pact's latest threat, the *Defiant* crew required immediate assistance. He stood back up straight and turned to the port side of the bridge. "Lieutenant Aleco," he said, "I want you to take a shuttle back to Bajoran space. Contact Captain Picard and inform him of what we've discovered. Tell him to order the *Venture* to join the *Defiant* inside the wormhole, and that I want him to station the *Enterprise* in the Idran system at the—"

"Captain," Dalin Slaine interrupted from the tactical station, tension in her voice. "I'm detecting another ship inside the wormhole, approaching from the Gamma Quadrant."

"On-screen," Sisko said.

On the main viewer, he watched with a measure of relief as the terrible red blight afflicting the Bajoran wormhole vanished. At the same time, Sisko feared that what replaced it might prove even more of a danger. It did not surprise him when the image of a Romulan warbird appeared.

"Captain," said Slaine, "they're running with weapons hot."

"Weapons?" Sisko said. "In the wormhole?" The idea horrified him. Even so long after his last contact with the Prophets, and even with the complex emotions he felt about them, the thought of a firefight within the Celestial Temple struck him as a profanity. More than that, though, such an incident would further endanger the beings who resided within the Bajoran wormhole.

"Sir?" asked Aleco, who had made it halfway to the portside aft door. He'd apparently stopped there when Slaine had interrupted Sisko's order to take a shuttle back to the Alpha Quadrant.

"For now, back to your post," Sisko said. He would not risk Aleco's life by sending out a shuttle with a Romulan warbird in such close proximity. He would have to find another way to thwart the Typhon Pact. "Commander Stinson, back us into the opening. Increase the extent of our shield envelope as much as possible. Move the ship as you need to, but we need to prevent that warbird from getting past us."

"Aye, sir," Stinson said, already working at his console to translate the captain's orders into reality.

As *Defiant* maneuvered into position, Sisko returned to the command chair and sat down. He had no idea how long he and his crew could prevent the Romulan vessel from entering the red wormhole, or, without firing their weapons, how they could permanently stop the warbird. He only knew that they had no choice but to make a stand.

Captain Picard sat in the command chair on the *Enterprise* bridge, peering at the panoply of stars on the main viewscreen. *Defiant* had departed only a few minutes earlier, but still Picard waited for the impressive display of the Bajoran wormhole to reappear. He knew that, in some manner, Starfleet would have to determine an ongoing way of protecting the spectacular natural resource.

Except that it's not natural, is it? Picard reminded himself. He didn't understand how or why Captain Sisko had lost his ability to communicate with the aliens who resided within the wormhole, but it seemed unfortunate that they could not be warned about the potential danger ahead.

"Captain, we're receiving a transmission," said Lieutenant Choudhury from the tactical console. Picard anticipated a report on the status of the wormhole from Captain Sisko, but *Enterprise*'s security chief told him something different. "It's from Bajoran Space Central," she said. "It's Captain Ro."

Picard exchanged a look of curiosity with his first officer, who sat to his right, then peered up at Choudhury. "Put her on-screen, Lieutenant."

Ro Laren appeared on the main viewer, situated within the confines of what appeared to be a very small office. "Captain Ro," Picard said. "What can I do for you?"

"Actually, I'm not sure, Captain," Ro said. *"A short time ago, we had something very peculiar take place here at Bajoran Space Central."* She paused, clearly not comfortable with whatever information she needed to reveal. *"You're familiar with Kira Nerys?"*

"Yes, of course," Picard said. "She was one of your predecessors aboard Deep Space Nine." Picard hesitated over the name of the station, not wanting to evoke the terrible events of less than a month earlier. The *Enterprise* crew had actually recovered Kira from DS9's wreckage, though Picard had not spoken with her. "She commanded for two years, I believe."

"That's right," Ro said, but then she looked away and shook her head. When she gazed forward again, Picard interpreted her expression as one that mixed concern and confusion. *"Kira's a vedek now,"* Ro continued. *"And if my chief engineer is to be believed, it appears that she just appropriated one of our runabouts."*

"What?" Picard said. He glanced over at his first officer. The captain knew that Worf had served for some time with Kira. The Klingon could only look back with a nonplussed expression.

Picard peered back at Ro. He did not appreciate having to address such a situation while in the midst of dealing with the far more serious issues at the wormhole. "Pardon me, Captain," Picard said, not hiding his displeasure, "but how does something like that happen?"

"It happens when you've got a ground-based facility masquerading as a space station," Ro said, not without an edge, *"and people who've known Kira Nerys for more than a decade not expecting her to hijack a spacecraft."*

Picard thought about that for a moment. He had to admit to himself that if, say, Will Riker or Deanna Troi wanted to transport aboard the *Enterprise* and purloin a shuttle, they probably wouldn't run into much opposition—not even from Picard himself. "All right," he said, softening his tone. "Where is Kira now?"

"Headed in your direction, Captain," Ro said. *"That's why I'm contacting you."*

"Do you have any idea why Kira would—"

"Captain," interrupted Choudhury, "we're being hailed by a runabout. It's the *Rubicon*. It's Vedek Kira."

"Did you hear that, Captain?" Picard asked Ro.

"I did," Ro said.

"We will retrieve your pilfered runabout and return it to you," Picard said. "I'll let you know what Vedek Kira has to say for herself."

"*Thank you, Captain,*" Ro said.

"Picard out." As the stars replaced Ro on the viewer, the captain turned to Choudhury. "Put the vedek on-screen, Lieutenant."

Picard immediately recognized the face of the woman who appeared on the display. He'd met and dealt with Kira Nerys on several occasions in the course of his career. She did not wear a uniform—she'd resigned from Starfleet five or six years earlier, as best Picard could recall—or the traditional vestments of a vedek, but a casual, albeit flattering, outfit.

"*Captain Picard,*" Kira said, a sense of urgency in her voice. "*I need to speak with you at once.*"

"Vedek Kira," Picard said, rising and moving to stand in the center of the bridge. "This is unexpected."

"*Yes, Captain, I know,*" Kira said. "*I'm sure Ro's contacted you by now to tell you that I borrowed one of her runabouts.*"

"I don't believe that Captain Ro used the word *borrowed,*" Picard said.

"*Fine, I stole it,*" Kira said. "*I'll gladly turn it over to you and surrender myself into your custody. But none of that matters right now. The important thing is that I need to speak with you about a critical issue.*"

"An issue critical to whom?" Picard asked.

"*I'd rather not reveal that on an open channel,*" Kira said. "*Will you give me an approach beacon so that I can land in your shuttlebay and we can talk in person?*"

At Kira's question, Picard glanced over at Choudhury, who appeared concerned. "Stand by, Vedek," he said, then motioned to the security chief, who interrupted the communication. "Lieutenant?"

"Sir, she *stole* a Starfleet runabout," Choudhury said. "It's unclear if we can trust her to land safely aboard."

Worf quickly rose from his chair and paced over to stand beside Picard. "Captain, I served with Kira on Deep Space Nine for four years," he said. "She is an honorable woman. If she took a runabout, she must have a very good reason for it. And she is not absconding with the *Rubicon,* but flying it directly to a Starfleet vessel and requesting a meeting with you."

Picard considered Worf's judgment, then looked back to Choudhury. "Lieutenant," the captain asked, "do you think that the vedek has suddenly become a terrorist?"

"I don't think that she's *become* a terrorist, sir," Choudhury said. "She has always been a terrorist."

Until that moment, Picard had forgotten about Kira's past under the Cardassian Occupation. Clearly his chief of security had not. The captain sighed, then said, "That was a long time ago, Lieutenant, and under very different circumstances. Since then, Kira has worn this uniform." He motioned to his own tunic.

"Vedek Kira is no longer in Starfleet," Choudhury said. "But even if she were, I would be remiss in my duty if I did not point out that people wearing the uniform have betrayed their allegiance before." Picard didn't know if his security chief specifically intended to make reference to Ro Laren, but the captain understood her point.

"How far away is the *Rubicon*?" Picard wanted to know.

"At its current speed," Choudhury said, checking her panel, "less than two minutes."

"And have you scanned the runabout?" the captain asked.

"Yes, sir," Choudhury said. "There's no indication of explosives or other weaponry other than what's standard for a runabout. The vessel does not appear to have been altered in any way, and it contains no passengers other than Vedek Kira."

"So no unusual readings?" Picard said. "No details that would alert our chief of security?"

"Other than the fact of the runabout's theft, no," Choudhury said.

Picard nodded. "In that case," he said, "I think we can give Vedek Kira the benefit of the doubt for now. But to respect your concerns, Lieutenant, we'll tractor her in."

"Aye, sir," Choudhury said.

Picard gestured toward the main screen, and the security chief reopened the channel to *Rubicon*. "Vedek Kira," Picard said, "we are transmitting an approach beacon for you, and we'll bring the *Rubicon* in using our tractor beam."

"*Understood, Captain,*" Kira said. "*Thank you.*"

"I'll see you shortly," Picard said. "*Enterprise* out."

Kira's image winked off the screen, replaced again by a view of the stars. Picard looked to Choudhury. "Make the necessary arrangements, Lieutenant."

"Sending out an approach beacon," Choudhury said, operating the controls of her console. But then she added, "Captain, I know that you and Commander Worf know Kira personally, but—"

"I understand, Lieutenant," Picard said. "If you feel it's necessary, send a security team to greet Vedek Kira and escort her to my ready room."

"I'll go," Worf said.

"Very good, Number One," Picard said. Then, looking to Choudhury, he said, "You have the bridge, Lieutenant." The captain started toward his ready room, but before he reached it, the security chief spoke up.

"Captain, the *Rubicon* has deviated from the approach beacon," she said.

"What about the tractor beam?" Worf asked.

"I was just about to deploy it when the runabout began taking evasive maneuvers," she said. "It's headed—" Choudhury stopped and peered over at the main viewscreen, where the Bajoran wormhole erupted in a rolling surge of luminous blue.

"Warn her off," Picard ordered, but too late.

Kira Nerys flew the *Rubicon* into the wormhole.

Morad stared at the main viewer on the *Vetruvis* bridge. On the screen, a Federation starship stood sentry between the Romulan warbird and the fulfillment of the mission. "What are they waiting for?" he asked, frustrated at what seemed like the final impediment to his success.

"I don't know," said Kozik. Once the crew had detected the presence of the Starfleet vessel in the entrance to the Tzenkethi wormhole, the commander had ordered *Vetruvis* to a halt. The Federation ship made no aggressive moves, but without its cloak, the Romulan warbird could not hide. "Is there room for us to fly past them?" Kozik asked.

At the sensor board, Reval worked her controls. "The Starfleet vessel is projecting its shields out around it," she said, "but they can only obstruct about half the entry."

Kozik nodded, but he said nothing more. Morad could not stand the inaction. "What are *you* waiting for?" he demanded of the commander.

Kozik slowly turned his head to peer at Morad. "Would you have us attempt to rush past the ship out there," he asked, "so that its crew can use its shields to force the *Vetruvis* into the wall of the wormhole?"

Morad said nothing. In his mind, though, he visualized the confrontation of which the commander spoke.

"Do you know what would happen in such a case?" Kozik asked.

"No," Morad responded meekly, though he imagined a catastrophic end.

"Neither do I," Kozik said. "Neither do any of us. Any more than we know what will happen if we fire energy weapons inside a wormhole."

From the weapons and defense console, Subcommander Analest said, "Commander, what about a tractor beam? If we sweep in as if to attack, perhaps we can surprise the Starfleet crew and capture their ship."

Kozik looked from Analest to the viewscreen, and then back again. "That is one of their *Defiant*-class starships," he said. "It has powerful engines."

"As does the *Vetruvis,*" Analest said. "But velocity is limited within the wormhole, anyway, and so an equal force for both ships. But our vessel has a greater mass than theirs, so we should be able to move them aside. We'd only need a matter of moments to clear them from the mouth of our wormhole."

Morad looked at the commander and studied his reaction. The Cardassian hoped that Analest's proposal made practical sense. Morad understood that the longer *Vetruvis* remained within the Bajoran wormhole, the more likely that Starfleet reinforcements would arrive and foil the delivery of the slipstream-enabling technology.

Kozik peered at the viewer once more, and then, quietly, said, "Yes." Then, louder, "Yes." Morad felt a rush of excitement as the commander stood up and made his way to the center of the bridge. "Lieutenant Natrel," Kozik said, "calculate a crossing run designed for an attack, but bring us in just close enough to engage our tractor beam."

"Yes, Commander," Natrel said.

"Analest," Kozik said, "when we're close enough, use the tractor to capture the Starfleet vessel and haul it out of the entrance to the Tzenkethi wormhole. Maneuver the ship out of our path and release it. Natrel, the instant we drop the tractor beam, take the *Vetruvis* inside."

Both the executive officer and the pilot acknowledged their orders. Morad waited anxiously while they made their preparations. Finally, Natrel said, "Course laid in, Commander."

"Tractor beam at the ready," said Analest.

Kozik returned to the command chair and sat down. "Execute," he said.

As *Vetruvis* leaped forward, Morad saw the Federation starship grow on the viewscreen. He expected phasers to erupt from the enemy vessel at any moment, but the ship only moved to alter its position relative to the warbird. On the cusp of attempting to dash past the Federation starship, *Vetruvis* suddenly slammed to a halt.

On the viewer, Morad saw hazy white rays shoot from the warbird, like the grasping tendrils of some deep-sea creature searching for its next meal. The Federation vessel lurched backward, farther into the Tzenkethi wormhole, but then *Vetruvis*'s tractor beam reached it and held it fast.

"Now," Kozik called out. "Full reverse."

But Morad heard that the sound of the engines had already changed. A great whine suffused the bridge as the warbird's engines strained to overcome those of the enemy vessel. For long moments, the two ships faced each other, connected by the white glow of *Vetruvis*'s tractor beam.

And then Morad saw the Federation starship begin to move. He watched eagerly as *Vetruvis* retreated from the entrance to the Tzenkethi wormhole, pulling the Starfleet vessel away from where it blocked the path back home.

The lighting panels on the bridge of the Jem'Hadar fighter had failed, leaving only the illumination provided by a number of active control stations and a sporadic series of sparks near where part of the overhead had collapsed. Odo hurried from one member of the crew to another, checking on their condition. Two of the Jem'Hadar had died in the attack, and several others had suffered serious injuries, but the Changeling knew that if the Romulan warbird hadn't broken off its assault, the destruction and death would have been total.

While Odo detested losing any of the crew, particularly as they carried out his orders, it pleased him to find that both Weyoun and Rotan'talag had survived the attack. The Jem'Hadar had already risen and moved over to work at one of the control consoles, where he followed the Changeling's order to attempt the restoration of communications.

Although Odo still felt obligated to complete the task he'd set himself, he wanted nothing more at that moment than to return to the Dominion. Since he had chosen to reside there after the war, the place had truly become his home, and even after the Founders had fled, it had remained so. Odo wished only to turn around and head back to the Dominion, where he could continue his efforts to elevate all its members, in preparation for the day that the rest of the Founders would return and re-form the Great Link.

But all of that will have to wait, he thought.

Odo crossed the compact bridge to where Weyoun spoke with the Jem'Hadar seventh, Vorgan'lorat. Odo listened as the Vorta issued orders. It pleased him to hear Weyoun focus on seeing that the crew received the medical attention they needed.

When the Vorta had finished his conversation and Vorgan'lorat hurried away, Odo asked, "What's our status?"

"We've lost main power," Weyoun said. "The warp drive and the sublight engines are off line, as is communications. We had a hull breach on Deck Two, but it's been sealed with a force field."

"What's the prognosis for repairs?" Odo asked.

"The Jem'Hadar report that, without assistance, the warp drive is irreparable," Weyoun said. "They may be able to restore the sublight engines though, and communications should be back on line shortly."

"What about main power?"

"That may take some time," Weyoun said, "but the backup batteries are in good condition."

Odo considered his options. He had to finish what he'd started, but he also wanted to ensure the safety of his surviving crew. "Make communications your top priority," he said. "As soon as it's restored, send a message to the Dominion and, on my authority, request two Jem'Hadar vessels to provide you immediate assistance. If you can repair this vessel within a day, do so. Otherwise, have it towed back to the Dominion. I want you to remain here with one ship to wait for my return."

"Founder," said Weyoun, his concern plain in both his voice and expression, "where will you be?"

"I have to deliver the message that the Romulans prevented us from transmitting," Odo said.

"But how can you be sure your message didn't get through to Bajor?" Weyoun asked.

"I requested a confirmation if it was received, but there's been no reply," Odo said. "Additionally, the Romulans targeted our communications equipment, and they also destroyed the Federation's comm relay. That tells me that they were intent on preventing my message from making it to the Alpha Quadrant."

Weyoun nodded in apparent agreement, but he continued to look stricken. "I see your point," he said. "But is it safe for you to travel on your own?"

Odo felt a swell of emotion for Weyoun, and pride for how far he'd come. Odo could tell from the way the Vorta had asked about his safety that Weyoun's apprehension came less from a creation's fear for one of his gods and more out of one friend's natural concern for another. "I'll be careful," Odo said. "I'll be fine." He looked toward the near corner of the bridge, to the hatch that opened onto the deck below. "I'll use the hull breach," he said.

"I understand," Weyoun said. "The crew have abandoned that section, so it's empty right now. Once you're there, I'll lower the force field for a moment."

Odo nodded his assent, then made his way to the hatch. He opened it, climbed down the ladder, then pulled it closed behind him. It did not take him long to locate the breach, a blackened gash that ran diagonally across two compartments. He stood in front of it and waited.

When the force field dropped along the breach, the restored atmosphere in the compartments rushed out into the void. Odo did not look outward, though, but inward, to the currents of motion that lived within him, that made him a Changeling, that exemplified his nearly limitless physical potential. He saw and felt rivers of movement, the never-still tides of possibility that formed his being, and with a conscious effort, he envisioned the change that he would become. His body softened and shifted, transformed from quasi-solid into the embodiment of thought, as he willed himself into a new series of shapes.

Odo poured himself through the fissure in the hull and out into the void. Humanoid in one instant, an amorphous spill of golden liquid the next, he continued to morph, his essence seeking to capture in itself a figure that Laas had first shown him. Satisfaction washed over Odo as he became a large, long, multifinned creature, a life-form that could move through space, its motion smooth and graceful. Odo fashioned parts of his new body into specialized sensory organs, mimicking those the creature used to detect the gravitational eddies caused by stars and planets, so that it could adjust its own mass and dimensions to propel itself through the void.

The spaceborne Odo moved quickly, utilizing the abilities of that which he had become to soar through the Idran system. He dived deep into the gravity well of one world, then hurtled around it and out again, deeper into the system. Asteroids aided him along his path, a comet, another world, and another. He knew his destination, could sense the increased wave intensities surrounding it, could feel the impact that the high quantity of protons had on the surrounding region.

In short order, Odo arrived. The great passage that linked distant parts of the galaxy opened for him, turning in loops to bare its radiant blue entrance. Powerful light gleamed from within.

Without hesitation, Odo swam into the Bajoran wormhole.

Through the runabout's forward viewports, Kira saw colors and shapes that did not belong in the Celestial Temple. She opened the blast doors on the lateral ports as well, but the wormhole appeared normal to either side. Kira worked the sensors on *Rubicon*'s main panel, searching for answers about what lay ahead. She hadn't known precisely what she would find in the wormhole, only that she *must* find it.

But that's not entirely true, is it? Kira asked herself. She did have one expectation for what awaited her: the Emissary. She did not retain her Orb experience in the way that people recall their dreams; in some sense, she did not recall it at all. But she felt it, a new, deeper part of herself, a partially submerged but still essential portion of her psyche, which housed the compulsion that had driven her from Bajor and out into space, to the home of the Prophets.

Kira surveyed the displays on the runabout's main console, observed the sensor readings as they danced, settled, fell apart. Among the noise of confused information, though, she spotted the identification beacon of *Defiant. Benjamin's old ship,* Kira thought, *and the ship to which he'd returned.* Sometimes, the Prophets draped the paths they weaved with poetry.

As Kira continued farther into the wormhole, the foreign colors and shapes became clear. She saw the gray, compact hull of *Defiant,* but not by itself. To her dismay, the ship had been caught in the gauzy white embrace of a tractor beam. Its captor, a great, grayish-green Romulan warbird, dwarfed the Starfleet vessel.

Smaller than either starship, *Rubicon* hurtled toward them both. Without hesitation, Kira pushed the runabout closer. Though still unsure of her purpose, she felt certain that the Prophets would guide her actions.

As she neared the two starships, another color, another shape crossed her view. The flame-red opening in the wall of the wormhole—of the *Celestial Temple*—repulsed her. Its tattered edges made it look like a lesion, a horrible injury that showed no signs of healing.

It's worse than just a wound, Kira thought. *It's a desecration.*

She stared at the vile red despoilment. She didn't know what had happened, what it meant or why, only that something terrible had taken place, and that there might yet be worse to come. Kira understood that she had been summoned to this moment, that the Orb of Destiny had changed her so that she could change what lay ahead of the runabout.

But she didn't know what to do. She searched *Rubicon*'s main console for answers and found none. She knew that she couldn't fire phasers or launch a microtorpedo within the wormhole, and given the relatively small size of the runabout, she couldn't hope to use its own tractor beam to help *Defiant* escape the warbird's clutches.

Feeling helpless, Kira stood up in *Rubicon*'s cockpit. She stared at the console, at all the controls, but nothing came to her. She looked frantically around the cabin for anything that might point the way to a solution. Seeing nothing of any use, she peered back out through the viewports. Just ahead, the warbird used its tractor beam not to pull *Defiant,* but to push it away from the hideous stain on the Temple wall.

But that stain, Kira saw, had depth. *Not something* on *the wall of the wormhole,* she realized. *Something attached to it from the outside.* She stared at it, tried to will herself to comprehend it. And as she did, it began to glow . . . a red light that grew to blot out everything else in her view, a light that came to encompass her—

The sun had dropped lower on the horizon, its orange-red face reflecting off the water and bathing Kay Eaton in its radiance. She squinted against the glare, then turned back around and resumed rowing. Her back ached, and the fatigue in her arms left them numb. But still she continued on. She had to save Benny. She had to save him for Cassie.

As Eaton had moved farther out into the river, she'd largely stopped trying to peer back over her shoulder to see Benny and Eli in their boat. Doing so broke her motion and slowed her down. Periodically, though, she would throw her chin over one shoulder or the other, allowing her peripheral vision to catch a glimpse of the other boat, just so that she knew that she followed along in the right direction, and that the two men had not been lost.

Farther away from shore, the river roughened. Rowing became harder for Eaton as swells rose higher and fell deeper. She had already pushed herself for so long, and exhaustion threatened to overcome her. *I have to be close,* she thought desperately. *I have to be.*

Eaton turned and looked.

Where the water swirled in the middle of the river, it had grown wider and deeper, she saw, and it had begun to spin faster. The whirlpool reflected the dying sun in tints of flaming red. In horror, she spotted Benny's boat teetering on the lip of the abyss, in jeopardy of falling into the gaping hole.

Benny moved in a blur of motion, hauling his oars through the water with visible effort, trying to pull away from the danger. Eaton had almost reached him. *If I can just get close enough to grab hold of his boat—*

Suddenly, a great wave rolled across the river and carried Eaton's boat upward. She rose higher and higher, until she could look down past Benny and Eli and see into the vortex. Within it, a strange green boat, shaped like a bird, rode the rim of oblivion. A man with scaled flesh rode inside, and, as Eaton watched, he reached up and clawed at Benny's boat. If he reached it, if he gained a grip on it, she knew that he would pull Benny and Eli down, dooming them.

As the wave settled, Eaton swung back around, turning her back on the scene once more. She drove her oars quickly through the water, powered by the certainty of what she must do. Her boat sliced through the waves, picking up speed. *I'm going to make it,* she told herself. *I'm going to save Benny.*

And then a tremendous cacophony roared up behind Eaton,

the sound of a collision. Her head snapped back painfully and she fell to her hands and knees. She struggled to right herself, but the boat pitched and tossed on the violent water. She tried again, steadying herself, trying to rise so that she could see what had happened.

Eaton peered over the side of the boat. It faltered on the edge of the maelstrom. Deeper still, though, the birdlike boat, which she must have struck, hurtled down into the red vortex.

Eaton looked to either side for Benny. Somehow, his boat had been thrown clear, and she saw him moving away toward shore—toward safety.

A smile bloomed on Eaton's face, even as something cold clutched at her feet. She looked down to see water pooling in the bottom of her boat. The collision had caused a leak. She turned around to see how badly the boat had been damaged—and instead saw Eli Underwood.

Could he have been thrown into my boat when we collided?

Except that something more than that must have happened, Eaton realized. Eli no longer looked like the decrepit man Benny had been so anxious to free from custody. Eaton gazed instead at a man who appeared strong of body and strong of mind, still recognizable, but no longer infirm. He did not have a young face, but one with character and experience. She supposed that his gray hair and the lines in his flesh had been well and honestly earned.

"How did you get here, Eli?" she asked, her voice barely audible over the sound of rushing water.

The newly invigorated man said nothing, but in reply, he stood up, reached forward, and hauled Eaton up into his arms. For a moment, she thought he meant to walk across the water and carry her to safety, but that seemed a mad idyll. Instead, he bent his legs, spun his body, and threw her into the air.

Eaton saw nothing but sky as she flew from the boat. She waited for the cold embrace of the river to swallow her in its depths, but then she landed on something solid. The impact pushed the air from her lungs. Even as she struggled to breathe, though, she sought to rise.

When she did, Eaton saw that Eli had managed to get her back to the shore. She peered out over the water, searching for the two men whom she had helped free from police custody, and had then pursued. She could not see her boat, or the one that looked like a bird. The vortex had vanished. She saw only Benny, rowing away, no longer in danger.

Eaton raised her hand and waved to Benny. Her eyes narrowed against the glare of the sun on the water, but the light grew brighter—

—and then the light faded, leaving behind the fiery depths of whatever had breached the wall of the Celestial Temple.

Through the viewports, Kira saw that the warbird had pushed *Defiant* back away from the red flaw. All at once, she understood that the Romulan crew meant to travel into that hole . . . into that *worm*hole.

And she knew that they had to be stopped.

Kira quickly sat down again at the main console and worked the conn. She brought the runabout up and over the Romulan warbird. From her new vantage, she saw that the tractor beam projected from the forward hull of the warbird— from the beak at the front of the vessel's long neck. Kira glanced down at the console, still looking for answers. Her gaze came to rest on the weapons controls, but she knew that could not be an option.

Running on instinct, feeling that she had no other choice, Kira lowered the bow of *Rubicon,* aiming the runabout at the Romulan vessel.

"The smaller Starfleet vessel is moving above us," reported Reval.

Though he could not say why, the timing of the second Federation ship's entry into the wormhole filled Morad with dread. He turned away from the viewer, even as it showed *Vetruvis*'s tractor beam forcing the Federation starship away from the mouth of the Tzenkethi wormhole. All Morad wanted to see were the stars of home.

"Ignore the smaller vessel," ordered Kozik. "We're just moments away."

The ship shook, and Morad waited for the devastation that would surely follow. *All of my efforts,* he thought. *All come to nothing.* He had lost every trace of confidence.

But the ship only trembled and remained intact.

"They're firing some kind of focused force beam," Reval said. "Minimal impact."

"Keep pushing," Kozik said. "Keep the tractor steady and keep moving that ship away. We're almost there."

"What . . . what is *that*?" asked Analest, her tone one of complete confusion. "Is that one of the aliens who live in the wormhole?"

Morad turned back to the viewscreen, his curiosity overcoming his fear. He saw what looked to him like a mammoth sea creature. It had a long, graceful body that trailed winglike appendages behind it. It moved sinuously, as though swimming through water currents. He watched it, fascinated despite the circumstances. He wondered idly if it would attack, and if so, how much damage it would cause.

But then the ship shuddered as a deafening noise filled the bridge. In his mind, Morad saw metal rending and sections of hull crushed. He crashed to the deck as the lighting failed.

Morad didn't know if he passed out, but he became aware of a terrible quiet. He heard the voices of the crew, mostly delivered as moans and cries for help. Other than that, the ship had grown deadly silent.

But that remained true only for a moment more.

"Try using the deflectors!" Sisko called out, searching for any means of beating back the Romulan vessel. He stared at the warbird on the main viewer, and at the tractor beam that had captured *Defiant.* Admiral Akaar had charged Sisko with preventing the Typhon Pact from utilizing their newfound wormhole-generation technology to acquire the tools to construct their own quantum slipstream drive, but it seemed likely that the Romulans stood on the threshold of accomplishing exactly that. Sisko knew that he had to stop the warbird, but the *Defiant* crew had so far been unable to break the ship free. Restricted to the use of impulse engines within the wormhole, and with the warbird's greater mass, Sisko and his crew hadn't been able to prevent the Romulan vessel from moving *Defiant* out of its way.

"Use the deflectors *how*?" asked Slaine.

Sisko strode over to tactical and leaned in over the console. "Try concentrating a narrow-beam deflector burst," Sisko explained. "Maybe if we can throw an unexpected punch, that will break us free."

"Captain," said Candlewood, "there's a runabout approaching."

A runabout? Sisko thought. *From where? From Bajor?*

"Attempting deflector burst," Slaine said.

Sisko looked over at the viewscreen and saw a slim white beam flash out from the bow of *Defiant* and into the Romulan vessel. The warbird quivered, but its tractor field did not falter. "Minimal effect," Slaine said.

"Try it with more power," Sisko said.

"We'll blow out the deflector array," Slaine said.

"Then blow it out!"

Suddenly, a creature appeared on the main screen. It glided past, but then traveled out of view. Sisko shook his head, wondering if he'd begun to lose his hold on reality.

Then he saw the runabout. It swept up and over the Romulan vessel. For a moment, it hung there, and Sisko didn't know what to expect next. But then it dived down toward the forward section of the warbird.

"No!" Sisko yelled. He could do nothing but watch as the runabout crashed through the neck of the warbird. The tractor beam ceased immediately. "Quickly," Sisko said, even as the bridge and forward structure of the Romulan vessel tumbled away from the decapitated remainder of the ship. "Move us back—"

That's when the Romulan warbird exploded.

Kira programmed a collision course with the Romulan warbird, executed it, and raced for the back of the runabout's cockpit.

And then a tremendous cacophony roared up behind her, the sound of the collision. Her head snapped back painfully and she fell to her hands and knees. She struggled to right herself, but the runabout pitched and tossed from the violent encounter. She tried again, steadying herself, trying to rise so that she could see what had happened.

Kira peered through the side viewports. The runabout faltered on the edge of the second wormhole. Deeper still, though, the forward section of the warbird, which must have been severed from the rest of the vessel when *Rubicon* struck it, hurtled down into the red vortex.

Kira looked to either side for *Defiant*. Somehow, the ship had been thrown clear, and she saw it moving away toward the Alpha Quadrant terminus—toward safety. A smile bloomed on Kira's face, even as she felt suddenly cold. Air rushed past her, toward the front of the cockpit. The collision had caused a hull breach. She turned around to see how badly the runabout had been damaged—and instead saw Elias Vaughn.

Except that Vaughn no longer looked like the decrepit man she had seen earlier that day in the hospice. Kira gazed instead at the man he had been, strong of body and strong of mind, still recognizable, but no longer infirm. He did not have a young face, but one with character and experience. She understood that his gray hair and the lines in his flesh had been well and honestly earned.

"How did you get here, Elias?" she asked, her voice barely audible over the sound of the atmosphere rushing out.

The newly invigorated Vaughn said nothing, but in reply, he stood up, reached forward, and hauled Kira up into his arms. For a moment, she thought he meant to leave the ship and carry her through space to safety, but that seemed a mad idyll. Instead, he bent his legs, spun his body, and threw her into the air.

Kira saw nothing but the overhead as she flew across the cockpit of the runabout. She waited for the hard impact of her body against the deck, but then she landed on something solid, but not nearly as hard. The impact pushed the air from her lungs. Even as she struggled to breathe, though, she sought to rise.

But then white light surrounded her. Her eyes narrowed against the glare, but the light grew brighter. In the end, Kira closed her eyes and accepted whatever her fate would be.

On the Vir-Akzelen asteroid, Nelzik Tek Lom-A saw the readings on her console and didn't understand them. In no context did they make any sense. She realized that the equipment must be experiencing an overload, and she hoped that it extended only to her monitor.

She called over to Vendez Tek Lom-A to ask his opinion. As he moved toward her station, Nelzik glanced up at the transparent superior floor of the lab. She saw the sky catch fire.

The wormhole burst into existence, not just a fiery red, but actually burning like the surface of a sun. Nelzik lived just long enough to register the forward section of a Romulan warbird career out of the wormhole and crash through the ceiling of the lab. And then fire took her too.

Picard judged that they had waited long enough.

"There's no response from the *Defiant*," said Choudhury.

"And still none from Vedek Kira aboard the *Rubicon*, I take it," the captain said from where he stood with Worf in the center of the *Enterprise* bridge. They had sent a message to Captain Sisko aboard *Defiant*, warning him about Kira and the stolen runabout, but they'd received no reply. They'd also tried to raise the vedek, without result.

"Lieutenant Faur, ahead one-quarter impulse," Picard said. "Take us into the wormhole."

"Aye, sir," Faur said.

Before the lieutenant could even operate the conn, though, the Bajoran wormhole thrust itself into normal space. Picard looked over at the main viewer at the unexpected burst of light. The wormhole did not open in its customary circular fashion, but *erupted*, as though carving a hole straight through the fabric of space-time. It still radiated blue, but the light seemed to burn and roil, as though somehow on fire.

Picard stared at the viewscreen, transfixed by what he saw.

As he looked on, a shape emerged from within . . . not stable, but tumbling. Another, smaller shape followed.

"The *Defiant*," he said quietly. "And the *Rubicon*."

A third shape appeared, though it did not look at all like a ship. It appeared more organic, like a living being.

"Analysis," Picard said. "What's happening out there?"

Before anybody could respond, the wormhole blazed even brighter. Then it fell in on itself, like a tunnel collapsing.

And then it was gone.

On Bajor, in the hospice at the Vanadwan Monastery, Elias Vaughn opened his eyes, closed them again, and then died.

Summa Summarum

Praetor Gell Kamemor walked down a wide corridor of Stronghold Telvan'rey, Uhlans Preget and T'Lesk following dutifully behind her. The footfalls of the trio multiplied against the stone floor and walls, the timber ceiling too high up to effectively suppress the clatter. The sound, thin and hollow and reverberant, somehow reminded Kamemor of historical times. She had no trouble envisioning the era before modern power generation, when only fire lighted the night, when simple flames would have thrown her shadows and those of her guards wavering across the ancient walls.

The stronghold, one of the oldest extant structures in Ki Baratan, stood on the outskirts of the city. Set atop a rise overlooking the Apnex Sea, the great edifice had once housed generations of Romulan royalty. With both its interior and exterior fully restored, and its updated infrastructure artfully hidden, the praetor could easily imagine that she had slipped the restraints of the complicated present and escaped into the undemanding past.

Kamemor knew that she romanticized history. She also understood that her enthusiasm for the bygone era stemmed at least in part from a desire to live in simpler times. As a public servant, and especially as praetor, she yearned to free herself of the intricacies frequently attendant with the performance of her duties. But she also recognized the lie in thinking that the lack of technological sophistication in earlier periods corresponded to a lack of political complexity.

Up ahead, at the end of the corridor, a large opening looked out on the sparkling sprawl of the nighttime city. The window lacked glass, but Kamemor knew that a force field protected the stronghold against the elements. As she neared the semicircular opening, Ki Baratan stood out in the night like a clutch of gems strewn upon a jeweler's cloth.

The praetor arrived at the last doorway in the corridor, set into the left-hand wall. The door itself, a collection of dark wood planks fastened together by steel bands, stood perpetually open, its function reduced to mere adornment. As with the window, a force field sealed the opening, but a row of metal bars also marched from one jamb to the other.

Kamemor had ordered the prisoner incarcerated in that specific cell because it possessed an unparalleled view of Ki Baratan. Such a choice might reasonably be deemed unkind, perhaps even cruel, but the praetor held no such malicious intentions. She did seek to make plain, though, the reason that her government would not tolerate the prisoner's crimes: the good of the Romulan people.

And really, not just the good of the Romulan people, Kamemor thought, pushing her populist stance beyond the borders of the Empire. *The good of* all *people in the Alpha and Beta Quadrants.*

As the two uhlans fell back and took up positions across the corridor from the praetor, Kamemor stepped up to the cell. The force field buzzed at her approach. She peered inside, at a room that, as best she could tell, appeared little different than it had when the stronghold had first been constructed centuries earlier.

The praetor knew that redundant force fields surrounded the cell, that its walls had been fortified by impregnable materials, and that transport inhibitors protected against beaming into or out of it. Further, subspace jamming devices prevented unauthorized communication, and Romulan Security kept both individual cells and the entire stronghold under continuous surveillance, the sensor perimeter reaching well beyond Telvan'rey's curtain walls and battlements. As far as Kamemor knew, since the repurposing of the stronghold in the modern era, no prisoner had ever escaped its confines—other than via the traditional Romulan method.

"Good evening," the praetor said.

Sela raised her head from where she lay on her back atop the stone slab that served as her bed. Clad in a distinctive yellow jumpsuit—*Not very different from the color of her hair,* Kamemor thought—she regarded the praetor for only a moment. Then she lowered her head back onto the slab.

Kamemor peered around and saw that the cell possessed few features: a simple stone sink, a half-wall that clearly sheltered a lavatory, and a barred window that looked out on Ki Baratan. Not for the first time, the praetor reflected on the differences in the ways that the Empire and the Federation housed and treated their prisoners. She wanted more information, not just about the UFP's holding cells and its processes of detention, but the reasons behind them. She resolved to seek out an expert in such matters; perhaps Nan Bacco herself would be gracious enough to provide a resource. Certainly the two heads of state had parted on better terms than any praetor and president had enjoyed in quite some time.

"It might interest you to know that your position as chairwoman of the Tal Shiar has been filled," Kamemor said, more to draw Sela out than to pass on the information. The new Tal Shiar leader had served in the elite intelligence agency for only a relatively short time—less than two decades—having first arrived there well into her middle age. Until the proconsul had brought her to the attention of Kamemor, she had met the praetor on only a couple of occasions, as part of a contingent delivering security briefings. But Ventel had attended university with the woman, and they had later served together for a long period as researchers and historians with the Imperial Library and Chamber of Records. The two had remained friends for years, and though quite a few of the others considered for the position had been more highly qualified, none possessed precisely the combination of characteristics the praetor sought: a keen mind, a dedication to duty, a belief in the rule of law and in the moral limits to the power of the government in general and the Tal Shiar in particular, and complete trustworthiness. "The new chairwoman is Tesitera Levat."

Sela immediately swung her legs from her bed and stood up. She paced over to the doorway, then bent down and reached to the floor, out of sight along the inner wall of the cell. The unexpected movement obviously caught the attention of the uhlans, whose footfalls resounded in the corridor behind Kamemor. She turned to see that they had drawn their disruptor pistols. The praetor waved them back, but they held their ground until Sela stood back up and displayed what she had retrieved from the floor: a bronze chalice. She slowly upended the goblet, spilling its viscous, silvery contents onto the bare cell floor beside her. The liquid spattered on the stones, several drops splashing against the force field with a sizzle.

The praetor turned and nodded to the guards, who holstered their weapons and returned to their positions across the corridor. When she looked back into the cell, she saw that Sela held the empty chalice upside-down by its circular base. The ex-chairwoman stared at her with what looked like untempered hatred.

"It was not my choice to place the goblet in your cell," Kamemor said. "In the case of your crimes, though, the law is quite specific."

"Of course it wasn't your choice," Sela said. "That would have been far too *Romulan* an action for you to take."

"And clearly far too Romulan for you as well," Kamemor said, gesturing to the puddle to the side of Sela's feet.

"*Nothing* is 'too Romulan' for me," Sela said. "My mother was human—" She spewed the word like an epithet. "—and yet I'm still more Romulan than you'll ever be."

"I think you and I have very different ideas of what it means to be Romulan," Kamemor said.

"Nothing's ever been clearer to me than that," Sela agreed.

The praetor had not chosen to visit the chairwoman to debate her, or to lecture her, or even to attempt to better understand why she had taken the rogue actions she had. Kamemor had come as a matter of her own conscience. She believed that she should accord Sela the right to know the potential fate that awaited her, so that she could then choose whether or not to face it. Still, long before she had been elevated to the praetorship, Kamemor had served as a professor, and so she still believed in teachable moments, even so far into Sela's life.

"I'm a Romulan because I was born a Romulan," Kamemor said. "But I was also born ignorant of the universe. Should I have remained that way? No, of course not. I learned as a child, taught at home by my parents and in school by my teachers. I believed what I was told, as most children do; it is an evolutionary trait, for children need adults for their very survival. But there is a difference between merely surviving and truly living, and if you learn only what you're taught in childhood, if there is no questioning of authority, no curiosity about the unknown, no pursuit of additional knowledge, then there is no growth, either for an individual or for a species."

"So you grew up," Sela said. "That's your idea of being Romulan?"

Kamemor hadn't intended to say exactly that, but she agreed with the sentiment. "More or less," she said. "Because I'm Romulan by birth, but also by culture. My brain has a certain capacity, my body has particular physical abilities, my emotions well-defined ways of reacting to situations, but our society also metes out expectations for the individuals it comprises. To be Romulan, then, I need to nurture the characteristics inside me, attempt to bring them to their fullest flower, but also to work outside myself, toward the greater good. I think you can say the same thing for half-Romulan, half-human hybrids."

"And for full humans, and Klingons, and Vulcans, and all the rest?" Sela said. "It's the same for all the galaxy in your mind, isn't it?"

Kamemor nodded. "And for Cardassians and Gorn and Ferengi and Tzenkethi," she added. "We are all more alike than unalike."

"That's the fatal flaw in your argument," Sela said. "It is also why the Imperial Senate *and* the Romulan people will eventually bring you down: you don't believe in the natural superiority of Romulans."

Kamemor shrugged. "I certainly don't believe in the superiority of *certain* Romulans."

Sela snorted derisively. "I agree," she said. She turned and walked the few steps to the other side of her cell. The goblet still dangled from her fingertips, a thick, silver drop occasionally giving in to gravity and falling from the rim to the floor. A drop, Kamemor knew, would be all Sela or any Romulan would need.

When Sela turned back, she said, "It is astonishing to me that you preach about the good of the Empire, while you continually undermine the security of Romulus, and castigate me for taking steps to protect it."

"It is difficult to accept that you actually believe that," Kamemor said.

"What?!" Sela erupted, moving back over to the doorway. "All I've done is fight to overcome the Federation's military advantage, and I've had to do that because the alleged leader of our people refuses to do so herself."

"Yes, I keep hearing about the quantum slipstream drive," Kamemor said, "and how it provides the Federation with a clear tactical advantage over the entire Typhon Pact. And yet, slipstream hasn't seemed to make much difference to the Romulan Empire—other than when you've taken pains to steal it. Starfleet has employed their new drive on some of their ships for some time now, and yet not once in all that time has a Federation force attempted to penetrate the Neutral Zone."

"Just because Starfleet hasn't attacked yet doesn't mean it won't," Sela said.

"I think it does mean that," Kamemor told her. "In fact, isn't past behavior the *best* indicator of future behavior? Even when you and Tomalak have given the Federation valid reasons to declare war, they haven't. That's because, for the most part, their people aren't like you; they may be different from Romulans, but they don't hate us for that difference."

"I disagree," Sela said. "The inferior always resent their betters."

Kamemor shook her head. "So we're back to that, are we? Romulan exceptionalism," she said. "That's such an outdated notion, and irrelevant, and I think wrong in so many ways. But let's assume for a moment that it's none of those things. Let's declare that Romulans are superior to humans . . . and to Andorians and to Vulcans and to all the rest. That leads me to a simple question: so what?"

Sela looked at her as though Kamemor had spoken in gibberish. Another silver drop fell from the rim of the chalice to the floor.

"If we are somehow 'better' than the people of the Federation," Kamemor continued, "does that mean that we necessarily must vanquish them, or subjugate them, or annihilate them? I say no. Wouldn't a truly advanced people help lift up the less fortunate, the less capable, the inferior?"

"I see our rightful place in the universe," Sela said. "Why can't you?"

"'Our' rightful place?" Kamemor asked. "Or *your* rightful place. Because it seems that your actions have in no demonstrable way benefited Romulus. Like Tomalak, you assert patriotic motivations, but in his case, it's a rationalization for self-aggrandizement. For you, I suspect it's a reaction to your self-loathing. I don't understand why you would choose to hate yourself just because your mother was different from your father—"

"Don't you dare talk about my father," Sela growled, taking a step perilously close to the force field. She looked down, apparently trying to calm herself. When she peered back up, she spoke normally once more. "What you say about Tomalak may be partially true—he may not be a patriot in the fullest sense—but he at least works toward goals that would benefit Romulus."

"So he claims," Kamemor said. "But no one will hear any of those claims for the rest of his life."

Sela smiled, an expression that seemed to convey pity rather than humor. "You really are a poor excuse for a Romulan," she said. "If you choose not to execute Tomalak, rest assured that his words will make it out into the public. And if you do put him to death, he will surely avail himself of the Right of Statement. Either way, he will be certain that the Romulan people understand how you have cowered from the Federation."

"Seeking mutual understanding and peace is not cowering," Kamemor said. "As for Tomalak, his words will not reach the Romulan people, and he will not employ the Right of Statement."

"That is a foolish assumption," Sela declared.

"It is not an assumption," Kamemor explained. "Tomalak will not use the Right of Statement because it is not a part of Federation law."

For a moment, Sela looked confused by the construction, but then understanding seemed to come to her. "You're not demanding that the Federation return Tomalak—once your own *proconsul*—to Romulus?"

Kamemor shrugged again. "Tomalak committed crimes against the Empire and against the Imperial Fleet. He betrayed his praetor and his duty. All the attendant charges will remain in force. But he murdered Federation citizens. He deserves to face their justice."

"You would let aliens—*humans!*—sit in judgment of a Romulan citizen?" Sela said. She turned and marched away from the door, lifting her arms up and then dropping them to her sides. Eventually, she glanced back over her shoulder, turning her head to be heard, but not looking at Kamemor. "You disgust me," she said.

"I will wear that avowal with honor," Kamemor said. "But don't be too upset about Tomalak. It's always possible that you and he will have adjoining cells."

"What?!" Sela said, whirling back around. Kamemor said nothing, but Sela clearly understood what she'd meant. "The Empire has no extradition treaties with the Federation."

"We didn't," Kamemor said. "But while I was on Earth interrogating Tomalak, and promising to bring him back to Romulus and grant him his freedom in exchange for information about Commander Kozik and the *Vetruvis,* I also took the time to speak with President Bacco. We came to a short-term agreement about delivering accused criminals into each other's custody. Given recent events and the importance of such an accord, both the Imperial Senate and the Federation Council have already ratified it." It occurred to Kamemor that, in some ways, she could be a Romulan like Sela, could behave like the Tal Shiar, for she had brazenly lied to Tomalak about securing his freedom in exchange for information.

The praetor stepped forward, as close as she safely could get to the force field and the bars separating her from Sela. "That's why I came to see you," Kamemor said. "To tell you that you will be placed in stasis tomorrow morning, loaded aboard a Romulan vessel, and delivered to the Neutral Zone. There, the crew of a Starfleet ship will take custody of you and bring you to Earth. When you are removed from stasis, you'll find yourself in a Federation holding cell. I thought that you should know before it happened."

An expression of horror passed over Sela's face. "You . . . you can't do that," she said. "You have to give me a choice."

"Sela, everything you've done to reach this point has been your choice," Kamemor said. "All that's left now are consequences."

Sela held the praetor's gaze for a long time. Kamemor did not shirk from it. Finally, Sela looked down at the chalice still suspended from her hand. Kamemor looked too, just as another silver drop fell to the floor with a small, empty sound.

"Jolan tru," Kamemor said. The traditional Romulan greeting and farewell rendered literally as *May you find peace.* Then she stepped back from the cell, gave a nod to her guards, and started back up the corridor.

As they walked through the old stronghold, the sounds of their heels echoing loudly all around them, Kamemor again thought about the ancient past. In so many ways, her people had come so far to reach the modern present. Sometimes, though, they acted as though they had yet to escape their treacherous, violent history, as though they had never left those dark, dangerous days.

When she reached the end of the corridor with the two uhlans, Kamemor stopped for a moment. She turned back and listened as their reverberating footsteps marched back into silence. Far off, she heard the ping of a small metal object against stone, and then what sounded like the dull thud of something much larger striking the floor.

Kamemor gazed in turn at each of the guards. Very quietly, Uhlan T'Lesk said, "She was never going to choose Earth."

"No," Kamemor said. "I suppose not."

Then the praetor continued on her way, the guards once more following behind her.

Odo stood in the shuttlebay of *U.S.S. Robinson,* examining the broken hull of the runabout *Rubicon.* Its bow had caved in where it had crashed through the neck of the Romulan warbird, and a fissure ran from below the starboard viewport all the way up to the overhead. One of its warp nacelles had been cracked and nearly torn from the hull. The runabout sat canted in the middle of the bay like a wounded animal.

"And you say there's no sign of her . . . remains?" Odo asked. He found it difficult even to consider Nerys's death, let alone to discuss it.

"We've run scans of the runabout's entire cabin," said Doctor Kosciuszko, *Robinson*'s chief medical officer. "Sensors picked up trace amounts of DNA, mostly from Deep Space Nine's crew, but also from Vedek Kira. Other than that, no, there are no indications that she perished while on board. But conditions within the wormhole are unusual even under normal circumstances."

Odo considered that. "What do you think, Captain?"

Sisko regarded *Rubicon* himself. At Odo's request, the captain had allowed the Changeling to board *Robinson* in order both to see the runabout and to hear the doctor's final report on it. It had been three days since the destruction of the Romulan warbird and the collapse of the Bajoran wormhole.

"I don't know," Sisko said, shaking his head. "Because of their communication with her and their own sensor readings, the *Enterprise* crew can verify that Kira was aboard the *Rubicon* when it entered the wormhole. They also scanned the runabout when it was ejected back into the Bajoran system and can confirm that it contained no life-forms at that time."

"I know she was aboard because I saw her there myself," Odo said. As he'd soared through the wormhole toward the unexpected tableau of vessels—*Defiant, Rubicon,* and the Romulan vessel that had eventually been identified as *Vetruvis*—Odo had seen Nerys through the forward viewports of the runabout. She'd been at the main console just before *Rubicon* had rushed toward its collision with the warbird. In the last moment he'd been able to see into the cabin, Odo thought he'd glimpsed Nerys hurrying aft—and then, for just an instant, he thought he'd spied somebody else there. Events had transpired so quickly, though, that he hadn't been sure just who or what he'd seen.

If Nerys was alone on the runabout when she entered the wormhole, Odo thought, *then how could somebody else have gotten aboard?* "What about the transporter?" he asked.

"Are you asking if Kira could have beamed safely off the *Rubicon*?" Sisko said. "I'm not sure if transporters can function within the wormhole, but even if they could, Kira never appeared aboard the *Defiant*."

"What about the planet?" Odo asked. When Sisko and Jadzia Dax had first discovered the wormhole almost a decade and a half earlier, they had reported their runabout alighting on a world within it.

"I don't know," Sisko repeated. "I'm not certain of the planet's physical reality. Since Dax and I first thought we landed there, there's been no other hint of its existence. It's possible that our experience took place only in our minds." He shook his head again. "Even if it did exist, and even if Kira somehow miraculously found it, there's still the issue of whether or not transporters can work in that environment, and my guess is that they can't. And there's no record in the runabout's computer of any last-minute transport."

Odo offered a grunt of acknowledgment. As troubling

as he found it to contemplate Nerys's death, he also found it fitting that she had faced the end of her life within the Bajoran wormhole—or as she thought of it, the Celestial Temple. It did not end Odo's pain, but he found solace in his belief that Nerys would have been pleased not only that her death had saved lives—and according to Sisko, possibly averted a war—but that her path had ended in the place she considered most sacred.

"Will there be anything else, Captain?" Doctor Kosciuszko asked.

"No, that'll be all, Ambrozy," Sisko said. "Thank you." The doctor headed for the nearest door and exited the shuttlebay. Once he'd gone, the captain faced Odo. "I'm sorry for your loss," Sisko said. "I know that, even though you hadn't seen Kira in some time, you still cared for her."

"Thank you, Captain," Odo said. "Nerys meant a great deal to me. And I know that you and she had a special relationship as well."

"We did," Sisko said. "I spent a little time with her recently, and I'm very grateful for that."

Odo nodded but said nothing more. The two men stood quietly with their thoughts for a few moments. Finally, Sisko asked, "What are you going to do now, Odo?"

Since the destruction of the Romulan warbird within it, the Bajoran wormhole had not reopened. Of greater import, none of the crews on the starships still patrolling the area had detected any signs of its continued existence. As best any scientists could tell, the wormhole had been completely destroyed.

"Since the Dominion is now seventy thousand light-years away," Odo said, "and since Starfleet isn't inclined to send a slipstream-equipped starship there, it doesn't seem like I'll be returning anytime soon."

"I'm sorry," Sisko said again. "I know how important it was for you to rejoin your people."

"Yes," Odo agreed. He considered sharing some of his experiences with the captain, and thought about telling him of the dissolution of the Great Link—of which he hadn't been a part in more than a half dozen years. But even though he considered Sisko a friend, it seemed too overwhelming to talk about the totality of his grief: he had lost what had meant the most to him in the Alpha Quadrant, and in so doing, he'd also lost any chance of regaining what had meant the most to him in the Gamma Quadrant.

"I know you're stranded here right now," Sisko said. "And it's possible that may never change. I haven't spoken with Starfleet Command about this, but if you want a place aboard the *Robinson,* I would welcome you here."

The captain's offer surprised Odo. "Thank you," he said. "I don't really know what to say. I think for the time being, though, I'd like to spend some time on Bajor."

"Of course," Sisko said. "But if you decide differently at some point, just let me know."

Sisko started walking toward the nearest door, and Odo followed alongside the captain. Before they reached the end of the shuttlebay, though, Odo stopped. When the captain turned to face him, Odo asked, "Is the *Robinson* departing from Bajor soon?"

"Not immediately," Sisko said. "The ship's just undergone a month of repairs at Starbase Three-Ten, and much of the crew's been on leave. We'll be here for a few more days until everybody's back aboard, then we're headed back to starbase to deliver the *Rubicon* for repairs."

"Would you mind, Captain, if I . . ." Odo hesitated, not comfortable with his request, which seemed overly sentimental, perhaps even foolish. He felt the need, though, and so he continued. "Would you mind if I spent a few moments alone aboard the runabout?"

Sisko blinked, obviously not expecting such a request. He paused, then said, "Of course. Take as much time as you need. I'll alert transporter room twelve to expect you later. They'll beam you down to Bajor whenever you're ready."

"Thank you, Captain."

Sisko turned and made his way to the door. When it had closed behind him, Odo immediately looked inward, finding the change he needed, the form he would become. His body softened and elongated, and he sent himself streaming upward, then down and around in a rapid, graceful arc. He directed himself toward the runabout, stretching through the air toward it. He narrowed the contours of his body and found the breach in *Rubicon*'s hull, sent himself slicing through it and into the main cabin. In its center, he regrouped, pouring himself back into the humanoid mold he had developed so long ago.

Odo gazed around the darkened cabin, the only light coming in from the shuttlebay through the viewports. *This is where Nerys died,* he thought. He wanted to tell himself that she had sacrificed herself in a final act of heroism, but her life from a young age had been one courageous effort after another— including allowing herself to develop feelings for somebody as vastly different from her as Odo. That she had died saving others did not mitigate his grief.

Odo stepped forward to the mangled main console. He sat down in one of the chairs there, where he had seen Nerys sitting when he'd spotted her in the runabout. He sat back and closed his eyes.

Alone in the cabin, Odo remembered everything he could about Kira Nerys.

Julian Bashir followed Jasminder Choudhury into the ship's security section. The *Enterprise* tactical officer wore her long, black hair pulled back in a ponytail that the doctor found particularly appealing. He wondered how Sarina's much lighter hair would look tied back in such a fashion.

Sarina.

She had been released from custody four days earlier, after the arrest of Rahendervakell th'Shant. Sarina immediately returned to the housing complex in Aljuli, where she and Bashir greeted each other passionately. Before she resumed her duties at Bajoran Space Central, he took two days' leave. They spent much of their first evening together in her cramped room, a tangle of heat and limbs and lips. Afterward, as night fell and the glow of Bajor's moons blanched their surroundings silver-gray, he lay in her bed, holding her body against his. He heard her breathing slow and deepen, his gaze following the unhurried progress of the pale lunar light across the walls. Lying beside Sarina but alone with his thoughts, Bashir found sleep elusive.

Can I trust her? he had asked himself countless times. Depending on the moment, he might answer, *Don't be a fool, of course you can trust Sarina* or *Don't be a fool, of course you* can't. Her involvement with Section 31 confounded him. Did she still belong to the covert organization, or did she merely pretend to be a member while she actually pursued its eventual demise? L'Haan's appearance in Bashir's own quarters and her desire to see Sarina released from custody demonstrated the operative's belief that Sarina still worked for them.

Or maybe that's just what they wanted me to think, Bashir had realized. His head ached with the possibilities. The wheels-within-wheels, ends-justify-the-means mentality of the organization made it virtually impossible to know their ultimate aims. *So maybe I should just trust the woman I love,* he'd concluded.

Concentrating on his thoughts, Bashir nearly ran into Lieutenant Choudhury when she stopped before him. They had passed a line of dark, presumably empty cells, but they had reached the single lighted one. "You have a visitor," the lieutenant announced to its occupant.

At the far end of the cell, th'Shant sat on the compartment's bed, his back against the bulkhead, his knees up. He looked over at Choudhury and Bashir. "I don't want to talk to anybody."

"What you want is immaterial, *Ensign*," said Choudhury. "Commander Bashir outranks you." Although th'Shant had been removed from duty after his arrest, he would retain his rank and position pending the outcome of his trial. Initially held in custody in Ashalla, he had been transferred to *Enterprise* for the journey to Earth. His trial could have been held on Bajor, but Bashir suspected that the sensitive situation between the Federation and Andor—not to mention the complications with the Typhon Pact—had driven the president, the Federation Council, and even Starfleet Command to want to more closely monitor the proceedings so that they could immediately deal with any fallout. When Bashir had learned that th'Shant would be taken out of the system, he decided to act on his impulse to speak with him. His chest still ached from where the heel of th'Shant's hand had sent him flying across the infirmary, just before Nurse Etana had brought down the fleeing Andorian with a phaser set to heavy stun.

"If you require any assistance, Doctor," Choudhury said, "please speak with Ensign Elvig." She motioned toward a Tellarite woman seated at a freestanding console in the middle of the security chamber.

"Thank you," Bashir said. He waited until Choudhury had departed before turning to peer into the holding cell and over at th'Shant. The Andorian wrapped his arms around his knees and said nothing. "I know you don't want to talk to me," the doctor said, "but . . . I want to try to understand why you did what you did."

"I don't care what you want," said th'Shant. "Nobody's bothering to explain to me why *you* did what you did."

"Why I . . . ?" Bashir said, puzzled.

"*All* of you," th'Shant said, flinging the back of his hand toward the doctor in a gesture paradoxically both inclusive and dismissive.

"I don't understand," Bashir said, "but I want to."

"Of course, you don't understand," said th'Shant, his voice rising. "Because there is no sense in racism."

The word struck Bashir like a physical blow. "Racism?" he managed to say, the charge not merely nonsensical to him, but offensive.

Th'Shant vaulted from the bed and across the deck. Despite the force field that sealed the ensign in the cell, Bashir took a reflexive step backward. "Don't bother to deny it," th'Shant said, pointing his finger accusingly at the doctor. Bashir saw his antennae straining forward, like wild animals tensing to attack. "In the Andorian people's moment of greatest need, the Federation turned its back on us."

Andor's secession nearly a year earlier had rocked the Federation. Bashir could not fully imagine what individual

Andorians—particularly those with lives entrenched outside of their culture—must have felt then, and what they must continue to feel. Since Andor's withdrawal from the UFP, Starfleet had lost more than a third of its Andorian officers to resignation.

"I understand your frustration," Bashir said, "but—"

"My *frustration*?!" th'Shant roared. "Your use of such a word demonstrates your insensitivity and complete lack of understanding about the situation. My people are suffering a reproductive *crisis*—not something *frustrating,* but a danger that threatens our existence."

"I know the situation is grave," Bashir said. "And whatever help the Federation could have provided to the Andorian people, it should have, of course. But my understanding is that they *did* do what they could, that nobody in our government, from the president on down, even knew about the Shedai genetic information." A century earlier, Starfleet had apparently discovered a massive, complex genome in the Taurus Reach, created by an ancient civilization known as the Shedai. Deemed too dangerous even for general research purposes, the entire catalogue of genetic information had been classified. Until the Tholians had revealed its existence, the Taurus Meta-Genome— and therefore its potential to address the Andorian crisis—had been unknown to present-day Federation scientists.

"Starfleet discovered it, but they didn't know about it," th'Shant said sarcastically. "And yet the Tholians provided that same information to the Andorian people. The Federation denied it to their allies of more than two centuries, to one of its own founding members, but the xenophobic Tholians made a gift of it to Andor."

"I understand why you're appalled by what's taken place," Bashir said. "I'm appalled by it too. It shouldn't have happened. Surely, you must realize that it wasn't intentional. But even if you believe that the Federation willfully withheld the assistance your people needed, I don't see how killing Federation citizens—innocent civilians and your own crewmates—I don't see how that could possibly help the situation. If anything, it makes it worse."

"How could anything make the Federation's racism worse?" th'Shant asked. "My people opted to secede, but *I* stayed." The Andorian rapped his fist against his own chest with a thump. "I didn't go home when so many others did. I stayed in Starfleet when others left. I continued performing my duties. But what did I get for my loyalty? I was accused of plotting against Starfleet, against Deep Space Nine, and as you say, against my own crewmates—all because of the color of my skin."

"Are you talking about what happened a few months ago?" Bashir asked. At that time, when two Andorian crewmembers had resigned their commissions and prepared to leave Deep Space 9, Sarina had overheard the departing Ensign zh'Vesk in a heated discussion with th'Shant, in which one of them threatened to avenge their people upon the Federation. Captain Ro had ordered th'Shant investigated—as well as Sarina, and the station's chief of security, Jefferson Blackmer. "The captain ordered a probe into your background and connections because she feared that somebody might attack Deep Space Nine—which you did."

"I hadn't done anything like that at the time, and I hadn't planned to," th'Shant said. "I had friends and family members who decried my misplaced loyalties when I chose to remain in Starfleet and not immediately return to Andor. My family begged me not to stay with bigots. I actually defended my crewmates, and then what did they do? I was accused and investigated because of the species I belong to."

"But that's not what happened," Bashir protested. "You weren't arrested. You were temporarily removed from duty until you could be cleared, and not because you were an Andorian, but because you were overheard participating in a conversation in which threats were made against the Federation."

"I never made any such threats."

"Which is why you weren't the only one investigated; two *humans* were also under suspicion," Bashir said. "And you were *all* cleared."

"When I was accused," th'Shant said, hissing the words through his clenched teeth, "it became obvious that my family was right: the people of the Federation hate Andorians." It seemed to Bashir that the ensign willfully ignored the facts of what had taken place. "So when a friend on Andor contacted me about the Typhon Pact needing help to restore the balance of power with the Federation, I listened—because the Pact, and especially the Tholians, had shown their willingness to help my people."

"Can't you see the calculation the Tholians made in doing what they did?" Bashir asked. "That they only helped the Andorians in an attempt to weaken the Federation?"

"Who cares why they did what they did?" th'Shant said. "If losing Andor weakens the Federation, then you'd think the UFP would do everything it could to help resolve our reproductive crisis. Even for their own self-interest, though, they didn't do that."

"No, but the Federation didn't *intentionally* withhold the information."

"What difference does it make whether or not their actions were intentional?" th'Shant said. "The Federation didn't help the Andorian people, and the Tholians did. It's clear who our friends truly are."

"So you were willing to kill your own crewmates?" Bashir asked quietly, still having difficulty accepting the cold-bloodedness of th'Shant's acts.

"The bombs were only supposed to cause the evacuation of the station," said th'Shant, his own voice dropping to a lower level, his eyes peering downward at the deck. "And if we did need to set them off, they were only meant to damage the reactors in order to require their ejection."

"That was a terrible risk."

"Don't you think I know that?" said th'Shant, looking up, his tone rising. "But . . ." He looked away again, as though searching for an answer. Finally, he shrugged, though unconvincingly. "Casualties are inevitable in war."

"I don't think you believe that, not as justification for what you did," Bashir said. He might not have known th'Shant that well, but even after all that had happened, he found it difficult to consider the Andorian a heartless killer. "Otherwise why would you have fired on the Typhon Pact vessels? And why would you have saved Captain Ro and the senior staff?"

Th'Shant stared at the doctor, but didn't answer any of his questions. Bashir wondered if a motive other than guilt or reclaimed altruism had driven the ensign to go into battle against the Typhon Pact ships, and to transport Ro and her senior officers from ops: plausible deniability. When Bashir had found him out—or at least when th'Shant believed he had—the Andorian had attempted to flee; clearly, he did not wish to face Federation justice. In the end, Bashir decided that th'Shant's aims didn't really matter—certainly not to the more than a thousand people who had perished on Deep Space 9, at least in part thanks to the ensign's actions.

"You're wrong about the Federation," Bashir told th'Shant. "But then I guess that the Federation was also wrong about you."

Th'Shant suddenly lunged forward. Bashir again reflexively stepped back. The Andorian's hands and head struck the force field, which flashed blue at the points of impact. His mouth contorted into a rictus of agony, his yell consumed by the grating electrical sound of the security screen.

As th'Shant fell back a pace, visibly stunned by his contact with the force field, Bashir caught movement off to his side. From her place at the security console, Ensign Elvig darted over to the cell. As she arrived beside Bashir, th'Shant rushed forward again into the force field, which erupted in more blue flashes and bursts of static. Whether the Andorian acted out of uncontrollable anger, unable to keep from attempting to attack the doctor, or he behaved out of remorse, wanting to punish himself, Bashir could not tell.

Elvig rushed to the bulkhead and tapped a control panel set beside the cell. A bright blue pulse flashed through the force field, accompanied by a high-pitched sound reminiscent of a phaser blast. Th'Shant froze, then fell to the deck. Bashir saw his chest rising and falling, indicating that he'd only been rendered unconscious.

The security officer activated her combadge. "Ensign Elvig to sickbay."

"Sickbay," came the response. *"This is Doctor Crusher."*

"Doctor, I'm monitoring the brig," Elvig said. "We've had a prisoner make prolonged and repeated contact with his cell's force field. I used a neutralizing charge to stop him. He's still breathing, but unconscious."

"I'm on my way with a medical team," the doctor said. *"Crusher out."*

"I'm a doctor," Bashir told the security officer, but she held up a hand to quiet him as she touched her combadge once more. "Elvig to Lieutenant Choudhury."

"This is Choudhury," replied the *Enterprise* security chief. *"Go ahead."*

Elvig repeated her story, then added that she had contacted sickbay.

"I'll dispatch a security team at once," Choudhury said. *"Do not permit medical personnel to enter the cell until security reinforcements arrive."*

"Understood, Lieutenant," Elvig said.

"I'll inform Captain Picard of the situation," said the security chief. *"Choudhury out."*

Elvig looked to Bashir. "Does the prisoner appear to be in distress?" she asked.

"No," Bashir said, gazing at the inert figure of th'Shant. "His breathing appears regular. I'm more concerned about how his contacts with the force field affected his antennae and central nervous system."

Elvig seemed to consider this. "We'll wait, then," she said. The statement impressed Bashir, not because she had chosen to wait for the medical and security teams, but because she had obviously considered violating a direct order and allowing Bashir to treat the Andorian. The doctor believed that if he'd indicated that th'Shant's health had been at risk, she would have lowered the force field and allowed Bashir to tend to him.

As they stood peering into the cell at the fallen form of Vakell th'Shant, Ensign Elvig asked, "Why do you think he did it?"

Bashir knew that the security officer specifically asked about why th'Shant had hurled himself into the force field, but the doctor's own thoughts ranged farther afield than that. He thought about the bombs planted on Deep Space 9, and the terrible destruction that had followed. So when he replied to Elvig, he answered many more questions than she'd asked.

"I don't know," he said. "I truly don't know."

Captain Benjamin Sisko stood from the command chair. He knew that below *U.S.S. Robinson,* the world of Bajor floated in space. Since the confrontation in the wormhole, and as Sisko awaited the return of all his crew, a monotony had arisen throughout the ship. That would change as soon as *Robinson* enjoyed a full complement and they headed the ship for Starbase 310, where they would deliver *Rubicon* and receive their new orders, but for the moment, the captain and his available crew had little to do but test and confirm all of the recent repairs to the ship.

Since the collapse of the wormhole—which still showed no signs of reopening, or even of whether it still existed—the Cardassians had reported a coincident explosion near their border. Investigation by Gul Macet aboard *Trager* uncovered readings that revealed the location of the other terminus of the Typhon Pact's wormhole. Evidence, though, confirmed that the wormhole itself, as well as the equipment that generated it, had been completely destroyed.

"Commander Rogeiro, you have the bridge," Sisko told his first officer, who sat to his right. "I'll be in my ready room."

"Aye, sir."

Sisko crossed the bridge, his thoughts wandering to Kira Nerys. Her loss had been a terrible blow. Still, despite his own bitter estrangement from the Prophets, he continued to hope that they had somehow survived the explosion within the wormhole, and that they had also managed to save Kira. On one level, it seemed like a wildly optimistic thought, but Sisko had experienced far more improbable events since he had first arrived in the Bajoran system nearly fifteen years earlier.

The captain entered his ready room. As he took a step forward and the doors closed behind him, though, he saw before him not the familiar environs of his personal workspace aboard *Robinson,* but a shabby, old-fashioned room. He halted in his tracks.

The area before him measured roughly the same size as his ready room, perhaps a little larger. To the right, he saw an old, threadbare couch; a chipped, wooden coffee table; a shaded standing lamp; and a chair placed beside a short filing cabinet. A hulking, metal typewriter sat atop the cabinet. On the other side of the room, Sisko saw a sink, a stove—on which two pots cooked—and an icebox lined up along the wall. Dishes and flatware had been set on a round table, next to which stood a highchair. He spied a closed door past the kitchenette, and two others along a short corridor leading away from the living area. Sisko didn't recognize the place, but he knew its style and the era from which it came.

The captain turned back around and, to his surprise, saw the doors to his ready room. Sudden vertigo caused him to lose his balance, and he lurched a step to one side before he caught himself. He peered down the length of his body to see the familiar black and gray material of his Starfleet uniform. Bracing himself, Sisko slowly rotated in place.

He could not identify the precise moment when his ready room somehow became a run-down apartment in Harlem, or even how he knew the place's location, but again, he felt light-headed. He tottered, then steadied himself by grabbing onto the back of one of the chairs at the table. Its legs chattered along the wood floor.

"Benny, are you all right?"

Benny closed his eyes in an effort to regain his equilibrium, then looked over to the couch. Cassie sat there in a black skirt and lavender blouse, a few white sheets of paper in her hand, with another small stack of pages sitting beside her. Becky lay asleep on the other side of Cassie, her small form a scatter of arms and legs.

"I'm . . . I'm fine," Benny said. He glanced down at himself and saw a pair of charcoal gray slacks and an olive-green, button-down shirt.

"Have you read Kay's new story? 'The Abjuration of Rough Magic'?" Cassie asked. "She does a terrific job with her woman first officer. She saves the day aboard the *U.S. Temple,* and it's just so good and so . . . I don't know . . . so *honest.*"

"No," Sisko said, knowing that he hadn't read the story, that he'd never even heard of it or of its author, but somehow also knowing the identity of its first officer character: Kira Nerys. "No, I haven't read it yet."

"You should," Kasidy said. "The report has a lot of unanswered questions." She sat on the sofa in *Robinson*'s ready room, holding a padd, and wearing one of the multi-toned jumpsuits she often favored during cargo runs. Rebecca, clad in a pretty floral-print dress, slept stretched out on the sofa, her head resting on Kasidy's thigh.

Benny pulled out the chair from the table and sat down hard. He hadn't felt this way—*fractured*—in quite a while. At the same time he'd been cleared of the charges of assault and battery on the orderlies at Riverdale, a court-appointed psychiatrist had pronounced him well enough to avoid his re-committal to the asylum. Since then, he and Cassie had married and moved into an apartment together with their little girl. Benny continued to write, mostly for himself, though he occasionally sold a story to Pabst over at *Incredible Tales* or to Quinn over at *If,* and he'd even managed to get a novelette into an issue of *Galaxy.* But for the most part, he worked construction, good, honest labor that he actually enjoyed, and which allowed him to take care of his family. In all that time, he'd felt *whole.*

"She's really becoming a very good writer," Cassie said, and Benny gazed over to see her holding up the pages of Kay's latest story.

"I'll read it," Benny said, but something nagged at him— something about Kay. He tried to think, tried to dredge up the memory he sought, but to no avail. He closed his eyes, but then someone knocked on the front door. "Who can that be?" he asked Cassie.

"It's Kay," Cassie said. "Don't you remember? She's joining us for supper."

"Oh," Benny said. "Of course." He didn't remember, though, which scared him.

Cassie took the pages of Kay's story and set them on the coffee table, then carefully extracted herself from where Becky lay. "Would you get the door while I go check on the stove?"

As Cassie crossed to the kitchenette, Benny rose a bit shakily to his feet. He headed past the living area and down the short hall. At the front door, he unlatched the locks, thinking that it would be good to see Kay. As the doorknob turned beneath his hand, though, he recalled what had eluded him earlier: Kay had been in an accident—a *terrible* accident.

He pulled open the door. Kira stood outside in the corridor. "Hello, Benjamin," she said. She wore a traditional, earth-toned vedek's robe. In one hand, she carried a curvy, elongated bottle filled with pale blue Bajoran springwine.

"Nerys," Sisko said. "You're all right." Relief flooded through him. He thought his friend had been lost.

"Of course, I'm all right," Kay said, wrinkling her nose up at Benny. "You didn't think a little accident would keep me down for long, did you?"

"I . . ." Benny started, but the feeling of his mind splintering had returned, and he had difficulty forming complete thoughts.

"Cat got your tongue, Benny?" Kay asked. "This oughta loosen it." She held up the bottle of red wine she'd brought with her. She entered the apartment, and Benny closed the door after her.

When he turned around, Sisko nearly walked into his desk. Kira peered at him from its other side, her hand on the bottle of springwine she'd set down between them. "Nerys?"

"It's time to celebrate, Benjamin," Kira said.

"That you're alive?" Sisko asked.

"We don't need to celebrate that I'm alive," Kira told him. "We need to celebrate that *you* are."

"I've got glasses," Kasidy said, returning from the replicator. She carried three delicate flutes with her, which she placed beside the bottle of springwine.

"I . . . I don't understand," Benny said.

Kay pulled the cork from the bottle and poured the deep-red liquid into three water glasses. She handed one to Cassie and then one to Benny. She took the third for herself and held it aloft before her. "To family," she said, then held her glass out, first toward Cassie, then toward Benny. "To mother, father—" She motioned toward where Becky slept on the couch. "—and daughter." When Kay and Cassie sipped at their glasses, Benny did too.

Sisko hadn't always enjoyed the taste of springwine, but during his time on Deep Space 9, he'd cultivated an appreciation of its subtle flavors. He'd even thought about growing *kava* on their land in Kendra Province so that they could produce their own vintage. He'd never gotten around to doing that.

There are a lot of things I haven't gotten to do, he thought. *A lot of things we haven't gotten to do.* "We're a mother and father and daughter," Sisko said, "but we can't be a family." Each time he uttered words to that effect, each time he considered the Prophets' warning, he hated it. He hated the situation, and he hated himself. But he had to protect Kasidy and Rebecca, and that meant that he couldn't spend his life with Kasidy.

"Yes, you can," Kira said. "You can be a family."

"Nerys," Sisko said. He placed his flute of springwine down on his desk. "You know how much I want that to be true, but you also know the Prophets' warning to me."

"I do know," Kira said. "You told them that you wanted to spend your life with Kasidy, and they told you that if you did, you would know nothing but sorrow."

Beside Sisko, Kasidy closed her eyes. He knew how badly the situation had hurt her—how badly *he* had hurt her. "As much as I want to, there's nothing I can do."

Kira smiled. "But you already have done something," she said. "You haven't spent your life with Kasidy."

Kasidy opened her eyes. "What are you saying, Nerys?"

"I'm saying that nearly eight years ago, the Prophets told Benjamin that if he spent his life with you, he would know nothing but sorrow," Kira explained. "But he defied their warning, and, eventually, the prophecy began to fulfill itself:

Benjamin began to know nothing but sorrow. But then he stopped spending his life with you, so there's no longer anything to be concerned about. You can be together."

"What?" Sisko said. "If I go back to Kasidy, we'll be right back where we started."

"No, you won't be," Kira insisted. "There's an old saying: you can't step twice into the same river." Sisko knew the aphorism, but thought that it had originated on Earth, not Bajor.

"What does that mean?" Kasidy wanted to know.

"It means that as a river flows, it changes," Kira said. "When you enter it for the first time, it's in a certain state. Every drop of water in a particular place, exerting a particular force on the drop next to it. But just by entering the river, you change it. If you leave it and enter it a second time, the drops of water have moved, their forces have changed, and it's not the same river."

"And time is a river?" Sisko said. He could hear the desperation in his voice disguised as hope.

"The Prophets say that it's a continuum," Kira said.

"You've spoken to the Prophets?" Kasidy asked. "Did they save you?"

"They've spoken to me," Kira said. She set her glass down on Sisko's desk. "Benjamin, they want you to know that you can enter your continuum again."

Sisko's heart began to beat rapidly in his chest. He felt his lips widen and spread of their own accord. He had never expected to feel such elation again. "I'm going to transport down to Bajor," he said. "I'm going to consult an Orb. I'll—"

"Benjamin," Kira said, casting her gaze downward.

"What?" Kasidy asked. Sisko could hear the fear in her voice, the belief that something would put the lie to what Kira had just told them. "What is it?"

"Benjamin, you have fulfilled your destiny," Kira said, looking back up at him. "At least, with the Prophets."

"They're done with Ben?" Kasidy asked, excitement rising in her voice.

Kira continued to peer at Sisko, but she didn't say anything. She didn't have to. He understood precisely what she meant.

He'd understood it for a long time, ever since the period since his last contact with the Prophets had begun to draw out longer and longer. He knew that he'd accomplished all the tasks they'd set him, and that they therefore had no further need to communicate with him, to be a part of his life.

Back when he'd first come to that realization, Sisko had been angry about it. He felt used, unappreciated, and abandoned. But how could he truly be sorry for all that he had been allowed—all that he had been led—to achieve in his life? Whether a mere instrument of the Prophets or not, he knew he had played a significant part in saving the people of Bajor, not just from the horrors of war, but from how they had lost their way, how they had lost themselves. He had helped guide the Bajorans back onto their collective path.

Sisko would miss that responsibility. He already did; even though many still regarded him as the Emissary of the Prophets, he hadn't been able to think of himself in those terms for some time. As much as that hurt him, though, Sisko would gladly forsake that role for another: husband.

"You're sure, Nerys?" Sisko asked. "About all of it? The Prophets are done with me, but I can safely go back to Kasidy?"

"I'm sure of it," Kira said.

Sisko looked at Kasidy. "Then we *can* celebrate," he told her. "If you'll have me."

Cassie held up her glass of red wine. "To family," she said.

"To family," Kay echoed, tapping her glass against Cassie's with a clink.

Benny reached forward and touched his own glass against the other two. "To family," he said, the single word as sweet as poetry to him. He lifted the wine to his lips, closed his eyes, and drank.

When Sisko opened his eyes, he saw that he held his empty hand up to his mouth. He dropped his arm back to his side and peered around his ready room. He stood behind his desk, alone.

What did I just experience?

Sisko walked over to the tall viewport in one bulkhead. He gazed out at the beautiful form of Bajor against the black backdrop of space, an oasis in the desert. *Was all of that real?* he thought. *Was it a hallucination? Was it contact with the Prophets?*

It seemed like none of those things. But it had felt . . . substantive. Important. *And if not real, then at least . . . honest.*

Sisko looked at Bajor. He could feel Kasidy's presence, and Rebecca's. He knew what he had to do—what he finally *could* do.

Sisko turned and hurried across his ready room, headed for *Robinson's* nearest transporter.

Kasidy Yates sat in her home office and regarded the face on the companel with appreciation. "Thank you, Jasmine," she said. "It's really important."

"*You're welcome, Ms. Yates,*" said Tey. "*I hope there's nothing wrong.*"

"No, not at all," Kasidy said, though in truth, she couldn't say for sure. She didn't believe anything was wrong, but she had to admit the possibility that she might be losing her mind. "It's just an unexpected appointment," she said. "I'll contact you in a little while to let you know when I'll be back, but I shouldn't be too late."

"*Take as much time as you need,*" Tey said. "*I never mind picking up Rebecca from school and spending time with her out at the house.*"

"Thank you," Kasidy repeated. "I'll talk to you later." She ended the transmission with a touch to the companel. "Computer, I want to contact—"

Kasidy heard the chime that signaled somebody at the front door. Without shutting down the companel, she stood up and raced from the room. She ran down the hall, past the dining area, and across the living room, until she reached the door. She immediately pulled it open, already knowing in her heart who would be standing there.

Ben looked in at her from the porch, as dashing as always in his Starfleet uniform. It required all of Kasidy's willpower not to step forward and throw her arms around him. She had to remind herself that she didn't really know what she'd experienced.

"May I come in?" Ben asked. "I really need to speak with you."

"Of course," Kasidy said. She closed the door, then turned to face Ben. "Actually, I was just about to contact you."

"Is everything all right?"

"Yes, everything's fine," Kasidy said. "I just needed to talk to you." She didn't know how she would broach the subject, or even if she really should, but what she'd been through had seemed so . . . *honest* . . . that she had to try.

"I hope it can wait, because I have to tell you something," Ben said. His sense of urgency seemed clear, since he made no move to sit down. "I don't really know how to say this, since it may not mean to you what it meant to me, but I *have* to say it: I just experienced a . . . I don't know what it was. A *pagh 'tem' far.* A vision. A dream. I don't really know."

Kasidy stared at Sisko. She felt dizzy—almost as much as she had earlier when she'd sat down on the sofa and looked up to find herself in a dilapidated, antiquated apartment. Almost as much as when she'd suddenly found herself aboard Ben's starship, in his ready room. "Tell me."

"We were in an apartment on Earth in the twentieth century," Ben said. "You and me and Rebecca."

"Except we weren't always us," Kasidy said. Her voice sounded to her as though it came from far away. "And when we were, we weren't in the apartment, but in your ready room aboard the *Robinson.*"

Ben's eyes widened. "How do you know that?"

Kasidy hesitated to say the words, knowing how preposterous they would sound. But then she said them anyway. "I was there."

For long moments, Ben only stared at her. When finally he spoke, his voice came out in a whisper. "Was Nerys there?"

Kasidy nodded.

"You heard what she said?" Ben asked. "That the Prophets are finished with me? That I have my life back? That we . . . ?"

Kasidy's vision blurred as tears formed in her eyes. She completed Ben's question. "That we can be together?" Then she answered it: "Yes."

Time seemed to slow. Kasidy knew they would have to work through all that had happened, not only since Ben had left, but in the months leading up to that point. She also knew they wouldn't be staying on Bajor, but what did that mean? Would she and Rebecca join him aboard *Robinson*? Once, Kasidy never would have considered such an option, but now it seemed like a real possibility to her. The *Galaxy*-class ships had even been designed to accommodate the civilian families of Starfleet personnel.

"Does that mean that you believe what Kira said?" Ben asked. "Does that mean that . . . that we can be together again?"

As an answer, Kasidy took a step forward and melted into his embrace. Her lips found his. She closed her eyes, sending tears spilling down her cheeks.

When at last they parted, Ben said, "I love you."

"I love you." Kasidy looked up at Ben, and for the first time in a long time, she saw in his eyes that everything would be all right.

September 2384

Ab Initio

Captain Ro Laren sat at the forward console of the runabout *Rio Grande*. Beside her sat Prynn Tenmei, never missing an opportunity to pilot one craft or another. Behind them, other members of the crew filled the cockpit: Cenn Desca, John Candlewood, Zivan Slaine, Jefferson Blackmer, Aleco Vel, Miles O'Brien, and Nog. Doctor Bashir and Sarina Douglas didn't hold hands, but their connection seemed clear.

"Well, Chief," Ro said, looking over at O'Brien, "it looks pretty good to me."

Through the forward viewports, Bajor's new space station gleamed. Construction hadn't been completed, and wouldn't be for another year. The first pair of fusion reactors had just gone online, though, and nearly half the interior space had been made habitable. The Starfleet Corps of Engineers had officially informed them that the crew could move into that portion of the station.

"It's coming along," O'Brien agreed. "I have to admit, I'm not going to miss that old Cardassian bucket of bolts."

"Me either," said Nog.

Standing beside Ro, Dalin Slaine cleared her throat. O'Brien glanced over at the Cardassian officer, and the captain saw his face flush in embarrassment. Nog also looked abashed.

"I think what you fail to understand," Slaine said, "is that the problems Terok Nor held for you had little to do with it being a *Cardassian* space station. It was that it was designed to be an ore-processing facility. Who would want to live or work on one of those?"

"Good point," Ro said, attempting to bail out O'Brien and Nog.

"Absolutely," said Nog at once.

"Point taken," said O'Brien.

Ro peered through the viewports at the new station. "I just hope we won't have to move it once it's completed," she said. Despite the collapse of the Bajoran wormhole a year earlier, Starfleet had opted to continue construction in the same location. Although Federation scientists had been unable to confirm the existence of the wormhole, everybody continued to hope that the aliens within had survived and would, if needed, make repairs and reopen the great subspace tunnel. If that didn't happen, then Starfleet Command would likely consider relocating the station to the orbit of Bajor.

"I hope we don't have to move her either," Nog said, "but if we do, she can take it."

O'Brien clapped a hand on Nog's back. "Spoken like a proud papa."

As *Rio Grande* neared the station and it grew larger in the viewports, Ro took a long look at it. Peering past the lattice of hemispherical modules from which the SCE staged its construction efforts, and past the flurry of engineers in environmental suits and the support craft that moved about, the captain gazed at the new structure. Despite the radical design, it shared many characteristics with other Starfleet facilities: the gray-white surface of its hull, the curves and proportions of its components, the familiar lettering along one arc that read UNITED FEDERATION OF PLANETS. The overall, essentially spherical shape of the station, though, reminded Ro of its predecessor. The new facility would ultimately comprise three rings, oriented at right angles to one another. They would all surround an inner sphere, connecting to it via half a dozen crossover bridges. The rings would provide docking and cargo services, while the sphere would house work, commercial, and residential sections. Ro decided that she liked it—and with apologies to Zivan Slaine, it would represent a marked improvement to the facility it would replace.

"Captain," Tenmei asked, "has Starfleet settled on a name for the station?"

"They have," Ro said. "Starfleet Command consulted with the Federation president and the Bajoran First Minister about it, and they all came to an agreement." Ro raised her hand and pointed through the viewports toward the half-constructed station. "Welcome," she told her crew, "to the new Deep Space Nine."